A Scholar of Magics

By Caroline Stevermer from Tom Doherty Associates

A Scholar of Magics
A College of Magics
When the King Comes Home

A TOM DOHERTY ASSOCIATES BOOK

New York

A Scholar of Magics

CAROLINE STEVERMER

Fiction
Stevermer

A SCHOLAR OF MAGICS

Book design by Milenda Nan Ok Lee

This book is printed on acid-free paper.

A Tor Book
Published by Tom Doherty Associates, LLC
175 Fifth Avenue
New York, NY 10010

www.tor.com

Tor® is a registered trademark of Tom Doherty Associates, LLC.

Library of Congress Cataloging-in-Publication Data

Stevermer, Caroline.
   A scholar of magics / Caroline Stevermer.—1st ed.
      p. cm.
   "A Tom Doherty Associates book."
   ISBN 0-765-30308-6
   EAN 978-0765-30308-0
      1. Magic—Study and teaching—Fiction. 2. Universities and colleges—Fiction. 3. Americans—
England—Fiction. 4. Sharpshooters—Fiction. 5. England—Fiction. I. Title.

PS3569.T4575S36 2004
813'.54—dc22

                                                                    2003061472

Printed in the United States of America

0   9   8   7   6   5   4   3   2

To Patricia C. Wrede

Acknowledgments

For their expertise, insight, and patience, I would like to thank eluki bes sha-
har, Charlotte Boynton, Frances Collin, Mary and Jerry Dahlstrom-Salic,
Amanda Dalcassian, Pamela Dean Dyer-Bennet, E. Ryan Edmonds, Beth
Friedman, Beth Hilleman, Ellen Kushner, Katherine Lawrence, Scott Lund-
berg, Alex MacKenzie, Ashley McConnell, Janet Myers, Shweta Narayan,
Mimi Panitch, Pen Rensley, Jenn St. John, Delia Sherman, Leslie Schultz,
Eve Sweetser, Jodi Tanji, Betty G. Uzman, Betty T. Uzman, Jo Walton,
Patricia Wrede, and Zack Weinberg.

Thanks as well to Leah Sinanglou Marcus, who wrote "The Milieu of Milton's *Comus*: Judicial Reform at Ludlow and the Problem of Sexual Assault,"
Criticism, fall 1983, vol. XXV, No. 4, pp. 293–327, and to Mary Blockley,
who sent me a copy long ago.

All chapter epigraphs are from *Comus*, a masque by John Milton.

I must keep alive in myself the desire for my true country, which I shall not find till after death; I must never let it get snowed under or turned aside. I must make it the main object of life to press on to that other country and to help others do the same.

—C. S. Lewis, *Mere Christianity*

A Scholar of Magics

"Peace, brother, be not over-exquisite"

Samuel Lambert, all too aware of his responsibilities as a guest, saw with dismay that there were loose bits of tea leaf in the bottom of his cup. Lambert was not easy to alarm. He had no objection to tea leaves as such, but their presence made it probable that his hostess would once again try her dainty, inexorable hand at telling his fortune.

Mrs. Robert Brailsford cultivated parlor fortune-telling as an excuse to bring out some of her intuitions, her observations, and on rare occasions, what amounted to impertinent remarks. Fragile, blond, and as fashionable as the wife of a Senior Fellow of Glasscastle University dared to be, Amy's refined exterior concealed a lively appreciation of the absurd. That she could sometimes behave with boundless absurdity herself was no small part of her charm.

Lambert liked Amy. He appreciated the hospitality shown to him by both the Brailsfords, and he respected Mr. Robert Brailsford, even felt a bit intimidated by him. But he *liked* Amy, and he felt quite sure that his liking was returned. In her, he found an appreciative audience for any reminiscences or observations he cared to make. She enjoyed his lapses into American speech and behavior. Indeed, she encouraged them.

Still, in the past six months Lambert had put up with Amy's examination of his handwriting, her analysis of the numerical value of the letters in his name, and an inspection of the bumps on his head that made him suppress a shudder every time he thought of it. Amy Brailsford's powers of divination had revealed that Lambert was a gentleman of keen perception, that he would take a long journey over water, marry well, and have seven children. Her evaluation of his handwriting was accurate enough to make Lambert reluctant to surrender to any more studies.

Enough was enough. Since his arrival at Glasscastle six months before, Lambert's experience of local etiquette had given him the confidence to brave most social perils. Afternoon tea was well within his capabilities. Impromptu fortune-telling was not. Lambert resolved to drink his tea with such fervor and dedication there would be nothing left in the cup to read. As Lambert took a deep breath and prepared to polish off his tea, leaves and all, the parlormaid joined them.

"Miss Brailsford has arrived, ma'am."

Amy Brailsford put her cup down on its saucer with such uncharacteristic force that the porcelain chimed in protest. "*Who?* That is, which Miss Brailsford?"

"Miss Jane Brailsford."

Amy looked askance at the maid. "Goodness. How extraordinary. Set another place at the table and ask Cook to cut a few more sandwiches. On second thought, make that rather a lot more sandwiches. And a fresh pot of tea. I'll be there in a moment." Amy turned to Lambert, eyes wide, to explain. "It's Robert's sister. The youngest of the family. She teaches at a school in France."

"A schoolteacher?" Lambert exclaimed. "That is, I meant to say, how interesting."

Amy looked puzzled by his response but continued, "We haven't seen her for years and years. It almost seems more likely that Robert's great-aunt Susannah left Cheltenham Spa to call on us than that Jane should visit. Excuse me, please."

Grateful for the unexpected reprieve, Lambert used the precious minute or so of solitude after Amy's departure to conceal the contents of his teacup in a brass pot that held a substantial aspidistra. When his sleeve brushed against the foliage, he roused a beetle from its afternoon nap. The insect flew low over the table, rose to an altitude just out of swatting range, and set itself to veer around the room for the rest of the day. After watching its erratic flight for several circuits of the room, Lambert helped himself to a few sugar cubes from the bowl. He wasted two shots before he got the hang of the insect's abrupt changes of speed and direction, but the third sugar cube closed its account. Lambert nailed the beetle on the wing at three paces, exactly over the tea tray. The corpse missed the milk pitcher with half an inch to spare and landed, legs to the sky, between the teapot and the sugar bowl. Uncomfortably aware that no etiquette book covered freelance insect extermination, Lambert retrieved the evidence. He deposited the dead beetle and the sugar cubes on top of the tea leaves in the aspidistra pot and resumed his seat.

Lambert was listening to the tick of the clock on the mantel and watching the progress of the afternoon sunlight across the oriental carpet when his hostess rejoined him. In Amy's wake was a woman somewhere in her early twenties, no older than Lambert was himself. She had clear gray eyes and smooth dark hair coiled and pinned into a large knot. Only a stray tendril here and there betrayed that she'd just taken off her hat. Her clothing, of good material and elegant cut, showed little sign of the dust of the road, but her half boots did. For all her elegant appearance, Miss Jane Brailsford had apparently traveled a considerable distance. Lambert rose as Amy performed the introductions and the maid arrived with the new place setting and a fresh supply of provisions.

"Jane, may I present Mr. Samuel Lambert? He is an American visiting Glasscastle to help Robert and his friends with some studies of theirs. Mr. Lambert, allow me to present Miss Jane Brailsford, Robert's younger sister."

"Ma'am." Lambert didn't have to strain for sincerity. "I'm mighty pleased to make your acquaintance."

Jane made the proper reply and took her seat. The maid withdrew. Introductions successfully concluded, Amy sat and devoted herself to meeting her guests' need for tea and sandwiches.

Jane removed her gloves and folded them in her lap. She regarded Lambert with interest as he returned to his seat. "Some studies of Robin's? I suppose it is useless to ask directly. What sort of studies?"

Lambert couldn't help smiling a little. "I'm the last one who could tell you. The boys in charge are all Fellows of Glasscastle. They give the orders. I just do what I'm told." He inspected his teacup before he took a sip. No leaves. Maybe his luck had turned.

Jane reproached Amy. "You shouldn't have brought it up if I wasn't to ask about it." She turned her attention to a plate of stuffed mushrooms. Lambert had given them a wide berth after his first, since he detected the faint fishy presence of patum peperium in the filling. Jane appeared to find no fault with them, nor with anything else on her plate. Her manners were impeccable, but her appetite was fierce.

Amy dimpled. "My dear, why do you think I said it? I'm curious too. All I know is, Mr. Lambert is here as a marksman. He's allowed to take tea, but no other stimulants. Coffee, alcohol, and tobacco are forbidden. They would interfere with the accuracy of his aim."

"No stimulants of any kind?" Jane gave Lambert a searching glance. "But surely tea itself is a stimulant?"

"I prevailed upon the committee. They granted Mr. Lambert the privilege of drinking tea, provided it is not too strong," Amy said. "After all, what would life be without at least an occasional cup of tea? Hardly worth living."

"I tried to make the same case for brandy," said Lambert. "I gave it a game try, but somehow my opinions don't carry the weight that Mrs. Brailsford's do. I am a greenhorn here, and I appreciate her looking out for me."

Jane studied Lambert for a long time before she spoke. Lambert expected her to take him up on the word "greenhorn," but instead she said, "Then you make the ideal guest. Even a chicken sandwich constitutes adventure."

Lambert met the challenge in Jane's tone with utter solemnity. "Mrs. Brailsford's company is intoxicating enough. I reckon any more excitement than that would upset the Fellows."

"I reckon it would." Jane didn't just match his words, she matched his sober expression with one of her own, but there was a distinct gleam of humor behind her gravity. Lambert warmed to her.

"Isn't he a perfect lamb?" Amy asked Jane. "He says things like that all the time. Unfortunately, neither he nor Robert take the slightest notice of a woman's natural curiosity. Whatever they're doing, it involves firearms. Mr. Lambert is a genuine cowboy, but he is here as a professional sharpshooter. A dead shot." Amy obviously relished the phrase.

"Are you indeed?" Jane looked at Lambert again, her surprise ill concealed.

Lambert was still wincing slightly from hearing himself described as a perfect lamb. Before he could answer, Amy went on.

"He was traveling with Kiowa Bob's Genuine Wild West Show, but when Glasscastle needed him, he obliged us and came here to stay." Amy beamed at Lambert. "Luckily for us."

Jane said, "How extraordinary. Is there really such a person as Kiowa Bob?"

"Yup. Well, his name isn't Bob and he's not really Kiowa. But the fellow in question was good enough to take me on and show me the ropes," Lambert replied. "I only came to the tryouts to keep a friend of mine company. My friend got in with his roping and riding and then dared me to try the sharpshooting. To make a long story short, I was hired. I'll always be grateful to Kiowa Bob for giving me a chance."

"Very amiable of Mr. Bob, I'm sure. Had it been a long-held ambition of yours to go into show business?" Jane asked.

"Nope. I liked it better than what I was doing before, though." Lambert didn't give Jane a chance to ask him about that. Instead, he pushed on. "Thanks to the Wild West Show, I've had a chance to see the world. We toured America, of course. Spent months in New York City. When Kiowa Bob decided to arrange a European tour, I thought I'd come along and see a bit more of the world."

Jane's gray eyes were keen. "If you loved it so much, what made you decide to leave and come here?"

"I was recruited. We heard there was a big shooting contest held in London every year. Kiowa Bob thought it might help plug our show, so I entered. First thing I knew, Mr. Voysey, Mr. Brailsford, and those other men from Glasscastle were there to sign me up."

"You won the contest, then?" Jane asked.

"Of course he did," said Amy. "He wouldn't be here if he hadn't."

Jane looked puzzled. "Surely it defeated the purpose to have you leave the show just as you were, er, plugging it. Didn't your employer object?"

"At first I reckoned I'd just come down here for a day or so, straighten out your Fellows, and head right back to the show. Kiowa Bob gave me permission to miss a few performances. Then, once I'd seen Glasscastle and found out more about the job, I decided to stay here, at least for a spell. Kiowa Bob could have made me work out my contract, but he was a gent about it. He let me go with his blessing."

"Remarkable." Unlike most people, Jane did not subject Lambert to a cross-examination on the subject of the personal habits of Indians, cowboys, or buffalo. Instead, she selected a cucumber sandwich from the offerings before her and began to consume it with obvious pleasure. Lambert was surprised at the degree of his disappointment. It seemed likely that Jane would ask more interesting questions than he was used to. What a pity she seemed so much more interested in the food.

Into the silence that ensued, Amy said, "Jane, it's wonderful to have you visit here at last. Robert will be so pleased. He would have met your train if only he'd known. You might have given us some hint you were coming."

Surprised, Jane paused in the methodical demolition of her sandwich. "I certainly might have. I might have neglected to do so; I'm quite capable of it. But in this instance, I am not guilty, upon my honor, m'lady. I sent a wire from London yesterday."

Amy frowned. "You did? How extraordinary. I wonder if Robert forgot to mention it to me. No, he wouldn't have."

"Preoccupied with his studies, perhaps?" Jane suggested. "Wires do go astray sometimes. Not often, I grant you. Where is our gentle Robin?"

It was Amy's turn to look reproachful. "You know he hates to be called that."

Jane merely smiled and took her time about selecting the next sandwich from the assortment before her.

"Robert is at a reception this afternoon. The new Vice Chancellor of Glasscastle is entertaining two cabinet ministers and Robert is there to help him. The plan is to establish warmer relations between the policy makers and those who carry out the policy. I quote." Amy gave Lambert a sidelong glance of mischief, and then added, "Mr. Lambert is here to keep me company while they are busy making their relations more warm."

Jane was the picture of innocence as she thought this statement over. "Goodness. Luckily, they should have no trouble on a day like this." After a pensive moment, she asked, "Which group does Robin think he's in? Not the policy makers?"

Amy looked scandalized. "Jane. As if there could be any question. All the official funding Robert's research project receives comes straight from the Home Secretary. It couldn't be more direct, or more vital to our imperial interests."

"I suppose I needn't bother to ask about the unofficial funding. You won't say anything you shouldn't. I really must get Robin to tell me what it is he's working on this time." Jane spoke half to herself, half to her cup of tea.

"There was a last time?" Lambert prompted.

Jane looked pleased with herself. "Inadvertently. He needed some help attaining permission to do research in a Breton archive. I was able to smooth the waters, so to speak."

"Your sister-in-law told me you teach at a school in France. In Brittany?"

"In Normandy."

"What kind of teaching do you do?"

Prompt came the reply, as the gleam of humor reappeared beneath Jane's gravity. Not for a moment did she seem to entertain the notion of giving him a simple answer. "Oh, Mock Turtle's arithmetic: ambition, distraction, uglification, and derision."

Lambert could tell she was quoting from something. It was a sensation he often had at Glasscastle, when an allusion was being made to something that the speaker thought must be as familiar as the alphabet. Nine out of ten times whatever was being alluded to was so far beside the point it wasn't worth the breath it took to explain it. The tenth time the allusion generally turned out to be too clever, or too strained, to make sense to him. Lambert had learned it was faster and more interesting to wait and ask his friend Nicholas Fell to explain later. Either way, letting things pass unquestioned saved him the effort of trying to look interested in the resulting clarification. Lambert thought of it in baseball terms. He was Honus Wagner taking a pitch, confident that the next conversational opening would be something he could handle. So Lambert let the gleam in Jane's eyes go unchallenged. "I take it the school year is not in session yet?"

"That's right. Michaelmas term starts in a few weeks. Until then I've chosen to spend my free time here in England. I haven't seen Robin and Amy for years. There's also the lure of visiting the celebrated precincts of the university of Glasscastle. I'm looking forward to seeing all the sights."

"But you must know—" An awkward pause threatened to descend as Lambert searched for words and came up dry. "You can't—"

Jane looked puzzled. After a moment, she prompted Lambert. "I can't what?"

"It isn't—They don't—For women—" Lambert gave it up.

Jane frowned slightly, apparently perplexed by his lapse into silence.

"Jane knows perfectly well," said Amy.

Jane relented. "I do know Glasscastle is off-limits for any but those properly escorted by members of the university and they man the gates with Fellows of Glasscastle to keep it that way. Very proper and sedate, this place. What about you? Are you able to range at will, or do you have a chaperon?"

Lambert found Jane's flippancy engaging. "Oh, I range at will—within reason. Though there are quite a few places they don't let me ramble on my own."

"That must have the charm of novelty for you," said Jane.

"Needing a chaperon? There are plenty of places where outsiders aren't allowed in Glasscastle. Just because they let us inside the gates doesn't mean we're welcome there. An escort provides a simple way to prevent me from delivering unintentional offense while I'm a visitor." Lambert broke off, conscious of how stuffy he must sound. He must have been spending too much time listening to the Fellows' dinner conversation in hall. Pomposity must be contagious. Lambert felt himself poker up.

Jane's solemnity was back, and the challenging look that went with it. "Intentional offenses only, I take it?"

Lambert didn't let Jane's solemn look fool him. He did let the gleam of challenge in her eyes tempt him to maintain his air of gravity as long as possible. "Maybe I should have said inadvertent," he added, with diffidence.

His meekness seemed to take Jane aback. "I hope I haven't—inadvertently—offended you. I prefer the intentional offenses myself."

"Oh, I agree. There's nothing more satisfying than delivering a sound, well-regulated insult. Only to those who deserve it, of course," Lambert added with deliberate piety.

"But whoever does deserve to be insulted?" Amy asked. "When one's intentions are properly taken into account, there is seldom cause to give or even receive an affront. It's all a matter of understanding one another's intentions."

"Some intentions," Jane replied, "are not well intended."

Amy countered, "How do you know that? You can't read people's minds."

"Of course not. But I can pay attention to what they say and what they do. Easier to read behavior than the shape of people's heads," said Jane.

The edge in her voice made Lambert wonder if Jane might have some experience of Amy's fortune-telling. Eager to keep a safe distance from that particular topic, Lambert changed the subject. "What do you aim to do while you're here in Glasscastle? Are there any special places you'd like to see?"

"Oh, yes. The Winterset Archive, for one. Some consider it holds the finest collection of magic texts in the world. I'm told there's a larger one in Peking, but not surprisingly, most of that library is in Chinese. For another landmark, the chapel of St. Mary's. I have quite a list, but much depends upon my brother. I'll need him to squire me. If he's too busy, I'll need to change my plans." Jane sounded distinctly wistful.

"Oh, really," murmured Amy. "Too heavy-handed of you, Jane."

"I could escort you," said Lambert. "I'd be glad to. I've been shown around myself. It would make a nice change to be the one to do the showing. St. Mary's is the place everyone starts with. I'm free to come and go as I please in most of the buildings around Midsummer Green, including the Winterset Archive."

"Excellent." Jane's delight was plain. "What else?"

"Do you know much about stained glass? The glass in St. Joseph's chapel is supposed to be old and fine, if you know about such things. I don't. The labyrinth in the botanical garden is famous, of course, but we'd need a Fellow of Glasscastle to escort us there. Everything in England seems old to me, but when they dug a reflecting pool in the garden at Wearyall, they found some Roman potsherds, so maybe Glasscastle will seem old to you too."

"I'd love to see everything," said Jane. "Tomorrow, perhaps?"

"Well, sure. Unless Jack Meredith needs me for a marksmanship trial. There are no tests scheduled tomorrow—that I know of." Lambert didn't let the pleasure Jane's enthusiasm provoked overrule his honesty. "I can't show you everything, but what I can, it'd be a pleasure."

"Two o'clock?" Jane suggested eagerly.

Amy rolled her eyes but said nothing.

Lambert asked, "Shall I call for you here?"

"That would be perfect. It will give me the whole morning to torment Robin. You're very kind, Mr. Lambert." Jane's smile was wonderful.

"It's nothing." Lambert thought it over. "It might be better to get someone with full authority to go with us. Then neither of us will miss any points of interest."

"It's all new to me. Amy, would you care to come with us? Robin must have shared the best bits with you, surely?"

"Oh, I have seen quite enough stained glass for now. You two will enjoy yourselves."

Lambert held Amy's mildly satirical gaze. "You should come with us. I ought to have thought of it myself."

"Perhaps another time," said Amy. "I've been shown the glass in the chapel of St. Mary's so many times I think I may scream if I must admire it again so soon. When Robert decides to show you the labyrinth in the botanical gardens, I'll come along. Except for that, I'd rather stay here and put my feet up."

The parlormaid joined them again, this time bearing an envelope on her tray. Amy added, "Here's your wire at last, Jane. You put the wrong house number, I see."

"I did not."

"Your penmanship, I suppose. No wonder it was delayed." Amy opened the envelope and read. In a moment, she looked up. "I understand the part about inviting yourself for a visit of indefinite duration. I understand the part about hoping to be here in time for tea. But what on earth do you mean by Luke 15:23?"

"'Bring hither the fatted calf.'" Lambert smiled crookedly at the stares this earned him from Amy and Jane. "I liked Sunday school, that's all."

"I'm glad someone knows the reference," Jane said. "I looked it up specifically for Robin's benefit."

Amy shook her head. "You're a strange girl, Jane."

Jane's good cheer was unimpaired. "Odd, that's what Robin always says."

Lambert left the Brailsford house to walk back to his rooms at Glasscastle. It was a bright, warm day. Only a brisk southwest wind kept it from being unpleasantly hot. The wind forced him to adjust his Panama hat to a less jaunty angle to keep it on. It was insistent, shoving him along, as if it thought he should be off doing something useful. Yet he had nothing to do, useful or otherwise, until dinner.

Whatever the residents of Glasscastle town were doing, they seemed to be doing it out of sight. Even the busiest streets were nearly empty. Here and there weeds grew in the center of the streets, the usual wear and tear of cart traffic in abeyance for the summer holiday.

To Lambert, the buildings of the town of Glasscastle circled the foot of Glasscastle Hill like a ring of stone. Set like a jewel in the bezel of that ring was the walled and gated university of Glasscastle, where magic lived and worked in the harsh light of modern day.

Holythorn was the senior college of Glasscastle, and every scholar of Holythorn was a Fellow, a full scholar of magic. St. Joseph's was a less exalted institution, for it and its sister Wearyall admitted beginners, young men who were just setting out in the study of magic. All three colleges were vital to the whole that was Glasscastle. No religious mystery of three in one was required. It was an arrangement as practical as a three-legged stool.

In its way, Glasscastle was its own religion. Those who taught and studied there were devotees of the study of magic, magic for its own sake, the purest of disciplines. Behind its gates, Glasscastle enfolded itself in halls and towers, greens and gardens.

Lambert found it a pure delight to walk the mile and a half from the Brailsford house to the great gate of Glasscastle. The sun would have been hot, but the morning's high clouds had refused to burn off. The overcast thinned the summer sunlight and gave it a silvery cast. There was just a suggestion of potential bad weather to come in that slight overcast. With a persistent stiff breeze, the sky should have been utterly clear, yet the high cloud lingered. Lambert savored the warmth of the sun on his back as he walked the cobbled streets. He savored the cool of the shade when the street he walked was overarched with trees.

Glasscastle Hill loomed over town and university alike, the long grass on the hillside shimmering green and gold as the wind made waves through it. At first, Lambert had wondered at the starkness of the hill. Why build all around the base and never upon the hill itself? His friend Nicholas Fell, in Lambert's opinion the fount of all knowledge, arcane and historical, had explained the phenomenon to him.

Long ago, the hill had been crowned with a prehistoric fort. Traces of the flat walkway that had circled to the top were still faintly visible, as if the hill had been terraced once. It was no longer possible to tell which had come first, the remains of ancient dwellings at the foot of the hill or the tradition that the hill itself was a place of power and not to be built upon.

"There are legends that the hill is hollow," Fell had said, when Lambert asked him about it. "Only legends, alas. About one hundred years ago, the Vice Chancellor of the day authorized an archaeological survey. He believed the ancient Phoenicians once had an outpost here and that the local legends were folk memories of a tin mine somewhere in the hill."

"What did they find?" How many thousands of years had men walked here? How many stories had been told of hollow hills and places of power? Lambert's imagination was afire with the possibilities.

"Potsherds, mostly. Nothing lasts like a potsherd because nothing much can happen to it. Even if it breaks, from then on you have two potsherds," Fell said. "There was some excitement about a find at the crest of the hill, right where the old fort once was. It turned out to be a stoneware bottle, probably for beer, quite recent."

"No tin mine, then?"

"No, nor any gateway to the hollow hill. No champions asleep until England's hour of need. Nothing but a few broken pots. Not exactly the stuff of legends."

"No, I suppose not."

"Tsk, Lambert. You seem disappointed. It's only to be expected. Modern methods elicit modern answers. If you want a legend, that's easily arranged. Climb the hill by moonlight and weave your own. Profit by past example and take some beer with you."

Lambert paused at the head of Hautboy Road to savor the view of Glasscastle at the foot of the green and golden hill. Behind the crenellated walls, the spires and towers of the place were peaceful. As they always did in his mind's eye, the stones of Glasscastle seemed more than simply gray to Lambert. They were a gray stained subtly with other colors: lavender, silver, and violet, as iridescent as a pigeon's feathers.

From what Lambert could see at a distance, there was no more activity within the gates of Glasscastle than there was without. It was a sleepy afternoon, but for that constant southwest wind.

Even as he neared the great gate, Lambert weighed the merits of going out again. He'd had enough of sitting still. Yet his stiff collar bothered him. The boots he'd put on for a formal call were too good to hike in. Despite his light flannels and the crisp breeze, he was sweating. Whatever he did for the rest of the afternoon, a change of clothing was the first order of business.

In the cool shade of the gatehouse arch, Lambert greeted the Fellow of the university on duty as gatekeeper, signed the visitors book, and crunched out into the sunlight along the pea-gravel path that crossed the green to Holythorn.

From inside its gates, Lambert could not help but think of Glasscastle as a labyrinth or a maze, walls within walls. Three paths that met at the great gate soon branched into many, as the broad stretch of Midsummer Green yielded to the shadowed passages of the colleges that flanked it. A man could get lost in those passages, Lambert knew. More than once, he'd been lost himself.

Lambert made his way to Holythorn College. Once indoors, he climbed stairs two at a time, eager to reach what he considered home, the rooms Nicholas Fell had invited him to share six months before.

Fell, as a Senior Fellow of the college, had three rooms overlooking a garden. The middle room, spacious and comfortable, served as a sitting room. It boasted a deep window seat overlooking the garden, a sound, well-designed fireplace with a Venetian mirror hung above the mantelpiece, and a handsome old clock ticking industriously on the wall. On either side of the sitting room was a bedroom, Fell's twice the size of the one he'd given Lambert.

Even though Fell had a study filled with books and other reference materials at the Winterset Archive, his rooms at Holythorn were still lined floor to ceiling with his books. Lambert had never seen so many books in one place in his life as he had the first time he laid eyes on Fell's sitting room. Later, when he saw the Winterset Archive, his ideas about what constituted a lot of books had been revised upward radically. Nevertheless, he still found Fell's books a source of abiding wonder and pleasure.

As Lambert had few possessions of his own, his small bedroom was ample in size. All he really needed was a bed and a wash stand, and there was a wardrobe besides. The sitting room held everything else he considered vital to support life: Fell's books, a comfortable chair, and a good reading light. Given free run of such things, the living arrangements at Holythorn suited him tolerably well. He liked Fell and he was grateful to him for his generous hospitality. Compared with life on tour or in a rooming house, life at Glass-castle was a revelation. Never before had Lambert known such comfort, privacy, or peace.

At the moment, however, Lambert found the cosiness of Holythorn, usually so pleasant, stuffy and hot. He needed to be outdoors. He would change his clothes, get back out into that wind, and let good fresh air clear his head and calm him down.

As Lambert had half expected it would be, the sitting room he shared with Nicholas Fell was empty, as was Fell's bedroom. The only sign of recent human habitation in the sitting room was one of Fell's stale cheroots left half smoked and teetering on a scallop shell that did service as an ashtray. That cheroot had been there two days now. Lambert had last seen Fell at breakfast the day before. Fell had said nothing at that time about any deviation from his usual routine, nor had he left any message for Lambert.

Lambert didn't permit himself to waste any time speculating about Fell's whereabouts. The man didn't need a nanny, after all, nor did he owe Lambert any explanation of his actions. Fell's scholarship—or to be exact, Fell's idiosyncratic notion of scholarship—drove him. That was explanation enough.

Lambert changed from flannels into a linen suit several degrees less impressive than the one he'd put on for tea with Amy. It was that much more comfortable and Lambert moved with ease as he took a circuitous path away from Holythorn. His route led Lambert behind the Holythorn kitchens, between the kitchen garden and the walled garden of St. Joseph's deanery, toward Pembroke gate, to the east side of Glasscastle, to the far side of the university from the Brailsford house.

There, in the shadow of Wearyall's cloister garden walls, Lambert sat on a stone bench and listened. The sound of chanting voices was clear and pure. There were more voices during the regular school year than there were now, so the volume was not as loud as it had been the first time Lambert came there. But the power in those voices had nothing to do with the volume. Many voices sang as one, intoning the pure tones of the chants. That was the source of the beauty, to Lambert. That such disparate young men could each bend his will to serve Glasscastle, that the individual could surrender himself for the good of the whole, that many could become one.

Lambert yielded to impulse and stretched out full length on the stone bench. He balanced his hat on his stomach and gazed up into the shimmer of leaves overhead. The wind in the trees blended with the chanting. Lambert stared upward. Beyond the leaves, the sky was raked with small scudding clouds. Yes, there was bad weather brewing out there somewhere, with more rain to come. Rainiest summer for years, folks said.

It had been raining when he first visited this spot. Lambert had arrived at Glasscastle in February. The grass had been just as green then, but the trees were bare and most of the flowers yellow, forsythia and daffodils within Glasscastle, gorse on the hillsides. The damp cold had sliced through Lambert's clothes courtesy of a wind that seemed never to ease or shift direction more than a degree or two from true north. It had been chilblain weather.

Lambert's arrival at Glasscastle had been in full cowboy regalia. He'd assumed that the men from Glasscastle, stern in their shiny top hats, meant to hire a cowboy sharpshooter, so he'd prepared accordingly. He'd worn his show costume, and he'd brought along the Colt Peacemaker, his most reliable weapon. The effect was all he'd planned. Heads had turned every step of the way, some with a nearly audible snap. It wasn't until he was inside the precincts of Glasscastle that he understood how he'd miscalculated. The Fellows of Glasscastle didn't want a cowboy, they just wanted a sharp-shooter.

Lambert considered himself an entertainer, thanks to his time with Kiowa Bob. He had never meant to give anyone as much entertainment as he did that day at Glasscastle. It could have been worse. His shooting was up to standard. But the intense amusement his costume inspired was more than Lambert had bargained for. On top of that, Lambert had to strain to keep his embarrassment from showing. That had never been a problem before, even back in his earliest days with the Wild West Show. Lambert told himself to perk up. It didn't help much.

Luncheon, when they got around to serving it, made up for some of the social discomfort. After the meal, the Senior Fellows, the men in the shiniest top hats of all, took Lambert around the grounds of Glasscastle, and that was where Lambert understood the magnitude of his error. He'd been standing just here beside the bench, watching the rain drip from the brim of his hat, when his escort paused to listen to the chants from Wearyall College.

The place was beautiful, that much Lambert had noticed at once. The bench was in a spot well sheltered from that tireless wind in winter, ordi-narily basking in the sun so that even on that roughest, coldest of days, snow-drops bloomed in the grass beside the ancient foundation stones. Lambert had been admiring the snowdrops in an absentminded way when the sound of chanting transfixed him.

Many voices raised as one, though not raised far, seemed to inhabit the trees, the grass, every mossy stone of the place—and illuminate it. The music filled Lambert's chest and stung his eyes with tears. It opened his heart the way only the sight of home and the sound of certain voices had ever opened it before. The change occurred with a speed that frightened him. One moment he was himself, waiting patiently for the tour to move on, and the next moment he was clinging to the chant, waiting with his whole soul open, breathless to discover how it would change him next.

Time went away for Lambert as he stood listening, but his escort did not. He stood rapt as long as his guides' patience permitted, but at last Lambert had to yield and let himself be led away, towed along to finish the tour. As the distance from the garden grew and the intensity of the experience faded, the chant became a separate thing again, something Lambert could think about objectively.

Afterward, Lambert couldn't account for the power the chant held for him, couldn't really believe it had seized him with such speed and force. When he was thinking with his head again, not his heart, it was the purpose behind the music that intrigued Lambert most. The notes held a meaning he felt he ought to understand. Lambert was sure of that, yet all the while his rational mind flipped and struggled like a trout to explain to itself how he could possibly know any such thing. How could he be so sure of something he had never encountered before, something he knew nothing about? How could he be so sure that this was the most important thing that had ever happened to him? What *had* happened to him?

The spell of that oddly uncomplicated music lingered with Lambert when he walked away. Lambert agreed to stay and help the top hats of Glasscastle with their marksmanship project. He didn't know what it was about the chanting that changed things so. He simply knew he needed to hear more. He needed to learn more. He needed to be there.

From that day on, Lambert had adopted the manners of Glasscastle as quickly and as sincerely as possible. He wanted to fit in there as best he could. He wanted to belong, but failing that, he wanted to spend every moment he could exploring the urgency that chanting roused within him. He had to put up with the teasing reminders of his debut, which embarrassed him a little more every time he remembered it. But they let him stay.

In two days, he was trusted to stick to the paths of the university open to him as a guest. The first chance he had, and every chance after that, he'd made his way back to the bench outside Wearyall. That was where he listened. That was where the music of the massed voices worked its way into his bones. That was where he first met Nicholas Fell.

It had been a miserable day, not raining but just about to, and the wind was unrelenting. After his first disastrous day at Glasscastle, Lambert had worn his best, most unobtrusive clothes, and after half an hour of sitting still, even his heavy topcoat did nothing to keep the chill away.

Lambert had been joined by a rumpled, wiry man with thick dark hair and a neatly trimmed mustache. It was hard to not stare at the dark hair, because the man was bareheaded. His voice, when the man spoke, was low, almost diffident.

"I'm terribly sorry to interrupt you," the newcomer said as he approached the bench, "but have you seen my hat?"

Lambert couldn't help taking a quick look around. There was the bench, the stone walls, the corner of garden, plenty of trees, and some snowdrops blooming. No hat. "Sorry, no."

The man sank down on the bench beside Lambert with a weary sigh. "Blast them. Where do they get these notions?" In reply to Lambert's look of inquiry, he explained apologetically, "My students believe I pay them insufficient attention. In reprisal, they have taken my hat. I thought I had interpreted the ransom note correctly. Apparently not." He thought it over. "It's a good hat. Worth going to some inconvenience to recover. But it isn't a remarkable hat. I may simply have to resign myself to its loss. My name is Nicholas Fell, by the way. You're the American, are you not?"

Lambert blinked. "I'm *an* American," he admitted cautiously.

"Around here, that means you're *the* American." Fell tugged at the corner of his mustache. "Beastly boys. I don't know where they get the time, let alone the energy."

"I thought the students of Glasscastle led an ascetic life." Lambert nodded toward the sound of chanting. "Rituals and all."

"Up at five o'clock in the morning to chant for hours, scrub the floors for a quick diversion, a cup of gruel and a good gossip for breakfast, and then off to attend their lectures?" Fell made a derisive sound. "That still leaves them hours to spend getting into trouble, the young animals. I liked that hat, damn it."

"If I find it, I'll be sure to report it."

Fell gave Lambert a long look. It was a piercing look, and Lambert wanted to squirm under the close scrutiny. "You are cold." Fell rose. "Come to my rooms with me and I'll give you a drink. Brandy all right?"

Lambert got to his feet. He was inches taller than Fell, but he didn't feel it, for all he loomed over him. Fell seemed to consider him an equal, someone of merit not for what he could do or where he was from, but just for who he was. "You're very kind. I'm not supposed to drink anything stronger than tea, though."

"Sorry. Tea it is, then. Come along." Fell beckoned Lambert and the pair of them walked together along the winding paths to Holythorn. By the time they finished tea, Lambert knew he liked Fell. Over the next few days, Fell made it clear that he liked Lambert well enough to solve the problem of housing by letting him share his rooms at Holythorn.

Six months now, Lambert had been at Glasscastle. Six months of working at whatever job he was given, trying to fit in. The work they wanted him for was simplicity itself, firing every kind of weapon they handed him as accurately as possible. The hard part was fitting in when he wasn't working. Fell was far from the usual mold of Glasscastle scholars.

At first the whole atmosphere of Glasscastle had seemed foreign to Lambert, more foreign at times than the places he'd visited in France and Germany. There was no chance of forgetting he was foreign in countries where he didn't speak the language at all. At Glasscastle, after the first weeks, similarities lulled him. In some ways, it seemed more like home to him than Wyoming had. The serenity and the seriousness of Glasscastle made Lambert feel as if he belonged there. Yet sooner or later, he was always yanked back to reality. He was a guest, a wayfaring stranger, where left was right and right was left. Even the accents in words fell in strange places, so that in speaking the same language, Lambert could sometimes hardly understand, let alone be understood. It was the people who made him feel foreign. Some of the people. Fell didn't seem to care if Lambert were an American or not. Amy seemed to revel in any symptom of cowboy colorfulness that Lambert could think of.

People like Yardley, on the other hand, made Lambert feel foreign. Yardley was a Senior Fellow of Holythorn. That Lambert spoke English was something Yardley seemed unwilling to concede. He would often cock his head and ask Lambert to repeat what he'd said, as if his accent were too thick to understand. Some words, such as "reckon," Yardley treated as if they were not merely unfamiliar but profane. When Yardley was gatekeeper, the spectacle of Lambert writing his name in the visitors' book all by himself made Yardley marvel aloud.

Yardley was in Vienna for the summer. Lambert wished the Austrians joy of him. If there were any justice in the world, Yardley would be treated as rudely as he treated others. Lambert held no hope of such a thing. He knew the people of Vienna were far more polite than Yardley. Wayfaring strangers there were much better off.

Although he was a stranger, Lambert had set himself to learn everything he could about Glasscastle. There was no method to his study. He picked up facts at random, like seashells at the shore.

Chants at Glasscastle were in Latin. Even the least promising student, fresh faced and new to the university, was able to memorize the words and music that powered the wards of Glasscastle. As the day moved on, so did the chants. The words and music changed throughout the day and night, with students chanting in shifts according to their schedules. The timing of the changes in the chants was drawn from the bells.

Bells were almost as common as snowdrops at Glasscastle. Full sets of bells hung in the spires of St. Mary's and St. Joseph's. They were augmented by individual bells in each college. Every day was divided by bells, simple music to mark the hours. Every night was bordered by bells, from the curfew that rang stray undergraduates home at midnight to the vigorous changes that welcomed every day at Prime, a joyous cascade of sound that began in the last moments of darkness and spilled over into the first gray shades of morning.

Lambert learned the trees of Glasscastle as well as he learned the bells. Every tree gave a hint to the direction of the prevailing wind, for even the noblest beech tree, straight and proud and silver, held itself at a slight angle, leaning south. Glasscastle was well endowed with trees, great old cedars and limes and oaks as well as the beeches. The famous thorn tree that had given its image to the Glasscastle university seal and its name to Holythorn College grew beside the church of St. Mary's, sheltered in its cloistered courtyard. If, as legend insisted, the tree was nearly nineteen centuries old, it did not look it. It had bloomed exuberantly at Easter and Lambert hoped he'd still be around when the tree bloomed again. Folks told him it bloomed at Christmas as well as Easter but he didn't see how that was possible. A tree could blossom once a year, not twice.

The year at Glasscastle was divided as carefully as the days. The first term of the year began in mid-January and had been well under way by the time Lambert arrived. The next term began after Whitsuntide and lasted well into the summer. The third term didn't begin for more than a month. At first, Lambert had enjoyed the relative peace and quiet of the days between terms. Now holiday sleepiness made the days seem uncomfortably long.

There were older universities in England than Glasscastle. Oxford and Cambridge had been granting degrees long before Glasscastle admitted students to St. Joseph's, the first of its three colleges, in the late fourteenth century. There were larger universities and richer universities, but no other institution in the country was devoted to the study of magic. In the wake of the pestilence, all the resources of Glasscastle's great library had been turned to research in hope of preventing the return of the plague.

Down the centuries, the focus had changed. Glasscastle still prided itself on the research done within its walls. But the walls themselves had taken on a greater significance. Glasscastle was protected by its own and in turn it protected the knowledge stored in its archives. Wisdom, or at least knowledge, had found refuge there almost as long as the thorn tree had grown and blossomed.

In some ways, a student of Glasscastle led a monastic life. Every student who matriculated as an undergraduate devoted himself for a set number of hours each day to the chants that gave strength to the protective spells around Glasscastle. The first-year students took it in turn to chant the wards. In his first days at Glasscastle, Lambert had dared to picture himself among them, rising before dawn to join the chanting, dividing his day between study, devotion, and simple physical chores, as an undergraduate of St. Joseph's or Wearyall, he didn't care which. Students retired early, in theory at least, and they did not indulge in the intoxications common in the world outside. In theory. It was all theory as far as Lambert was concerned. He had dared to picture himself as a second-year student, increasing the time spent in study as his place in the chants was taken by newer students. He had even dared to imagine himself passing the tests administered at the end of the ninth term, three years on, to earn the robes of a scholar of Glasscastle. Anyone could dream. In theory.

Lambert let the sway of the treetops lull him into a doze. Only a deep voice speaking almost in his ear brought him back to full attention.

"You. I might have known. You do know you aren't supposed to be here without an escort, don't you?" The voice belonged to Jack Meredith, like Fell and Voysey a Fellow of Holythorn, the man who administered the tests of marksmanship Lambert was given. Meredith was tall and strong enough to make his words sound like something of a threat, even to someone Lambert's size.

"I stay on the gravel path." Lambert was in no hurry to sit up. If Meredith had ever felt inclined to exercise the authority vested in him as a member of the university, Lambert had never detected a sign of it. "Were you looking for me?"

As soon as there was room on the bench, Meredith sat down next to Lambert. "Not you in particular, no. When I see someone sleeping on a garden bench between terms, I feel obliged to ask if he needs some sort of assistance. During the term, of course, I assume it is an exhausted under-graduate."

"What kind of help do they get?"

Meredith looked surprised by the question. "None. Anyone too weak to sustain our academic rigors is welcome to find more congenial surroundings."

"Right. I should have seen that one coming."

"Where's your Fell friend?" Meredith looked around as if he expected Nicholas Fell to spring up from the path before him. "I suppose Voysey and Stowe and Stewart have wheeled him out to impress the visiting ministry. All ancient and legendary glories of Glasscastle to report on the double."

Lambert took his time about deciphering Meredith's words. Fell was older than Meredith, but he didn't think Fell qualified as ancient any more than Meredith did. Meredith might be using slang to mean just the opposite of what he actually said. He often did. "I don't think Fell's off drinking fine old brandy with Voysey and the boys. I haven't seen him at all today. Or even yesterday. Doesn't seem likely that he'd impress any of the government bigwigs. Or vice versa. Voysey should probably keep Fell at a safe distance from anyone he wants to butter up."

"I couldn't agree more. Fell wouldn't impress my maiden aunt. That doesn't mean the Provosts would leave him out of it, though. Perhaps that's why Fell's playing least in sight. To keep out of their way."

"Lying low, you mean? You're probably right. Well, if you see him before I do, tell him to write home, will you? I miss him."

Meredith said, "There's no accounting for taste. If Voysey ever offered me some of that fine old brandy, I'd be there early and often. It's a pity they make a point of keeping the likes of us well away from the dignitaries."

"Next time, maybe."

"Cold comfort, Samuel. By next time, they'll have finished all the brandy. Mind you, I've no doubt they need the brandy to get through the whole agenda. Wiston is the world's biggest bore and Fyvie's not much better. Voysey will be lucky if he doesn't doze off between speeches."

"What's it all about, do you know?" Lambert asked.

"Of course I know. Nobody gossips like an undergraduate, except perhaps a Senior Fellow. Voysey doesn't want old Wistful or Lord Fiver interfering with the project, but come next budget season, he doesn't want them to neglect us either. He invites them here so he can wine them and dine them on the premises. A reminder of what it means to have your research done in the true Glasscastle style."

"Wouldn't it work the other way?" Lambert protested. "If you let on to the ministers how comfortable we are here, they'll cut the budget. Won't they?"

Meredith's scorn was cheerful. "Not those two. They don't mind the hospitality a bit, but what really matters to them is the deference. Their support for the Agincourt Project lets them come here and soak up some gracious living."

"Surely they have plenty of that wherever they come from?"

"Oh, they do. They do. But the Agincourt Project isn't competing with their clubs. It's competing with Sopwith, Roe, and Cody and the other mad aviators. There's talk of a military air trial with a cash prize for the designer of the winning aeroplane. Wiston and Fyvie might well be carried away by the glamour of mankind in flight, so Voysey means to remind them that air trials are likely to involve hours of standing fetlock-deep in a muddy pasture somewhere. Much more comfortable to support the tireless efforts of Glasscastle."

"They can't take funding away from us—" Lambert caught himself and rephrased his thought. "They wouldn't take funding away from the Agincourt Project before the device is designed and built, would they? That's just throwing money away, to cut the budget before the project is done." If the ministers did cut the funding, would they be cutting him too? Lambert wondered.

"You're right. But there are a lot of other projects out there competing for the money, and ministers are notoriously fickle beasts. Watch and see." Meredith sprang to his feet. "Now, do stop cluttering up the place. I can't just walk off and leave you here. Come along."

Lambert rose slowly. "You're wasted in this job, Meredith. You'd make a wonderful mother hen."

Meredith struck a pose and adopted what he obviously considered to be an accent right out of the wild west. "'When you call me that, *smile*.'"

Lambert just shook his head despairingly. "Just about everyone's read that book, haven't they?"

"They have now." Meredith laughed a little to himself.

Lambert came quietly. The popularity of Owen Wister's novel *The Virginian* never ceased to amaze him.

———

By the time dinner was served, Jane Brailsford was feeling quite at home in her brother's house. Amy's standard of domestic comfort was high. The guest room was delightful. Jane's luggage was unpacked. The grime of the journey had been washed away. She had changed into her favorite gown. Best of all, Robin was home at last.

Robert Brailsford believed in the importance of precision. This belief revealed itself in many ways. To his sister, the most obvious symptom was his careful choice of clothing. Though he dressed simply, preferring plain black and white in all things, it was the nuance of his choice of garb that betrayed the care he lavished on his appearance. Even relaxing at home, he looked severely elegant, from the gloss of his dark hair, combed straight back, to the gleam of dull-finished gold shirt buttons against the starched perfection of his white linen shirt.

"You might have given us more notice you were coming," Robert told his sister. "Amy would have appreciated it." Precision in speech was another of Robert's habits. He overenunciated his words. Even when he wasn't being reproachful, the emphasis gave his words an accusing air, and on this occasion, he certainly intended to be as reproachful as possible. "It's August. We might have been away ourselves. As it is, it's sheer luck I wasn't obligated to attend the dinner for the ministers this evening."

Jane kept her tone suitably penitent. "I sent you a wire from London as soon as I arrived. I'm sorry I appeared before it did. It's just as well I never expect the fatted calf, isn't it?"

Robert frowned. "Oddly enough, I have no recollection of a prodigal sister anywhere in Scripture. I must say, your rackety ways seem to agree with you. You look splendid."

"Thank you. So do you. Amy, of course, is looking particularly splendid these days." Jane glanced across the table at her sister-in-law. "She always sets a high standard." Amy had the complexion and coloring of a china doll but there was far more to her than met the eye. Neither her flaxen ringlets nor her wide blue eyes were her best feature, rather it was the gleam of lively common sense that lit her from within.

"Jane brought me this brooch from Paris." Amy modeled the delicate cameo for her husband. "Isn't it pretty?"

"Exquisite," said Robert, after a brief but loving inspection of his wife. "Do your duties at Greenlaw permit you to spend much time in Paris, Jane?"

"It is on the way," Jane said. "You've reminded me. Uncle Ambrose sends us all his love."

"Dear old boy. I must write to him soon," Robert said. "Have you come home to see the family? Unfortunate timing, if you have. Mama and Papa are in Scotland. Thomas is with his regiment and the last time he bothered to write, Alfred was in Orvieto. Something to do with studying the construction of a well they have there. He plans to spend the winter in Italy, I gather. Lord knows where Thomas's regiment will be."

"What on earth are Mama and Papa doing in Scotland?" Jane asked. "I thought they could be counted upon never to go farther afield than Tunbridge Wells."

"They're to stay with the Desmonds for the shooting."

"Ah, yes. Shooting. Amy tells me you have an American to help you shoot things for your studies, Robin." Jane saw no reason to beat about the bush. It was just the three of them at the table, after all. "What are you studying? Ornithology?"

"*I'm* not studying anything," Robert replied. "Discretion, Amy. Discretion is vital."

Amy smiled sunnily at her husband. "Why, darling, how can that be? You must have noticed by now that I haven't a shred of it."

"Must you insist others notice it too? Oh, never mind. Yes, Jane. For the moment, I have Mr. Lambert on my staff. Let him alone. He's working."

"What is he working on?"

"Curb your feminine curiosity just this once. Suffice it to say, there is work to be done, work vital to our imperial interests. You don't need the details."

"Oh, very well." Jane felt unusually indulgent toward Robert. She was happy to see her eldest brother again. It had been several years and he had far less hair than she remembered. In addition, he'd grown more solid, positively substantial about the midsection. Perhaps the excellence of the family cook had something to do with that. Certainly the happy combination of food and wine played a large part in Jane's tolerant mood. "Since you feel so strongly about it, I'll leave your wild colonial boy to his own devices. I'm only making the sacrifice for you, though. He seems delightfully unpretentious compared with the usual Glasscastle man."

Robert looked severe. "Lambert isn't a Glasscastle man, Jane, no matter what repellent stereotype that phrase may signify to you or to members of the popular press. He's a guest here and he's been good enough to help us with our research. That's all."

"He's not a student, in other words?" prompted Jane.

Robert frowned. "Certainly not. Did he give you the impression he was?"

"Of course he didn't," Amy said. "He's been put in his place quite thoroughly, Robert. You needn't worry about Mr. Lambert."

"Not if he has you to defend him, obviously." Robert beamed fondly at Amy as he tasted his wine. After a contented pause, he continued. "I was not worried about Lambert in quite that sense. It's the expert pestering Jane's capable of that concerns me. You let that man alone, understand? He works hard and he can't satisfy your curiosity about what we're doing, so no interrogations. Understood?"

Jane surrendered with reluctance. "Understood."

Robert studied her with as much intensity as he'd brought to his appreciation of the wine. "You haven't paid the slightest attention to my invitations to visit for years. What's brought you here now? It can't be pure family feeling."

"Can't it?" Jane tried to look offended. "Why can't it be?"

"Because I know you, Jane. You were happy to leave the bosom of the family when you went off to France and you've been happy to spend most of your holidays on the Continent since. If you're here in Glasscastle instead, it's for a very good reason." Robert kept up his scrutiny. "Honestly, now. What's the ulterior motive, Jane?"

Jane gave up on righteous indignation and settled for a confiding air. "I'm thinking of buying a motor car. A Blenheim Bantam, I thought. Small but sturdy."

Robert snorted. "A Blenheim Bantam? Nonsense. Those things are barely big enough to warrant four wheels. If you were fool enough to try to drive one in London, you'd be crushed like an insect. No, if you're going to bother at all, you'd do far better to buy yourself a real motor car while you're about it. When did you take up motoring?"

"I learned last winter. Now I want something small I can keep at Greenlaw for runs to the railway station and back, things like that." For once, Jane felt unalloyed fondness for her brother. He might be full of opinions about what sort of motor car was worth driving, but it would never cross his mind to tell her that she ought not drive one.

"Nonsense. You'll want a proper motor car if you need one at all, which I doubt. I'll show you mine, give you an idea what you'd be missing."

"*You* have a motor car, Robin? You astound me." Jane had always viewed her brother as the third last person in the world to welcome any form of innovation. The last two people would be Mother and Father.

"Not just a motor car. A Morgan Minotaur. Purrs like a cat, growls like a lion, and—on a suitable stretch of racetrack—it can do thirty-five miles per hour. I'll take you and Amy for a run on Sunday afternoon. You'd like that, wouldn't you, Amy?"

Amy looked delighted by the idea. "I would. We might go to Wells. We could take a picnic lunch."

Jane smiled at them both. "Robin, I have misjudged you. That sounds delightful."

When the possibilities of a Sunday afternoon picnic had been thoroughly discussed, a companionable silence fell over the dinner table.

After a suitable pause, during which she made neat work of removing the worst of the bones from her portion of fish, Jane asked, "Do you know someone named Nicholas Fell? I understand he's a Fellow of Glasscastle."

Robert looked exasperated. "Fell? Yes, of course I do. Save yourself the effort of questioning him. He has nothing to do with what we're working on."

"No?" Jane looked up from her fish bones with interest. "What does he do, then?"

"He's a Fellow of Glasscastle, Jane." Amy smiled tranquilly from Jane to Robert. "One might as well ask what a swan does, floating along the river."

"That's not a bad analogy," Robert conceded. "It's the effect we all strive to attain, certainly. To the world we present a facade of such effortless indif-ference that we might as well not be capable of magic at all. All seraphic calm on the surface, whilst among ourselves we know that underneath one paddles furiously, seeking one's own advantage all the while. Fell's not that sort."

"Not a paddler, do you mean?" Jane asked. "Or not calm?"

"I mean he's not focused entirely on his own advancement. Unlike some I could mention. On the contrary. At times Fell hardly seems interested in advancement at all. He's not the sort to volunteer for extra duty on the gate, mind, but he is devoted to Glasscastle. Doesn't let anything distract him from his studies."

"Mr. Fell doesn't care much for outward appearances," said Amy. "His paddling is in the interest of pure scholarship."

"A bit too pure, at times," said Robert. "One might wish him to pay a trifle more attention to his students, but one can't have everything. Fell was invited to help with the project at the outset. He soon grew bored with us and went back to his own work. One favor he did us first, though. He volunteered to host Lambert. The two of them are even sharing Fell's quarters. Good luck, that, since it lets Lambert stay close by yet keeps him isolated from the inquisitive. No one is less curious about the project than Fell, so Lambert doesn't have to worry about letting information slip inadvertently." Robert gave Jane a meaningful look. "You've promised, now—no interrogations."

"I've promised," said Jane. "Mr. Lambert knows Mr. Fell quite well, then?"

"Oh, yes. Not precisely David and Jonathan, but they seem to be good friends." Amy said.

"Most considerate of Mr. Lambert, offering to call for me tomorrow afternoon." Jane permitted herself to dwell on the thought of Mr. Lambert for a moment. There was something very striking about him. Of course it was only natural that she would find him attractive. So would she find any man that athletic, anyone who moved with such instinctive ease, anyone whose eyes held such utterly disarming modesty. Still, it would never do to let herself be distracted.

"Poor fellow just doesn't guess what he is in for. He's not afraid of you. Not yet." Robert seemed inclined to drop the subject in favor of devoting himself to his meal. "Give him time."

2

"Therefore when any favoured of high Jove
Chances to pass through this adventurous glade,
Swift as the sparkle of a glancing star,
I shoot from Heaven to give him safe convoy"

It was too hot that evening for the customary menu of meat and two vegetables, comprehensively boiled, but out of sheer habit Lambert ate dinner in hall just the same, right down to sampling the tray of cheeses offered as a final blow to the digestion. Even if he didn't eat much, it restored him to be in the company of other people. Even if he didn't say much. There wasn't much chance.

Despite the weight of the meal, conversation at the table was lively. Lambert found himself between Cromer and Palgrave, Fellows of Holythorn for only a year, but pompous enough to have been there all their lives. About three times a week, they argued about the Bible. On the days they didn't, they argued about the weather, Chinese politics, and horses. Lambert didn't know anything about Chinese politics, but judging from their opinions about the Bible, weather, and horses, Lambert didn't set much store by anything either of them said. It turned out to be a Bible night.

"You can't argue that Scripture shouldn't be subject to scholarship." Palgrave had a better head for claret than Cromer did. "Why should the Bible be different to any other book?"

"I never said it should." Cromer said, "I never said it shouldn't be subject to whatever analytical method you choose. I said scholarship alone proves nothing. You may rank your hypotheses from least unlikely to most unlikely.

That is the use of scholarship. You cannot understand Scripture in hypothetical terms."

"I disagree. No rational man understands it in any other way," said Palgrave. "Even if your approach made sense, which it does not, what is it good for? Where does it take us? Back to Bethlehem? Please."

"Talk all you like about the historical Jesus." Cromer calmed himself with more claret. "You're missing the point."

"The point is, you prefer to believe the fairy tales. Three kings bear gifts of gold and frankincense and myrrh to a child born in a manger." Palgrave laughed to himself. "God put Adam to sleep and made Eve from one of his ribs. You'd rather believe folktales than admit that man has evolved like every other creature on this earth."

"Who wouldn't?" Cromer countered. "As for utility, you must admit we learn more about women from the story of Adam and Eve than we do from anything in the pages of *On the Origin of Species*."

The argument lasted precisely as long as the cheese and biscuits held out. When the meal was over, Cromer and Palgrave concluded their debate with the verbal equivalent of tennis players shaking hands at the net and went their separate ways.

As the room emptied, Lambert tried to picture anyone from Kiowa Bob's show taking part in such a polite disagreement. Chinese politics, maybe. But if the subject were something they cared about, say, the rival merits of a ham sandwich over roast beef, it would have been profanity for sure and fisticuffs quite likely.

That was one of the true ancient and legendary glories of Glasscastle, Lambert decided, an atmosphere where men could differ strenuously over matters both vital and trivial. No one needed to resort to force to get his ideas across. No one needed to defend himself on any level but that of his ideas. No argument was final. It would all be fought through again, perhaps not three times a week but whenever there was fresh information, or fresh energy to explore the subject.

Lambert caught himself. Pomposity must be contagious. If it was, Lambert hoped he would catch something else along with it. Detachment, maybe. Or objectivity. Or plain persistence.

Alone, Lambert left the dining room. The place had cleared out early this evening. Too hot to linger. Lambert wished for a moment that Cromer and Palgrave had gone in for arguing about the weather instead of the Bible.

With the change in the wind, from southwest to north, how could anyone mistake the break in the weather that was coming? Unless Cromer and Palgrave didn't read the signs the same way he did?

Lambert returned to the quarters he shared with Fell to find no trace of his friend. The rooms seemed unnaturally quiet. Lambert had to chide himself out of a fancy that the place was waiting for something to happen. Any anticipation was his own. Any sense of impending doom was nothing but a shadow cast by his own impending indigestion. The steady tick of the clock on the wall held no significance. The chime of the Glasscastle bells, complex and comforting, meant only that the time for bed approached.

At midnight, still with no word of Fell's whereabouts, Lambert retired with a faint sense of unease. There was nothing extraordinary about Fell's absence, let alone anything sinister, but it was not like Fell to leave for days without mentioning his plans. Even Fell knew how to send a telegram, after all.

Nightfall had done little or nothing to ease the warmth and stuffiness of Lambert's little room. It was hard to bear the heat. Lambert thought back to his first night at Glasscastle. It had been cold that night. He had spent the whole day playing the cowboy, thinking they'd be through with him and send him on his way afterward. Instead they'd put him up in luxurious guest quarters, the kind of place they used for visiting dignitaries. Vice Chancellor Voysey had shown him there in person and asked if he had any questions.

Voysey was young for his post, hardly forty, but he had great dignity just the same. He was as lean as a whippet, at least an inch taller than Lambert, and held himself proud as Caruso. Not one to hide behind old-fashioned whiskers to try to enhance his authority, Voysey was clean-shaven, his wavy red-brown hair untouched by pomade. He dressed the same way everyone else at Glasscastle did, but Voysey's clothing seemed subtly different. There was a certain drama about Voysey, a bit of extra sweep to his academic robes, a bit of extra gloss to his top hat. Compared with the other men of Glasscastle, Voysey seemed to have good reason to be convinced of his own importance. Oddly, he seemed less smug than either Victor Stowe, Provost of St. Joseph's, or Cecil Stewart, Provost of Wearyall.

Lambert hadn't been impressed with the guest quarters. He liked the fine old furnishings, the coal fire smoldering in the fireplace, the dark green velvet curtains that covered the deep windows. All of that looked nice, but it felt miserable. The draughts in the room made the velvet curtains stir a little in the windows. He'd expected Glasscastle to be full of people who thought they were important, and it was. He'd expected they'd live in a place that looked fancier than the Ritz, but why did it have to be cold as an ice house?

Any questions? Voysey had asked. Lambert decided not to ask that one. "I am curious," he admitted. "I've been wondering why you brought me here. Why target shooting at a school that teaches magic? Couldn't you and your friends come up with some kind of magic that would eliminate the need for shooting?"

Voysey waved Lambert to one of the brocade chairs and folded himself into another. "In a way, that is why we brought you here. To help us with that very task. You're here to help in the search for knowledge. Pure research."

Lambert frowned over this. "But you are using magic?"

Voysey leaned forward in his chair. "We're just beginning to learn the best ways to use the scientific method to explore the world. Someday we'll know all there is to know about everything. Until then, there is a certain discipline called, for want of a better word, magic." Voysey's expression invited Lambert to smile at the use of such an old-fashioned term.

"All right." Lambert thought it over. "Where are the wizards?"

Voysey laughed aloud. It made a world of difference to his long face. "That's an antiquated term. As well go into a room full of chemists and ask where the alchemists are. But for lack of a better answer, here I am."

"*You're* a wizard?" Lambert had expected Voysey to be a bit less matter-of-fact about it.

"I study the discipline we haven't yet found a modern term for, yes." Voysey scrutinized Lambert as if gauging how much listening he could do at a sitting. "I began my studies here as an undergraduate of St. Joseph's. My work found favor with the Vice Chancellor and Senior Fellows of the day and upon my graduation, I was invited to stay on as a Fellow of Holythorn. Since then, I have continued to study as I took on more responsibility and authority. Let me emphasize that word. *Study.* We all study here, students, faculty, everyone."

"You mean you study magic." Lambert returned Voysey's inspection with his own. "Were you able to do it before you came here or did you have to learn it on the premises?"

"What little I have mastered, I learned here at Glasscastle." Voysey sounded modest, but under his words ran pure confidence. Lambert judged

Voysey was sure that what he called small magic would seem like a great deal to an outsider. He wondered if Voysey ever played poker. If he did, Lambert wondered how well he did at it.

"How did they know you could learn to do magic when they took you on?"

"Oh, they didn't know. Not with utter certainty." Voysey's modesty took a turn toward the smug. "Though I showed as much promise as any arriving student."

"Does Glasscastle pick students by how much promise they show?" Lambert asked.

"Not entirely. One day there will be a scientific test to determine aptitude. For now, we can't be absolutely sure of any student's capacity. We admit or reject a student on the basis of his background and his previous education. He's given a year of the scholarly regime to demonstrate a capacity for magic. If he does no more than chant for three terms, he has earned his room and board and repaid the efforts of his teacher. But if he does no more than chant, if we detect no aptitude for magic of any kind, he's dismissed at the end of the third term."

"That chanting—" Lambert hesitated. He knew he could find words to describe what the chanting had seemed like to him, but he wasn't sure he could do it without betraying more emotion than was seemly. "Is that magic?"

"You heard the chants?" Voysey seemed pleased. "I thought you were given the standard tour. Did they take you into one of the student chapels too?"

"No, I heard them from the garden. It was—I never heard anything like that before."

"Once you leave Glasscastle, I don't suppose you ever will again." Something in Lambert's expression seemed to soften Voysey. "I'm glad you appreciated the experience. Chants are a vital part of Glasscastle."

"Those are just regular students doing it? You don't pick them for their voices?"

"Lord, no." Voysey chuckled. "We don't want opera singers. We look for young men who can work well as part of the whole. The reliable, rather than the exceptional."

"So—in theory—anyone could spend at least one year here? Once he was admitted?"

"In theory." Voysey hesitated, then went on with gentle firmness. "Admission depends on more than mere interest. We look at each student's background and education. There are certain academic requirements, literacy in Latin, for example."

Voysey's choice of words brought Lambert up short. "Background? What does that mean?"

Voysey looked uncomfortable. "I think you can deduce that from the students you've met. There is a certain, how shall I put it, a certain tone to the Glasscastle man. You'll learn to recognize it when you've spent more time here."

Lambert thought he guessed what Voysey left unsaid. There was no room at Glasscastle for men who came from the working class, nor from beyond the boundaries of the United Kingdom. "Does Glasscastle admit any foreign students?"

Voysey seemed relieved at the question. "Oh, of course. Within the standards I've already described. It's a curious thing, nationality. I have a theory. One of the traditions folk ignorance has insisted upon down the ages is that witches detest water."

"I thought the tradition of ducking witches was based on the notion that water detested witches. Witches floated because the water wouldn't let them sink." Lambert had read that in one of his mother's history books, he couldn't remember which one.

"Quaint, these folktales, aren't they?" Voysey spread his hands. "Scientifically, we're investigating a relationship between the practice of magic, possibly even the aptitude for the practice of magic, and the degree of discomfort occasioned when crossing large bodies of water. Our knowledge is limited now, but as the scientific principles are discovered, I believe this is one of those cases where superstition foreshadows fact. One day we'll be able to show that those hardy souls who colonized the New World were those who survived the ocean voyage—survived when many other travelers sickened and died on the way. It has been established that those, like yourself, who descend from that hardy stock have so little detectable aptitude for magic that we are safe in generalizing that no one from Canada, the United States, or any other part of the New World will show any skill at magic."

"You really have proof of that?" Lambert thought of some of the things he'd seen traveling with Kiowa Bob's show, some of the stories the Indians told, and he wondered what Voysey would make of them.

"Not yet," Voysey replied. "I have every confidence that in a few years, the advances of science will show us the precise wording of the natural law. In the meantime, we simply apply it as a rule of thumb. We didn't know why the apple fell from the tree until Sir Isaac Newton gave us the calculations. But we did know that the apple would fall."

"So only those who come from the right side of the ocean have the capacity to learn magic," said Lambert, "and only those who study at Glasscastle actually do learn magic."

"Perhaps I've oversimplified." Voysey frowned. "Things are not nearly as clear-cut as that. For one thing, of those who might have the capacity to learn magic, only a few do. For another, there is more than one kind of magic, just as there is more than one place magic is taught. If you were a Frenchwoman, God forbid, you could study magic at Greenlaw. If you believed in the lore of kitchen maids, there is a whole body of knowledge to be gained from study of the way one pares an apple. If you believe in fairy tales, there are the four wardens of the world, who balance and protect all earthly realms by neutralizing our magic with their own. Even if you don't believe in fairy tales, from time to time, often in the very oldest families, a wild talent occurs."

"What is a wild talent?" Lambert asked, after a moment of interior confusion involving the parable of the talents.

Voysey's frown deepened. "Wild talent is the capacity to work magic without any preliminary training. One could hardly conceive of anything more dangerous. Scholars believe the conflagration in Pudding Lane originated when someone with wild talent tried lighting a candle with a fire spell."

Lambert took that pitch, waiting in silence for Voysey to explain.

"The Great Fire of 1666 originated in Pudding Lane," the older man said kindly. "Half London burned."

"Some candle," said Lambert.

"It was a windy day," said Voysey. "Fortunately, wild talent is a rare phenomenon. One day our research will tell us why. There will be a reason, one as sensible and solid as the reason a few animals are albino. We just don't understand the scientific principles behind the magic yet. But we will. One day we will." For a moment, Voysey stared beyond Lambert into the glow of the coal fire. Then, as if with an effort, he brought his attention back to Lambert and rose from his chair. "You will have a long day tomorrow. I'll leave you to get your rest. But a word of advice is in order. We want you for your skills as a marksman, not your skills as a showman. Save the spurs and *chaparejos* for Kiowa Bob. Wear something respectable. I think you'll find it far more comfortable."

Any chill Lambert had felt was cured by his embarrassment. "I'd worked that out for myself, Vice Chancellor."

"Good luck tomorrow, Samuel." Voysey had left Lambert counting the hours until he could get away from Glasscastle.

Remembering that cold night on this hot one, Lambert wondered what would have happened if he hadn't seen the garden that first day. If he'd never heard the chants from Wearyall, would he still be hanging around Glasscastle? Kiowa Bob's troupe had gone on with the European tour. Lambert could have been in Italy by now. He might have been to the opera at La Scala. If there was more than one kind of magic in the world, how many kinds of music must there be?

For a time, during those first days at Glasscastle, it had seemed to Lambert as if a door had been opened. He'd been invited into a world where knowledge and mystery were entwined, where music held unsuspected might, where the horizon of the possible was limitless. Lambert knew his welcome in that world was entirely conditional. The door was open for him to contribute his skill. It wasn't there for him to come and go freely. He would stay by that door, though, as long as he could hear the music from within.

There was indeed a thunderstorm during the night. Next morning, the air was as clear and soft as the bells and birdsong that woke Lambert. He went down to breakfast frowning, for there was still no sign of Fell, nor any message from him.

On his way back from breakfast, Lambert decided to look in again at the Winterset Archive, where Fell conducted his research. Lambert had checked Fell's study the day before. Not likely that Fell had returned to the study without returning to his rooms first, but it wasn't out of the question. Fell could be lurking there, so lost in some academic pursuit that the passage of time meant nothing, or he could be hiding out to avoid Vice Chancellor Voysey's ministers.

If Lambert had been a Fellow of Glasscastle, or if he had been accompanied by one, he would have walked straight across the green and into the archive building. As it was, he had to crunch his way around the green, Holythorn to the gatehouse, the gatehouse to Winterset.

As he passed the great gate, Lambert heard a woman call his name. He turned back to follow the voice, walked through the gatehouse arch, and saw Jane Brailsford. She sat alone on one of the stone benches reserved for visitors who had been refused entry. It was a spartan place for the visitor to wait for Glasscastle to come to them, but it served its purpose of isolating visitors until their escorts came to claim them.

Miss Brailsford seemed as well entertained as if she were in a box at the opera. She was dressed in what Lambert could only assume was the latest Parisian mode, since he'd never seen anything quite as sleek in his life. Her hat alone must have cost a month's pay. Only high style could get away with doing that to a bird. Her attitude, as she waited, was no different from the ease she'd displayed in her brother's house. Her enjoyment of the passing scene was clear to see. There was not much in the way of cart traffic in the cobbled street outside, but there were pedestrians and bicyclists in plenty, not to mention the robed Fellows and students who came and went through the arch.

Lambert pulled himself together. "Miss Brailsford. A pleasure. Am I late or are you early?"

"You are blameless, sir. As, in this instance, am I." Jane smiled up at Lambert. "My brother's memory is at fault, I fear. He had a committee meeting first thing this morning so he left the house without me. Prodigiously important meeting, I gather. I was to follow at a more civilized hour and he would collect me for my tour. I have followed his instructions to the letter. The committee must have adjourned at least an hour since. Robin promised to meet me here thirty minutes ago. Yet here I languish."

Lambert had half convinced himself that he'd been imagining the gleam he'd seen in Jane's eyes, but here it was back again. He was glad to see it. "That's languishing, is it?" Lambert thought it over. "My experience with this sort of thing is limited. Forgive me if I get it wrong. But you aren't languishing very hard, are you?"

"I'm just a beginner," Jane explained. Her deadpan expression was perfect. Lambert promised himself he would never play cards with her.

Lambert consulted his pocket watch. "I don't think you can blame Brailsford's memory. Those committee meetings can be the devil. It could still be going on."

"Truly?" Jane looked chastened. "Poor Robin."

"Is there something I could do?" Lambert sat down beside her.

"If you aren't expected elsewhere, I'd appreciate your company. If you are . . ." Jane trailed off.

A small silence stretched between them. Lambert ended it. He didn't like to admit how little honest work there was for him to do at Glasscastle, but it was the truth, so why shrink from saying so? "No, no. I'm at your service. I have no tests today. I was at a loose end, I promise. Let me show you some of the sights of Glasscastle. You'll be doing me a favor."

"No tests of marksmanship, perhaps," said Jane. "Research takes many forms."

Something of Lambert's wariness must have shown on his face, because Jane seemed to relent. "Forget I said that. Last night Robin told me not to ask you about the project. Don't worry. I'll be discreet."

"I'm not worried about your discretion. Mine might be questioned."

Jane grimaced. "Dear me. That will never do. I don't mean to interrogate you. Would you like to interrogate me instead? Just to be perfectly safe?"

Lambert took this in the flirtatious spirit it was obviously intended. "Very much."

"Oh, good." Jane settled herself more comfortably. "Do your worst."

"Yesterday I asked you what subjects you taught. You said Mock Turtle's arithmetic. I don't know what that means."

Jane shook her head slightly. "I was being silly. Amy brings it out in me sometimes. I meant I teach mathematics."

Lambert tried and failed to conceal his surprise. "You teach mathematics?"

"Why? Don't I seem scholarly enough?" Jane gazed at him tranquilly and if anything her eyes were wider and more limpid than Lambert remembered them being the day before.

Lambert didn't let Jane's innocent look or mild tone deceive him. There were tests and then there were tests. She was a schoolteacher, after all. He chose his words with care. "You don't seem anywhere near old enough."

"I am quite old enough." The innocent look remained, but Jane's tone had gone tart.

"Are people ever surprised to learn you teach mathematics?" Lambert could guess the answer from her tartness. Jane had held this conversation often enough to be tired of it.

"People are usually surprised that a woman knows even the rudiments of mathematics." Jane looked as if she would like to say more, but she let it stand at that.

Lambert thought it would be a good idea to get off the topic before her willpower failed. "What other subjects do they teach at your school?"

Jane's elaborately innocent look was gone. She answered as to an equal. "Greenlaw was founded on classical lines, so both the trivium and quadrivium are offered."

Lambert knew he was gaping like a fool when Jane added, "Arithmetic, music, geometry, astronomy, grammar, rhetoric, and logic."

Lambert waved the list away. "Excuse me. I hadn't realized that you taught at Greenlaw. Your sister-in-law said it was a French school. I'm afraid I didn't make the connection with Greenlaw. It's nearly as famous as Glasscastle as a school of magic."

"Nearly?" Jane looked amused. "Magic is taught there. Not languishing, honesty compels me to admit. But we do teach magic, along with decorum, which includes how to sit on a stone bench and make it look as if it were a feather cushion. I don't teach decorum myself. I have studied it."

"But you've studied magic as well." Lambert didn't try to keep the respect out of his voice. It was hard enough to conceal the envy. "True magic."

Jane looked down and Lambert noticed she had gone pink. It was surprisingly becoming. "I only teach mathematics."

"How long have you been a teacher?"

Jane appeared to give this question careful thought. "Not long."

"I didn't think so." Lambert hesitated, then yielded to temptation. "You aren't pompous enough yet."

That brought her attention straight back to him. "You don't know that. I might be pompous as anything when you get me on mathematics."

"It isn't a subject that lends itself to more than one interpretation. Your true pomposity shows itself best where any opinion could be the right one." Lambert thought of Cromer and Palgrave, and added, "Though somehow, no opinion ever turns out to be."

Jane said, "That's all you know. There are many theories of mathematics."

"How can there be? As long as numbers are numbers, the truth is the same."

"But *are* numbers numbers?" Jane countered. "What is truth?"

Lambert held up a hand to stop her. "Don't get fancy on me now. Two plus two equals four. There's an eternal verity for you."

The feathers on Jane's hat bobbed and danced, such was the enthusiasm with which she took issue with him. "You're oversimplifying things. Even eternal verities can change sometimes. It depends on how you perceive them."

"Do you think this particular eternal verity will change?" Lambert gestured at Glasscastle's great gate. "Outsiders kept away while the scholars of Glasscastle pursue their studies in isolation?"

Jane looked blank. "How could it change? Glasscastle wouldn't be Glasscastle without its walls."

"Don't you want it to change? To permit—others to study here?"

Jane's eyes narrowed. "Were you going to say women? Are we going to discuss the rights and privileges of education for women in general? Or shall we go straight to the comparison between Glasscastle and Greenlaw?"

Lambert answered honestly. "I was going to say . . . outsiders. I didn't mean just women, though. I meant—anyone."

"No point in arguing that. Just anyone can't study what Glasscastle studies. Certain skills are required. If those skills belong to a woman, she's better off at Greenlaw. Nothing in Glasscastle compares."

A stocky man in a bowler hat walked close as he passed Lambert and Jane on his way toward the gatekeeper. He paused, his back to Lambert and Jane, at the visitors book. Lambert didn't let his attention waver from Jane for a moment. "How do you know? You've only been here a day. Not even that long."

"Oh, I know." Jane's eyes were as steady as her voice, and as sure.

Lambert said, "Your brother may be trapped in that meeting all day. Why don't we start without him?"

Jane's eyes brightened at the invitation. Lambert permitted himself a moment of deep satisfaction. He might be a wayfaring stranger at Glasscastle, but he could do this much kindness. He presented himself to the gatekeeper, signed his name and Jane's in the book, and won them admittance. There was no delay, for the man in the bowler hat who had gone in ahead of them was already out of sight.

Together Lambert and Jane walked through the outer quadrangles of Glasscastle. It was a glorious morning. Ivy covered the stone walls, green against gray freshened by last night's rain, and deep within the foliage, leaded glass windows gleamed as diamond panes of glass caught the brilliant morning light. The place smelled sweet, a combination of the morning's baking, the rosemary in the perennial border, and the sun-warmed roses.

Everything looked grand to Lambert, though he supposed a purist might find fault. Maybe the ornamental borders were not at their best. Profusion of shape and color had been worn down by months of rain until only the toughest blossoms were unscathed. The thunderstorm the night before hadn't helped. Still, the pale graveled paths were more geometrically precise than usual, with fewer students around to trample the precincts of the university. Only the minimum number required to chant the wards remained through the summer. The rest of the undergraduates were off on holiday. This was a piece of good luck. There was no question that Jane's visit would be more comfortable with fewer young men staring as she passed. As he let Jane walk ahead of him through a narrow passage between ornamental borders, Lambert had to reconsider that. Something in the line of Jane's attire, utterly correct though it was, hinted that she might not mind being stared at by a lot of polite young men.

"This is where most visitors begin." Lambert hesitated at the threshold of St. Mary's. "It looks like morning service is over. We ought to be able to look around for quite a while without bothering anybody. Would you like to?"

Jane, it seemed, was enthusiastic about church architecture. She followed Lambert into the peace of the church, then led the way as they moved from nave to aisle, transept to choir, through the sweet scent of the incense used during the morning's service. When they stood in the crossing, Jane pivoted on her heel, head back and eyes bright as she took in the splendors of the place. She put one hand up to hold her extravagant hat firmly in position while she gazed.

"Look at this." Jane kept her voice down, but the excitement and pleasure in it carried her words to Lambert vibrantly no matter which way she turned. "See the ratio between the length of the nave and the length of the transept? That's two to three. The ratio of the nave to the choir is four to three."

"How do you know that?" Lambert asked. Once his attention was drawn to the proportions, he could see the harmony of it. If Jane could pick out distance with that accuracy, Meredith might want to give her a few tests of marksmanship too.

"Mathematics."

"I mean, you can tell just by looking?" Lambert knew very few people had an eye for distance like his, but he hadn't given up hope of finding one.

Jane shook her head. "I've read the architectural studies. The men who built this place knew their mathematics. See the height of the columns and the distance between the base of the columns and the first molding, the plain one there? Compare that with the height of the piers. That's the golden section."

Lambert noticed the line of Jane's throat. He thought how much younger she looked this way. She might have been a schoolgirl, spinning herself dizzy as she gazed up into the heights overhead. Well, except for the hat. Lambert asked, "The golden section? What's that?"

"The Greeks thought it was the key they needed to measure the whole world." Jane glowed with enthusiasm. "If you divide a line such that the length of the shorter segment to the longer is the same as the ratio between the longer and the total of the two, that's the golden section. You can keep it up forever if you want to, and if you map the coincident points, it makes a lovely spiral."

Something stirred far back in Lambert's memory. "Oh, is that the chambered nautilus?"

"That's the one." Jane looked pleased with him.

"What's golden about the golden section?"

"What's golden about the Golden Rule?" Jane countered.

"'Therefore all things whatsoever ye would that men should do to you, do ye even so to them,'" Lambert quoted. "Matthew chapter seven, verse twelve. It's a pretty good rule, don't you think?"

"You have quite a memory," Jane said dryly.

"For some things." Lambert made himself look away and concentrate on the stained glass windows. He was careful to ignore Jane's scrutiny, but he could still feel it.

"I suppose you had the Scriptures drummed into you as a child."

"That's how I learned to read. My mother taught me."

"Oh, that's right. She was a schoolteacher, you said. Like me."

Lambert had to laugh a little. "I don't think you teach at the same kind of school."

"Why? Because Greenlaw teaches magic, do you think it's so different?"

Lambert looked squarely at Jane. "Fifteen students in eight different grades, all mixed together in a room no bigger than a box stall? One room with a potbellied stove for heat and a kerosene lamp for light? If Greenlaw isn't different, I feel sorry for you."

Jane looked right back as she thought it over. "Running water?"

"All you want, in the creek at the bottom of the hill. There's a bucket and a dipper by the door."

"I see. Yes, Greenlaw is different. Is that the kind of school you attended?"

"That's right, and a lot of people had to work mighty hard to get that much. We were lucky to have any kind of a school." Lambert gestured vaguely. "Something like this—it's more than I can believe sometimes, that a place like this exists at all, let alone that it has existed for hundreds and hundreds of years."

"It must be very different from what you are accustomed to."

Lambert couldn't help laughing. "It is. It's different here, but I like it. Who wouldn't?"

"It can't be very exciting for you. They won't even let you join the old duffers in a glass of brandy."

"There's more than one kind of excitement. It would be something, to be able to work here. Centuries of effort, all to one end. The men of Glasscastle did all that men can do to protect the wisdom of the ages." Lambert took another look at the dimensions of the place, the sun through the vivid glass. "It's safe here."

"Safer than under lock and key." Jane gave Lambert a look of keen assessment. "They protect themselves from all kinds of things, these Glasscastle men."

Together they strolled through St. Mary's. Jane paused to read every memorial set into the walls, to admire every change in the vaulting overhead, and to step as carefully as possible around the brasses and inscriptions in the floor.

"That was excellent. What's next on the grand tour of Glasscastle?" Jane asked when they had examined every feature of the place.

"Well, it's up to you. You want to see the Winterset Archive, I reckon. After that, would you rather see the stained glass in St. Joseph's or stop to take a look at some of the buildings on the way?"

"Oh, by all means, we must stop on the way. Any chance of having a little snoop behind the scenes? Watching the scholars of magic as they conduct their research?"

Lambert considered showing Jane around Fell's study. She'd enjoy it if Fell weren't there. Maybe even if he was. If Fell were there, he'd hate to have his work interrupted by sociability. Being polite to Jane might be fit punishment for making Lambert worry. Savoring the mental image of Fell's pained reaction to Jane's hat, let alone a whole visit from such a fashionable young lady, Lambert steered Jane out of St. Mary's and along the path toward the Winterset Archive.

"Isn't it a lovely morning?" Despite her stylishly narrow skirt, Jane matched Lambert stride for stride with no apparent effort. "Amy tells me this has been the rainiest summer she can remember. She said the university boat race had to be canceled and rowed over. I can't imagine it. She says Cambridge sank at Harrod's wharf and Oxford only made it as far as Chiswick Eyot before they sank too."

Lambert stopped in his tracks, and said, "That's odd."

There was a main door to the archive building but the side door, facing out on Midsummer Green, was visible from their vantage point on the neatly swept path. To his surprise, Lambert recognized the man leaving the archive building by cutting across the green to the quadrangle path as the stocky man in the bowler hat he'd seen at the gate.

"That's very odd. That man must be a Fellow. No one else is qualified to walk on the grass all by himself. But he was just ahead of us to sign in at the gate."

"He *does* seem in a bit of a hurry, doesn't he?" Jane watched the man's rapid departure with interest. "One doesn't often see a man in a bowler hat actually bustling. They always look as if they're just about to, but they seldom really do."

"Excuse me." Lambert approached the corner where the man's route would intersect their graveled path. "May I help you? Sir? *Hey!*"

Without a second glance at them, the bowler-hatted man broke into a run. In moments he was through the stone arch of the great gate, lost from sight.

"How extraordinary!" Jane started back toward the gate, then hesitated as she noticed Lambert wasn't coming with her. "Who was that? Do you know him?"

Lambert stood staring after the man. Downright peculiar, that had been.

"I wonder what he was doing in there," said Jane. "Shall we follow him or shall we go investigate?"

The rate the man had been running, Lambert calculated he'd be long gone by the time they cleared the gate. "It's probably nothing. But I think we should at least take a quick look in the archive, just to make sure everything's in order. Whoever he was, I don't think he belongs here."

Lambert and Jane entered the Winterset Archive by the side door, since the man in the bowler hat had left that way. They paused in the doorway to listen. The customary silence of the archive held sway. There was a distinctive quality to the quiet there. Lambert had noticed it on previous visits. It was a very busy silence, a silence composed of human concentration, not only of the activity of the moment but somehow of the long years of concentration that had gone on there since the construction of the building. The place smelled of books and book bindings, wood and wax. To Lambert, it smelled like wisdom.

Lambert led the way through side passages to the foot of the main staircase and started to climb. Three steps up the creaking wooden stair, Lambert noticed Jane wasn't following him. He turned back. Jane was still at the foot of the stair, gazing up at the height of the coffered ceiling, the depth and detail of the linen-fold paneling on the walls, and the angle and sweep of the staircase. Her expression was far more reverent than it had ever been in St. Mary's. Jane seemed to have forgotten all about the man in the bowler hat in her worshipful admiration of the surroundings.

"Are you coming?" Lambert asked.

Jane shook herself out of her reverie, adjusted her hatpins, and followed Lambert upstairs. "Just thinking. Sorry."

The splendor of the place only increased as they rose from the ground level to the first-floor reading room. From floor to ceiling the room was lined with shelves, each rank served by a spiral staircase of intricate ironwork. More shelves were arranged throughout the room, yielding at intervals to great long tables of polished wood, each like a clearing in a forest. There were brass study lamps in plenty, each with its green glass shade, but they were unlit, for the room was flooded with light from the skylights overhead.

There were only two men at work in the place, one in the robes of an archivist and the other in the short poplin gown of an undergraduate. Neither looked up as Lambert and Jane hesitated on the threshold.

The archivist was speaking to the undergraduate. "All our senses rely on the spirit. Ficino says so quite clearly. Each sense employs its own form of spirit to convey its message. Music is transmitted through air, and air is the medium closest to the spirit itself, therefore hearing is the highest of our senses."

"What sort of message does smell convey?" asked the undergraduate.

Lambert could tell from the undergraduate's manner that they had stumbled across yet another of Glasscastle's civil disagreements.

"Smell is one of the lower senses," the archivist replied patiently. "Taste, smell, and touch are inferior to sight and hearing."

"Is not smell transmitted through the air?" the undergraduate asked.

Lambert debated the merits of asking the archivist if he'd noticed an intruder but decided to do so later, if at all. It took a lot of intruding to get someone to notice an outsider here. Better to run a quick check of the scholars' studies that filled out the remainder of the building.

This time Lambert had to take Jane's elbow to get her to follow him away from the reading room. Even so, she looked back wistfully over her shoulder as they went on.

"None of that," said Lambert as he started up the more modest stairs to the studies on the topmost floor. "Remember what happened to Orpheus and Eurydice."

"That was hell. This is heaven." Jane followed Lambert. "You've studied Greek, then? Or at least the Greek myths?"

"I told you where I went to school. Must you make me come right out and admit I never studied much of anything?" Lambert urged her on. "When I was in London, I went to Covent Garden a few times, that's all. I saw the opera there."

"Did you like it?"

"It was pretty good." Lambert couldn't help smiling. It had been wonderful.

"What on earth led you to the Royal Opera?" Jane asked.

"Well, I went to the Metropolitan Opera House in New York City quite a few times. That's how I found out I liked opera."

"But what made you decide to go in the first place?"

"It was a stunt to plug the show back when we were playing New York. Some of us went along in full costume to see that new one by Puccini. *The Girl of the Golden West.*"

"You liked that one?"

"Never laughed so hard in my whole life. But the music was kind of pretty." After a moment, Lambert added, "Yes. I liked it."

On the next floor, a corridor ran in a rectangle around the perimeter of the structure, with small rooms opening off either side. Each Fellow of Glasscastle had a right to a room devoted to his own research somewhere on the premises. Fell's study was just one of many in the orderly warren of the place. Even here, the peaceful energy and scholarly hush of the place was undisturbed.

"What's your favorite?" Lambert asked softly.

Jane looked puzzled.

"Your favorite opera," he prompted.

"Oh." Jane took her time about thinking it over. "*The Magic Flute*, I suppose. Though some aspects of the magic bear as much resemblance to what they teach at Greenlaw as *The Girl of the Golden West* bears to your true golden West."

Lambert did not dare open any of the doors that were closed, for fear of annoying possible scholars within, but he led Jane through a quick survey of those rooms with doors ajar. None seemed a bit out of the ordinary. There might be books stacked on the floor until there was no room to walk to the desk. There might be scholarly journals stacked in the corners like straw or hay. But there was order to the disorder everywhere they looked. Nothing seemed to have been disturbed. Nothing, that is, until they reached Fell's study, where the door had been left open a few inches.

Lambert rapped on the door as he opened it farther and peered inside. "Uh-oh. Fell is not going to think much of this." The room was deserted Lambert sidled in and took a good look around.

From one side of the room to the other, papers littered the confined space. A study lamp had been knocked to the floor, its green glass shade broken, though no oil remained in it to cause a fire hazard. If there had been a robbery, nothing seemed to have been taken and many objects of considerable value remained. There were gleaming brass astronomical models in each corner of the room, three armillary spheres and an orrery. An astrolabe lay half buried in paper on the desk. The glass-fronted bookshelves seemed undisturbed but every other surface was in complete disarray.

Among the chaos covering Fell's desk, Lambert found a set of plans, drawn with painstaking care, for a weapon that appeared to combine the properties of a telescope, a cannon, and a slide trombone. Either the cannon was incredibly small or the gun sight incredibly large. Lambert didn't waste a moment figuring out the scale. He scanned the mechanical drawing long enough to spot the words "gun sight," "Egerton wand," and in larger letters "confidential" stamped on each sheet. He folded the papers hastily and slipped them into his pocket while Jane inspected the door lock.

"What kind of a scholar of magic needs a lock on his door?" Jane's disapproval was clear. "A very ordinary lock at that."

"Was it forced open?"

"Judging from the marks here, yes." Jane traced the gouged wood and scratched metal. "It wasn't locked. Someone didn't even bother to try the knob first, just slid a knife blade in and pushed."

"He must have been in a hurry." Lambert started picking up papers and stacking them in no particular order. It would be easier to clean the place up once the floor was clear.

Jane studied the room with sharp-eyed interest. "Whoever works here is a devil for armillary spheres." She flicked a speck of dust from one of the nested rings of the largest armillary sphere and set the gleaming metal into silent motion. "Is this an orrery?" She moved along to the mechanical model of the solar system. She touched the crank and glanced up at Lambert. "Shall I give us a little extra spin?"

Lambert said, "It's an inaccurate model. The earth isn't really in the center. The sun is. Earth and the other planets spin around it."

"Just like Glasscastle, in other words." Jane moved the crank gently until the polished wooden planets eased into motion around the ivory orb representing the earth. Old as it was, the device had been well cared for. The mechanism made only the softest of clicks and whirrs to accompany the stately motion of the model.

"What?"

Jane watched the planets slow. "Glasscastle stays unchanged while England spins around it, the British Empire spins around England, and the rest of the world spins around the British Empire." The planets stopped.

Lambert tried to decide if Jane were serious or not. "That's an exaggerated view of the importance of England, don't you think?"

"But not of Glasscastle?" From Jane's expression, she was only serious about hearing Lambert's reaction.

Lambert hesitated. "Well, Glasscastle is part of England, after all."

"No, it isn't. Not really." Jane gave the crank a more vigorous turn and the planets took up their smooth clockwork dance again. "The Fellows of Glasscastle ransomed it from the Crown at the Dissolution. Paid for the cost of the lead on the roofs and settled down in comfort and privacy to master the theory and practice of magic."

"They aren't just working for themselves." Lambert wondered what Fell would make of Jane's cynical reading of Glasscastle's history. Mincemeat? Or would he have an even more satirical version? Probably. "They swear fealty to the Crown."

"Diplomatic to a fault. They give each new monarch a fresh bit of invention as a coronation gift. A microscope here, a telescope there. The Fellows of Glasscastle are loyal only to Glasscastle."

"That's not true. The Fellows of Glasscastle devote themselves to the advancement of human understanding."

"Oh, yes. Of course." Jane's attention was entirely on the motion of the planetary model. She seemed amused by it. "Did you say a friend of yours works in this room?"

"Nicholas Fell. He's going to be tolerably cross about this. He doesn't like anyone disturbing his work and I've probably set him back six months just tidying up his papers."

"What is Fell working on? Do you know? Our friend in the bowler didn't visit this room for nothing." Jane lost interest in the orrery and leaned forward to make a cursory inspection of the papers spread across the desk. "Is there anything that should be here that isn't?"

"I don't know." Lambert frowned at Jane. "Can we be sure that's what really happened? The man comes in here, throws things on the floor, and leaves in a big hurry? Even if that's what he really did, *why*? What was he doing here?"

"Is there anything here that shouldn't be?" Jane seated herself behind the desk and began working through the papers in earnest. "What *is* your friend's field of study? To judge from this, it looks like he makes clocks."

Mindful of the plans stuffed into his pocket, Lambert decided to ignore Jane's first question for the time being. "History of magic. But for the past few months he's abandoned his thesis completely to study the measurement of time."

"What kind of work is he doing?" Jane looked puzzled. "Physics?"

Lambert shrugged. "Just—time. He's interested in it."

The orrery ran down again and Jane frowned at the arrangement of the planets without seeming to see it. "That man in the bowler was looking for something—or he found it."

Lambert looked again at the surrounding mess and winced at the thought of what Fell would have to say. "We'd better report this."

"You're right. I shouldn't have delayed you. I'll wait here until you find the proper authority." Jane went back to her careful examination of the papers.

Lambert hesitated, then gave up on any attempt at tact. "Please come with me. I don't think Fell would approve of me leaving you alone with his papers."

Jane looked surprised. "Why? What harm could I do?"

"No harm. Not that." Inspiration struck Lambert. "But this way, we can be witnesses for each other's good behavior."

"Do you think me capable of anything less?" Jane's words held a distinct edge. "What are you implying?"

"I'm not trying to imply anything." Lambert settled for absolute honesty. "If I leave you here alone, I think you might snoop."

Jane bristled. "Oh, do you?"

"Forgive my bluntness, Miss Brailsford, but I try never to underestimate a woman. Particularly not an Englishwoman."

Lambert was perplexed by Jane's sweet smile in response. "Very well, Mr. Lambert. In that case, I concede that I am quite capable of snooping. Let us go and find the proper authority together."

It took Lambert some time to track down the right person to inform of the disturbance in Fell's study. The young man responsible for the reading room sent to someone with more authority, who sent for someone else. Finally Russell, one of the senior Fellows, arrived and took a look at the place.

"To be honest, it doesn't look much worse than usual." Russell poked at a stack of papers. "Fell can make a formal complaint if he notices anything is missing. Leave it alone until then."

"What about the man in the bowler hat?" Lambert asked.

"If you see him again, ask him to come in and answer a few questions. Not much we can do unless he returns." Russell ushered them back out to the corridor. "It was very conscientious of you to report this." To Lambert, his tone made it plain he thought Lambert and Jane were a pair of officious fussbudgets intent on making a mountain out of a molehill.

Lambert noted with interest that Jane seemed to interpret Russell's tone just the way he had, for she looked peeved as Russell escorted them out of the archive and left them on the front steps.

"That's that, then." Jane surveyed the prospect before her with no sign of enthusiasm. "Vigilant Glasscastle at its finest."

"That's a sour look, Jane." Robert Brailsford hailed his sister cheerfully as he and Adam Voysey joined them on the steps. "Lemons for lunch, was it?"

"I haven't had anything for lunch." Jane brightened considerably at the mere thought. "Is it already time for lunch?"

Robert greeted Lambert, and said to Jane, "I see you've found a more congenial guide to squire you through the place. I might have guessed you would."

Lambert hadn't noticed the resemblance between Jane and her brother until he saw them side by side. Their coloring was not dissimilar, but the set of the head and the line of the jaw clearly marked them as kin. Beside Vice Chancellor Voysey's lean height, Robert Brailsford seemed stocky, compact yet not unathletic. In Jane, economy of build turned to grace.

Jane's attention was all on her brother, and most of it was reproachful. "You forgot me, didn't you?"

Robert did not hesitate. "I did. Completely and utterly. Jane, may I present the new Vice Chancellor of Glasscastle and Provost of Holythorn, Adam Voysey? Adam, allow me to present my sister Jane Brailsford, a scholar of Greenlaw."

Voysey's dignity came to the fore. Jane might have been a duchess, such was Voysey's courtesy. Lambert watched with reluctant admiration. As Vice Chancellor, Voysey spoke for all of Glasscastle. He was a busy man. Yet Jane might have been the only person in the world, the way Voysey treated her. Bearing like that could never be learned. It was innate courtesy improved by years of polish.

Under Voysey's admiring eye, Jane's mood seemed to improve. She returned compliment for compliment, saying nothing in particular, yet saying it with elegance and poise.

"And you, Samuel," Voysey said at last. "What of you? Perishing with hunger, I've no doubt?"

Lambert had long since grown used to Voysey's informality toward him. It had been Voysey's idea to recruit the best possible marksman and he seemed to view Lambert as a kind of honorary younger brother. The advantage of such informality was that Lambert could be honest. "It has been a long time since breakfast."

"I think, if we devote ourselves to the quest, we might find something to sustain us. Now that Lord Fyvie and Mr. Wiston have returned to their native heath, my time is my own again, thank goodness. Will you be my guest, Miss Brailsford? This time of year, the cooks at Holythorn do an extremely good smothered quail on Tuesdays."

For an instant, a pert rejoinder seemed to tremble on Jane's lips. Lambert could almost see the thoughts move behind Jane's changeable face as she considered an assortment of replies. Whatever the temptation, good manners won out. With decorum, she accepted Voysey's invitation and the four of them adjourned to the common room of Voysey's college to dine. Lambert was surprised at the small but distinct pang of regret he felt. Now he would never know what sort of saucy remark Jane had been about to make to Voysey.

Jane tried not to look peeved, but inwardly she was seething as Voysey and Robin bore her off with Lambert in their wake.

It had been forethought, planning, patience, and a smattering of luck that brought Jane to the gates of Glasscastle in time to be waiting there when Lambert passed. To have her campaign sidetracked by her brother, of all people, made her want to swear.

To get Lambert talking about Fell had been well worth the time spent in admiration of Glasscastle's—admittedly admirable—architecture. To see Fell's study had been an unlooked-for benefit, and to be first on the scene to find the disruption there was as intriguing as it was alarming. She had intended to get Lambert to herself again as soon as the authorities were located and dealt with. To be forced to become an official guest again, officially escorted and officially patronized, was all the more annoying since it dashed her hopes of learning more about Fell from the man who seemed, so far, to know him best.

At the common room table, where the food was every bit as good as Vice Chancellor Voysey had promised, Jane found herself engaged in conversation by Voysey and James Porteous, a Senior Fellow of mathematics. Porteous was older than either Voysey or her brother by at least fifteen years and his gravity of manner was proportional.

"You will forgive me, Voysey," Porteous decreed, "for monopolizing the young lady. You take it for granted that we may share hospitality with a lady. To me, a member of a more sheltered generation, it has the charm of the exotic."

Jane caught Lambert's eye. "I'm not the only exotic guest, surely. You have Mr. Lambert among you every day."

Lambert looked mildly disgusted to be brought to Porteous's attention. "I'm not as exotic as all that."

Jane wondered if Lambert's response was distaste for attention in general or Porteous's attention in particular. She suspected it might be the latter.

"No comparison at all, dear fellow," Porteous agreed. "Where have you taken Miss Brailsford? I trust you let her fully admire the beauties of St. Mary's?"

"First thing," said Lambert.

Porteous turned to Jane. "You'll have been more interested in the tombs or the stained glass, I suppose, but there are some extremely subtle things in St. Mary's. For example, if you compare the length of the nave to that of the choir, you get a ratio of four to three. That's the equivalent of a musical fourth. The whole place is music if you know how to read the intervals." After a dreamy pause in which he seemed to be contemplating music only he could hear, Porteous returned the subject at hand. "But I suppose such things are a bit more abstract than the stained glass and the stone carvings."

"I've always been fond of misericords myself." Jane risked a simper. She judged that misericords would rank with playing with dolls or cuddling puppies to a man of Porteous's interests.

Lambert looked mildly stunned. Jane wondered if her simper was responsible or if Lambert was remembering the architectural lecture she'd given him in St. Mary's.

Porteous, it was clear, lived down to Jane's expectations. "Harrumph. Yes, very droll, some of them. In an obvious way. Quite vulgar, some of the others. Your brother tells me you are a teacher at Greenlaw, Miss Brailsford. Perhaps I ought to say, Dame Brailsford? I believe that is the proper form of address at Greenlaw? What branch of magic is your specialty?"

"I teach mathematics," Jane said. "We don't teach magic directly."

Porteous seemed taken aback. "You teach mathematics."

"I do," said Jane briskly. "I find it quite satisfying. You've no notion."

Porteous chose his words with evident care. "I'm confident you teach your subject most competently, Miss Brailsford, yet if you do not instruct your young charges in the fundamentals of magic, who does?"

"I cannot generalize. It's a highly individual matter," Jane replied. "The curriculum is planned with great care, lest anyone suffer through having their own idiosyncratic talent subsumed into the whole."

"Idiosyncratic poppycock," said Porteous. "If the individual is not subsumed into the whole, where is the power behind the spell to come from? Eh? And for another thing, how do you get the chants to work together if the theory isn't properly drilled into your students from the very start?"

"Greenlaw doesn't use chants the way Glasscastle does," said Jane.

"No chants?" Porteous looked horrified. "No chants whatsoever?"

"Greenlaw operates on its own methods," Voysey put in smoothly. "I believe there are considerable differences in the theoretical structure of the curriculum."

"In other words, what Greenlaw uses as a curriculum is probably full of the sort of modern nonsense you favor," Porteous retorted. "Never have I known you to subject one of your theories to full formal analysis before you share it with the world. You enjoy shocking people too much to refine a hypothesis."

"At least I'm open to the implications of the new work being done. Then again, I'm not considered one of the finest minds of the eighteenth century." Voysey's inflection made it clear that he was referring to Porteous.

"Very droll, dear fellow. You mean that as a joke but I take it as an accolade," Porteous countered.

Jane thought it best to bring the subject of the discussion back to magic. "Just as there are considerable differences between men and women, there are considerable differences between the way their magic works. Men must work together, if what I gather from my brother is true. Women must work alone. If magic is to work for either, it must work its own way through us."

Voysey smiled. "*Vive la différence,* eh, Porteous?"

"Yes, yes. Of course." Porteous lifted his wineglass to Jane. "The lady is always right. One of those verities of life, eh, Brailsford?"

For a fleeting but vivid instant, Jane longed to slap the smug expression off Porteous's face. She caught Lambert's eye for a moment. With unsettling clarity, she felt he read her impulse exactly and was waiting calmly to see what she would do. There was no hint of disapproval, merely interest and appreciation. Jane couldn't help feeling nettled. With perfect self-possession, Jane turned to her brother. "The lady is always right. Why have you never learned that particular verity, Robin?"

Perhaps alerted by something in her tone, Robert regarded her warily. "But I did, my dear. It's covered in the very first lessons at Glasscastle. If Greenlaw's classes don't teach the same material, there's a flaw in Greenlaw's curriculum, not in ours."

Jane tried to keep the crisp annoyance out of her voice. "Another verity, then. Glasscastle is always right." She lifted her glass as she made the toast.

Lambert gave her a speaking look as he raised his glass of water, but maintained his silence. Jane gathered that even in jest, Lambert would not say those words. Or perhaps, Jane thought, Lambert did not consider Glasscastle to be something one jested about.

Porteous beamed at her. "True, Miss Brailsford. Very true."

"If I understand the nature of Greenlaw's curriculum, and I'm sure you'll correct me at once if I misstate the matter, Miss Brailsford," said Voysey affably, "it contrasts with that of Glasscastle in the nature of intelligence. The power of Glasscastle resides in trained intelligence. Mere native intelligence is all very well in its way. Yet the more it can be refined, the greater the source of power."

"What do you mean by 'trained' and 'refined'?" asked Jane.

"Perhaps 'cultivated' would be a better word than either," Voysey replied. "Merely stuffing a student with facts accomplishes nothing. It is the student who learns to question established belief, the student who poses questions of his own, who makes the ideal scholar of magic."

"Perhaps Greenlaw and Glasscastle are not so far apart on some points after all," said Jane. "We don't look for magic in books either."

"There is no royal road to magic. No textbook to follow slavishly. Books may even act as a damper. A distraction, in fact." Voysey's enthusiasm was plain.

Jane thought of the way a whole dormitory of energetic young women, dangerously restless with spring fever, could sometimes be soothed by a suitable three-volume novel. "A very welcome distraction at times."

"I agree there is no royal road to magic." Porteous made no effort to conceal his disapproval of the direction the conversation had taken. "That's as far as I go with you, Voysey. I see no point in breaking rules unless you learn them first. For one thing, it's dangerous."

"True," Voysey conceded.

Robert added, "For another, it's far more entertaining to break the rules intentionally than inadvertently."

"Why, Robin," Jane turned to her brother in mock astonishment. "Break the rules? *You?*"

"A shocking revelation, isn't it?" Robert was smug. "Is it enough to make you question my authority?"

"That's the key," said Voysey. "That is what makes Glasscastle great. Its scholars have the ability to question all manner of authority. Indeed, they have the responsibility to do so."

"If they do so without overstepping the bounds of prudence," Porteous added.

Jane glanced across at Lambert to see if she could catch his eye, but all his attention was on Voysey and he was nodding slightly. Jane felt mildly disappointed in him.

"Agreed," said Robert. "So you see, Jane, we are all models of intellectual and moral decorum. Therefore we endorse your previous statement, which I suspect you made with your tongue in cheek. Glasscastle *is* always right."

Jane said, "I am left speechless by what passes for logic here."

"Then let me provide the toast." Robert lifted his glass and the others joined him. "Glasscastle is always right. Amen."

3

*"And the gilded car of day
His glowing axle doth allay"*

After yet another boiled dinner in hall that evening, Lambert slowly climbed the staircase to the empty quarters he shared with Fell. Still no sign of his friend. The conversation between Voysey and Jane earlier in the day had given Lambert the chance to let Robert Brailsford know that there was something important he needed to tell him. The need to get Jane out of earshot had made it tricky, but her spirited conversation with Voysey and Porteous lasted longer than their meal did. Eventually the three of them strolled far enough ahead that Lambert could mutter to Brailsford and pass him the plans with a brief explanation of where he'd found them.

"Good gad, man. What was Fell doing with these?" Brailsford tucked the papers away hastily. "He washed his hands of the project long ago."

Lambert didn't like the critical note in Brailsford's voice. "I'd lay odds Fell doesn't even know they were there. If it turns out he does know, I reckon he just doesn't think they're anything important. He's never given two pins for the project anyway."

Brailsford shook his head in mock despair. "*Tuppence.* The idiomatic phrase should be 'He doesn't care tuppence.'"

Happy that Brailsford had let himself be distracted, Lambert continued to play dumb. "He doesn't give two cents for it either."

Whatever Brailsford had in common with his sister, a sense of humor was not included. "I'll tell Voysey as soon as Jane is safely out of the way. I don't suppose you'd like to show her the glass at St. Joseph's, would you?" Clearly, Brailsford thought it most unlikely that anyone would willingly choose to spend time with his sister.

Lambert didn't have to think it over. "I would."

"Capital." Brailsford started to move toward Voysey, Porteous, and Jane, caught himself, and turned back to Lambert. "Would you really?"

Lambert nodded.

Brailsford frowned slightly. "That's good. That's fine. Just—don't take her too seriously. Jane was rather strange as a child. Fanciful. When it suits her purpose, she can be most—convincing."

Lambert had puzzled over that piece of advice for the rest of the afternoon and evening. Much of the afternoon he'd spent in Jane's company, as Porteous showed them around some of the more restricted areas of Glasscastle. Jane had seemed a bit subdued, politely attentive to Porteous no matter what flights of architectural or philosophical fancy he took them on. Any talent she had for convincing people of things they ought not be convinced of remained hidden. Lambert could appreciate any brother's urge to protect a sister, but the warning seemed intended to protect Lambert from Jane. Odd, that.

There had been a moment that afternoon, although no more than a moment, when Jane's courteous attention to Porteous had faltered. It occurred during Porteous's lecture upon the architectural excellence of the Wearyall College chapel.

"There are complexities upon complexities all around us as we stand here," Porteous told them. Back to the wall, he faced the entrance and his voice boomed beautifully around the empty space of the chapel. "Every element we see tells us something about the way the architect viewed the world. No, let me rephrase that. Not the stained glass windows. Those are a recent restoration and quite extraordinarily insipid at that. But I digress. The use of space here can hardly be understood by the untrained eye. It requires years of study to comprehend and to appreciate the place fully."

Lambert tried to catch Jane's eye and failed utterly. Meekly, he settled for a murmur of polite encouragement and Porteous surged onward.

"This is where the genius of Glasscastle has been made not merely visible but audible. To hear a fully sung service here at Easter is to witness the auditory equivalent of a glimpse of the gates of paradise. Chanting was not discovered here, but it has certainly been brought to a state of perfection at

Glasscastle." Porteous beamed. "Architecturally, musically, aesthetically, the sum is greater even than its parts."

Jane smiled brightly. "Oh, yes. This is where the Yell Magna was perfected, wasn't it?"

Jowls quivering, with indignation, Porteous drew himself up to his full, not very impressive height. "I *beg* your pardon?"

"I read about it somewhere." Jane's expression was demure. "Baedeker, perhaps."

"You refer, I imagine, to the Vox Magna, the technique that matches architectural space to the acoustics of the human voice in the performance of magic?" Porteous was ponderously sarcastic. "I can assure you, Miss Brailsford, that your little red Baedeker can do no possible justice to one of Glasscastle's greatest achievements."

Unruffled by Porteous's massive indignation, Jane said to Lambert, "It's for opening doors."

"Opening doors?" Porteous goggled at her effrontery. "My dear child, is this what they taught you at Greenlaw? By no stretch of the imagination is the Vox Magna for 'opening doors.'" His voice echoed ominously throughout the chapel.

The acoustics were first rate. The place gave Porteous's bellow something close to beauty. Lambert wondered what the vibrations of Porteous's voice would be the auditory equivalent of. A bull moose, maybe.

"It's for unlocking things, then," Jane conceded.

"Oh, is it?" Belatedly, Porteous seemed to detect something suspicious in the utter gravity of Jane's demeanor. His indignation subsided and mild sarcasm took its place. "If one could be permitted to describe the guillotine as a device for the radical adjustment of one's hairstyle or for the drastic reduction of one's hat size, then perhaps one might say the Vox Magna could be used for unlocking things. Perhaps, I say."

Belatedly, Jane seemed to remember her manners. Her deference returned and the remainder of the tour was without incident. Lambert had admired the unobtrusive ease with which she undermined Porteous's self-control. He wondered if she could do the same to her brother.

The ticking of Fell's clock seemed unnaturally loud. Even with the windows open to coax in any night breeze meandering by, the sitting room was stuffy.

For a luxurious moment, Lambert allowed himself to picture Fell's annoyance if he came home to find the clock silent and the pendulum stopped. Fell was not a patient man. The smallest things sometimes made him cross. Interfering with his clock, just to stop the minor nuisance of its repetitive ticking, would not seem a small thing to Fell. Lambert put temptation aside and distracted himself with the day's newspapers.

It was, as usual, difficult to make out what was happening in the world from what the newspapers said. Against all odds, the Republic of China had lasted five months and if the much-discussed China Loan ever floated, seemed likely to last for six. The ocean liner *Titanic* had broken her own trans-Atlantic record. Lord Fyvie had delivered a speech in the House of Lords demanding the Imperial Defence Committee deal with the question of aerial navigation. Someone else had delivered a better speech about the need for fiscal restraint in these difficult times. The fortunes of the British Empire were detailed in flattering terms. The court calendar figured prominently. Countries far away and ineffectual received short shrift indeed. Lambert read the society news with the same care and attention he gave to the account of an expedition sent to explore the depths of a jungle.

An item in the society column made Lambert sit up straight in his comfortable armchair. The Earl of Bridgewater, a man sufficiently famous and fashionable that the newspaper saw fit to report his lightest deed, had delivered a speech to the Royal Society the day before. Among the members mentioned as addressing questions to the speaker afterward was Nicholas Fell.

Lambert was startled at the relief he felt. No unexplained disappearance after all. Bridgewater had spoken on the history of the armillary sphere, with particular emphasis on the one handed down through generations of his family. Fell's interest in armillary spheres was not as intense as his self-education in the measurement of time, but it was more than sufficient to send him to town to attend a speech without mentioning his plans. If he had bothered to leave Lambert a message, it had somehow gone astray.

Lambert put the newspaper down, surprised at how late the hour had become. A trip into town might be a good idea. Fell was probably doing research there. Lambert knew which club Fell favored. The intrusion into his study at Winterset would annoy Fell considerably. He would want to know about it sooner, not later.

There was the possibility Meredith might have more tests of marksmanship for Lambert planned for the next day. If so, Meredith would have to

postpone them. Lambert would make sure he left before any possible summons might come from that quarter.

Sleep came easily to Lambert that night. London first thing in the morning, that was the plan. Lambert always felt happier when he knew what he
was going to do with himself. A day in London would make a bracing
change.

In the morning, London still seemed like a good idea. Lambert let himself
out into the cool early silence. Glasscastle had only begun to stir itself. The
sky was clear. Lambert thought it promised to be another warm day.

Glasscastle Station was inconveniently distant from both the university
and the town itself. The strategy, Lambert had once been told, was that the
harder it was for the undergraduates to get to the railway station, the harder
it would be for them to abandon their studies to go live it up in London.
Whether the strategy worked or not, and it seemed by and large not to,
there was no question that it was a long walk to the railway station.

Lambert walked down Silver Street as far as the Haymarket before he
struck it lucky with a drayman he knew from previous venturesome mornings.

"You're out early." The drayman made room on the box to give Lambert
a ride to the station. "In trouble, are you?"

"Not this time." Lambert gauged the driver's degree of disappointment at
that news and searched for some bit of entertainment to offer in return for
his ride. "I knew a fellow once. You could say he got in trouble."

The driver looked pleased. "Bison, was it? Or bears?"

"Worse than either," said Lambert. "Women."

"Ah." Deep satisfaction from the driver.

Lambert took that as permission to carry on spinning his yarn. "This fellow was named Max and he was sweet on a girl called Agatha, but Agatha's
pa didn't think Max was the man for her. He set up a shooting contest. Winner takes Agatha."

"This Max was a cowboy?" The driver looked dubious. He turned down
Barking Lane on the way to Headstone Road and eventually the railway station.

Lambert had the advantage of aimlessness. He had no particular train in
mind so it didn't matter if he were late or not. He'd take the drayman's
meandering route to the station and whatever train came next, that would be
his. "Yup. Best shot you ever saw. But he wasn't so sure of himself that he'd

risk his girl. So he listened to his friend Caspar. Caspar was a cowpuncher who had traveled in some mighty strange places, and he came back with a Sharp's rifle and five cartridges that he swore would hit anything he wanted them to. He promised Max that he'd loan him his rifle for the shooting contest." Lambert knew perfectly well that the driver would put him off the box and make him walk if he admitted that this yarn had its origin in one of Lambert's visits to the opera at Covent Garden.

"Ah. What was in it for this Caspar bloke?"

"You guessed it. Caspar had sold his soul to the devil for that rifle and those cartridges, and he knew the devil would be coming around to collect pretty soon. It was his idea that he'd give the devil Max instead."

"Ah."

"Max didn't know any of that. He took Caspar up on his offer and he used four of those cartridges to win the shooting contest. The fifth cartridge was ready and waiting when Agatha's father told Max to make one last shot. There was a dove flying past and he told Max to shoot that."

The driver shook his head. "That's never good luck, shooting at a dove."

"It's bad luck in Wyoming too."

"Did he hit it?"

"He did. But it was Agatha who screamed and fell down."

"Dead, was she?"

"Looked that way. Agatha's father was mighty upset."

"His own fault, that was." The driver spat to express his opinion of a shooting contest as a basis for matrimony and gave Lambert an amused look, as much prompting as Lambert required to get on with the story.

"Women are tough, you know."

The driver nodded. His expression made it plain that he had good reason to know.

"Agatha had only fainted. She wasn't dead after all. But by the time she was back in her right senses, Max had thrown down the Sharp's rifle and gone for Caspar's throat. It was quite a scrap. None of the other boys who'd come for the shooting contest could break them apart. The fight only ended when the devil came to collect Caspar's soul."

"Not Max's?" the driver asked. He'd reached the station but instead of pulling in, he drew rein and sat waiting to hear the rest of the story.

"Max was all right, as he'd been innocent of the whole scheme, so he got off free and clear. The devil took Caspar, though."

"Didn't Max agree to cheat by using that Sharp's rifle?" the driver countered. "Doesn't sound innocent to me."

Lambert decided the driver had a point, and he made adjustments accordingly. "That's what Agatha thought. By the time the dust had settled, she was feeling more herself, and she came to see what her father had known all along. Max wasn't the man for her after all."

The driver looked dubious. "She didn't marry him?"

"She didn't marry anyone. She settled down to take care of her father instead. When he died, she took over his ranch and ran it herself."

"What, lived alone and died a spinster?" the driver demanded.

"I never said she was dead. She's living in Wyoming yet." Lambert gauged the driver's tolerance for embellishment with care. "It's a fine spread too. About fifty miles out of Medicine Bow."

"Off my rig and get along with you," said the driver, disgusted. "That's never how the story goes."

"It's how it goes in Wyoming," Lambert said, climbing down from the box.

The drayman spat again, shook his head, and drove on.

The train to London was mercifully quick. Lambert found himself squarely in the thick of London by midday. In contrast to Glasscastle, the streets were jammed and dirty. Great buildings crowded wide streets. People of every degree jostled their way through the press as if they had been born knowing where they had to go and what they had to do once they got there. If there was ever a season in which London was supposed to be quiet, it was mid-August. To Lambert, the place seemed about as quiet as a stockyard on market day.

By one o'clock, Lambert had elbowed his way through the mob to present himself at Fell's club, a leather-bound retreat well supplied with rubber trees and aspidistras. After a brief wait, he was shown to one of the club rooms, where Fell had covered an entire table with his papers.

As usual, Nicholas Fell looked as if he had slept in his clothes. There was nothing wrong with the cut of his gray flannels, but something about Fell's posture made it impossible for him to stay tidy looking for long. He had obviously been immersed in his work, for when Fell looked up at Lambert, he wore the abstracted air of a man trying to listen to a voice from far away. Fell tugged at a corner of his neatly trimmed mustache and greeted Lambert.

"There you are," said Lambert.

"Agreed," Fell countered. "And here you are. Not your usual choice of outing, is it? May I ask why you have come, Lambert?"

You disappeared and I was worried about you. Lambert felt a bit sheepish, now the moment to explain his presence had arrived. "I thought you should know that there was an intruder in the Winterset Archive yesterday. Someone was in your study."

Fell had gone back to his papers. With no annoyance, only mild curiosity, he asked without looking up, "Whatever for?"

"I don't know. But whoever he was, he tore the place up some." Lambert's stomach growled. "Have you eaten lunch yet? I'll tell you all about it while we eat."

"Luncheon? Of course I haven't. I've only been here—by Jove—" Fell broke off as he consulted his pocket watch. "It has been a bit longer than I thought." His apologetic tone gave way to crispness. "What a refreshing change, to be allowed to get on with my work in peace." Fell surveyed Lambert from head to foot. "Relative peace, that is. Still, I'm glad you're here. Otherwise I might have missed my appointment. I'm to meet the Earl of Bridgewater for luncheon. You may join us."

"Are you sure?" Lambert hesitated. "Won't he object at having a stranger join you?"

"Let him object," said Fell. "It was his idea to invite himself to lunch with me. He seemed to have the idea that we should meet somewhere posh and make an afternoon of it. Just because he has time for such frivolity doesn't mean anyone else does. I insisted he come here. There's nothing wrong with the food at this place, I'll say that much."

"What time were you supposed to meet him?"

"One o'clock." Fell rose and clapped Lambert's shoulder. "Come along. He's far too polite to object to you. It's only thanks to your interruption that I remembered the appointment at all."

Fell did not hurry down to meet his guest. Nevertheless, the nobleman was waiting patiently when they arrived.

"My lord, allow me to present Mr. Samuel Lambert, our advisor on the Agincourt Project. Lambert, please let me present the Earl of Bridgewater," said Fell. "Mr. Lambert will be joining us for lunch."

The Earl of Bridgewater was an imposing man. Well over six feet tall, clean limbed, with a mane of flowing hair that must have been raven black in his youth but was now brindled like a badger with white at his temples, the man could have played Merlin as easily as King Arthur. To Lambert, Bridgewater had all the elegance of the long-limbed aristocrats featured in the *Illustrated London News*. Sidney Paget himself could have drawn no more imposing a profile. Bridgewater's eyes were benevolent yet piercingly clear, his long face kind.

"Never mind the formalities," said Bridgewater. "I'm pleased to meet you, Mr. Lambert. Mr. Voysey speaks of you often. I've heard only praise for you and your extraordinary natural eye. You and your abilities make an invaluable contribution to the Agincourt Project."

Lambert stared. "You've heard of the Agincourt Project? I thought it was supposed to be a secret."

"So it is." Bridgewater looked amused. "Perhaps I ought not to have mentioned it, even in relative privacy. Forgive me. I take a proprietary interest in the matter, as I have provided some of the resources, financial and otherwise, that Mr. Voysey required."

"You're a backer?" said Lambert. "I didn't know."

"How could you?" Bridgewater led them to the club dining room. Effortlessly, he caught the eye of the host, who showed them immediately to the best table in the room. Fell showed no sign of noticing that Bridgewater had taken the initiative from him. "I play the dilettante, after all. Nevertheless, when imperial duty calls, a man must answer."

"Imperial fudge," said Fell. "Contrary to the opinion of the Vice Chancellor, the safety of the empire does not hang on the success of the project. A bit of luck for us all, given how many times the designers have changed their minds about the very nature of the thing. I'm sick of hearing that the project's inspiration is simple patriotism, when in truth it is mere love of gadgetry."

"Do you often mock simple patriotism?" Bridgewater inquired stiffly.

"Only when it wraps itself in the Union Jack and strikes dramatic attitudes for my benefit."

Accustomed to Fell's brusque response to any form of interruption of his studies, Lambert watched Bridgewater's reaction to Fell's rudeness with interest. The momentary stiffness vanished and was replaced with smooth courtesy.

"That was hardly my intention," said Bridgewater gently.

"No," Fell agreed, "no need. That's why we have the popular press, after all. Leave that sort of thing to the people who excel at it."

If anything, Bridgewater's gentleness increased. "You're in a tart mood this afternoon. Perhaps a good meal will mellow you."

They ordered and in due time the courses began to arrive. Bridgewater made pleasant conversation until they reached the end of the meal. Then, as he and Fell enjoyed their coffee and Lambert looked on wistfully, Bridgewater addressed Fell. "I hope you have given my offer your serious consideration. My library remains at your disposal. You are welcome to arrive when you please and to stay as long as it is convenient for you."

"You are hospitality personified," said Fell, his mood visibly softened by the excellence of the meal he'd enjoyed. "I thank you, but I must decline. As fraught with distraction as Glasscastle can sometimes be, I do my best work there."

"The invitation stands. If you change your mind, merely notify me." Bridgewater turned to Lambert. "My mission has failed. If you can prevail upon your friend to accept my invitation to visit, I'll be in your debt. Gentlemen, thank you for your time." Bridgewater took his leave.

As Lambert and Fell left the dining room, Lambert marveled. "Yes, you're the dutiful one, aren't you? You do your best work at Glasscastle. So why did you light out for London without a word to anybody?"

"I did, didn't I? Didn't I?" For a moment, an apology seemed to tremble on Fell's lips. "No, wait. I must have left a note or you wouldn't have known I was here."

"You didn't." Lambert told him about the newspaper's society column.

"What on earth possessed you to read rubbish like that? You have too much time on your hands. I should speak to Voysey about accelerating the tests." Fell's eyes brightened at the thought.

"If you think it's rubbish, why do you take that newspaper? Lucky I did read it. I was ready to report you as a missing person."

Fell's brows went up. "You're right. It was lucky. You'd have found it most embarrassing, had you reported me missing. You don't care much for embarrassment. I've noticed that."

"Nobody does. What brought you here anyway?"

"I came up to hear Bridgewater address the Royal Society. I had one or two questions to ask him afterward. For some odd reason, he thinks I should stay with him for a fortnight at his ancestral seat. His invitation was very flattering. It was all I could do to think of a reason to refuse."

"Why should you refuse?" Lambert asked. "I'm glad you didn't just disappear for a fortnight without a word to anyone, but why shouldn't you if you felt like it?"

Fell looked disapproving. "I didn't feel like it. He's the sort who thinks it's all very well that the sun never sets on the British Empire, but if we put our minds to it, we could do better. Always detecting fresh menace from overseas, going on about the threat posed by the Pan-Germanic party. As if the Pan-Britannic party isn't just as bad. He makes me tired. More than that, I can't spend a fortnight away from my work. Nor do I dare to leave you to the tender mercies of those fellows you keep company with. What has Meredith had you doing while I was away? Throwing harpoons?"

"As for your work, you have a bit more of it on your hands. You need to sort out the mess in your study." Lambert gave Fell a quick summary of the incident of the man in the bowler hat, including the plans he'd given to Brailsford.

"By Jove." Fell thought for a moment. "Wait here while I fetch my things. We're leaving at once."

"For Glasscastle?" Lambert asked.

"Didn't I say? Of course we're going to Glasscastle. I won't be five minutes."

Lambert was as lucky with trains on his return as he'd been that morning. He and Fell not only caught an express, they had a compartment to themselves.

"There's nothing extraordinary about that," said Fell, when Lambert remarked upon it. "Even if the train were full, I can always get a compartment to myself when I want it."

"You can, can you?" Lambert doubted it. "How? Do you show your credentials to the conductor when you board?"

"Hardly. No, if the train looks like filling up, I merely make a point to smile and nod as I beckon strangers to join me. I've discovered that people will go to considerable lengths to avoid me."

"I'm not surprised." Lambert had purchased a selection of newspapers to read on the journey. He opened one at random. From an inside page, the name Bridgewater leaped out at him. "I see your friend Bridgewater has been named a patron of the Royal Hospital."

Fell looked up from a scholarly journal. "He's not my friend. A man in Bridgewater's position doesn't have friends."

Lambert snorted. "Don't be ridiculous. Of course he does."

"He doesn't. Not unless he made them before he inherited his title. I suppose that might explain why men of Bridgewater's station are so often sentimental about their school days." Fell brushed at a fleck of soot on his cuff. "When he was a schoolboy, Bridgewater made discreet inquiries about admission to Glasscastle. He was told he'd have to take his chances like anyone else. This put him off, apparently. He never did apply."

Lambert frowned. "How could Glasscastle have turned a man like that away? If anyone ever had the right background, Bridgewater has."

"True. But the Fellows of Glasscastle couldn't guarantee it in advance and Bridgewater refused to risk rejection. This came as a great relief to the Fellows on the admission committee at the time. It seems his great-grandfather had displayed an uncomfortable amount of initiative as a student here. A case of enthusiasm outrunning discretion, I gather. Given the way talent sometimes runs in a family, they were glad to avoid the potential awkwardness of a similar situation with Bridgewater. Fortunately, he has kept up his family's tradition of generous support to the university."

"If Bridgewater never went to Glasscastle, why is he interested in the place?"

"I can't imagine. Unless Bridgewater was piqued that Glasscastle did not immediately fall at his feet in gratitude for his slightest attention. I'm sure it is the only institution that hasn't. A unique and refreshing experience for him. Bridgewater is the sort of man who relishes a challenge. Given his resources, he doesn't find many." Fell returned to his journal article.

Lambert went back to reading the newspapers. The Board of Trade had proposed a bill to make wireless installation compulsory on oceangoing steamers. The British-Atlantic project, which would connect every continent by wireless, had announced a new receiving and transmitting station to be built in Shropshire. The American news was dominated by a spirited criticism of President Taft and his proposal to nullify parts of the Hay-Pauncefote Treaty. American efforts to curtail English shipping through the Panama Canal were misguided at best and inflammatory at worst. If Taft's government did not understand its folly, it must be made to understand.

Lambert sighed and turned the page.

When they descended at Glasscastle, the five o'clock train to London was steaming in at the opposite platform.

On their way up from the platform, Jane Brailsford and her brother hailed them. They met in the center of the walkway and exclaimed at the coincidence.

"Fell, good to see you." Robert Brailsford addressed Fell a bit formally, then turned to his sister. "Jane, may I present Nicholas Fell, Master of Arts and Fellow of Glasscastle. Fell, allow me to present my sister, Miss Jane Brailsford."

Lambert wondered what Jane would make of Nicholas Fell. Fell's one distinguished feature was his voice, deep and musical. To the uninformed observer, Fell was easily overlooked. His usual expression was one of faint apology, replaced only at rare moments with one of interest keen to the point of intimidation. He was only an inch or two taller than Jane, his build, his coloring, and even his neatly clipped mustache all average. If Jane treated Fell the way she had Porteous, Lambert didn't want to miss a moment of it.

"Has Lambert told you about the disturbance in your study?" Robert asked Fell.

"He came all the way up to town to fetch me." Fell tugged at his mustache. "I'll be interested to see the result."

"I wish I'd known you'd be back." Robert eyed the outbound train with some anxiety.

"Robin is going to Shropshire," Jane explained. "Amy was indisposed, so I'm putting him on his train."

"Nothing serious, I hope?" Lambert asked.

"Not at all," said Brailsford.

"She will feel better later," Jane added.

"Jane fancies herself my chauffeur," Brailsford said. "It's absurd. I'm sound in wind and limb—perfectly capable of getting myself to the train and back again without assistance."

"With bag and baggage? Ridiculous, when you have me to drive you."

Brailsford was firm. "It's my motor car, Jane. Just remember that. After all, you promised me."

Jane's manner was patient as she repeated terms with which she was evidently well versed. "No speeding and no detours, just drive straight back home."

"And don't sound the horn," Brailsford added.

"I remember, I remember."

"While you're remembering, bear in mind that it is a proper car and not one of your Bantams. No wedging it into spaces too small."

"I'll insist on a wide berth," Jane promised.

Fell eyed Jane with disbelief. "You drive a motor car?"

"One of the things I've come home to do is buy one of my own," Jane confided.

"I must go. No need to come with me to the platform, Jane." Robert kissed his sister's cheek and departed.

Jane asked, "May I offer you gentlemen a ride in from the railway station? It's rather a long walk back to the university gate from here. I'll just wave Robin off first."

"That's very kind of you," said Lambert.

"Please, it would be my pleasure. This is the first time Robin has trusted me with his Minotaur. It's enormous. I'll put you in the back and play chauffeur."

Brailsford's train pulled out as Jane waved and Fell and Lambert watched in amiable silence. When the train had gone, Fell said pensively, "I suppose you might mean *chauffeuse*."

"Trust me," Jane replied, "if I had meant chauffeuse, I'd have said chauffeuse. But if it will make you more inclined to accept my offer, consider me to have said chauffeuse."

Fell asked, "You won't drive fast, will you?"

"Define fast," Jane said.

Fell said, "By Jove, Lambert, you've fallen among Amazons. I suppose we have no alternative. Polite refusal would imply a lack of confidence in her skills. Hardly courteous behavior, that. I've had enough of issuing polite refusals lately."

Stowed in the backseat with the light baggage, both Lambert and Fell watched with interest as Jane negotiated with a sturdy youth to have the crank at the front of her brother's vehicle turned vigorously. The motor caught with a roar. Dexterously she manipulated the levers and pedals that allowed her to pull smoothly out of the station.

Once she had eased the Minotaur into the flow of traffic, Jane drove with complete aplomb. She contrived to miss, albeit narrowly at times, pedestrians, bicyclists, cabs, carts, draymen, and other motor cars. Even during the long holiday between terms, there was enough traffic to make the drive a sporting challenge. So novel was the rate of speed, so fascinating was the spectacle, it took Lambert several moments to notice that Jane had missed the turning for the road back to Glasscastle.

"I'm afraid we're headed for Ilchester," Lambert called over the racket of their passage. "Glasscastle is the other way."

"There's a first-rate coaching inn at Nether Petherton," said Jane. "By the time we get there, they will be serving dinner. I'm told they do a very nice steak pie." Clear of the town, the road was almost empty. Jane picked up speed. "Part of the route follows a Roman road, nice and straight, so with luck I'll be able to open her up a bit too."

"But you promised your brother there would be no speeding and you would go straight back." Lambert couldn't help the edge in his voice. He sounded downright plaintive. It was embarrassing. Lambert reminded himself that the speed probably wouldn't bother him if he were the one at the wheel. As it was, he had to fight the urge to shut his eyes until it was over.

"I know. Disgraceful, isn't it?" Jane spared enough of her attention from the road ahead to look back and give Lambert a reassuring smile. "Once we reach Nether Petherton, I have a message for Mr. Fell. It is of paramount importance."

Lambert had to raise his voice to be sure he was heard over the roar of the motor car and the wind slicing past them. "Can it be more important than your promise to your brother?"

"I also promised Amy I'd be home in time for tea. I think that promise is doomed to go overboard too." Jane's tone turned serious. "I've promised something else, to someone else, and it takes precedence over everything."

Lambert had been driven in motor cars before, but seldom over such abruptly rolling terrain, and never at so great a speed. When Jane drove up an incline, she did so with such abandon that the ascent continued for a split second after they reached the crest. The sensation this created in the pit of Lambert's stomach convinced him he would have no interest in dinner whatsoever.

Fell said, "Do you realize, Miss Brailsford, that the route you've proposed to Nether Petherton will take you along the Roman road at a time of day when the sun shines directly into your eyes? You may not be able to achieve the velocity you desire without sacrificing safety."

In his reading, Lambert had once or twice encountered the term *glee*. He had never seen it firsthand until he saw Jane Brailsford's expression as she glanced back to reassure them. "Oh, that will be no trouble at all. I have tinted goggles."

The Roman road was all that Fell had warned it would be. Jane pulled her green goggles into place and forged along pitilessly. "Robin says she'll do thirty-five at top speed," she announced, "but I think we can do a good deal better than that."

Lambert closed his eyes. The sunlight made red flashes against his lids. If Jane said anything more to him, it was lost in the rising noise of the engine. There was nothing else in the world but wind tearing at Lambert's hair and clothing, and regret tearing at his heart. Why hadn't he insisted on walking back to Glasscastle from the station?

A clear road, a sunny day, and not a police constable to be seen. Jane gave the Minotaur a chance to show its paces on the way to Nether Petherton and wondered if Robin might have a point. There was something to be said for massive motor cars. Vastly more automobile than she needed, the Minotaur was a treat to drive.

Jane pulled up at the Bunch of Grapes and looked to see how her passengers had weathered the journey. They were windswept, dusty, and pallid. Jane hoped the tint of her goggles was responsible for their greenish aspect and not her driving.

Fell leaned forward, eyeing the switches and dials on the dashboard. "What was our ultimate velocity, can you tell me? Did we travel at thirty-five miles per hour?"

"We did." Jane removed the goggles and with a few deft touches restored order to her traveling ensemble. "For a fraction of a mile, we were going faster. Thirty-seven miles per hour, if you can credit it. If we take the same route home, we could try to better our record."

Lambert made a small, probably involuntary, sound of protest.

Jane relented. "No? Perhaps another time, then. Now, if you'll permit me to arrange a meal for us, to be served in conditions of privacy, I have a question for you, Mr. Fell."

"Very well." Fell leaned back in his seat with a deep sigh. "It was a good run while it lasted."

The Bunch of Grapes was as comfortable as Jane had been led to believe. Although there was no private dining room, their table was in a nook off the private lounge, with no other diners within earshot. The room itself was inviting, dark timbers close overhead, ivy at the deep windows countering the heat of summer sunlight, and flagstones cool underfoot. She ordered for her companions and when the food and drink came, they found it excellent.

Once the meal had been cleared away, Jane turned to Fell. "I've been charged to deliver a message to you. Forgive my bluntness but I must know—what have you been *doing*? You've been the new warden of the west since January and you've done nothing. It's disgraceful."

Lambert blinked at her. "Warden?"

"The warden of the west," Jane explained. "The new one. The old one died in Paris in January."

Fell touched his mustache and glanced down at the tablecloth. "I'm not a warden."

Jane leaned toward him and kept her voice low. "You are."

Fell looked up and away, apparently fascinated by the beams overhead. "I should have said I'm not a warden yet."

"There's no point in arguing the matter. It's time you did your duty. You can't leave all the work to the others indefinitely."

"It isn't that simple." Fell wouldn't meet her eyes.

Jane suppressed the urge to pound the table with her fist. "Then please explain why not. Answer one of the letters or telegrams Faris Nallaneen sent you from Aravis. Would that be simple enough? I've had to cross the Channel to have it out with you and that's something I do not undertake lightly. You have ways to communicate that surpass anything I can muster. All I ask is that you do your duty as a warden or explain why you're doing nothing. This lurking about in the groves of academe is hardly the way to behave. I was starting to get the idea you were avoiding me."

"Had I known of your existence," said Fell, "believe me, I would have. I've been avoiding every other form of communication with the wardens."

"I wrote to you. I wired you. How could you fail to know of my existence?" Jane demanded.

Lambert looked from Jane to Fell. "Wardens?"

"She thinks I'm one of the four wardens of the world," Fell explained.

"You are. You're the new warden of the west, God help us all," said Jane.

"But there's no such thing as wardens of the world," said Lambert. "That's only a remnant of folk belief. Cromer and Palgrave were arguing about it at dinner just last week."

"Don't believe everything you hear," Jane advised. "The new warden of the north sent me here and I can promise you, *she* exists."

"Miss Brailsford must have it wrong. Tell her." Lambert appealed to Fell. "You've studied the history of magic for years. You're an authority on the subject. Aren't you?"

Fell looked glum. "At one time I was considered an authority on the prevailing studies of that subject. My monograph, 'Evidence for the Existence of Historical Wardens,' was favorably reviewed. Recently, er, it has been made manifest to me that I am supposed to play a certain role in the structure of the world. In simpler times, the term was warden of the west. You needn't stare, Lambert. Imagine my feelings on the subject. I can hardly express the mortification I felt when I learned I'd been mistaken all along."

"If you know you're the new warden, why have you been avoiding me? Not to mention ignoring Faris," Jane added. She knew from personal experience just how difficult it was to ignore Faris Nallaneen for more than a few minutes at a time. Truculent and touchy, the young noblewoman from Galazon had been Jane's fellow student at Greenlaw.

Fell folded his arms. "I know I am intended to be the new warden. I'm not yet prepared to enter that particular prison."

Jane stared. "It's hardly a prison."

"Whatever it is, I have my own priorities. There are more important matters I must see to." Fell was firm.

Lambert looked from Fell to Jane and back again, as if taking in a tennis match.

"More important?" Jane knew that with a little more provocation, her unruffled demeanor would be a thing of the past. Already she felt a faint warmth in her cheeks. She suspected that she might be coloring unbecomingly. The knowledge did nothing to soothe her. "You've been ignoring Faris because you have more important things to see to?" Jane fell silent, because she feared her voice would tremble if she said another word.

Jane had helped Faris to come to terms with Faris's expulsion from Greenlaw. On the journey back to Faris's home in Galazon, Jane had been one of Faris's few allies. From Galazon, Jane had accompanied Faris onward to Aravis. Through discomfort and danger, Jane had helped Faris Nallaneen all she could. Things had simplified somewhat when Faris took up her full duties as warden, with authority to match her responsibilities.

Faris's first duty as warden had been to close the rift created when the previous warden of the north destroyed herself with an overly ambitious spell. The rift torn by the miscast spell had been growing slowly since

1848. By the time Faris closed it, the wardens of the west, south, and east had been trapped in their wardenships for more than sixty years. Faris had freed them.

Jane knew how reluctant Faris had been to accept her new role as warden of the north. For Fell to cavil at the responsibility infuriated her.

Lambert looked as if he couldn't decide which astounded him more, Jane's behavior or Fell's tranquil acceptance of the existence of the wardens of the world. "You're the warden of the west," he said to Fell. He sounded as if he were trying out the words, testing them, yet not believing them. "You're the new warden of the west."

"Please, Lambert. Don't rub it in. That is the idiom, is it not?" To Jane, Fell said, "If anyone in my position has ever had a more realistic notion of the duties this entails, I'd like to see the documentation. It's intolerable. Furthermore, it's untenable."

"Delay is futile." Jane was stern. "What good does moaning about it do? The other wardens are doing their part. Time you did yours."

"The other wardens are welcome to please themselves." Fell met Jane's glare with resolute calm. "I refuse to further the imbalance. I can't take up my duties as a warden until the distortion is rectified. It would be worse than futile."

"What imbalance? The rift is mended. Surely you must have noticed." Jane had been in the vicinity when Faris mended the rift on the heights of Aravis. She could not imagine anyone, least of all another warden, failing to notice. Jane struggled to find words to describe the experience. Wild geese going over in numbers that darkened the sky and the best hat she'd ever owned exploding like a time bomb—Jane gave up on description and settled for bald fact. "That is why it was possible for the wardenships to change."

Fell's keen expression was belied by the chill in his voice. "The rift itself may be good as new. Something, however, is very wrong. Sixty years of imbalance since the rift originated have created a distortion within the structure of the world itself."

"You mean there's an imbalance independent of the rift?" Jane asked.

"The imbalance was caused by the rift. The wardens who remained when the rift was torn could not move on. Their efforts to hold the structure of the world intact lasted until the rift was mended. When the rift was mended, the wardens moved on. The new wardens are left to deal with that imbalance. It must be rectified."

"Working together, all four of the wardens should be able to rectify anything," said Jane.

"I disagree. I think that if all four wardens carry on balancing the world from here, the distortion will be impossible to erase. For all I know, it may be impossible to erase no matter what anyone does." Fell added, "My conscience, however, is not so flexible that it permits me to ignore the problem or to behave as if it does not exist."

"I must admit it is better to have a warden who regards the position with suitable respect than with greed for power, but I'm sure Faris never contemplated a warden who is too skittish to assume his duties." Jane didn't try to keep the coldness out of her voice. "What makes you so sure there's a distortion?"

"Close your eyes," Fell said.

After only a moment's hesitation, Jane obeyed.

Fell struck a match, let it burn for a few seconds, then shook it out. "Open your eyes," Fell ordered as he disposed of the blackened remains of the match. A tendril of smoke twisted in the air between them and then dissipated.

Jane looked around. Fell was impassive. Lambert looked puzzled. "You decided against smoking in here?" Jane asked dryly.

"Is that what I did?"

"You lit a match."

"How do you know?"

Jane's voice was perfectly level but the effort it took to keep it there was starting to tint the edges with annoyance. "I closed my eyes. I didn't lose consciousness."

"Your senses informed you, in other words."

"Is that what you're telling me? Your senses informed you of the distortion? Couldn't you have said that more directly?"

Fell nodded. "Certainly. My first impulse was to poke the back of your hand with a fork, but they took all the cutlery when they cleared the table."

"Probably wise to keep pointed things right out of reach," Lambert muttered.

Fell ignored him, all his attention focused on Jane. "What I'm trying to convey to you is that I am as aware of the distortion as I would be of the discomfort if I put my shoes on the wrong feet. It's there. I'm aware of it."

Jane scowled at him. "All right. I believe you. Tell me about the distortion. When did you first become aware of it?"

Fell let out a long breath. "Immediately. You seem well versed in matters concerning wardenship. One can no more ignore impending wardenship than one can ignore falling out of bed. The moment my situation dawned on me, I was aware of the distortion as an unseated discomfort. I can't say what it would seem like to another warden, one who accepted the position without hesitation. To me, it is like music out of key, or an itch I dare not scratch. For a time, such was my mortification at the position in which I found myself, I was too distracted to fully appreciate the discord—or discomfort, rather. Unfortunately, either the imbalance is intensifying or my sensitivity is increasing."

Jane didn't like the abstracted look Fell was wearing when he mentioned discomfort. "You're in pain?"

"No." Fell seemed embarrassed by the mere suggestion.

Jane pursued the point anyway. "But your discomfort grows?"

"Yes. It is made worse by the cold truth that I can't possibly teach myself enough about the structure of the world to rectify the problem before I'm forced to accept the wardenship in full. My studies have been cursory at best. As it is, it takes most of my attention to refrain from being the warden."

"Could you bring yourself to communicate with the other wardens?" asked Jane. She knew from Faris's account that with mutual consent, wardens could communicate directly, despite the vast distances separating them. It was the failure to establish such communication with Fell that had driven Faris to ask for Jane's help.

"Not directly. Not without becoming one of them. If I knew their precise locations, I suppose I could compose a message and send it by telegram. It would be lengthy. I'm not concerned with the cost," Fell hastened to add, "but with the accuracy of the transcription."

"I'll tell Faris," said Jane. "She can speak with the others. Well, perhaps speak isn't the right word. She'll do whatever it is wardens do. She'll communicate with them."

"You seem very sure of her cooperation," said Fell.

"I am. I'm also certain of Faris's interest in the subject. It's your cooperation that interests her most keenly." Jane added, "From your description, she must be aware of the distortion herself."

"I suppose she must." Fell seemed far from convinced of it. "You'll send her a wire?"

"Don't worry. I'll be as accurate as possible when I communicate your point of view," Jane said absently. If conditions were right, communicating with Faris could be far more direct than sending a telegram. Far more swift, too.

Fell's earnestness grew. "I trust your accuracy. I trust your discretion as well. Permit me to offer you advice: use some form of code or cipher in your message. I prefer my problems remain my own."

Jane's brows shot up. "Who is spying on you?" If Faris and the other new wardens weren't the only parties interested in Fell, that changed matters. Jane congratulated herself on taking the precaution of questioning Fell well away from Glasscastle. "Was that why the man in the bowler hat broke in to your study?"

Lambert said, "He didn't break in. The door wasn't locked."

Fell replied, "I'm afraid your insistence upon the urgency of this conversation has delayed my inquiries into that incident, Miss Brailsford. There may be a connection, although I doubt it. Yet to err on the side of caution does no harm."

Jane had the distinct impression Fell was holding something back, as if unwilling to make an accusation he couldn't prove. She let his denial go unchallenged, but resolved to tax him with it as soon as he was suitably off guard. "I'll be discreet," she promised. "I'll be prompt, as well. In fact, the sooner I inform Faris of all this, the better. If you gentlemen are ready, I'll run you back to Glasscastle now."

Fell gathered himself. "Yes, I have work to do."

"We'll be there in record time," Jane assured him.

"Oh, splendid," Lambert murmured as he followed them outdoors.

Jane's hearing was excellent. She stopped to look up at Lambert. "Are you referring to the weather?"

Lambert smiled crookedly. "Nope. Just thinking that if I had known that was going to be my last meal, I would have had a pint of ale to go with it."

Fell echoed Lambert's concern. "Our velocity on the way here was a matter of research, purely in the pursuit of knowledge. To what excessive speeds will you force that motor car now you have reason to hurry?"

Lambert said, "I can't help but wonder what you'll do to that motor car now your heart is in it."

"I've been warned the twenty-miles-per-hour speed limit is strictly enforced here," said Jane. "Don't worry. You're both perfectly safe with me."

4

" 'Tis most true
that musing meditation most affects
the pensive secrecy of desert cell"

Fell and Lambert extricated themselves from the Brailsford motor car in the street outside Glasscastle's great gate. With a flutter of gauzy scarf, Jane drove jauntily off, leaving them with their baggage. No sooner were they past the gatekeeper and through the gate than Fell touched Lambert's sleeve to halt him.

"I intend to send the baggage with a scout. I have something more important to do than unpack."

Lambert waited while Fell summoned a scout, issued orders, and sent the man off to the rooms in Holythorn with a bag in each hand and one tucked under his arm.

"Well, aren't you the Tsar of all the Russias." Lambert watched the scout go. "Why can't we carry our own bags? We're headed that way ourselves."

"No, we are not." Fell led Lambert in the opposite direction. "First, I think we need to take a turn around the botanical garden."

Despite Fell's sudden fit of decisiveness, he seemed in no hurry as he followed the paths around Midsummer Green and then as carefully around the quads in front of Wearyall and St. Joseph's. Lambert measured his steps to match Fell's stride. The leisurely pace Fell set made a contrast to the sense of urgency at Nether Petherton. Although Lambert preferred to be moving under his own volition, after motoring with Jane their progress along the gravel path seemed almost unnaturally slow. "You didn't have to be back at work so urgently after all, I take it."

"Oh, I'm back at work now." Fell sauntered through the open gates of the garden and under the triumphal stone arch that marked the only way in or out of the botanical garden. The shadow of the arch was surprisingly cool after the warmth of the afternoon sun, but the momentary chill faded as soon as they were in the garden itself. "We're both working."

"We are?" Lambert followed Fell through the first garden, a complicated knot of lavender, rosemary, and about fifty other herbs he didn't recognize, and down the central path of the second garden, an axis that cut a sun-drenched promenade through fiercely pruned roses. Even in late summer, the scent was dizzying. "Nice work."

Fell did not pause to admire so much as a single blossom. He held his pace through the second gate, this one set in a wall all but concealed by ivy. Pear trees heavy with fruit lined the inner walls, pressed up against the masonry as if they were being punished. At the heart of the innermost garden grew a labyrinth of boxwood groomed with topiary precision into a maze only waist high. Patiently turning and returning as the path twisted its way through the right angles of the pattern, Fell led Lambert into the center of the green labyrinth.

Lambert had been to the botanical garden before. This time, prompted by Jane's architectural lecture, he took a good long look. Sure enough, the sum of the lengths of herb garden and rose garden was to the innermost walled labyrinth as the length of the walled labyrinth was to the whole. The golden section held true even here.

There were cherry and plum trees at the far corners of the garden, their middling height a relief to the stern geometry of the boxwood hedges, but they were not tall enough to cast much shadow. No shade disrupted the sunlight that flooded the place, no breeze stirred the foliage, and in the drowsy warmth of the afternoon, the loudest sound was the hum of bees. Lambert looked but saw no bees, nor any blossom to tempt bees near the hedges. The place was full of light and warmth, the scent of sun-warmed greenery, and the changeless sound of the bees. So clear was the sunlight that Lambert felt he could see the gray-blue shadow of each individual leaf of the boxwood hedges, each small pebble on the graveled path. Though the labyrinth was level, Lambert felt he was at the center of a bowl of light.

Lambert tried and failed to remember a time in his experience when bees had ever held to just one note, had ever stayed so still. The drone never rose or fell, but held to one constant pitch. That unchanging drone, too perfectly stable for any sound in nature, brought him to a standstill. Despite the sun's warmth on his shoulders, the back of his neck went cold.

As if he sensed Lambert's discomfort, Fell looked back. "Don't be alarmed. We're safe here."

"Hear that?" Lambert cocked his head. "You do hear that?"

"Of course. It's Glasscastle itself you hear. We're very near the wards here, the heart of its protection. It will protect us, I hope."

"From what?" Lambert felt goose bumps come out on his arms.

"I don't yet know. But this close to the wards, there should be no chance we are overheard." Fell halted in the six-sided space paved with flagstones to mark the center of the labyrinth. He turned to Lambert, eyes keen. "Describe the man you saw leaving the archive."

Lambert did his best to repeat the account he'd given Fell as they rode in the Minotaur. It was hard to concentrate. The warmth of the place, the brilliance of the sunlight, and the steady sound had worked together to blanket him with comfort. A groundless sense of well-being had conquered the unease he felt, and the chill at the back of his neck was all but forgotten.

Fell frowned. "No, I mean really describe him. Tell me everything you remember, every detail, no matter how unimportant it may seem. Think of it as one of Voysey's tests and spare nothing."

Lambert thought back. "Not a big fellow, but sturdy. Moved like a ferret. Even when he ran, he didn't seem to be in a hurry, but he covered a lot of ground. Kind of a lope. Fast and easy at the same time. His clothes looked all right, nothing to attract attention there."

"You're not the best judge of that," Fell pointed out. "If we were in the streets of Laredo, I'd trust your opinion, but not here."

Lambert considered reminding Fell that Laredo was not in Wyoming. Or that not everyone in America came from Texas. It didn't seem worth the effort. "Miss Brailsford didn't seem to notice anything out of the ordinary, and I reckon she is a reliable judge of such matters. She said something about his bowler, that's all." After a moment's consideration, he added, "I've never been to Laredo."

Fell was still focused on his study and the intruder there. "You saw the man arrive. You saw him leave. How long do you estimate that to have taken?"

"Miss Brailsford and I walked around part of Midsummer Green while we were talking. We went into St. Mary's. By the time we saw the man leaving the archive, I suppose a half an hour might have passed, no more than that."

"Not long. Not long at all, given the amount of material in my study. Was anything else in the archive disturbed?"

"We didn't have the authority to look in any closed rooms. So as far as I know, only your room was touched. Russell didn't seem to find anything in the incident to bother himself about. I didn't tell him about the plans I found on your desk."

Fell's eyes gleamed. "Ah, yes. Those plans that weren't there when I left. I thank you for your discretion. I'll have to see if there's anything else he brought me."

"Why would he turn the place upside down if all he wanted to do was leave something?"

"Isn't it interesting to speculate?" Fell tugged hard at his moustache. "Whoever the intruder was, he must have known just where to look. I wonder who told him which was my study?"

"Why would anyone have to tell him? Maybe he just picked yours at random. You hinted to Jane that someone was keeping an eye on you. Who do you think it is?"

"I don't know. If I did, I would have a word with him, whoever he might be. But someone must have arranged for your man in the bowler to have the credentials he showed the gatekeeper, don't you think? Whoever did that might have given him directions." Fell clapped Lambert on the shoulder. "That's your task for the afternoon. Find the gatekeeper he spoke with and see what he has to say."

"Oh, that's my task, is it?" Lambert didn't try to conceal his exasperation. "While you'll be doing God knows what, I suppose. What is all this tomfoolery about you being warden of the west?" Lambert remembered Meredith's joke. "Is that what makes you an ancient and legendary glory of Glasscastle?"

"A bit less of the ancient, if you please. Believe me, you could not possibly find it less likely than I do." Fell looked sheepish. "A voice woke me from a sound sleep one winter morning. Although I was alone, someone spoke to me and it was not a voice for my outer ear. It was a voice inside my head, thought to thought. It said four words, no more. I shall never forget the message, though it is not a voice I have heard before or since. *See to the clocks*, he said."

"See to the clocks?" Lambert blinked. "What clocks?"

"I wish I knew. There is something about an order, some quality of tone perhaps, that often makes one peculiarly reluctant to obey immediately."

Lambert tried to imagine Fell ever obeying an order, any order, without at least a cursory protest or demand for clarification. Lambert failed.

Fell continued, "I was suspicious of the voice. Once I was awake, I had the conviction that someone, or something, was prying at my mind. A most unpleasant sensation."

"I smell an understatement," said Lambert.

Fell acknowledged Lambert's accuracy with a faint smile. "At first I hoped it was a nightmare, the aftermath of too much Stilton or one glass of port too many. Alas, I could not reason myself out of it. The sensation did not ease until I took a few old-fashioned measures to banish intruders from my thoughts. My studies since then have confirmed the source of the intrusion is the wardenship. If I yield to the intrusion, at the very least, I will be confirming things as they are now."

"What choice do you have? How can you do anything else?"

"I don't know. I have exhausted my own resources. I have exhausted the resources of Glasscastle as well, at least insofar as the resources I trust without reserve. Since that first night, I have overcome the reluctance to follow an order. I put my faith in the message I received in the very beginning. I know nothing about clocks and less than nothing about time. But that's where I hope to find a hint of what I should do and how I should do it."

" 'See to the clocks,' " Lambert repeated. "Why don't you ask Miss Brailsford if she knows what it means?"

Fell's tone turned stubborn. "Miss Brailsford is hand in glove with the warden of the north. I dare not look to her for help, lest she pull me into the wardenship too soon."

"Would that really be so bad?"

"It's difficult to express how wrong it feels. It's more than discomfort. It's more than disquiet. It's a deep-seated conviction that things should not be this way. Something needs to be done. I only wish I had some idea what."

"Could you ask one of the other wardens?" Lambert marveled that he could make the suggestion with a straight face. "Somewhere I suppose there must be a warden of the south and a warden of the east."

Fell looked glum. "I dare not come closer to the wardenship than I am now. It is all I can do to refrain from yielding to the sensation."

"But haven't you even tried to find out how to stop it?"

"I know how to stop it. Surrendering would stop it. But what would happen then? I have no desire to surrender." Fell's stubborn expression did not budge. "I'd appreciate it if you would keep all this entirely to yourself."

"Don't mention anything to Miss Brailsford, you mean, in case she tells the warden of the north?" Lambert found it troubling to think of Jane as a potential spy.

"Don't mention it to anyone at all. Even if you're questioned on the subject."

"Who would do that?" Lambert was starting to find Fell's vague warnings as annoying as they were alarming. "Who would bother?"

"I have no idea. But if anyone does bother, you will tell me, won't you?"

"Of course." Reluctantly, Lambert surrendered the idea of asking Voysey or one of the Provosts for help. It must have occurred to Fell. Perhaps he'd done so by now. "I'll try to find the Fellow who was doing duty as gatekeeper yesterday, see if he noticed what was going on."

"Excellent idea."

"I'll see if he remembers anything I don't about the man or his papers." After a moment of silence, in which Lambert hoped Fell might volunteer something of his own plans, he gave up and prompted him directly. "What will you be doing?"

"Me?" Fell was all innocence. "Oh, I'll be back at my studies."

"Cleaning up your study, you mean. Russell was kind enough to offer to let you make a formal complaint if you find that anything's missing. Big of him, wasn't it? I'll come by later and help you tidy up."

Fell shook his head. "No need for that. Kind of you to offer, though."

"Kinder than you think. You haven't seen it yet."

Lambert left Fell in the botanical garden and went to find the gatekeeper who had admitted yesterday's intruder. It didn't take long, as the same man was on gate duty again, Tilney, a Fellow of Wearyall. Lambert introduced himself and explained what he wanted to know.

Tilney said, "I remember you, no question. You were with the young lady who talks. There was no one ahead of you."

For no more than a moment, Lambert let himself savor that description of Jane. What a pity she wasn't along to hear it. "Not immediately ahead of us, perhaps. But the person you let in just before us—"

Tilney spoke slowly and distinctly. "There was no one just before you. The last visitor before you and the lady arrived during breakfast."

"That's impossible. There was a man who came in just before us— bowler hat—"

"Look in the visitors book if you don't believe me." Tilney spun the heavy volume on the counter so that Lambert could read the entries. There, in chronological order, were neatly ranked entries for each of that morning's visitors to Glasscastle, along with times of arrival or departure.

Lambert persisted. "He was just in front of us. He stood right here. What else was he doing, if he didn't sign in?"

"There was no one in front of you. I remember because of all the talking the young lady did." Tilney flipped back to the previous day's page, found the spot in the list, and stabbed it with his index finger. "Use your eyes."

At the spot Tilney marked, Lambert found his own handwriting, his name followed by Jane Brailsford's. The entry before theirs, as the gatekeeper had insisted, was from more than an hour before. Lambert turned pages back and forth to make sure the sequence of pages and days was uninterrupted. "There must be some mistake."

Tilney scowled. "If there is, I didn't make it. There is the possibility that I've falsified the records in some way. That is a serious accusation. Extremely serious. I should think carefully before I said anything that implied as much. Now if you'll excuse me, I have work to do."

Lambert took out his puzzlement on Meredith's targets in the temporary shooting gallery set up on one side of South Quad. Meredith had him use his favorite weapon, the Colt Peacemaker, and the noise he made went a long way toward settling his temper.

"Not your best work today." Meredith finished marking the sheets on his clipboard. "The light will be gone soon. Perhaps we'd better try again tomorrow."

"Six more cartridges," said Lambert. "Then I'll stop."

"Please yourself."

Lambert stood at his mark and took a few deep breaths. The light was deceptive. He put his attention on the target, leveled the Peacemaker, and cleared his mind of everything. Six shots clustered at the heart of the target.

"Much better." Meredith made notes. "Pack it in now, will you?"

Without protest, Lambert sat down beside him and started the soothing routine of cleaning the weapon.

Meredith watched him work. "Fell's back, I hear."

Lambert nodded. "He took it into his head to go to London to hear a lecture."

"Without telling you?"

"Without telling anybody." Lambert shrugged. "He's a grown man."

"So he is. With the responsibilities of a scholar. One or two of his students are still waiting for him to mark their papers so they can find out if they passed Schools this term."

Lambert winced. "Impatient, are they?"

"Not half." As Lambert finished with his task, Meredith gathered up the bits of cloth and bottle of gun oil, stowing them with the clipboard in the case he carried. "They call him Sabidius, did you know? From that Latin jingle that means, when you cut to the heart of it, 'I do not like thee, Dr. Fell.'"

"They could call him worse than that before Fell took any notice." Lambert thought back. "Though they'd better not try swiping his hat again. That made him cross."

"You'll remind the old boy to see to them, next time you get a change?"

"I'll remind him. I can't promise that he'll do anything about it."

"No one expects miracles." Meredith looked thoughtful. "Listen, I can do my paperwork anywhere. Would you like to visit Upton's room?"

"They let you do your paperwork in Upton's room?" Lambert pretended to marvel at Meredith. "I don't even know why they trust you with the key to this place."

"I promise to be tidy. Come along." Meredith beckoned Lambert to follow him to Upton's room. "It's a good place to think."

"Do I look like a man with thinking to do?"

"To be honest, you shoot like a man with thinking to do." Meredith retrieved the key from its guardian and signed for it. Together he and Lambert climbed the narrow stairs to a room on an upper floor of Albany House, one of the Wearyall College buildings. The key turned easily in the lock.

Lambert followed Meredith into Upton's room. Upton's shrine was a more accurate term. Philip Upton had been Vice Chancellor of Glasscastle for thirty years. Since his death in 1870, his room had been preserved almost untouched. Like the botanical garden, it was an area off-limits to all but the Fellows of Glasscastle and their guests. Lambert had only been there a few times, always strictly chaperoned, but he treasured the experience. He welcomed, as vividly as on his first visit and every visit since, the sense of peace that filled the room. To Lambert, it was the silent equivalent of the heart-lifting music of the chant.

Meredith sat at the desk and began filling out his paperwork. Lambert took the chair opposite and let himself ease into the quiet of the place.

It was a small room, by Glasscastle's standards, but the ceiling was high. There was wall space above even the tall bookcases. The height of the ceiling prevented any sense of being hemmed in or confined. Instead, the solid run of books on every wall gave the room a cozy feel. To judge from the arrangement of titles, Vice Chancellor Upton had possessed a highly idiosyncratic sense of what book went with what, but his sense of order was evident.

"They really don't mind if you do paperwork here?" Lambert asked.

"Of course not, if it means I'll do my paperwork better." Meredith worked placidly on. "This place is for anyone who needs it. That's why the room has been kept the way it was when he used it."

"Just to let people sit here?"

"Sitting is optional. Thinking is mandatory. Upton was a good thinker. Some dark days he saw Glasscastle through. You could do worse than pick up a bit of Upton's thinking."

"You sound as if he left it lying around like a paperweight." In fact, there was a paperweight lying on the desk, a ceramic tile glazed with a shield blazoned with three red hearts. Lambert toyed with it idly.

"Of course he did. It's in the walls, most likely. Every strong personality leaves an influence." Meredith took the paperweight away from Lambert and put it gently back on the desk. "That was Upton's device, his sign, three hearts for the three colleges of Glasscastle. His friends said it was because he had three times more heart than most people."

"Upton died more than forty years ago. No one's personality is that strong."

"But when he was here, he was *here*. For thirty years. It hasn't worn off yet, believe me." Meredith went back to his paperwork.

The room felt as if Upton had gone only a moment ago, as if he might be back at any time. Lambert let himself relax in his ladder-back chair. What would it have been like to study at Glasscastle in Upton's day, before modern theories had come along to overturn the serene assurance of the past? Would it have been easier or harder to live in a world without Darwin and Malthus, a world without Voysey's scientific principles?

The peace of the place sank in. Lambert gave himself up to it. With only the small scratch of Meredith's pen to break the silence, it was easy to let questions and concerns fade as the angled light of sunset dimmed. Whoever Upton had been, whatever Upton had done, those hundreds and hundreds of books had not belonged to a man afraid of questions. The wear on the bindings attested to that.

Lambert sat with Meredith until it was too dim to work without a light any longer. Meredith put his pen away, and said, "Time to go, I'm afraid."

"Yes. Thanks."

"I thought it would help."

"It did."

Meredith locked the room up again, returned the key, and the pair of them went their separate ways into the deepening twilight.

In hall that night, Lambert found himself back in the neighborhood of Cromer and Palgrave's thrice-weekly debate. Fortunately, it wasn't a Bible night, as this time a guest joined Cromer and Palgrave for dinner. Louis Tobias was no older than Cromer or Palgrave were. He was as dark as Brailsford and as personable as Voysey.

"We mustn't overlook Colonel Cody," Tobias was saying to Cromer as they took their seats.

Buffalo Bill Cody had been Kiowa Sam's hero and the inspiration for his Wild West Show. The familiar name caught Lambert's attention. He looked up with interest.

"But the man's quite mad," said Cromer. "They say he sometimes takes a passenger along when he flies."

It took Lambert a moment to figure out the man Tobias referred to was not Colonel William Cody but Colonel Sam Cody. Sam Cody was yet another American to leave the Wild West for green Great Britain. He'd given up on his career as a cowboy showman, but had been making headlines as an aviator ever since. Necks didn't get risked any more regularly than Sam Cody risked his.

"Cody may have been the first, but these days he is not the only aviator to take up a passenger," Tobias replied. "Far from it."

Lambert said, "When he leaves his aeroplane, Cody tethers it to something, just as if it were a horse. That's what they say."

Tobias grinned at Lambert. "The man is an American, after all. One must make allowances." He turned back to Cromer. "Remember, he was the only man flying a British plane even to finish the round-England race. He won the Michelin Cup, after all. We don't count him out, even if Haldane did."

"Tobias has come all the way from the airfield at Farnborough to spy on us," Cromer informed the table at large. To Tobias, he said, "I think I speak for everyone here when I say that we feel very honored by your presence, sir."

"He isn't a spy," Palgrave countered. "He's gathering intelligence."

"A nice distinction." Tobias looked amused.

"Where better to gather intelligence than where the intelligent are gathered?" Cromer finished.

"That's the last time I let Lord Fyvie make my travel arrangements," said Tobias amiably. "Next time it will be a sneak attack."

"By air?" asked Palgrave.

"Certainly by air," Tobias replied. "In the future it will be the only viable form of warfare, you'll see."

"I can't wait." Palgrave looked gloomy. "It will be interesting to see which causes more damage, the objects the pilots drop overboard or the bits of equipment that fall off the aeroplane itself."

"Or possibly the impact of the aeroplane itself as it hits the ground," said Cromer. "Seriously, what brings you here?"

"Oh, espionage." Tobias was wide-eyed with sincerity. "Everyone knows that you Glasscastle men have the inside track with the ministry budget. I'm just here to pick up a few pointers."

"The vital thing," said Cromer, as he signaled for more wine, "is to keep the men with the money well oiled at all times. Hospitality, that's the watchword. Hospitality, simple self-confidence, and remarkable visual acuity," he added, with a nod toward Lambert.

"And mental acuity," said Palgrave. "That never hurts."

"Don't forget pluck," Lambert put in. As more claret arrived, he prepared to excuse himself from the table. There was very little in the world less interesting than watching other people get drunk.

"And pluck," Palgrave agreed. "Pluck is always good."

"And sheer animal cunning," said Cromer. "That about sums it up, I think. Do you think you can remember all that?"

"I think so," Tobias said. "The operative concept being self-confidence to the point of self-delusion and far, far beyond."

"Well put," Palgrave said. "But then, if half what I've heard about foolhardy aviators is true, that's your stock in trade, isn't it?"

Tobias seemed to find no fault in that statement, nor in the remainder of the evening's hospitality. When Lambert left them, the three were lingering at the table, highly entertained by their own wit.

Jane drove away from the great gate intent on her errands. She had to purchase a bottle of India ink, replenish the petrol in the Minotaur's tank, and return the Minotaur to its safe berth in the Brailsford carriage house. To Jane's dismay, once home she learned that Amy had invited a few of her friends to tea to meet Jane. Jane's impromptu sojourn in Nether Petherton had lasted too long. By the time Jane returned, the last of the guests had departed.

Such was Amy's agitation, her back hairpins were coming loose. "Did I say a word yesterday when you joined Robert for luncheon in hall without sending a message here? I did not."

"I apologize." Jane was meekness itself. "That was very rude of me."

Amy nodded with such vigor that a hairpin fell to the floor behind her. "Do I say a word when you take Robert to the railway station, a fifteen-minute journey at the very most, and then simply disappear with his motor car? I do not."

"I'm sorry. There's no excuse—"

Amy sprang another hairpin. "Do you have any idea how embarrassing your inconsiderate behavior is? What will I tell my friends?"

"Please apologize to them on my behalf." Jane had a shrewd idea that Amy's friends had found talking about her misbehavior more entertaining than they would have found talking to her, but she was careful to keep that thought to herself. "Do, please, tell me you accept my apology."

Amy relented before her coiffure came undone completely. In an effort to make amends, Jane helped Amy count linens.

"It's good of you to help with this," Amy told Jane. "I find it's wonderfully soothing, making sure that all the sets of sheets are in order, and all the tablecloths are put away properly."

"Soothing, indeed." Soporific was the word Jane would have chosen.

"Table napkins, on the other hand, are always a trial. I can't think what happens to them. One would think they were made of lint, the way they go to the laundry and never return." Amy counted out another dozen. "I know it's silly to be worried that Robert hasn't sent a wire yet. He can't have been there long, after all. For all I know, he may have sent one hours ago and it hasn't yet been delivered. Only I spilled the salt today, and that's never a good omen."

Jane folded and unfolded, counted, recounted, and sympathized with Amy until it was time for bed. It was pleasant enough work and by the time they were finished, their hair and clothes were scented with lavender from the sachets they'd handled. To Jane, the smell of lavender and clean linen seemed the very scent of domestic peace. She felt a pang of unaccustomed envy for the serenity Amy and Robert had achieved in the house they shared. There might be more appeal to such companionship than she'd suspected.

Did lavender grow in Wyoming? Jane dismissed the thought with a private chuckle. That was the sort of thing Amy would want to know.

That night, long after the rest of the Brailsford household was asleep, Jane sat writing letters at the desk in her room. When midnight struck, she put her work aside. On the blotter she centered a dinner plate she'd borrowed from downstairs, Royal Worcester patterned with flowers and butterflies within a wide band of blue within a narrow band of gold.

Murmuring softly but distinctly, Jane opened the new bottle of India ink and poured the contents carefully onto the plate until it was full to the band of blue. For a few moments, the glossy darkness reflected her face and part of the brass fixture of the gas light overhead. Then the reflection vanished and there was nothing before her but matte blackness. At the very edge of Jane's perception, she felt the steady discord of Glasscastle's bounds, too close for comfort even halfway across town. With determination, she focused on the absolute darkness, filtering out the interference of the bounds as a distraction she could not afford.

"Jane?" Faris's words were in Jane's inner ear, an interior voice, bodiless, small and remote as letters printed on a page.

Jane pitched her voice just above a whisper. "Were we far enough from Glasscastle? Could you hear us?"

"Heard and saw." Faris sounded tired. *"He's right. Blast him."*

"Mending the rift didn't mend the rift? That hardly seems fair." The news took away most of Jane's pride and pleasure in the success of her spell casting. "What's wrong with the way you did it?"

There was a pause, as if Faris were selecting her words with great care. Then the answer came. *"Sand in an oyster. If you wait too long, take the grain of sand away, the pearl is still there."*

"But the sand *is* gone? For good?"

"Oh, yes. That's taken care of. The trouble is, even if Fell can stay out of the wardenship, I don't think there's any way the rest of us can do anything about the pearl."

"What about Fell? Can he mend the distortion by himself?"

"Doubt it. Still. He's far more aware of it than the rest of us were. That's something. All that power he isn't using, since he isn't letting himself yield to the wardenship, ought to be compounding like interest. He should be able to put it to good use when at last he sees fit."

"What shall I tell him?" Jane could feel the spell yield within her as her concentration waned. "Any message?"

"Keep trying." The fatigue in Faris's response was unmistakable. As the strength of the communication began to fade, the ink on the plate began to dry from the edge inward, until, as the center dried completely, the final word trailed off into silence.

Jane glared at the dried, blackened plate as she rubbed her aching temples. "Thank you for the depth of your wisdom," she muttered to no one. "I'm so glad you're the warden and I'm just here to help count the linen." Without much hope of salvaging the Royal Worcester plate, she put it in her washbasin and poured water over it. The ink *might* soak off. Given enough time. Otherwise, she'd just have to buy Robert and Amy another to replace it. Amy would probably forgive her for the act of domestic vandalism eventually.

Jane went to bed with a headache.

5

"Then down the lawns I ran with headlong haste
Through paths and turnings often trod by day"

The next morning, as soon as it was decently possible to pay a call, Lambert visited the Brailsford household. He found that Mrs. Robert Brailsford was indisposed again. Miss Jane Brailsford received him in the morning room, a good sunny spot, and offered him tea. She looked fine in white linen with a filmy bit of lace for a collar, too demure to burst a soap bubble.

"Amy isn't downstairs yet." Jane handed Lambert a cup of tea mercifully unsullied by milk, sugar, or stray tea leaves. "Shall I ring for something more substantial? With Amy's excellent cook, you never know your luck. There might even be muffins."

Lambert sat back and put his cards on the table. "I only came to tell you that we seem to have imagined the man in the bowler hat."

"Did we?" Jane was intrigued. "How completely irresponsible of us. Tell me."

Happy to have such a good listener, Lambert related the gatekeeper's account, concluding with his own further investigations. "I thought there had to be some misunderstanding, so I went back and talked to Tilney again. Made him good and cross with me for doubting him. Then I questioned two other people he said were in the vicinity at the time. Fellows of Glasscastle are steadfast witnesses. I've never met people so sure of themselves in my whole life. Neither of them saw the man in the bowler hat either. Nobody did."

"How provoking." Jane seemed to be thinking hard.

"Yup. Even if one of the witnesses does remember something later, all three have already sworn up and down that no one went through the gate at that hour of the day but us. Once they issue an opinion, no one at Glasscastle likes to change it without a full-scale debate."

Jane looked irritated. "What does your Mr. Fell think of all this?"

Lambert grimaced. "Oh, Fell thinks I ought to question everyone at Glasscastle. In alphabetical order. Possibly by height. He likes it when I leave him alone. Which I have done to the best of my ability. When I tried to ask about it after dinner last night, he pretended he was deaf. Then he pretended he was asleep. A neat trick, as he was smoking a cheroot at the time."

Jane looked sympathetic. "How hard Mr. Fell works. Do you think he'd care to go for another outing in Robin's motor car? It might help clear his thoughts."

"You could ask him."

"I will. Wait while I write him a note. If Mr. Fell doesn't want a jaunt in the motor, bring him to tea instead. I must speak with him today, and the sooner the better." Jane rang for the maid and sent for paper and ink. While Lambert finished his tea, she dashed off a brief letter of invitation, blotted her signature carefully, and folded the paper as soon as the ink was dry. "Do make sure he knows I need to speak with him today, please. It's very important to me."

Lambert put the letter in the breast pocket of his jacket. "You don't wish to come back with me? You could question the gatekeeper yourself, if you wanted." *The young lady who talks, Tilney had called Jane. Well, it might serve Tilney right to have a little of that talk headed his way.*

"I'd rather see Mr. Fell outside the confines of his college," Jane replied. She looked at him through her lashes. "I am sure you learned more from the gatekeeper than I would."

"You being a mere female and all, of course." Lambert didn't even try to keep the sarcasm out of his voice. "Cut it out, will you?"

Jane laughed. "Are my languishing glances too much for you, Mr. Lambert? That's odd. You seem invulnerable to my charms. One might even say impervious."

"I'm supposed to stay away from stimulants, remember? Save your feminine wiles for the rest of the world. You don't need 'em on me. You win. I'm buffaloed."

"What does that mean? Something to do with your Wild West Show? Buffaloed." Jane tried the word out as if she were tasting it. "Buffaloed."

"You've bamboozled me, that's what it means."

"Me? Bamboozled you?" Jane shook her head. "On the contrary. You're the one doing the bamboozling, Mr. Lambert. You're gallant when it suits you to be, and gauche only when you decide to disarm the opposition."

"While you, Miss Brailsford, consider every man in the world fair game for your femme fatale act. I don't blame you, I guess. Too bad you don't have the run of Glasscastle just because you're a girl. If it makes you feel better to make a monkey out of every man who lets you, fine. Just don't waste it on me. You may look like you're made out of spun sugar, but if the way you drive a car is anything to go by, you're about as fragile as a piece of boiled leather. Your brother says you're fanciful. From what I've seen, you're about as fanciful as a pint of vinegar."

"Who put the bamboo in this bamboozle?" Jane was staring at him, her amusement plain. "What could I possibly have said to give you the impression I want to have the run of Glasscastle? To get up at some unearthly hour of the morning and sing myself hoarse for the greater good of the community? To eat gruel at two meals out of three? No, thank you."

"Doesn't it bother you to be shut out? To be let in only on sufferance, and then to be forced to walk only where walking is allowed, and only when your presence is permitted?" Lambert broke off, abashed by the force of his words. He hadn't meant to give away so much.

Jane eyed him narrowly. "No, it doesn't bother me. Not particularly. But I think it bothers you. It must bother you very much."

"Me? Doesn't bother me a bit. I know the rules." Lambert put his half-empty cup down. "It's a privilege for me just to be here in Glasscastle. Until I came here, it never dawned on me that there were such places. Places where magic is taught, same as if it were needlepoint or chemistry."

"Those are novel parallels to draw. How did you think people learned it?" asked Jane.

Lambert shrugged. "The first time I ever saw true magic done, I figured it was just something a man was born with. I never associated it with education."

Jane looked intrigued. "What sort of magic was it?"

"I don't know a name for it. I was in Paris with the show. Sometimes Kiowa Bob would issue a challenge to a cavalry regiment to see if any of their men could ride one of our horses. The broncos, I mean. The horses that buck." Lambert checked to see if Jane was following him.

"I understand," said Jane.

"Very seldom was there a cavalry-trained rider who could. Fine riders, one and all. It was a matter of experience, you see. It's one thing to learn that kind of riding over time. To pick it up in one try, when there's a wager on the line, and with all your friends watching you—well, it isn't easy."

"I can imagine."

Lambert went on. "This particular occasion, the cavalry officers brought one of their horses out, a bald-faced roan. It's strange how often a bald-faced horse will turn out hard to handle. The French cavalry officers challenged any of our bronc riders to try to stay on him. Three of our best riders tried him and they all but broke their necks."

"The French officers must have been pleased."

"They were looking mighty smug. But you can also imagine how wild this horse was. Eyes rolling, foam flying—it was painful to watch." Lambert frowned at the memory.

"Painful to handle him too, I suspect."

"Painful to try, that's for sure. Bite, kick, he did it all. While the boys from the show were deciding who would be the next to try to ride him, a stranger came up and asked if he could take a look at the roan. He wasn't one of the officers and he wasn't with our bunch. He was well dressed and mannerly, quite ordinary in a respectable way. Except there was a calm about that man that I had never run across before. Something special about how quiet he was. I can't describe it any better than that. He asked if he could see to the roan. Something about the way he asked made everyone take a step back and let him. He didn't make a sound. He hardly touched the horse. But there was true magic worked as he stood there. I've never been as sure of anything in my life."

"Why? What did he do?"

"Nothing. No mumbo jumbo, no gestures. Nothing I can put into words. But there is no doubt in my mind that he did *something*. He took the reins away from the men who were trying to hold the roan. Then he just stood there, quiet and peaceful. At first the horse had the reins pulled tight, trying to back away from him, but little by little his head came down and his ears

came forward. Pretty soon he came up square and stood there, calm as anything. Then the man ran his hand down the roan's neck, from just behind his
ears all the way down to his shoulder. The horse didn't mind it. Didn't mind
anything. Just stood there, nice as pie."

"Did he ride the horse himself?"

"Didn't have to. He just patted the roan, handed the reins back to one of
the officers, and walked away. That officer rode the horse around the ring a
few times, just to see how he behaved. But from that moment on, that horse
was tame."

"Did your mysterious man get a reward?"

"No, and once he helped that horse, he didn't stay around long either. Just
as well, because a man with skill like that could have put our bronco busters
clean out of business in under an hour."

"My goodness. What makes you so sure he was using magic?"

"I can't explain. It was a new kind of calmness he had. New to me. I never
felt anything like it before. I never thought I'd feel anything like it again. I
didn't. Until I came to Glasscastle. Even then, it wasn't until I heard the
chanting the first time." Lambert brought himself back to the present with a
shake. "Why are we even discussing this? I'll take your message to Fell, see
what he says. If he wants to go riding around in that fancy motor car of your
brother's, I guess he will let you know."

Jane's scrutiny did not falter. "Robin told me a bit about how you came to
be here. Glasscastle sent observers to a contest of marksmanship, looking
for someone with a good eye."

"The Sovereigns. You know, I thought it was named for royalty. More
than one king, something like that," Lambert confided. "I didn't even know it
was named after the prize money."

"One hundred golden sovereigns for the best marksman in the country. A
generous sum for an afternoon spent target shooting."

"One afternoon of the year," Lambert agreed, "and all it takes to win is a
lifetime of preparation. Some of the finest shots in the world were there for
the contest. Men who learned to shoot from their fathers, and their fathers
had won the Sovereigns in their day. Made me wonder if everything isn't
handed down, father to son, the way Darwin says it is. Survival of the keen-
est eye."

"Is that where yours came from? Did you inherit your keen eye from your
father?"

"No, I don't think so, for all he had a good one. I think I get it from my mother. To this day, she keeps the pests out of her garden with a Colt Peacemaker. Many is the time I remember she would look up from the laundry tub to see some foolish young jack rabbit, full of self-conceit and the neighbors' carrots, come for a sniff round her peas or her cabbages. She'd dry her hands on her apron, take aim, and we'd have rabbit pie for dinner. One rabbit, one cartridge. That was her rule."

"My goodness."

"Her father was a gunner in the artillery. That's where she had her eye from. I suppose everything is handed down, one generation to the next."

"So you won the Sovereigns. Quite an honor."

Lambert shrugged. "I only won because Miss Oakley doesn't shoot any more. If she'd been there, things would have been different. I wonder what the Glasscastle men would have done then? Do you think they would have signed her up to help them with their research? I don't."

"The Agincourt Project." Jane nodded. "Robin told me about it. Just a bit. Enough to keep me from asking awkward questions." At Lambert's look of skepticism, she went on. "I'm not trying to—buffalo you into thinking he told me more than he did. They went to the Sovereigns specifically to find the best shot they could. By studying the human mechanics of accuracy, they plan to enhance the accuracy of their device. What good is a cannon, no matter the size, if you can't trust the accuracy of its aim?"

"It's a cannon?" Lambert let all his uncertainty about the project show. "They haven't told me any more than they've told you. Not as much, maybe. But I'm starting to wonder if anything they've told me is just the way they say it is."

"There's nothing wrong with that policy," said Jane. "Given Robin's love of secrecy, the device could be anything. But I suspect that whatever the weapon may resemble, the degree of accuracy is vital. After all, you're the only outsider they've consulted on the whole project. The one man with a skill so vital, he can't be permitted to drink so much as a cup of coffee lest he spoil his aim. Is it true you can shoot the center out of an ace of spades at thirty paces?"

"No." Lambert was honest. "Though I wouldn't be surprised to hear Miss Oakley could do so. But if I can see my target, I can try to hit it."

"According to Robin, if you try to hit it, you do hit it."

"Depends on the weapon. Given a decent gun sight, I can do pretty well. Archery is hard. Can't seem to get the feel of the bow. Voysey had me try a crossbow once. That was a little better. I wasn't too excited the time he had me try throwing knives."

Jane looked surprised. "It isn't just guns, then?"

Lambert suppressed a smile. "I was at my best with a slingshot when I was a kid. Did my best work ever back then. Dead-eye Sam Lambert. Wasn't a squirrel for miles could sleep through the night for worrying about me."

"Does Robin know that? Did they test you with that one too?"

"It seems to have slipped their minds so far. They haven't asked me to throw a fastball, either. I used to hope I'd be the next Christy Mathewson, but that doesn't seem to be in the cards." Lambert took pity on Jane's confusion and explained. "Pitcher for the New York Giants. Finest right-hander in the game. A baseball player. Never mind."

Jane looked only slightly less confused. "Oh. Baseball. That's rounders, isn't it?"

"Approximately." Lambert rose. "I'll go back to Holythorn and see what Fell thinks about another outing in your motor car."

"Encourage him to accept. I'll stay well within the speed limit this time. I promise."

Lambert's powers of persuasion went untried, as Fell wasn't at Holythorn. Their quarters had been tidied up. Once again, only the tick of Fell's clock provided any sign that the rooms were actually a place of human habitation. Lambert knew the rule. If Fell wasn't sleeping, he was working. Without a pause, Lambert emerged again and headed for the Winterset Archive.

Despite the season, there were half a dozen undergraduates gathered at the entrance of the archive. They looked underfed, underslept, and moody. One had a scale model of an aeroplane in his arms, paper and balsa, as delicate as a box kite and even less useful. Lambert brushed past them and entered.

As he climbed the creaky stairs up to Fell's study, Lambert heard a substantial crash, as of a glass-fronted bookcase falling over. He took the rest of the stairs at a run.

"What the hell?" Lambert came through the half-open door of Fell's study. At first he couldn't see anyone, then he saw Fell was on the floor behind his desk, grappling with the man in the bowler hat. One bookcase had been knocked over in the struggle and the cascade of fallen books and broken glass added to the difficulties involved in wrestling beneath a large wooden desk.

Fell was not a tall man but he was wiry. Fighting on the floor minimized any disparity in strength, and he held his own against the intruder with pure doggedness, bad language, and an assortment of unsportsmanlike tactics.

Lambert waded into the struggle and pried the man off Fell. The bowler hat went flying as Lambert shook the man and demanded, "What's going on here?"

Weasel-fast, the man turned in Lambert's arms, landed a kick and a flurry of blows that doubled Lambert over gasping, and twisted away. His quick footsteps made the wooden steps squawk as he fled. Lambert caught breath enough to swear, looked at Fell, who seemed neither seriously injured nor particularly alarmed, and gave chase.

The steps squeaked as much for Lambert as they had for his quarry. The door at the foot of the stair was closing as Lambert reached it. Lambert emerged, elbowed past the undergraduates still loitering there, and stumbled down the stone steps outside. The bowler-hatted man had just left the gravel path to cut across Midsummer Green on his way to the great gate.

The whole world narrowed to panting breath and pounding steps as Lambert pursued the fleeing man at top speed. The yielding crunch of gravel beneath his feet gave way to the velvet softness of grass. Two strides and Lambert fell, wind knocked out of him, knees buckling beneath him. The world tilted and spun and dimmed at the edges as he fought for breath.

So this is why they warn us not to walk on the grass, Lambert thought, as he tried and failed to make his legs obey him. He couldn't even make himself inhale. He twisted and gasped, crowing for air. From somewhere beyond the edge of his vision, footsteps neared. Strong hands braced him and helped Lambert scramble back to the gravel path.

After what seemed an endless time of choking and gasping, Lambert caught his breath and blinked up at Fell. "Thanks," he tried to say, but all that came out was a hoarse whisper.

"Better?" Fell's concern was clear, though his voice was as calm as ever.

"I'm not in strong convulsions yet. Whatever they are. Where did he go?" Lambert craned his neck to peer around. There was no one in sight but the huddle of undergraduates watching him, curious as a herd of steers.

"I have no idea." Fell pushed him flat again. "Nor do I care, to be honest. Whoever he is, he seems able to come and go as he pleases. Let's just assume he'll be back the next time it suits him."

"He attacked you." Lambert decided that his ability to breathe was back to stay. He started to get up.

"Yes, I know." Fell helped Lambert to his feet. "Extraordinary behavior."

Lambert's vision fogged as he stood and he lowered his head while he waited to recover. Magic was a fine thing to think about in the abstract. To experience it in person was bruising. In a few moments, his head cleared and he was able to think again. "I'll notify the authorities." Before he could take a step, Fell's grip on his arm stopped him. "What is it?"

"Not now. I'll see to all that later." Fell turned back toward the Winterset Archive. "Come with me."

Mystified yet obedient, Lambert trailed Fell back to his lair. There, amid the scattered debris of the attack, Fell picked up his toppled chair, dusted the seat, and offered it to Lambert. "You'll feel better soon."

Lambert frowned at Fell but took the offered chair. "I feel fine now," Lambert lied. There was a headache gathering behind his eyes, the way the likelihood of thunder gathered when a summer afternoon grew hotter and more humid. He ignored it. He had his wind back, that was the important thing.

"Do you? That's fortunate." Fell peered under the desk. He found the bowler hat and inspected it inside and out. "Hm. Good quality." He left the hat on his desk and started picking up papers from the floor.

"Don't cut yourself." Lambert looked around for something to use to clean up the broken glass. As cluttered as Fell's study was, there was nothing remotely resembling a broom.

"Too late, I'm afraid." Fell held up one hand for Lambert's inspection. The scratches and cuts were minor but messy. "Nothing serious."

"Exactly what happened, anyway?" Lambert demanded.

"I'm not quite sure. He wanted me to go with him." Fell righted the bookcase and gingerly began to put shards of glass into the wastepaper basket. "He neglected to mention where."

From the slight unsteadiness of Fell's hands, Lambert could tell he was more upset than he let on. "Why? Who is he?"

"He didn't mention that either. In fact, he hardly said a word." More rummaging around under the desk and Fell came up with a gun in his hand. "He dropped this."

Lambert sprang out of his chair and took the pistol away from Fell. "Watch where you point that thing." He unloaded the weapon and put it carefully down beside the bowler hat. "Careless of him, leaving that behind."

"It was." Fell studied the pistol. "Careless of him to come back, for that matter."

"But now we can be sure about what he was doing here before. He was looking for you." Lambert rubbed his head. There was a spot over his left ear that was tender but he didn't remember getting hit there. Already the details of the fight were beginning to blur.

"Yes. He wants me, specifically. I wonder why." Fell was intent on the objects left behind. "Perhaps I should have played along until I found out more."

"Bad idea." Lambert felt his headache diversify to add a deep throb at the base of his skull.

"Perhaps." Fell didn't seem to be listening.

Lambert asked, "If that's what happens when you walk on it, how do you ever mow the grass here?"

Fell gave Lambert a sharp look. "Are you quite certain you're all right?"

"I am. Honest. I just wondered, that's all." Lambert felt sheepish. He hadn't meant to blurt out his question that way. He hadn't meant to say anything.

"The Fellows of Glasscastle take it in turns to tend the greens. It's all part of the egalitarian nature of the place. Undergraduates chant to sustain the wards while the Fellows keep the gates and tend the grounds. It keeps us humble." Fell seemed to believe every word of it.

To his own consternation, Lambert chortled. Humble? *Fell?* He bit the laughter back with difficulty. "Well, I don't know about that, but the place does look nice."

"Perhaps I should help you to the infirmary. We should have a doctor take a proper look at you," said Fell. "It's not a good idea, breaking the rules of Glasscastle."

"I'm fine. I won't do it again. I didn't mean to do it in the first place. I got carried away. Hot pursuit and all that."

Fell went back to studying the bowler and pistol, tugging at his mustache in concentration. "Strange that only you were affected."

"Same as last time, the way he cut across the grass. Didn't seem to bother the sidewinder at all." Lambert wished he'd done more than grab the man's collar and give him a shake when he had pulled him off Fell. A solid punch in the bread basket, for starters.

"Yet only a Fellow of Glasscastle may walk alone on the grass of Midsummer Green, or any other college quadrangle."

"He didn't look much like a Fellow of Glasscastle to me. More like a weasel."

Fell arched an eyebrow. "That fellow was no Fellow of Glasscastle." He scooped the cartridges up and put them in one pocket, stowed the pistol in another, and tucked the bowler under his arm. "Come along."

Lambert winced as he got to his feet. His muscles had begun to stiffen even in the short time he'd been seated. "Where are we going?"

"London," said Fell. "It's a good deal easier to hide in a big place than a small one. If you need me to explain why I want to hide, I will take you to the infirmary after all."

"Oh, thank you for such concern." Lambert didn't bother to conceal his irritation. He reached in his breast pocket for Jane's note. "Before we leave, you'd better read this."

Fell read it and frowned. "I'll wire her from town."

"She'll be disappointed." Privately, Lambert thought Jane would be furious, but he knew the idea of Jane's anger would neither impress Fell nor deter him.

"Unfortunate but unavoidable." Fell dropped the note on his desk. "There's a train in half an hour. Pack quickly." As an afterthought, he retrieved the note and put it in his pocket, the one with the cartridges. "And do be sure to travel light."

At a discreet distance, Jane followed Lambert from the Brailsford house back to the great gate. Wettest summer in years or not, it was a pleasant day, with a breeze out of the north to moderate the heat, and Jane had no difficulty in giving the impression she was merely out for a morning stroll.

At the gate, of necessity, Jane waited. If her guess was correct, Fell would try to elude her. If he chose to leave Glasscastle through Pembroke gate, he would succeed. But if, as was his apparent wont, Fell chose the great gate, she would have a chance to pounce upon him, and once she treated him to a brief scold on good manners, to pass along Faris's message to him.

There were other possibilities. Lots. Lambert might persuade Fell to see her, even to accept her invitation. Fell might listen to Faris's message with attentive courtesy. Pigs might actually fly. Jane was willing to keep an open mind. Or Lambert might fail to find Nicholas Fell at all. Fell might have gone to ground somewhere overnight. Or Fell might have seen the error of his ways and taken up the wardenship of his own free will.

Jane waited and watched the gate.

To Jane's dismay, the bowler-hatted man, this time without his bowler hat, was the first to appear in the arch of the great gate. He paid no attention to the gatekeeper, nor did the gatekeeper seem to take any notice of him. Without a break in stride, without a sign of pursuit, the man ran past Jane. He looked annoyed, but he did not seem upset. If anything, he looked as if he could run all day and not notice. He reached the street. There wasn't much in the way of traffic outside, but at his speed, he could lose himself to view down a side street in a matter of moments.

Jane chose not to permit him to do so. She followed him for a few yards, just far enough to clear the shadow of the gate. Then, wincing at the waste of energy she undertook in trying a spell so close to the confines of Glasscastle, she altered the appearance of a small heap of horse droppings. In their place, a small heap of golden guineas caught the morning sunlight.

The man without a bowler hat swerved toward the money, drawn by the lure of gold. He stopped in his tracks and leaned forward to grasp the coins. As he did so, Jane caught up with him. She was hardly able to see for the pain in her head the spell caused her, but when she had barreled into him, she knocked him off balance. Once he was down, Jane was able to bend his leg back, get a firm grim on his ankle and toe, immobilizing him, and then keep him down by dint of sitting on him.

"Get off me!" The man struggled to dislodge Jane's weight. When he failed, he waxed profane.

"Help!" Jane could not wave to attract the gatekeeper's attention but when the situation warranted, she had excellent lung capacity and a penetrating voice. Shouting for assistance all the while, Jane released her spell. The bareheaded man uttered a cry of disgust and began to swear even more volubly as the golden guineas he clutched turned back into horse droppings.

Jane wanted to swear, herself. Her headache was worthy of the strongest language and the gatekeeper's reluctance to come to her aid filled her with rage. Whatever Glasscastle chose to pride itself on, however devoted they were to the inconvenience of guests in the name of systematic exclusion of visitors, the basic notion of security was nowhere on the list.

6

"Why are you vexed, Lady? Why do you frown?"

Lambert was no novice in the art of the quick getaway. During his years on the road, he'd learned that few possessions were irreplaceable. Of those few, even fewer were worth compromising the ability to travel light and fast. His essentials fit into a small valise with room left over for half a dozen clean collars. The collars weighed almost nothing, but Lambert faltered. *Take what you need and let the rest go.* Lambert had always believed that was the key to travel, but now he learned there was a more important tenet. The true key to travel was the desire to go. Lambert didn't have the slightest wish to leave Glasscastle. He hesitated, the collar box in his hand.

It was simple. Fell needed to leave. Lambert didn't want him traveling alone. Lambert packed the collars, closed and locked his valise, and left his room without a backward glance.

Fell was already packed and ready to travel. Such efficiency on Fell's part made Lambert wonder just how many times in his life Fell had needed to make a quick exit.

The pair of them, Lambert still limping slightly, walked through the great gate as the bells of Glasscastle began to strike eleven. To Lambert's surprise and Fell's visible dismay, Jane Brailsford was waiting on the stone bench. She wore a becoming straw hat, which she was just adjusting to a better angle as they arrived.

Jane greeted them with a smile that did nothing to conceal the steely glimmer of her annoyance. "Good morning, gentlemen. I thought you might come this way. Mr. Lambert, I blush to confess I followed you from Robin's house. Forgive the impertinence. At least it was warranted impertinence."

"You followed me?" Somewhere beneath the confusion caused by his headache and the unusual formality of Jane's manner, Lambert was tolerably sure he'd been insulted. "Didn't you trust me to deliver your message?"

"I was certain you'd deliver it." Jane eyed Fell. "This was precisely the sort of response I expected."

"You'll forgive us if we don't stay to socialize, Miss Brailsford," Fell said firmly. "We have a train to catch. As you surmise, we're leaving. Now. It's a matter of some urgency."

"Fine, I'll walk with you." Jane's tones were dulcet. "I'm so glad you didn't arrive fifteen minutes sooner. I would have missed you. By the oddest coincidence, that man Mr. Lambert and I saw, the one who appears so skilled at eluding the gatekeeper's notice, departed while I was waiting here at the gate. For some reason, he seemed in a tearing hurry. I suppose you have no idea why?"

"You saw him?" Lambert turned to her. "Did you see which way he went?"

"Oh, yes. The authorities took him away for questioning. I thought of going along, but I didn't want to risk missing you, Mr. Fell."

"By Jove," said Fell. "They caught him?"

"What sort of authorities?" Lambert demanded. "What kind of questioning?"

"Strictly speaking, I caught him. Nicked him, that is." Jane's self-satisfaction fairly shone out of her. "I believe they've taken him to the police station. The nick, they called it. Strange, the way one word can mean many things, some contradictory. It must make being a criminal so confusing."

"How did you catch him?" Lambert asked.

Jane inspected the gloves she wore and clucked disapprovingly over the stain that marred one. "Fortunately, he did not have a mind above money. I feared he might."

Lambert met Fell's eyes. "Do you get the feeling she's enjoying herself?"

"Oh, yes." Fell sighed. "Still, she's earned it. Very well, Miss Brailsford. We surrender. Victory is yours. Your audience is rapt. Take pity on us and tell us exactly what happened."

"Are we going to walk all the way to the train station?" Jane asked. "I only ask because Mr. Lambert is limping. The police station is even farther than the railway station. Wouldn't you rather stop at Robin's house and have it all out in comfort first?"

"I am not limping," said Lambert.

"Lead on, young Amazon," Fell replied. "We follow."

When they were settled in the Brailsford parlor, gloves off and the obligatory cups of tea in hand, Jane relented. "Such attentive listeners. You're very good to humor me this way. I'll drive you to the police station as soon as we're finished. Or perhaps you'd prefer to stay to lunch? I think it's chicken divan and duchess potatoes. I'll drive you there after lunch, if you prefer."

Lambert felt cheered by the mere thought of lunch. Although his headache had been banished by the cup of tea, his bruises were still coming out like stars. Lambert remembered he'd been in a hurry all morning and last night's dinner had been very long ago.

Fell didn't yield an inch. "I see no need to delay matters for a meal. Please tell us what happened."

"Very well. I took the precaution of following Mr. Lambert back to the university since I thought you might be reluctant to accept my invitation." Jane eyed Fell over the rim of her teacup. "As I told you, I hadn't been waiting long when I recognized the man rushing through the gate as the mysterious caller from the day before yesterday. The gatekeeper paid him no attention, even though he was bareheaded. Enough to make anyone stare, a grown man out without a hat."

"He left it in my study," said Fell. "Go on."

"Did he? I'd like a chance to inspect it, if you have no objection. I've found that headgear can be unexpectedly informative at times." For a moment, Jane seemed lost in pleasant memories. When Fell cleared his throat, she continued. "I'm not at my best here, so near the barriers of Glasscastle, but I was able to put my training to good use. He broke stride and I was able to catch him. Once I had him down, the gatekeeper summoned two constables. The local police are reluctant to have anything to do with matters within Glasscastle, I gather, but I was able to persuade them to make an arrest."

"Glasscastle has its own methods of dealing with miscreants within its walls," said Fell. "Vice Chancellor Voysey and the other Provosts have jurisdiction there, not the constabulary."

"The police seem delighted to leave anything within the gates of Glasscastle to the Provosts." Jane looked thoughtful. "When I informed them of the circumstances of the man's previous visit to the archive, they agreed to take him into custody. They promised me they would summon the appropriate officials from Glasscastle to deal with the matter immediately. I hope they don't deal with it so promptly that we miss our chance to help."

"You still haven't told us how you caught him," Lambert pointed out.

Jane's eyes glowed at the recollection. "I made a small illusion, a trifle really, but luckily, an effective one."

"You used an illusion on our very doorstep?" Fell was taken aback. "Was that wise?"

"Perhaps not. But once I had the man down, I was able to locate another illusion." Jane produced a small object, well wrapped in a man's handkerchief. "He had this in his pocket."

Fell took the object, handkerchief and all, and inspected it. To Lambert it looked like a cylinder of dark wood, the same diameter but only half as long as one of Fell's cheroots, intricately carved. "Intriguing," said Fell. He began to put it in his pocket.

Jane held out her hand and Fell surrendered the object with reluctance. "Isn't it?" Jane admired the carving a moment longer, then folded the handkerchief back over it and put it away in her embroidered drawstring bag. "Until I removed it, the gatekeeper seemed unable to see what all the fuss was about. That is, it was plain that I was behaving appallingly. But once he saw the man I was sitting on, he became much more helpful."

"That's gratifying," said Fell. "Though I'm not sure helpfulness should always be the first duty of a gatekeeper."

"Wait," said Lambert, "you mean the gatekeeper didn't know why you'd stopped the man?"

"No, I mean he didn't know that I *had* stopped the man. He didn't see him until I removed this interesting object from his pocket. Very rude the chap was about losing it too, quite profane." Jane patted the bag in her lap. "I look forward to studying it in more detail."

Lambert frowned. "What *is* it?"

Jane dropped her voice to its softest, lowest register. "It's magic, my dear Lambert. I don't know where it comes from, or precisely what it's for, but I think it's designed to permit an outsider to come and go without anyone from Glasscastle the wiser. A cloak of invisibility, if you like."

"What for?" Lambert scowled impartially at Jane and Fell. "Why would someone who had power like that waste it on a doodad to let him walk on the grass?"

"Oh, I don't think our visitor made it himself." Jane turned to Fell. "Only someone from Glasscastle could circumvent the barriers so neatly. Who would wish to do such a thing?"

"Why?" Lambert persisted. "Why would they do it?" It was his turn to round on Fell. "Just to get you away?"

"Perhaps." Fell was pensive. "The intruder gave me the strongest impression that he wanted me to accompany him somewhere. Yet the possibilities for mischief inherent in something like this are boundless. Odd, to use it just for my benefit."

"Why would they use it on you?" Lambert asked.

"He's the warden of the west," said Jane.

"Not at the moment, I promise you." Fell applied himself to his cup of tea. "The intruder was careless coming up the steps. I am all too familiar with the sound of someone coming to see me, as the staircase squeaks deplorably. At first I couldn't see him. That interested me."

"It worked on you too?" Jane asked.

"At first. I was looking directly at the doorway and although I distinctly heard his approach, I could not see him until he was within a few feet of me. Most unsettling it was too. One moment he was absolutely invisible. The next, he was absolutely visible, and reaching out to me."

"Reaching out?" Jane looked intrigued. "To touch you? Did he have anything in his hand?"

"No, nothing at first," Fell replied. "He seemed intent on getting me into some sort of wrestling hold. I asked him what the devil he meant by it. He seemed very surprised that I could see him. When he understood that I meant to resist, he threatened me with a gun."

Jane looked appalled. "It's dangerous to threaten a warden."

"Very likely," snapped Fell. "I, however, am not a warden, so I had to resort to physical resistance. Fortunate you turned up when you did, Lambert."

"You and I could see him all along, because neither of us are Fellows of Glasscastle," Lambert told Jane.

Jane looked nettled. "Thank you. I had grasped that much."

"It only worked for him," Lambert continued, thinking aloud. "It doesn't make anyone else invisible."

"Do we know that?" Again Jane removed the bundle from her bag. "I didn't have time to try it myself." With deliberation, she unwrapped the cylinder, and held it in her bare hand as she looked at Fell. "Anything?"

"I see you perfectly," Fell informed her. "But then, I saw the intruder once he came close to me."

"Drat." Jane handed the cylinder to Lambert, who turned it over thoughtfully. "I wish Robin were here. He might be able to tell us more about the thing."

"There is one quick way to find out whether it works or not." Lambert inspected the carving closely. A pattern of ivy leaves spiraled around the cylinder. He liked the feel of the carving and the cool weight of it in his hand. "I could try walking on the grass again."

"That's a bit drastic, surely," said Fell.

"We'll test it some other way," said Jane. "But do we want to try it immediately or should we question our intruder first? I'm sure the authorities will let us help them in their investigation if you ask them nicely, Mr. Fell."

"I'm not interested in helping them in their investigation," Fell said. "I have my own work to do."

"Don't you want to know who is responsible for breaking into your study twice?" Jane held out her hand for the cylinder and Lambert turned it over to her. "Insolence, I call that. Sheer insolence."

"You'll have to give the authorities some kind of statement," Lambert said. "Trespassing is one thing. Attempted abduction, that's serious."

"You too, Lambert?" Fell looked peeved. "Very well. I'll go with you. But this is all futile, a mere distraction from my work."

"Fine. Intruder first, then when we're finished at the police station, you and I will go back to Glasscastle to perform a few tests on this thing, Lambert." Jane put the cylinder away again, rose, and shook out her skirts with brisk decision. "I'll drive."

Advance the spark, Jane told herself, as Lambert cranked the engine into a coughing roar. *Retard the petrol lever. Just take it easy.* It would be too embarrassing to flood the motor with Fell and Lambert right there as witnesses to her mechanical lapse. Two cups of hot sweet tea had banished the worst of her headache, but remnants were still there to remind her not to overdo things.

Lambert clambered into the passenger seat and Jane checked to make sure Fell was comfortably ensconced in the backseat before she pulled out. There was something peculiar about Fell's devotion to his studies. The aggravating man didn't even seem curious about the intruder's motives. Fell had been annoyed at the interruption, no more. Annoyed to be caught on his furtive way out of Glasscastle too, Jane thought.

"Mind the rain barrel," said Fell.

Jane negotiated the domestic obstacles between Robert's carriage house and the street and set forth across town to the police station. Where had Fell been headed with luggage in hand? Somewhere he could pursue his studies in peace, no doubt. Jane fought the urge to grind her teeth in frustration with him. It would only encourage her headache to return.

Perhaps she should have let Fell go through the gate unchallenged, let him take Lambert and go on his merry way. She could have followed them. Lambert was sharp-eyed, no question, but Jane knew ways to make herself utterly unobtrusive, even in London.

Jane winced at the thought. She had left what she devoutly hoped was a sufficiently diplomatic note to warn Amy that there might be two guests for lunch, or she might not be back for lunch at all, and she couldn't honestly guess which was more likely. Consigning this message to the maid with all the trepidation such misbehavior warranted, Jane had led the way to the Minotaur without daring a look back.

Fell leaned forward to speak sharply in Jane's ear. "There's a pony cart. You do see that pony cart?"

With what sounded like studied casualness, Lambert added, "Plenty of traffic out today."

Jane corrected her course to allow for the sudden indecision of a nanny pushing a perambulator. "Don't worry." It would have been nice, Jane reflected as she ran the gauntlet of blind, deaf, and generally heedless bicyclists all along Haycock Street, to have had a good look at the bowler hat the intruder had worn. There was no time for such luxuries before they reached the police station. But it would have been amusing and instructive. Jane promised herself the treat later, as soon as she'd had a chance to talk Lambert into bringing her the hat. They could test the invisibility cantrip at the gate and find out if it worked for anyone. Jane was almost positive that it was a cantrip that would only work for one person, but it would be worth the effort to find out for certain.

If the cantrip was designed to work only for the intruder, what would it take to convert the spell to something that would work for Jane? Very handy it would be, Jane thought, to have the power to come and go freely at Glasscastle. Worth quite a bit of trouble.

What if the same style of cantrip worked to circumvent the wards set to prevent intruders at Greenlaw? Unlikely, but a possibility. If Glasscastle could be clandestinely invaded, nowhere was truly safe.

Jane turned down the street that held Glasscastle's police station. It was easy to find a spot for the Minotaur, as the road was nearly deserted, barren but for a few horse droppings. She had seldom seen a more dismal urban prospect. The police station was liver-colored brick, lavishly gabled on both ends and in the middle. The mere look of the place gave new life to her headache. While Lambert and Fell clambered out of the motor car, Jane took a moment to collect herself. The sooner she found out what the intruder had wanted with Fell, the sooner she could leave this beastly place. Jane squared her shoulders. There was plenty of interesting work to be done. First things first. She would start with a spot of interrogation.

7

"O if thou have hid them in some flowery cave,
Tell me but where"

To Lambert, the Glasscastle police station seemed surprisingly modern. The architecture was centuries newer than Glasscastle University itself, and aspired to a hygienic, if utilitarian, philosophy of design. Ceilings were plain white and of uniform height. Though clean, the floors were oddly slippery underfoot. Fresh paint was lavished everywhere, but it was all in shades of muted brown, drab yellow, and pea-soup green. Despite its evident newness, the place somehow managed to smell old, a compound of boiled cabbage and institutional soap.

Porteous was there ahead of them. "Ah, Fell. The Provosts are meeting with Voysey, something about a memorandum from Lord Fyvie. They have delegated me to come see about this. I've asked that the chap be charged with trespassing. It's a start, at least."

Lambert glanced at Fell, prepared for the list of charges against the intruder to grow much longer. Fell said nothing. Lambert was surprised by his silence but not by the look of mulish resolve on Fell's face.

"May we speak with the man?" Jane sounded crisp and businesslike.

"Why?" Porteous countered. "Thoroughly bad hat, it seems to me. Remarkable work, capturing him—I'm not clear on how you managed it." He gazed fixedly at Jane, who stared back impassively.

"We would like to question the man if possible," said Fell. "If you can't grant our request, please tell me whose authority will suffice. I'm sure Voysey will lodge the petition for me if you force me to disturb him."

"No need to go over my head." Porteous's wide eyes bulged with indignation. "Are you sure all you want to do is question him? He's *been* questioned. Bloke won't say a word. Not a syllable. In fact, they're not even sure he *can* speak."

"He can swear. I'll vouch for that." Jane's half smile softened her voice as well as her expression.

"Oh, he can speak." Fell looked grim. "Please arrange it."

Fell had to ask several more people several more times, but eventually they were shown into a room almost filled by the table in the center and the chairs surrounding it. The man in the bowler hat, now handcuffed and bareheaded, sat at the table looking placid. Porteous and police officials sat in some of the chairs. A solicitor sat in another. Lambert, Fell, and Jane took the chairs that were left. After the scraping of chair legs on the tile floor subsided, the room was oddly quiet, given the number of people it held. The room was close and warm, and as the one small window high up on the wall was shaded, it was dimly lit as well.

Lambert found himself listening for any sound at all. From beyond their room, muffled by the closed door, he could hear heavy footsteps, a distant bell ringing, and the sound of someone laughing not far off. Lambert wondered what anyone had to laugh about in a place like this. The few noises dwindled and diminished, then trailed off into silence. Belatedly, Lambert noticed that almost everyone in the room had fallen asleep.

Fell was sitting completely still, but the intense interest in his expression assured Lambert that he was entirely alert. Jane was serene, gazing with tranquil kindness at the captive. Everyone else at the table, including Porteous, whose mouth was slightly open, was asleep sitting up. The man without a bowler hat snored very gently where he sat.

Fell caught Lambert's eye and raised a finger to his lips to hush him. To Lambert's surprise, it was Jane who spoke, her voice scarcely a whisper. Lambert could not make out the words at first. They didn't sound like any kind of English Lambert had ever heard. But as the warmth and silence in the room increased, Jane slowed, and Lambert began to understand what she was saying.

"Tell us who sent you. Tell us who you are. Tell us who gave you the cantrip I took from you. Tell us where you were to take Fell. Tell us everything you can, sir, tell us all and all."

The words whispered like silk in the wind, until Lambert's vision began to blur. He thought he would close his eyes a moment, just to ease them while he listened to Jane's murmur. A hand clamped his wrist. With a start Lambert sat up in his chair. Fell shook Lambert's arm gently, just enough to be sure he was roused from the drowsiness of Jane's soft litany.

Lambert stared at Jane. Though the words came softly and evenly, her breathing was labored and her face was flushed. It was as if she'd been running for miles when all the while she'd been sitting there serenely. Her temples were damp and as Lambert watched, a tiny rivulet of sweat trickled from her hairline. At last, with visible effort, she produced a pencil and small notebook from her reticule. Still whispering, she tore a leaf from the notebook, put it down before the captive, and folded the man's limp fingers around the pencil. She kept her hand over his, as if too fond of him to let him go.

The rhythm of Jane's whisper changed. It was back to the unfamiliar language, whatever it was. As her effort intensified, her voice dropped until there was hardly any sound, only the movement of her lips.

With a convulsive shudder, the captive's hand moved, jerking the point of the pencil against the ragged sheet of paper. The paper slid a little too, and without a thought, Lambert put out his hand to hold the paper still. Another twitch, and the pencil moved across the page. One word: "Ludlow." Then the pencil dropped from limp fingers and rolled a few inches across the tabletop.

Jane fell silent as she released the man. Her hands went to her temples and pressed there, as if by pressing she might keep her head from flying into pieces. Fell seized the pencil and paper and tucked them away.

Lambert sat back, marveling as the small sounds from outside gradually returned and the warmth in the room diminished little by little. For another moment or two, the quiet in the room held. Then the sleepers stirred and woke, seemingly unaware that any time had passed, still less that anything untoward had occurred.

For form's sake, Fell asked the captive who he was and who he worked for, a simulation of the questioning that Jane had conducted by stealth. The man kept up his silence. By no change of expression, however slight, did he betray that he even heard the questions.

"This is a ridiculous waste of time," Porteous announced at last. "The man's incorrigible."

"The only charge against him is trespassing," said the man's solicitor. "Unless you wish to accuse him of something more substantial, I think our course of action is perfectly routine."

When Fell said nothing, Porteous gestured to the policemen flanking the intruder. "Take him away. I'll finish the paperwork. We'll let the judge decide what's to be done with him after that."

Fell led the way out of the police station, Jane at his heels. Lambert followed. On the steps outside, Jane swayed for a moment and looked around as if bewildered. The color in her face was gone, replaced by a chalky pallor.

Lambert moved fast, tucked his hand under her elbow, and took her weight as she leaned heavily against him. "I've got you," Lambert murmured. "Take it easy."

At the foot of the steps, Fell noticed he was alone, looked back, and asked, "Admiring the view?"

"Just hold on a minute," Lambert called. "Some kind of dizzy spell, I think. She needs to take it easy for a minute."

"I'm fine." Jane didn't sound sure about it. She leaned on Lambert as if she needed to gather all her strength before she made the effort of going down the stairs.

"Headache?" Fell guessed. "I'm not surprised."

"Do you need a doctor?" Lambert demanded. He didn't like the way Jane's gaze seemed to wander.

"No, it's nothing." Jane covered her eyes with her hand. "I just overdid things a bit. It happens sometimes."

"You're not driving," Lambert stated. To Fell, he called, "Flag down a cab, will you?"

"What about Robin's motor car?" Jane asked. She descended the steps without mishap, but her lack of protest told Lambert all he needed to know about her state.

"If the police can't look out for one motor car, what good are they?" Lambert asked. "It will be safe here until you're ready to collect it."

Fell summoned a hansom cab and the three of them bundled themselves in for the ride back to the Brailsford house. When they arrived, Amy Brailsford was at the door to greet them.

"Jane, what's happened? You look like a ghost."

"I'm fine. Truly." Some of her color was back, but Jane still spoke as if it were an effort to get out more than a few words at a time.

Amy's alarm was clear. "You're not. Mr. Lambert, Mr. Fell, I do thank you for seeing Jane home. Jane, I insist you go to your room. You must lie down while I send for the doctor."

"No. I don't need a doctor." Jane held her sister-in-law off. "I'm fine. Truly. I just need a moment. I don't need to lie down. Really."

"Don't listen to her," Lambert told Amy. "She needs to rest."

Jane shook off their support. "Nonsense. I need to talk to Mr. Fell and Mr. Lambert."

Amy relented. "Are you certain you're all right?"

"I'm fine." This time Jane sounded quite sure about that. She gestured toward Lambert and Fell. "Whatever happens, don't let those two out of your sight. They were doing a bunk when I caught them at the great gate. Let them go now and we may never find out what's afoot."

Judging from the sudden gleam in her eyes, that struck a chord with Amy. "If you don't wish to go to your room, you needn't." Amy swept them all before her into the parlor and rang for the maid. "We will all have a nice cup of tea and then you may question anyone you please, Jane."

Lambert began to feel as if he'd been sentenced to drink tea in the Brailsford parlor for all eternity. The sunlight on the Oriental rug, the aspidistra in its brass pot, and the daintily appointed tea table were all too hideously familiar. What he'd give for some bread and cheese and a couple of pints of bitter. Glumly, he took the place Amy assigned him and composed himself to wait for the ritual to begin again.

"Unless you haven't eaten?" Amy interrupted her orders to the maid to ask. A single comprehensive glance at the three of them gave her the answer. "Good gracious, why didn't you say something? Lunch you require and lunch you shall have. Wait here while I have a word with Cook. I'll be back in a moment."

"Amy's feeling better." Jane took off her hat and subsided into the corner of the settee where her sister-in-law had left her. "That's something."

"What about you?" Lambert asked.

"Oh, I'm fine." To Lambert, Jane still seemed too pale, but her dour expression made it clear she intended to ignore her discomfort.

"Of course you are," said Lambert, with the gentle air of one humoring the insane.

Fell gave Jane a look combining reproach and severity. "That was quite an exhibition, young woman. Do you make a habit of such conduct?"

"You mean the way she mesmerized everyone but us?" Lambert asked.

"Us?" Jane's smile was wobbly but genuine. "I like that. If it hadn't been for Mr. Fell waking you, you'd have slept through it yourself."

"It was a reckless expenditure of power," said Fell. "If you'd faltered a few minutes earlier, there would have been some awkward questions to answer."

"He held out longer than I thought he would. It would have been easier to question the man in privacy, before the authorities arrested him," Jane admitted. "This was the best I could manage under the circumstances. At least we have something to show for our pains."

"Your pains," Lambert reminded her.

"This won't last long," Jane assured him. "The hardest part was keeping all those other parties asleep without letting them know I'd done it."

"I'm not surprised that turnip Porteous went under so easily," said Fell, "but I would have expected a bit more vigilance from the constabulary. Don't try anything of that sort again. They are certain to notice your work eventually."

"If any awkward questions are asked, I'll be happy to explain my misdeeds." In a more acid tone, Jane added, "Should it ever occur to them I could possibly be the one responsible."

The Brailsford dining room was not quite as familiar to Lambert as the parlor, but he'd been there several times, though never for such a simple meal. The table setting was as fancy as ever. Only the menu betrayed the suddenness of the invitation. They began with a clear soup served in very small portions so there was just enough to go around. The next course was an omelette stuffed with mushrooms and chicken—exactly enough chicken for two if it had been presented in chicken divan. After that came sandwiches, surprisingly simple ones, in great abundance. Something about eating sandwiches melted their reserve.

"Perhaps you'd like to tell me what you've been doing with yourselves." Amy's tone made it more a command than a request. "Jane?"

Jane gave Amy a full account of the capture and interrogation of the intruder. Fell and Lambert earned Amy's displeasure when she understood their plan to leave without telling anyone. She relented only when Jane explained how scrupulously kind they had been about seeing her home.

"I should hope they saw you back here safely." Amy turned her disapproving gaze on Jane. "Although I think using your magic on that man was perfectly disgraceful. I wouldn't be surprised if it counts as some sort of miscarriage of justice. He was a helpless prisoner and you rummaged through his brain in plain view of the authorities. That can't be right."

"Whatever my crime, I think I've been punished enough. I don't mind the headache—much—but this time my ears were ringing fit to deafen me." As if to prove she had made a full recovery, Jane helped herself to another cheese-and-pickle sandwich. "Horrid sensation."

"*This* time?" Fell pounced on the phrase. "So you do make a habit of it. Foolhardy of you to try something like that here in Glasscastle."

"But I wasn't inside the bounds of Glasscastle itself," Jane said. "I was a bit close to the barriers when I stopped our intruder, but that was a small spell, and the situation was an emergency. The speaking spell was far more demanding. I only dared try it because the police station is all the way across town from Glasscastle."

"It worked, that's what matters," said Lambert. "You got something out of him. *Ludlow*. Whoever—or whatever—that might be."

"The man was under a compulsion to silence, and a very powerful compulsion at that. I might have had better luck if I'd thought to try the pencil sooner. As it was, by the time I thought to try it, I was nearly done up." With a crunch of pickle, Jane disposed of another bite of her sandwich.

Amy frowned. "Ludlow. That's where Robert has gone. At least, that's where he was going. He's still not wired me that he arrived safely. He never fails to do that."

"Why did he go to Ludlow?" Jane asked. "Robin told me he had some research to do for the project. What sort of research, do you know?"

"I can't be certain." Amy looked troubled. "He wired the Earl of Bridgewater. The Earl was in London, but he invited Robert to stay at his house in Ludlow as long as he liked."

"The Earl of Bridgewater was involved with the inception of the project," said Fell. "Most of the work has been done here at Glasscastle, but Bridgewater's library in Ludlow contains some valuable resources. The Earl is generous to a fault and his hospitality can be difficult to refuse."

"Was that why Robert went to Shropshire?" Jane asked. "To visit a library?"

"It must have been a matter of some urgency," Amy said. "He canceled an appointment with the dentist in order to leave on the first train yesterday."

"Any excuse to avoid the dentist is a good one," Lambert pointed out. He winced at the very idea of voluntarily scheduling a visit to the dentist.

"Very true, Lambert. Though not all of us are forbidden to accept the laudanum if an extraction is necessary. All the same, it wasn't a trip Robert had planned to take, I gather?" Fell asked Amy. "When did he change his appointment, do you know?"

"Robert sent a message to the dentist's office just after he and Jane returned from the tour of Glasscastle." Amy turned to Jane. "Don't you remember? At the last *possible* moment, you and Robert sent word that you were going to stay to lunch in the common room rather than come home to eat here."

"I remember." Jane looked apologetic. "Sorry."

"I should think so," said Amy.

Lambert thought hard. "He said nothing about leaving Glasscastle until then? Could it have had something to do with the plans?"

Jane's eyes widened. "Plans? What plans?"

"Plans for the device—the delivery system for the Agincourt Project. I found them in your study," Lambert told Fell. To Jane, he said, "I gave the plans to your brother. Whatever the Agincourt device is, it looks like it's going to be small but awkward."

Jane's eyes narrowed, but she said nothing.

"I never had plans for anything associated with the project in my possession." Fell helped himself to the last of the cheese-and-pickle sandwiches. "I haven't been granted clearance to see any of the designs. Not that I wanted access to any of it. I have enough to do with my own work."

"Brailsford seemed surprised," said Lambert. "I'm sure it was something he recognized."

Jane and Amy exchanged a look of mutual inquiry, then Jane said, "He didn't mention anything about it to either of us."

"He might have mentioned it to Voysey," said Lambert. "I'll ask him."

"Yes, do that," said Fell, in a tone that suggested he meant just the opposite.

The maid announced the arrival of a visitor. "Mr. Adam Voysey, ma'am. He's brought the motor car back."

The four of them exchanged startled looks. "We'll move to the parlor," Amy told the maid. "Please show Mr. Voysey there."

When Voysey joined them in the parlor, Jane was the first to speak. "How kind of you to fetch Robin's motor car for us. I assumed I would have to go back for it."

Voysey looked mildly discomfited. "It was forward of me, I admit. The police helped me with the crank and the ignition switch. As soon as I was out of my meeting, I took Porteous's advice and visited the police station. What an extremely taciturn man that is. Shocking, the thought of an outsider making free with Glasscastle's archive. We may have to change the whole arrangement of spells on the most vital buildings. When I recognized Brailsford's motor car, I hoped he too had been summoned and was there before me. I was disappointed to find that he was not, though Porteous seems to have managed things very capably. In fact, the primary reason I returned the Minotaur is to see Brailsford. One or two questions have arisen as a result of the arrest. I hope he can shed some light on the matter."

"Robert isn't here," said Amy. "He left for Ludlow yesterday morning."

"Ludlow?" Voysey's surprise was plain. "Why, if I may ask?"

"He had some research to do, I believe," said Amy. "Is there some reason he shouldn't have gone?"

"Heavens, no." Voysey hastened to reassure Amy. "Will you let Brailsford know as soon as he returns that I have a matter of some importance to discuss with him? I'd hoped to clear it up before now, but Lord Fyvie has been monopolizing my time. Things are settled for the moment, but I find myself wishing for Brailsford's advice."

"I will tell him." Amy looked troubled. "I don't know when he plans to return. I haven't received any word from him since he left."

"That doesn't sound much like the Brailsford I know," said Voysey. "He's scrupulous about that sort of thing. I suppose there might be some difficulty with the trains?" He didn't seem convinced of the likelihood of that explanation. "Or with the telegraph, possibly?"

"Your wire from London went astray," Lambert reminded Jane.

"It was only delayed. But you're right. There's sure to be a good reason for the wait," Jane told Amy bracingly. To Voysey, she said, "Does the matter you need to discuss with Robin have anything to do with the arrest of that stubborn man?"

"I can't answer that, I'm afraid." Voysey looked genuinely regretful. "Anything you know about him would be extremely helpful to us."

Lambert started to speak, but Fell caught his eye and frowned slightly. Lambert stopped himself and turned his words into a throat-clearing cough. If Fell didn't want to help Voysey, there was probably a good reason.

Voysey turned his attention to Fell. "I don't suppose I could persuade you to rejoin the project? Given this new and potentially alarming development, that is?" His expression was frank, sincere, and with very little effort, might have been pleading.

"My time is spoken for, I'm afraid." Fell didn't seem a bit apologetic about it. He was crisply polite, but it was all too plain that Fell's courtesy was only a thin veneer over his dislike of Voysey. "My research has been subject to constant interruptions. Time I gave it the concentration it deserves for a change." He seemed to be addressing Jane at least as much as he was Voysey.

"I understand. We all have duties we must carry out," Voysey agreed smoothly. "Still, a matter of imperial security takes a high priority, don't you agree?"

"You know perfectly well that if I agreed that the security of the empire was the greatest of all possible public goods," said Fell, "I would still be involved in the project."

Voysey sat up straighter. "That's clear enough, even for me." He stood. "I'll take my leave, then. Mrs. Brailsford, thank you for your hospitality." He kissed Amy's hand as she rose to accompany him to the door. "Dame Brailsford, gentlemen, I bid you good day."

"What would be so wrong," Lambert muttered to Fell, once Voysey had departed, "about asking the most important man in Glasscastle for his help?"

"I don't like him. The man never stops recruiting," Fell replied as Amy rejoined them. "There's a fine line between persistence and pestering."

"If you weren't so obstinate," said Jane, "you wouldn't be as well acquainted with precisely how fine the line is."

Fell regarded her with disfavor. "It doesn't surprise me that you'd be on the side of pestering."

"I didn't say that," Jane said.

"Can't you stop sniping at each other?" Amy exclaimed. She put her hand over her mouth, looking horrified at her own outburst. "Oh, dear. I didn't mean to say that."

"Of course we can stop," said Jane cheerfully. "In fact, we will. Immediately."

"I wish Robert were here," Amy said. "He would know what to do."

"Come to that, we know what to do." Fell rose. "It's time Mr. Lambert and I followed Mr. Voysey's excellent example." He forestalled Jane's protest with a lifted hand. "You needn't fear that either of us will do, as you so colorfully put it, a bunk. Send to Glasscastle if you need us. I'll be in my study. *Studying.*"

Without further ado, Fell led Lambert away and they left the Brailsford house to walk to Glasscastle. Lambert was happy to leave behind whatever domestic storm was about to break there. Fell seemed in no hurry. He merely strolled along, preoccupied by his thoughts.

As he shortened his strides to match Fell's, Lambert asked, "Are you really going back to your research?"

"Eventually." Fell looked sour. "First I will need to find someone with a broom. There is a great deal of cleaning and tidying to be done before I'll be able to go back to work."

"What happened to getting lost in the big city?"

"I've changed my mind. The sooner I finish my work, the sooner I can put a stop to whatever nonsense is going on here."

After she checked over the Minotaur to make certain Voysey had returned it in good order, Jane went up to her room in hope that a quiet moment of reflection would banish the last of her headache. Nothing she had done was difficult under normal circumstances. Unfortunately, working her magic with the magic of Glasscastle so near made Jane feel as if she were walking into a high wind at all times. She felt weary just from the effort involved in compensating for that energy, let alone from the spells she'd performed, as though her hair had been disheveled, blown loose and into her face, blinding her, ever since she'd begun. Her eyes burned and her skin felt peppered, as if she'd been walking into wind-blown sand. Her neck ached and from time to time her ears seemed to stuff up, then clear themselves with a faint, unpleasant popping sensation.

Jane had tried all her usual remedies. She'd had a nice cup of tea. She'd eaten a sustaining lunch. Thanks to these tactics, the worst of her symptoms had diminished. Yet the small discomforts remained, reminders of her unaccustomed weakness.

In her room, Jane checked on the Royal Worcester plate. Soaking overnight and most of the next day had done it a world of good. The ink had dissolved into the water, not uniformly, but in a random spiral threading black through the water in which it was suspended. Jane admired the strange beauty of it for a moment, then dispersed the whorls and tendrils of ink into chaos as she removed the plate from the basin and dried it. "Might need you again," she murmured to it, as she put the plate away with care. *I'm glad Lambert forgot about testing the invisibility cantrip*, she thought. *Makes my head hurt just thinking about it. We can run a few tests first thing in the morning. If it doesn't work for just anyone, I'll have the rest of the day to see if I can make it work for me.*

Lambert had been most considerate, steadying her as they departed from the police station. In almost anyone else, the act of taking charge, bringing her home as if she were a parcel to be delivered, would have been infuriating. Jane marveled that Lambert's behavior did not infuriate her at all. Quite the contrary. Amy was right. He was a bit of a lamb.

Jane took off her shoes and unpinned her hair. Although her hair was not really wind-tangled, it still felt good to brush it out. Then, despite the fact it was merely afternoon, and no one lay on a bed in midafternoon unless one were sick unto death or disgustingly slothful, lazy to the point of vice, Jane took a nap. She had a dream.

Jane dreamed she was having tea in Number Five Study, back at Greenlaw College. Faris Nallaneen, looking precisely as rawboned and gawky as she ever had in the school days before she'd become warden of the north, was across the table. Under the black poplin of her academic gown, the frayed cuffs of Faris's made-over dress showed plainly. One of the cuff buttons was dangling from a thread.

"You're going to lose that button," Jane observed.

Faris glanced at the button and frowned. "Things don't stay mended, have you noticed?"

"Did you sew it on yourself?" Jane asked.

"Several times. There are constant interruptions." Faris pulled the button off and put it in her pocket. "You have something very important to say."

"I do?" Jane knew she did. It was urgent as well as important but her mind was a blank and she could not recall what it was she ought to say. "I do, don't I?"

"Tell him to get to work. But first, he must see to the clocks." There was a thunderous knocking at the door to Number Five Study. Faris looked annoyed. "Never a dull moment." Faris reached in her pocket. "Damn, I've lost that button again."

With that, Jane awoke. So vivid was the sense that someone had been knocking at her bedroom door, she went to answer it. When she opened the door, no one was there. The spacious hallway was empty, the house silent.

Jane hesitated, then walked downstairs in stockinged feet, hair loose over her shoulders, to open the front door. Mindful of her unconventional appearance, she peeped timidly out into the street. No one was there. The sense of peace within the house was profound. In the world outside, late afternoon had drowsed itself into the hush of early evening. Not a carriage in the street, not a breeze to stir the leaves, nothing moved. There was only birdsong and the measured tolling of a distant bell.

Jane locked the door and went back upstairs to put on her shoes, aware that her headache had vanished. She was surprised that the nap, a few hours according to the delicate carriage clock on her dressing table, seemed to have done her more good than a whole night's sleep. The rest had restored her sense of well-being and of purpose. With deft fingers she combed out her hair and pinned it up afresh. There was no time for laziness. She would have to beard Fell in his lair. She had to nag him on Faris's behalf anyway.

Jane permitted herself a small smile of anticipation as she selected just the right hat for her next foray to the great gate of Glasscastle. Lambert seemed to appreciate a good hat. It was wide brimmed, of pale Parisian straw, with a filmy veil that tied under her chin. After all, one never knew when a veil might be useful. She pulled on her favorite pair of afternoon gloves and saw with a stab of annoyance that one of the buttons was missing.

For a moment, Jane frowned. The dream had dwindled away but she knew the missing button reminded her of something. She knew there was something of grave importance she had to tell someone—Faris? She could not remember why she thought so, or what that message could possibly be. She only knew that Faris needed Fell's help.

Jane found a fresh pair of gloves and put them on. It was time to go find Fell and see how he had spent his afternoon. There might even be something she could do to aid him in his efforts. Inspect his intruder's bowler hat, for instance.

8

"If those you seek
It were a journey like the path to Heav'n,
To help you find them."

Lambert returned with Fell to the rooms they shared. For once, there was no chance to hear the soft persistent ticking of the clock. Fell was a one-man flurry of activity as he came into the sitting room, dropped his valise in the middle of the floor, and went to the card tray and its small stack of accumulated mail.

"Message for you, Lambert." Before Lambert had time to cross the room, Fell had already ripped open an envelope of his own. "Ha. Ridiculous. When did people forget how to take no for an answer?" Fell put the letter in his pocket without even bothering to fold it again. The heavy paper crumpled audibly as he crushed it. "I'm off back to the archive. There's work to be done. Don't interrupt me before it is time for dinner."

Lambert shook his head over Fell's single-mindedness but left the valise where it was. His own message was a summons from Voysey. Lambert was to report to Egerton House to participate in an unscheduled accuracy trial for the Agincourt Project, which amounted to target practice in the intense sunlight and shadow of late summer afternoon. Meredith wouldn't be there. Voysey felt they could manage without his help. Lambert hoped he was right.

Egerton House, a square gray Georgian structure designed around the courtyard set in its heart, was a ten-minute walk from Lambert's quarters. It was one of several buildings at Glasscastle built in and around gardens that encompassed the green lawns forbidden to any but the masters of Glasscastle. The only way through for Lambert involved a circuitous path along the maze of graveled paths. When he arrived at Egerton House, only a few minutes late, he had a brief conversation with the porter who lurked inside the doorway of the great stone edifice.

The porter knew Lambert, since the courtyard inside Egerton House had been the site of several of the early accuracy trials, but he didn't let that interfere with the careful check of Lambert's identity and authorization. Lambert tried not to let his impatience with the slow bureaucracy show. After all, it was high time to be more careful about such things, given the way the man in the bowler hat had wandered in, out, and around as if he owned the place.

"Just sign here. And here, if you please," said the porter, as he directed Lambert to the spot where he needed to add his signature. "Very good. Mr. Voysey and his guest are waiting for you."

Guest? Lambert wished he'd been told as much in the note. He hadn't bothered to change clothes for target practice and the heat of the day on top of his morning's exertions had done nothing to freshen Lambert's appearance.

Lambert became acutely conscious of all his shortcomings as he was brought into the sunny quadrangle where Voysey and his guest were already inspecting an assortment of weapons arrayed on a folding table.

Voysey's guest was a solemn man with the gleam of an enthusiast in his dark eyes. He possessed luxuriant side whiskers and wore a canary yellow waistcoat with his summer flannels.

"Timothy, allow me to present Mr. Samuel Lambert, our resident sharpshooter. Samuel, this is Mr. Timothy Wright, an expert who will be helping us today." Despite the heat, Voysey himself was even more immaculate than usual.

Lambert shook hands with Wright. It was like shaking hands with a blacksmith. Lambert suppressed the urge to double over, clutch his right hand, and whimper. He confined himself to wincing silently at the man's grip.

"We have a treat in store today," said Voysey. "Mr. Wright has kindly offered to help our research by permitting us to experiment with his Baker rifle. We'll save that for last. Meanwhile, let's just run through the routine Meredith usually gives you."

Obediently, Lambert took off his hat and jacket, put his cuff links safely away in his pocket, and rolled up his sleeves. He scanned the table. "Where do I start?"

"Begin with this." Voysey handed over a derringer of the lightest possible caliber. It was small enough to be palmed or concealed up a sleeve. "Careful."

Lambert inspected the tiny thing thoroughly. "Oh, a toy." He held it at arm's length and squinted at the sight. "What's the ammunition? Tin tacks?"

"Perhaps you've been spending too much time with Meredith. It's nothing to joke about." Voysey picked up a clipboard and ushered Wright to the observation point. "A weapon is a weapon. You can kill a man with this just as well as any of the others."

"By shooting him with it? I think I'd have better luck if I threw it at him." Lambert took his place at the mark. He was firing from bright sunlight into shade. It made hitting the three of hearts Voysey had mounted on the target a challenge, but despite the ferocious kickback of the little weapon, Lambert succeeded to Voysey's satisfaction. Wright was polite, no more, about Lambert's marksmanship. Lambert rubbed his hand and shook the sting out as unobtrusively as he could manage.

It was cool in the courtyard when Lambert stood in the shade. When he stood in the sunlight, the heat threatened to plaster his shirt to his back. Sweat trickled down his spine. The kick of the little handgun made Lambert's collection of bruises reverberate unpleasantly. He wiped his forehead with his handkerchief and wished he could take off his collar.

The rounds with the Colt Peacemaker went as smoothly as usual. The Colt had a kick of its own, but Lambert was used to it. He was pleased to note that Wright seemed mildly impressed by his accuracy.

The last weapon Lambert was assigned for the day's trial was at first glance even less efficient than the derringer. It was a muzzle loader, at least a hundred years older than Lambert himself, and he handled it gingerly, treating the antique with the respect it deserved.

"No tin tacks this time." Voysey gazed at the weapon as if it were made of gold. "All thanks to Mr. Wright, this is a Baker rifle. There was a day when arms like this ruled the world. At its foundation, our empire still rests on what such weapons won for us."

Lambert said, "It wasn't weaponry alone. It never is."

"That's true," said Mr. Wright. "It always comes down to the courage of the men who fight."

"I have nothing but respect for the men who hold the weapons. Brave men, all," Voysey said, "yet superior armament never yields to gallantry alone. We are here today on behalf of brave men to come. Mr. Wright, if you will do the honors?"

In silence, Mr. Wright demonstrated the fine art of loading a Baker rifle. His strong hands were surprisingly deft as he prepared the weapon, doling out gunpowder and placing the leaden ball with an artist's delicate care. Voysey's enthusiasm for Wright's expertise made a sharp contrast to Meredith's pragmatism. Lambert wondered if he might not have become a little spoiled by Meredith's calm efficiency. With Meredith, firearms deserved the utmost respect, but the point of the exercise was to shoot things. With Voysey and Wright, firearms seemed to hold a fascination that went past respect to border on veneration.

As Voysey and Lambert, with Wright's expert assistance, worked slowly through Voysey's checklist, the change in the angle of the sun made the shadows deeper. This time the target was a standard size, but the rings were hardly more than pencil lines, impossible to see at a distance.

Lambert took his time. He had to. Wright could reload with dexterity, but Lambert needed the recovery time to nurse his shoulder. The kick of the weapon was formidable. When he was finished, he'd put three shots into the heart of the target, after another three that ringed the center at three, six, and nine o'clock, and had collected six new bruises, each atop the last, for his trouble. After the kick of the Baker rifle, the fight in Fell's study, and his sojourn on the forbidden grass of Winterset Green, Lambert felt ready for a hot bath, a tot of brandy, and a bit of horse liniment. Lambert knew he was unlikely to get anything but the horse liniment, and it did nothing to cheer him up.

"Not bad at all," Wright conceded. Before Voysey had the target down, Wright was already cleaning his treasured antique.

Voysey was as satisfied with the result as Wright was. Lambert initialed the spot beside his name on the ammunition inventory, claiming responsibility for fifteen cartridges for the derringer, six for the Colt Peacemaker, and for the Baker rifle, what the inventory described as *six projectiles*. The projectiles looked like lead musket balls but might, given the unpredictable enthusiasms of the Agincourt research committee, have been anything from solid silver to the magical bullet from *Der Freischütz*.

The whole exercise took hours. By the time he had gone back to his quarters, washed, and changed for dinner, Lambert had just enough time left before the evening meal to look in at the Winterset Archive. Fell might know where Lambert could get some horse liniment for his shoulder. Lambert was also curious about what sort of progress his friend had made bringing order out of the chaos in his study.

"Fell, are you there?" Lambert pushed the half-open door wide.

No answer. Lambert regarded the deserted study with disbelief. Every object in the room gave mute testimony to the work that had been interrupted. Books were on the floor, some open, spines straining and pages bent. Papers, more than Lambert remembered, were scattered everywhere. Broken glass had been swept into a heap, but the heap had been scattered as if by a careless misstep. The armillary spheres had been tipped over in one corner, worlds within worlds jostled recklessly together.

Fell was gone.

The study windows were open to the warm twilight, but no breeze stirred the heavy fabric of the institutional brown curtains. Not a floorboard squeaked. Lambert could hear nothing but random birds chirping and the distant sound of bells as they struck the quarter. The room might have been deserted for five minutes or five hours. There was no way to tell.

For an hour and twenty minutes, Lambert searched the desk, the floor, and the bookshelves. He scanned every bit of paper he could find, looked for any juxtaposition of objects that might convey a message, and found nothing. The bowler hat was gone. Fell was gone. Lambert could find no other clue. At last he sat at the desk and rested his chin on his clenched fist.

If Lambert had come sooner, there might have been a chance of interrupting the intruder, if there had been another intruder. If Lambert had thought faster, there might have been a point in alerting the gatekeepers, or notifying the authorities of Glasscastle immediately.

But had there been an intruder? Could Fell have left of his own volition?

Lambert knew that Fell hadn't been back to the rooms they shared. Or if he had, he'd disturbed nothing. If Fell had been called away, it would have been the work of a moment, if he wished, to leave some kind of message. But what could have called Fell away? Who would have? What reason could Fell have for leaving without a word, if he had left willingly?

Did the man in the bowler hat have a partner? Had Jane's friend, the warden of the north, resorted to more direct methods of persuasion? Could Jane herself have played some role in Fell's disappearance?

Lambert caught himself. That line of thought was ridiculous. Jane was honest, if anyone was. She had her reasons for pestering Fell, but she was on the square about them. In fact, her keen interest in Fell probably made her Lambert's best ally in the search.

Lambert found the idea of a second intruder a more likely scenario. If one man could be provided with a cantrip to equip him to come and go through the gates of Glasscastle, why not another? Fell might have left of his own free will. Lambert chose to think otherwise.

When at last Lambert yielded to the urge to swear, it took him several minutes to cover the full situation. He swore because it was human nature, because he wanted to, because he could, and most of all because it was time yet again to visit the Brailsford house. Four times in a single day was well over his limit. His only consolation was that it was far too late for anyone to offer him a cup of tea.

The sun was long since down and the late summer twilight was deepening to evening. The intense shadows of afternoon had run together and mellowed into a general chiaroscuro as the light faded. The day was at that point between twilight and evening when all but the most vivid colors yield to shades of gray. The spires of Glasscastle, each tipped with its finial as a flame tips a candle, took on a sharp edge, black against the deep blue of the sky, proud and graceful as wildflower spikes of agrimony. Bells and birdsong provided counterpoint as the world grew quiet. Through the beauty of the twilight, Lambert walked muttering under his breath, his language as blue as the sky.

As Jane approached the great gate, she removed one glove, put her hand inside the drawstring Dorothy bag she carried, and drew out the intruder's cantrip, handkerchief and all. She put the handkerchief back and held the wooden cylinder in her bare hand. It would be a good test of the cantrip to see if it worked for her as well as it had for the intruder. Jane stepped softly. It wouldn't do to have an unwary footfall betray her presence.

As Jane drew near the gatekeeper, he looked up and smiled. "Nice to see you again, miss. Just wait at the visitors' bench until your escort comes to meet you."

Hopes dashed and feeling foolish that she'd ever let them rise in the first place, Jane turned back to the bench. She would need a moment to put the silly thing away and get her glove back on. Then she'd send for Fell. If Fell ignored her, she'd send for Lambert. If neither came, she'd wait. She would grind her teeth, but she would wait.

So resigned was Jane to this program, she was astonished and delighted to see Lambert stalking through the arch before she'd buttoned up her glove again. He saw her and changed course to join her at the bench. Her pleasure was squelched by Lambert's thunderous expression. "What is it? What's wrong?"

"Fell's gone." Lambert spoke softly but his anger and concern were unmistakable. He seemed oblivious of the incongruity of their situation, a gentleman dressed for dinner accosting a lady dressed for a late afternoon stroll in the very shadow of the great gate.

"He's *gone?*" Jane forgot about buttoning her glove. "What happened?"

"All I know is, his study is a worse mess than ever. If he left a message, I sure can't find it." Lambert looked at her sharply. "What are you doing here?"

"I came to see Mr. Fell." Jane met Lambert's challenging gaze and watched it soften. "You're worried about him."

"Hell, yes." Lambert shook his head as if to clear it. "Sorry, ma'am. Didn't mean to use that kind of language. Yes, I'm worried. He's gone, but his valise is still right where he dropped it when we got in this afternoon."

"This morning, not to put too fine a point on it, Mr. Fell tried to run away," Jane reminded him. She couldn't keep a touch of waspishness out of her tone.

Lambert glowered. "He wasn't running away. He was leaving. There's a big difference."

Jane raised an eyebrow. "You were both doing a bunk."

"Fell wanted to go to London." Lambert's face cleared as he pushed his hat back on his head. It gave him an air of utter harmlessness. "I didn't want to let him go alone."

Jane turned away from the gate, back in the direction she'd come. "Walk with me." Lambert fell into step beside her. For a hundred yards they walked side by side in silence, each consumed by their own thoughts.

Jane touched Lambert's sleeve and he stopped beside her. "You're concerned for Fell's safety. Yet we don't know that he's come to any harm."

"Concerned? I'm scared stiff." Lambert held out his hand to show Jane the slight yet distinct tremble in the fingers. "I don't even have a vice to blame this on. It's all me."

"What are you going to do?"

"I was headed to your place to ask you that."

"Who else knows?" Jane gazed up at Lambert, wishing for more light. "You are going to report this to the authorities, aren't you?"

"I guess I should, shouldn't I?" Lambert sounded resigned. "I have to. But I haven't told anyone yet."

"Good." Jane took Lambert's arm for a moment, just enough to draw him along beside her as she set forth for her brother's house again. "Let's think this over before you do. The police won't take you seriously until Fell has been missing for more than twenty-four hours, so you aren't behindhand with them yet. Who would you tell at Glasscastle?"

Lambert rattled off the names without hesitation. "Voysey, Stowe, and Stewart. Brailsford, only he's not here to tell. Porteous is sure to find some way to push his nose in where he doesn't belong. I should see Voysey first."

"Yes, you should, but not yet." Jane wished Robin were there to advise her. The relative merits of Glasscastle's wise men were difficult for her to discern. To Jane, they all seemed alike, marvelously pleased with themselves and inexplicably certain of their own superiority over the rest of the world.

Lambert went on, "Why shouldn't I? Fell is gone. The bowler hat is gone too. But nothing else seems to be."

"The hat is missing? Oh, dear. I had great hopes of that bowler." Jane castigated herself for not insisting that she conduct an immediate examination of the hat as soon as the intruder was in custody. A little excitement and a large headache were no excuse for neglecting the fundamentals. Now she would have to think of a way to get back in the police station to question the intruder again. It made her tired just to imagine the effort it would take to conduct a reprise of her spell.

"If Fell left, why would he go without taking anything else? Just the bowler hat?" Lambert sounded frustrated.

"Put that way, it does seem unlikely. But what if Fell isn't really missing? What would he say if you'd raised the alarm prematurely?" Jane cautioned.

"What would—" Lambert stopped in his tracks, all indignation. "I thought you believed me."

"I do, I do," Jane assured him. She tugged at his sleeve again, just enough to get them moving.

"That's a good point about the false alarm," Lambert conceded. "Fell would hate it if we kicked up a fuss for no reason."

"Too bad if we did. It would serve him right, if he was that careless about leaving a message for you. Not only is it foolish for a warden to be so cavalier, it's rude."

"But neither one of us really thinks this is a false alarm."

It was Jane's turn to concede the point. "No."

"What should we do?" Lambert looked as frustrated as he sounded. "I know what I'd like to do. I'd like to turn the whole place upside down and shake it. Either we would find Fell or we would know for sure that he isn't there. But unless I can persuade a Provost or a Senior Fellow to authorize it, that's not allowed."

"We will plan the best way to search for Fell, I promise." Jane used her most soothing voice. "But first, we'll have a nice cup of tea."

Far from being soothed by this prospect, the suggestion made Lambert touchier than ever, but by the time they walked to the Brailsford house, she had talked him around. There was no time for a restorative cup of tea, however. Jane and Lambert were scarcely inside the door when Amy joined them. Despite the hour, she still wore that morning's delicately filmy white dress and her hair had come unpinned in the back.

"Thank goodness you're back." With only a moment's hesitation, Amy welcomed Lambert in. She touched her hair. "I'm sorry I'm in such a state."

"You look fine," Lambert said stoutly.

Amy gave him an absent smile, and said, "James Porteous has just sent a message here for Robert, Jane. He has had word from the police station. That man you caught has fallen into some sort of trance. They're sure it's magic but they can't identify the source or the nature of the spell."

"Oh, dear," said Jane. Another source of information gone the way of the bowler hat. This was what happened when she yielded to her own weakness. She should have continued her interrogation, no matter the risk of discovery.

"It's not something you did to him, is it?" Amy asked.

Jane was horrified by the very suggestion. "Please remember that I am thoroughly trained in my discipline. I would never use a spell unless I were confident of the result."

"You are rather a confident person, though," said Amy. "Aren't you?"

Jane bristled.

"Do you have the message?" Lambert asked. "May I see it?"

Amy handed him the note and Jane read it over Lambert's shoulder. Porteous had used a great many more words than Amy had, but the meaning was the same.

"Oh, dear," said Jane. "This is most distressing."

To judge from her stance, all but a-tiptoe, Amy had more to tell them. "There is something else I must show you at once. Come into the library."

"It *isn't* anything you did to him, is it?" Lambert asked Jane sotto voce, as Amy led the way.

"Here's a scriptural reference for you," Jane retorted. "'O ye of little faith.'"

"Matthew 8:26, I think," said Lambert, after a moment of silent cogitation. "So it wasn't you?"

Jane wrestled with exasperation and won. "No. Did you really think it was?"

"No." Lambert gave her a long, measuring look. "I figure if there's anyone in this world I can trust to help me with this, it's you."

Lambert's gravity took Jane completely off guard. "Oh."

Jane and Lambert followed Amy into the small library Robert Brailsford used when he worked at home. Across the table in the center of the room, Amy had arranged tiles painted with letters and numbers. A tiny ivory drop spindle was tied to a stout cord of braided white horsehair. Amy dangled the spindle over the tiles.

Lambert stopped in his tracks. "Uh-oh."

"Oh, no." Jane recognized the props with mild revulsion. "Not divination. There's no point to this, Amy."

Amy looked mulish. "You do your magic, don't expect to stop me doing mine. Now, silence, both of you, or it won't work."

"Do we have time for this?" asked Lambert.

"Just let me show you." Amy held the spindle's cord steady and waited.

Jane suppressed the urge to deliver a terse lecture upon the unreliability of the domestic enchantments. It might relieve her temper and her conscience, but it wouldn't accomplish anything else. Amy was a devotee of parlor magic, and this device to spell out messages was among the least effectual of any of the sociable magics.

After a long pause, the spindle began to swing. It moved slowly at first, almost imperceptibly, but with time, the movement became more pronounced. The spindle swung out and back from the central point. At the height of its arc, it indicated the tile marked *L*.

Frowning, Jane watched the pendulum swing of the spindle closely.

Amy was triumphant. "There, you see? *L* for Ludlow. I asked it where Robert is. It spells out the rest of the word, but it's terribly slow. You must be patient." The spindle continued swinging, not bothered by Amy's explanation.

Lambert was looking embarrassed. "We'll be sure to include this in our report to Voysey."

That brought Amy's attention to Lambert. "What report?" The spindle kept swinging relentlessly despite her distraction.

"Fell is missing. We'll have to tell the authorities. If he were here, your husband would be the first one I'd tell."

"If Robert were here, no one else would be missing. Nor in a trance." Amy glanced meaningfully in Jane's direction. "He would have things well in hand."

"*L*." Jane ignored Amy and kept her attention on the spindle and the scattered tiles. "*U. D.*"

"There it goes," said Amy. "I told you." The spindle picked out the rest of the letters in turn: *L-U-D-L-O-W*.

Jane looked from the spindle to Amy with respect and resignation. "I'm glad it knows how to spell. So often they don't."

Lambert continued, "We'll have to tell Voysey and Stewart and Stowe."

The ivory spindle was swinging wildly now. Amy ignored it, focused entirely on Lambert. "No, you mustn't. They put Robert out of the way for a reason. Don't trust them."

Lambert was dogged. "There's a logical explanation for Mr. Brailsford's disappearance. And for Fell's. We'll find out what it is."

The horsehair slipped from Amy's fingers and the spindle flew across the room to lodge in the aspidistra. Amy gasped and clapped her hand over her mouth. Tears welled up and she stifled a sob. Lambert helped her to a chair and patted her hand.

Reluctantly, Jane took off her gloves, plucked the object out of the aspidistra's pot, and let the spindle dangle from its long cord like a dead mouse by its tail as she inspected it. It was old ivory, worn smooth with use, and could have been mistaken for a child's miniature top. Jane touched the ivory. To her consternation, the spindle felt distinctly warm to the touch. "Amy, where did you get this thing?"

"It was my grandmother's," Amy said in strangled tones. She produced a lace handkerchief and delicately blew her nose. "It never did that before."

"No, I don't suppose it did." Jane ignored the efficient soothing Lambert was administering to Amy while she continued her analysis. "Most interesting. Where did the cord come from? It looks like horsehair."

"It is. I made it. I had a gray pony when I was a girl," Amy replied. "Orlando, I called him. When I was thirteen, I went out to the stable by the light of the full moon and I clipped a bit of his tail with my silver embroidery scissors."

"What a shame you never had a proper education," Jane said, with injudicious honesty. "I think you must have great aptitude. With the right kind of training, you might have been a powerful magician."

"I don't want power," snapped Amy. "I only want things the way they should be. A bit of peace and quiet, a well-run house, that's all. I want my husband and I want as many children as possible." Amy put her handkerchief away and added defiantly, "When it comes to the really important things in life, I'd back my education against yours any day. I had an excellent governess."

Sharp rejoinders occurred to Jane but she let them all fade away unspoken. The spindle was cool between her fingers now. She wound the cord neatly around it. "I don't suppose your grandmother had any formal education either?"

"She taught me all sorts of things," said Amy. "Natural magic, not that stuff with foreign invocations. Very dangerous, that sort of magic."

"She was right about that," said Jane, with heartfelt agreement.

Slightly mollified, Amy unbent. "She talked to the bees. They told her things."

True country magic of the oldest kind. Jane was impressed.

"Is that magic?" Lambert looked intrigued. "My grandmother said that about bees too."

Jane nodded. "That's the genuine article. What else?"

Amy thought it over and added, with an air of mild defiance, "She was very good at reading one's character from the shape of one's skull."

"Oh." Jane noticed Lambert had withdrawn and found a chair of his own. Apparently he now considered Amy sufficiently soothed. How typical of Amy that she valued her grandmother's craft no higher. There had been real skill involved in the construction of the spindle's cantrip. It was simple but durable and had a strength that would long outlast more complex and sophisticated magics.

Jane released the spindle and let it spin free at the end of the horsehair cord. "Let's see if it works for me." She took a deep breath and centered her attention on the ivory spindle, ignoring the tiles scattered across the table beneath. She steadied herself, emptied herself of expectation, and simply stood there with the pretty bauble motionless at the end of its cord.

The tableau lasted no more than three silent minutes. Amy was just about to speak, possibly to offer advice, when Jane forestalled her. "Where is Nicholas Fell?" she asked.

At once, the spindle began to twist the cord. Jane felt her fingertips prickling as if they had fallen asleep. Slowly at first, then with increasingly swift rotation, the spindle began to turn so fiercely that the cord twisted out of Jane's grasp. The spindle arched across the room, hit the wall with a sharp thud, and then fell back to lodge in the aspidistra.

"See?" Amy was triumphant. "It really works."

"Oh, dear." Jane rubbed her fingers until the prickles ebbed away. "It must be a great bore to have to spell things out. I don't blame them for cutting corners now and then."

"All right. What just happened here?" Calmly, Lambert retrieved the spindle and cord from the aspidistra and put it on the table. "Just who is *them*, if isn't rude to ask?"

Jane waved her hand in a vague gesture that took in about half the ceiling. "*Them.* Those who come when you don't call."

"Spirits?" Lambert looked as if he were trying not to laugh. "Mediums and their controls, you mean? I thought that was all a copper-bottomed fraud."

"The mediums are. They only get what comes when they call. Most don't even bother to call. They can't spare a moment from their trickery, the malignant scum." Jane caught herself at the edge of a lecture and relented. "Just because the world is full of frauds doesn't mean there isn't more out there than we can understand. There are other forces, not that they are usually worth half the trouble they cause. Five hundred years ago, even here in a bastion of learning, there was hardly a spring that didn't have its tutelary spirit, and plenty of people glad to honor it. No one has ever properly catalogued all the different kinds of natural spirits. That would be a thesis worth writing, even if one only did the locals." Jane picked up the spindle again. "As for what just happened here, Amy, point in the direction of Ludlow."

Amy pointed, without hesitation, in the direction of the aspidistra.

"Thought so. Mind if I borrow this?" Jane wrapped the cord tightly around the spindle.

Amy's suspicion was clear. "Why? You're not going to take it apart to see how it works, are you?"

"No. If this cantrip of yours can tell us which direction Fell has gone, and Robert too, it might be helpful on the journey. But since you reminded me, I do have something I've been meaning to take apart." Jane put the spindle in her bag and produced the handkerchief that contained the carved wooden cylinder she'd taken from the intruder.

Lambert regarded her bleakly. "What journey?" He sounded like he already knew the answer to the question he was asking and he didn't like it.

"I'm going to Ludlow. Do you have a knife, by any chance?" Jane put the handkerchief on the table and unwrapped the cylinder with care.

"Why?" Lambert searched his trouser pockets, scowling.

Jane found a crevice in the cylinder's carving and ran a fingernail along it. "I think it's time to do a bit of dissection on this thing. I tried it on the gatekeeper earlier and it didn't work at all."

"Not that." Lambert handed her his penknife. "I mean why go to Ludlow?"

"To look for Fell. And for Robert, of course," Jane added, with an eye toward Amy's incipient protest. "Who am I to ignore these signs and portents? Something—or someone—wants me to go to Ludlow. I don't see any way to find out why unless I actually go there."

"Oh, I knew you were worried too," exclaimed Amy, and enfolded Jane in a sisterly hug. "Oh, thank goodness. Oh, I'll help you pack for the train."

"Not for the train," Jane said, still engrossed in the cylinder. "For the motor car."

"Great." Lambert leaned close to Jane, watching as she poked gingerly at the intricate carving. "Are you sure that's the proper tool for the job?"

"Don't cut yourself." Amy was watching too. "That knife looks very sharp."

"No point in carrying a dull one," said Lambert. "Watch it, there."

Jane did her best to quell Lambert with a glance. "Quiet, you. I'm still recovering from my disillusion. If ever I thought someone could be relied upon to carry a Bowie knife, it's you." Jane teased the edge of the knife blade into the crevice and loosened a plug at one end of the cylinder. Once she had it uncapped, she shook the contents of the cylinder out among the tiles. What emerged was about half an ounce of water and something that seemed to be fine splinters of wood.

"I had a Bowie knife once," said Lambert. "Lost it, though. Stuck it in a bear and the bear ran off. It seemed like a good swap at the time."

"What is that?" Amy asked. "It looks like someone put a piece of drift-wood in there and it just fell apart."

"So it does." Jane prodded the wet wood with the tip of the blade, then gave the penknife back to Lambert. She rubbed her palms together and mur-mured an incantation as she cupped her hands over the wet wood and the cylinder. After a long silence to absorb the impressions in full, she brushed her hands palm to palm again and clapped them lightly to close the spell.

Jane folded her hands. "What a pity Robin isn't here. He could tell so much more. I think it's not pure Glasscastle magic. There's a vein of Glass-castle magic running clear through it, the way that carved vine winds around the cylinder. But the wood and the water, that's new to me. It's fresh water, by the way. Not salt water, nor holy water. The wood isn't driftwood, though it does look it. More than that, I don't know. I don't think there's any chance of adapting it to work for us. Pity."

"You wanted to use it yourself?" Lambert asked. "A bit of magic to let you come and go through the gates of Glasscastle without supervision? Miss Brailsford, I'm shocked."

"Oh, so innocent. Don't pretend the thought never crossed your mind." Jane mopped up the water with the handkerchief she'd used to wrap the cylinder, then put the splinters back and plugged the cylinder again. "You will loan me the Minotaur, won't you?" Jane asked Amy, as she stowed the little bundle in her bag.

"Borrow anything of ours you please," said Amy. "But do be careful."

"You can't go motoring off all by yourself," said Lambert. "For one thing, it's pitch-dark."

"I'll leave first thing in the morning. It will take me quite some time just to pack and make a few basic preparations." Back to the ink bottle, Jane thought. She couldn't leave without telling Faris what she planned to do. Just as well she'd kept the Royal Worcester plate in her room.

Lambert said, "You really can't drive off all alone."

"How kind!" Jane beamed at him as if he'd made a wonderful discovery. "No, it would be much better if you came too."

Lambert looked taken aback. "*Me?* No, I can't go."

"I'd go," said Amy, "but I have an appointment. The doctor will be here to see me tomorrow." She touched the slight swell of her belly. "It's important."

"We understand." Jane patted Amy's hand soothingly. "Everything will be fine."

"Perhaps Lambert could bring a pistol or two along with him, just in case of emergencies," suggested Amy. She smiled at him with great sweetness. "Since the bear ran away with your Bowie knife."

"Yes, what was all that about the bear?" Jane's interest was unfeigned. "Did you think we weren't listening?"

"I think I'd be forgiven for reaching that conclusion." Lambert looked nettled. "I crossed a stream and worked my way downwind. When he couldn't smell me any more, the bear gave up."

"Lambert tells the most wonderful stretchers," said Amy fondly. "It's a bit like feeding a squirrel. If you pretend you don't notice, he sits right down beside you and then the stories just come out, as naturally as breathing."

"I remind you of a squirrel?" Lambert's indignation was profound. "Why didn't you mention this before?"

"Because I love every moment of it," Amy assured him. "The story about the man who sells his soul for a rifle and five magic bullets is my absolute favorite." Amy turned to Jane. "You really must get him to tell you that one."

"I *might* have stretched a point here and there," Lambert admitted stiffly. "You never let on I was boring you. I wish you had."

"You weren't! I wouldn't have missed a single word, not for anything. Oh, don't look so embarrassed." Amy patted Lambert's shoulder. "You only do it to please me, because you know I enjoyed reading *The Virginian* so much."

Lambert muttered something that sounded very much like "Damned embarrassing book," and then "Sorry, ma'am," and then fell silent.

Jane thought it best to change the subject. "You may come along with me if you're here, ready and waiting. Otherwise, I'll go alone."

"If I get told off for drinking a pint of lager on a hot day, just think how overjoyed they're going to be when I disappear completely. In a motor car. With firearms." Lambert was no longer muttering, but he was still far from his customary good humor.

"I think Amy was being facetious. You don't really need to bring any pistols along," said Jane.

"I wasn't being a bit facetious," Amy protested. "I think it would be quite a good idea."

Jane ignored her. "I'll leave at sunrise."

Amy consulted an almanac from one of the library shelves and spoke directly to Lambert. "The sun rises at three minutes to six tomorrow. Don't be late. She means it. I can tell."

9

*"By the rushy-fringed bank,
Where grows the willow and the osier dank,
My sliding chariot stays"*

Lambert hurried back to Glasscastle from the Brailsford house. Voysey was not in. Neither was Stewart, Provost of Wearyall. Lambert sent a message in at the lodgings of Victor Stowe, Provost of St. Joseph's, and was fortunate enough to catch him just as he returned from his dinner.

Stowe led Lambert into the tower room that served as his study. From the second floor of the tower, the windows opened onto St. Joseph's Green like a box at the opera. It was dark, but even Glasscastle by night made a fine view. Stowe waved Lambert to a chair and sat at a writing table beside the window. "What brings you here, young man?"

Lambert matched Stowe's directness. "Fell has disappeared."

"What, again?" Stowe seemed pleased with this comeback. "Some of his students have been making that complaint since the end of the summer term."

"I want to make certain the authorities know about this. I think something has happened to him." Lambert made sure Stowe knew about the intruder and went on to describe the state of Fell's study. "I'm going to look for him."

"Dear me, where? It's a big country, and Mr. Fell is free to go where he likes in it." Although Stowe's expression was serious, Lambert was sure he was being humored.

"Is Fell free? I know he refuses to work on the Agincourt Project, but he knows the project exists. We don't know where he's gone or who he's with.

Won't that trouble the men in charge of imperial security?" Lambert countered. "Shouldn't you tell someone?"

"The project concluded yesterday," said Stowe. "Its importance has diminished considerably since the ministry announced its decision to redirect the funding to the aviation project at Farnborough."

"Concluded?" Lambert felt as if he'd been punched in the stomach.

Stowe looked rueful. "I suppose it violates the basic tenets of imperial security to admit as much. But Meredith always spoke highly of you. I'm surprised he didn't tell you himself."

"Tell me what? I had an accuracy trial just this afternoon. Mr. Voysey and Mr. Wright worked with me for hours. The project can't have concluded."

"Did they? Are you sure?" Stowe frowned. "Meredith must have persuaded them to pursue an ancillary line of thought. Must be an addendum to a memo somewhere. Blast. I can't keep up with the paperwork." He rifled through the documents heaped on the table before him. "Meredith's stubbornness is notable. I believe he's gone to London to try to speak with Lord Fyvie directly."

"When did Meredith find out the funding was to go to Farnborough?" Lambert was remembering the peace he'd felt in Upton's rooms. Had Meredith guessed the project was coming to a close? Was that why he'd suggested that visit?

"Blasted paperwork. I can't find it." Stowe gave up and shoved his stacks of paper back into place. "First thing this morning. The Vice Chancellor told Stewart and me after dinner last night. That's why I was rather surprised to see you now. Thank you for reporting Fell's departure. I'll make it known to the appropriate authorities."

"Thank you." Lambert spoke at random as he rose and started for the door. He didn't know what to say next, let alone what to do next.

Stowe followed him, abruptly solemn. "As of now, I'm officially informing you that the project is complete. Should you be needed for any further studies stemming from the project, you will be invited to resume your duties as an expert marksman, so be sure you leave a forwarding address with the Bursar before you go. You will need to see him anyway, to collect your wages." Stowe shook Lambert's hand and his formal air vanished as quickly as it had come. "Congratulations. You have been a great help, you know. What will you be doing after this?"

Lambert blinked and frowned. "The project is finished. I'm leaving."

"Not immediately, old man." Stowe chuckled. "We aren't turning you out in the street, you know. No need to catch the very next ship that sails. While you are making your travel plans, I suggest you keep your eye on the newspapers. I think we'll let a few of the finer points out in rumor, just to keep the boys at Farnborough on their toes."

Through his stampeding thoughts, Lambert could make sense of only one thing. This was the end of his time at Glasscastle. After this, he was exiled for good.

"You can have a pint or two to celebrate," offered Stowe, as he saw Lambert out. "It must be a long time since you've had a chance to sink one."

"Yes, of course. All sorts of luxuries I can take up again," Lambert replied, and was proud of how normal he sounded, only mildly strangled. "Can't wait."

"That's better," said Stowe, "that's the spirit. Good luck, eh?" He shook hands with Lambert again as he let him out into the moonlit night. "Good luck."

Adrift in the dark, at first Lambert walked at aimlessly, the pea-gravel path crunching underfoot. Not until he recognized the peppery scent of the marigolds in the Holythorn kitchen garden did he realize his heart had taken him back to the bench outside Wearyall. He sank down on the bench and let the evening chant ease his mind to emptiness.

Lambert sat there for a long time. He let the music fill him, knowing it would have to last him all his life. The leaves shifting ceaselessly overhead rustled silver behind the golden thread of the chant. Around him in the shadows, all the beauty and power of Glasscastle slept unseen in the dark.

Maybe Voysey was right. Maybe Glasscastle was not for the likes of Lambert. But something in that deep music had awakened something deep in him. The only true failure, Lambert promised himself, would be to forget that one had ever awakened, to permit oneself to sleep again. *Take what you need and let the rest go.* In his brief time at Glasscastle, it had been granted to Lambert that he discover the existence of such music. Nothing could take that knowledge from him. On this side of the River Jordan, one had to travel light. Therefore, Lambert must let even Glasscastle go, and take with him only the changes the music had made in him.

At last, with slow steps, Lambert returned to the rooms he had shared with Fell. The valise he'd packed approximately one hundred years ago—in other words, that morning—was at the foot of his bed. He opened it and stared at the neatly packed contents. These things had been indispensable mere hours ago. With a sigh, Lambert emptied it all out on the bed, ready to start over.

There was a knock at the door. Lambert answered it, trying hard not to hope it was a message from Fell. It wasn't. Two young men stood there, unmistakably undergraduates. Both were fair, but one was built like a string bean, the other a potato.

"Pardon the intrusion," said the string bean. His tone made it clear that he did not care if anyone pardoned him or not. "My name is Herrick. This is Williams. We're here to speak with Mr. Fell. Please ask him to be so good as to see us."

"I don't have to ask him. He can't see you. He isn't here." The undergraduates showed every sign of wanting to elbow past him into the room but Lambert did not budge. "It's mighty late for a social call, don't you think?"

"This isn't a social call," Herrick said. "We must see Mr. Fell."

Williams, the potato, was more polite, almost apologetic. "You see, he hasn't sent our marks to the Registrar yet. We don't know if we're still students of Glasscastle or if we've graduated. I don't mind staying on for the summer, not at all. Chanting clears my mind, you see. I like it. But Michaelmas term is coming up in a few weeks and it would be so embarrassing to be here if we're not supposed to be. Terribly embarrassing."

"I see your problem. Too bad someone else is going to have to solve it." Lambert was about to shut the door on them when a thought struck him. No chance of Glasscastle hushing up Fell's disappearance if the undergraduates knew about it. "Mr. Fell has been abducted. Ask the Provosts if you don't believe me. Now, go away." Lambert closed the door and locked it while the young men were still gaping at him, mouths working like fish. There was more knocking, but Lambert ignored it. In fifteen minutes, they had given up and gone.

Lambert returned to his room. The bed was strewn with the contents of his valise, most of which he tidied away in the wardrobe. His shaving things he put back on the washstand, ready to use in the morning, then repack. He wrapped his Colt Peacemaker in his oldest shirt and tucked it in a corner of the valise with a generous supply of cartridges, then added a compass, a box of lucifer matches and a change of underclothes. Lambert studied the result. Travel with Jane was sure to be a very different proposition from travel with

Fell. For a moment, he regretted his long-lost Bowie knife, then he topped off the valise with two clean collars and went to bed.

The sun was coming up when Lambert reached the Brailsford house. The late summer sunrise changed color moment by moment as the world turned toward the light. By the time Lambert rang the bell, the sun had edged clear of the horizon and the gaudy colors of cloud and sky had faded. A fine summer day had begun, the first day of his life after Glasscastle. Lambert had precisely one minute to contemplate that milestone before the door opened.

"You're late." Jane joined him on the doorstep. "Let's go." She was wearing a plain linen motoring coat over a gray dress, driving gloves like gauntlets almost to her elbows, and the largest hat he'd seen yet. Its broad brim strained against the gauzy motoring veil she had stretched over it and knotted beneath her chin.

"You look like you're ready for a hard day's bee-keeping." Lambert winced the moment the words slipped out, but it was too late to take them back.

"How kind of you to say so," Jane replied tartly. "You look as if you didn't sleep a wink last night."

Behind them, the door opened and Amy peered out. She wore something white and graceful. With her hair loose down her back, she looked like Lucia di Lammermoor, about to run elegantly mad. Lambert had no trouble keeping that thought to himself, for before he could speak, Amy hushed them both.

"You said you'd leave at dawn," Amy reminded Jane. "Go. Find Robert for me!"

"We're going, we're going." Jane replied. Lambert waved farewell to Amy and followed Jane back to the carriage house where the motor car waited. Something bulky filled the boot and rear seat, but Lambert couldn't tell what it was, as canvas had been tied down over it to protect the cargo. "What's all that?"

"Just my luggage," said Jane, sliding into the driver's seat and donning her goggles. "Give it a twirl, please?"

With private gratitude that he hadn't brought more than one small satchel, Lambert wedged his valise into the Minotaur and went around front. Lambert cranked up the motor and took the place beside Jane. She reversed smoothly out into the street and headed out of the town as the sun climbed the sky to their right.

Lambert decided he was either more comfortable sitting in the front seat than the back, or Jane's driving style was more conservative this morning. She took her time leaving the confines of the town. Lambert, intent on savoring what might be his last drive through the place, was glad he had a clear view from the passenger's seat. He wanted to appreciate the look of things in the early light, not watch it go past in a blur. Gray stone walls seemed to glimmer silver. Greenery still damp with last night's dew set off the brilliance of blossoms opening to the sun.

At that hour, the streets were nearly deserted. Down a side road, Lambert thought he glimpsed his drayman on morning rounds. Here and there a cat was tucked up waiting on a doorstep. Otherwise, they had Glasscastle town almost to themselves. It was a lovely sight, ivy over stone in the rising day. Lambert reminded himself that he would return, if only to fetch his remaining possessions, but the pang of departure was sharp.

"Nice place," Lambert said, when all that remained was the silhouette of Glasscastle Hill in the distance behind them.

"Not bad," said Jane. "Get out the map case, will you? We're on the Wells road. From there we bear north for Bristol, but we must cross the Severn eventually."

While extracting the leather map case from beneath his seat, Lambert noticed Amy's spindle dangling from one of the knobs on the dashboard. He eyed it narrowly, but there didn't seem to be anything more to its motion than the steady sway natural to their momentum. "Did Amy make you bring that along as a good luck charm?"

"You never know. It might be useful. I'm not sure of our precise route yet."

Lambert watched the spindle swing aimlessly from one direction to the next. "If it starts pointing to Ludlow, what do we do?"

"I suppose we go to Ludlow." The goggles made it impossible to read Jane's expression but she didn't sound any more serious than Lambert. "I hope it won't take offence if we stick to the road."

"I brought my penknife. If it gets out of hand, I'll cut it loose." Lambert wrestled with the clasp on the map case. In less than a mile, he'd managed to pry it open and peer inside. After a few more miles of shuffling through the contents of the case, he stopped to stare at Jane. In addition to the usual two-shilling Bartholomew's sections, mounted on linen, two miles to the inch, the case held other maps. "Quite an assortment you have in here."

"It's Robert's map case. I thought it seemed a bit heavy. Why, what's in there?"

Lambert went through them in order. "An ordnance survey map of the Welsh marches with something marked in scarlet. Roman ruins, the key says. The Romans didn't get very far with the Welsh, did they? A map of the entire United Kingdom with geologic substrata marked in grease pencil. Which smears when you touch it, so be careful. Here's one that might actually be some use—another ordnance survey map, this one six inches to the mile, of the immediate Glasscastle area." Lambert unfolded it. "I think we drove off the edge of this one about five miles ago." He folded it up and put it back. "Here's the Southwest of England with most of the rivers marked in black. Your brother likes that grease pencil far too much."

"Try that one for now," said Jane

"Rivers it is. Are you expecting the radiator to overheat?" asked Lambert.

"No. It is possible that our excursion may attract a modicum of attention. Running water would help us avoid unwelcome notice."

"Sometimes it works on bears." Lambert thought it over. "Does this have anything to do with why witches float or why people who work magic are supposed to have a hard time crossing water?"

"Witches don't float. They do have a hard time crossing water," Jane replied. "A location spell works by finding changes in energy between the seeker and the sought. You match your perception of the changes with your perception of the world around you until you've found what you are looking for. Does that seem clear so far?"

"So far."

"Running water doesn't just change the energy. It renews it completely. If I were seeking you with a location spell, you could elude me each time you crossed running water. If you were on the water, say in a punt or a rowing boat, I'd never find you at all."

"So if we stay close to a river," Lambert said slowly, "we could cross it every time you think we're being sought by a location spell."

"That's it." Jane sounded pleased.

Lambert frowned. "What makes you think we're being sought by a location spell?"

"At the moment, I don't think we are. Even if I'm wrong about that, we're probably in the clear until we cross the Severn. But I'd like to know where the rivers are just the same."

Lambert consulted the map. "I found your Wells road. On to Bristol from there?"

"That would be best."

"The road to Wells is fairly straight. Are you planning another speed trial?" Lambert overplayed his suspicion and was glad to see it made Jane laugh. "You would warn me, wouldn't you? Though, come to think of it, it might not seem quite so bad if I can sit up here with you."

"Don't worry. No speeding today." Jane slowed the Minotaur as they topped a rise. "I promise."

As they left Wells behind, the land rose steeply. The road veered a little to avoid the worst of it, but kept more or less straight on northeast. Lambert knew they would have to pick up a road heading north to get to Bristol, but he wasn't sure which would be best. Reading the network of fine lines representing roads and railways was like reading a spiderweb, a task made more difficult if Jane happened to be changing gears at the time. "Farrington Gurney, I think we want. How long until we reach Bristol?"

"Not very long. Why?" Jane was intent on the Minotaur's climb.

Lambert folded the map down to a size he could read without the wind getting at it. "I missed breakfast. Come to think of it, I missed dinner too. If we find a pub, we can eat something."

"No need to suffer. There's a luncheon hamper back there somewhere. I thought we could have a picnic rather than put ourselves at the mercy of whatever pub we find."

"Thanks for reminding me. As I'm off the Agincourt Project and can do what I please for the first time in six months, we will definitely stop at a pub. I haven't had beer in so long, I've forgotten what it tastes like."

Jane kept her eyes on the road but it was clear from the slackening of her speed that her attention was focused entirely on Lambert. "You're off the project? You quit?"

"The project has concluded. My services are no longer needed." Lambert didn't try to keep the bitterness out of his voice. "I was officially informed last night. No one thought to mention it to me until then."

"The project has concluded? I can't believe it. The Agincourt Project is over?"

"Those ministers Robert was trying so hard to impress decided to give the funding to the aviators at Farnborough instead. There must be some details left to finish up on the Agincourt Project, or Voysey wouldn't have had me shooting a Baker rifle yesterday while Meredith was off in London. Voysey knew the project had concluded before anyone else did. Stowe told me."

"Stowe. Provost of St. Joseph's, isn't he? I haven't met him. What's he like? As oblivious as our friend Porteous?"

"I don't think he's *that* oblivious. Is anyone? Stowe seemed mildly embarrassed that I didn't already know I was fired. He was quite polite about breaking the news to me."

"I should think he would be. What did Voysey say?"

"Voysey wasn't there. Nor Stewart. It was all Stowe, concerned that I see someone in the Bursar's office to collect my pay."

"Oh, dear." Jane's concern showed despite her goggles. "The Bursar's office probably doesn't open for hours yet and here I've rushed off with you on my crupper."

"That's all right. I'll make the Bursar pay up when I go back for the rest of my clean socks. Don't worry."

"You sound a bit grim about it."

"I wasn't expecting a medal or anything. But the lack of efficiency irritates me. Why call me back for more shooting if the project had already concluded? It was stupid. The whole thing was stupid."

"Odd, to say the least." Jane picked up her speed again. "I wonder why Voysey was still recruiting Fell to the project if he knew it had concluded."

"Do you think Stowe knows something about the project Voysey doesn't?" Lambert folded the map into a new and better accordion. "I don't."

"It would be more likely—" Jane began, but she did not finish her thought, for at that moment the motor car swerved toward the hedge at the side of the road. Jane braked and brought the Minotaur to a halt. "Drat! Puncture."

"What?" Lambert was still recovering from the alarm their swerve had caused him. Things had been exciting there for a moment.

"Help me with the jack?" Jane clambered down from the driving seat and found the tool kit. "Please? It won't take a moment."

Of course it took far more than a moment to place the jack and get the wheel off the ground. By the time the damaged wheel had been removed and replaced with the spare, almost two hours were gone, along with quite a lot of the skin from Lambert's knuckles.

"I should have let you use the wrench," Lambert told Jane, once they were on their way again. "You have the gauntlets for it, after all."

"I'll do the honors next time," said Jane. "I don't think I would have taken any longer than you did."

Lambert let Jane's criticism pass. "Let's hope next time holds off until we have the first puncture mended."

"Let's hope next time doesn't happen at all."

In Bristol, at midmorning, Jane stopped to buy more petrol and have the tire mended. While they were waiting, Lambert persuaded her to try a pub nearby, the Blue Boar. It was too early in the day to order food, but despite the hour, Lambert could not resist trying the beer.

Jane took no spirits, declaring that behind the wheel she needed her wits about her at all times. Lambert could not argue with that. He drank two pints of lager, one quickly and one slowly, and wished he had a plate of toasted cheese to wash down with it. Beer tasted even better than he remembered. On a sticky August day devoted to the accumulation of road dust, the cellar-cool tang of the beer made him feel life might not be so bad after all. The strange lightness he felt afterward warned him that his capacity for liquor had dropped alarmingly. There had been a time when he wouldn't have noticed a gallon of beer, let alone a quart, even on an empty stomach. After his months of abstinence, the lager made the whole world lift a few degrees and take on extra color and mild spin. Lambert considered what such indulgence was likely to do to his aim and concluded with regret that he was better off without strong drink until Fell was safely home again.

Refueled, repaired, and restored, Jane and Lambert left Bristol behind. With the map half-unfurled in his lap, Lambert directed Jane through the city traffic and the maze of streets until they emerged on the northern edge of the city and meandered toward the estuary in the direction of Aust.

Jane was dubious. "Are you certain this is the right road?"

Lambert checked the map. "I'm certain this is the right road for Aust."

Jane slowed the motor car. "Why are we going to Aust?"

"Because that is where the map says we catch the Chepstow ferry."

Jane said nothing but she halted the Minotaur and let it purr to itself by the side of the road, to the great disgruntlement of a bicyclist close behind them. She stared at Lambert, but with the goggles it was hard to read her expression.

Lambert said, "We have to cross the Severn somewhere. You said so."

Jane spoke very slowly, as if she were dealing with a child. "We can't cross here. We're barely out of Bristol. There can't be a bridge within forty miles."

A gloomy thought struck Lambert. "Won't they take a motor car on the ferry? Even as freight?"

"I don't care if they take motor cars or not. I'm not crossing the Severn on a ferry."

"What's the matter with the ferry?"

"Nothing's the matter with it." Jane put the Minotaur back into gear and began to drive again. From the way she craned her neck, it was clear she was looking for a spot to turn the motor car around. "Nothing is the matter with the Channel ferry, but every time I use it, I feel sick for three days. I'm not going on any ferry if I can avoid it. And in this case, I can avoid it. We're driving upstream until we find a bridge."

"Is this something to do with that theory about crossing water?" Lambert asked.

"In my experience, it isn't a theory." Jane's tone was crisp.

"Ah. In that case." Lambert studied the map. "Watch out for signs to Alveston. We'll head in the general direction of Gloucester. Looks like we won't be able to cross the river until we get to the bridge at Over."

"Over it is," said Jane, and drove on.

It wasn't as easy to pick up the road to Gloucester as the map made it look. At times the hedgerows on either side brushed against the Minotaur as Jane negotiated the tight space, wincing and muttering over the probable damage to the motor car's paint. At times, their road met what looked like the road they wanted, but after a hundred dwindling yards, it became clear Lambert had directed them down some farm track.

Lambert kept the Severn on his left. Eventually, they found a road of respectable size that seemed to be going their way. By the time they crossed the bridge at Over, it was past two in the afternoon. "Only fifteen miles to

Ross-on-Wye." Lambert held out the map to Jane. "If you're tired of driving, we could probably find a place to stop for the night there."

"It will be light for hours and hours." Jane ignored the map. "Why would we stop for the night?"

Lambert winced. The beer in Bristol had been a bad idea. Drinking it had helped to pass the time until the Minotaur was ready, but it had given him a headache. Even if it hadn't, Lambert had already had enough of wind in his face and dust in his eyes and mouth for one day. Possibly for a month. "Sorry. I thought you might be tired by the time we get there, that's all."

"We aren't stopping for the night." After almost perfect silence for more than an hour, Jane was as forceful as if they'd been having an argument for miles. "There's no need. We have acetylene lamps. There's even a smaller one to illuminate the back number plate. We would be perfectly safe and perfectly legal even if we drove the night through. We aren't stopping."

Jane's words were so clipped, Lambert wondered if she had a headache too. He considered and discarded several responses, finally settling for mildness. "Not even when we get there?"

"We should be there by now." Jane braked to avoid a ewe that had wandered out into the road ahead.

"We should," Lambert conceded. Discarding mildness, he yielded to temptation, and added, "If you had bothered to mention that you don't believe in ferries, or if you'd spent less time packing a picnic and more time planning a sensible route, we probably *would* be there."

"If you could read a map properly, we wouldn't have taken an hour to find our way out of Bristol," Jane said.

Lambert stared at her. "I can't believe you plan to drive all afternoon without stopping. Won't you miss a meal?"

Jane bristled at his tone. "What is that supposed to mean?"

"For one thing, if the sandwiches go off, it will be a sad waste of that picnic basket you brought along, won't it? Or are there any sandwiches? Is the whole cargo taken up with your silver tea set?"

"I did pack a tea basket," said Jane levelly. "No point in bringing a lunch basket without a tea basket. You needn't have any tea if you don't care to. You needn't have anything."

Recklessly, Lambert continued. "What else do you have stowed back there? What is all that luggage? Hats?"

Jane looked peeved but said nothing. Evidently she had decided to ignore her traveling companion and concentrate on the driving.

The silence between them might have held indefinitely. Instead, somewhere between two and three o'clock, a wasp misjudged its death flight toward the windscreen of the Minotaur, caught the slipstream into the left side of the front seat, and stung Lambert on the eyebrow. For an instant, Lambert had the wild thought that he'd been struck with a hot poker. He swatted at his forehead instinctively, but the insect was already gone, leaving only a painful welt to mark its passage. Lambert swore.

"What is it?" Jane drew the motor car to a halt by the side of the road. They were alone in a country lane, near the bend of a pretty little river. Lambert didn't know which river it was, nor did he care, as long as it wasn't the Severn.

"Nothing. Something stung me, that's all." Lambert wanted to swear, but he took what comfort he could in preserving a stoic facade. With every pulse the sting hurt more, and he could feel it swelling. He wondered if it would end by obscuring his vision.

"Let me look." Once she'd pulled the Minotaur over and set the brake, Jane held Lambert's chin in one gloved hand, tilting his head ruthlessly this way and that as she inspected the injury. "That needs seeing to."

Jane found a spot at the edge of the road with enough grassy verge to park the vehicle safely. The little knoll sloped away gently toward the running water. Only the fresh droppings left behind by sheep grazing in the area posed any challenge to a picnicker.

Jane untied the canvas shroud over the backseat, removed the wicker tea basket, and unbuckled its lid. "I'll get some cold water for a compress. Just sit tight for a moment, will you?"

"Something stung me, that's all," said Lambert. "I'm not crippled or anything."

"Be quiet. Arguing with a ministering angel never got anyone anywhere he wanted to go," Jane said.

"Oh, is that what you are?" Lambert spent the time it took for Jane to clamber down to the stream and back in trying to envision Jane as either a literal angel or as the late Miss Florence Nightingale. He failed miserably at both.

On her return, Jane soaked one of the linen napkins from the picnic basket in cool water and gave it to Lambert to apply to his injury. With many a flinch and wince, Lambert put the cold compress in place. While he waited to see if it helped, he watched Jane out of his good eye as she unpacked the tea basket. Since he had a hand to spare from his compress, Lambert, noble in his suffering, helped her unfold and spread the thick woolen blanket. They were careful to avoid sheep droppings.

Mercifully, the weather was fine and showed no sign of change to come. The clouds overhead were the puffy white stuff of daydreams. Borne on a brisk west wind, they changed from shape to shape as Lambert lay on the blanket and gazed tranquilly upward. "Look, that one has Porteous's nose."

"Oh, don't. You'll spoil my appetite." Jane had removed her goggles, her gloves, and most improperly, her hat and veil. Bareheaded as a schoolgirl, she seemed younger than ever as she set to work, apparently intent on proving that a watched pot boils no later than any other kind.

Lambert found it pleasant to rest on the blanket, free of the roar of the motor car. With only the occasional distant bleat of a sheep to punctuate the steady rush of the river, it was a tranquil spot. No other traffic came from either direction, horse-drawn or motorized. The astringent scent of the spirit lamp burning under the tea kettle mingled with the smell of bruised grass under the picnic blanket. It was perfect—except for the relentless throb of his eyebrow. After thinking it over for a while, Lambert asked, "Is this all the ministering I get?"

Warily, Jane looked up. "Why, what were you expecting?"

"You had magic to spare when it came to dealing with our friend in the bowler hat. Couldn't you use a little on me? Get rid of the sting altogether?"

Jane returned her attention to the ritual of brewing up. "Sorry. Not my sort of magic. I doubt it would help. It would probably just make things worse."

With Jane in a more friendly mood behind her tea basket frontier, Lambert concentrated on distracting himself from the discomfort of the wasp sting. The sandwiches were excellent, the eventual tea strong and sweet, and when Jane produced thick slices of stem ginger cake, sticky and dark as molasses, Lambert decided he forgave her. Her tea might have none of the subtlety of Amy's fragile Chinese potions, but it was strong enough to trot a mouse on, and it cured his headache completely.

"You planned this well," Lambert said thickly. The stem ginger cake made clear diction an unnecessary luxury.

Jane accepted the olive branch and offered one in return. "I'm glad you're feeling better. Your eyebrow has swollen beautifully. You look as if you've been in a prizefight."

"Thank you." Lambert devoted himself to brushing cake crumbs off his waistcoat. That led to brushing crumbs off the blanket. At last, exhausted by these labors, Lambert lay down again. He gazed up at the clouds drifting overhead.

"It's nice here." Jane sounded a little sleepy.

Flat on his back, full of tea and cake, Lambert made an inarticulate sound of agreement as he arranged his hat so that the brim shaded his eyes without interfering with his wasp sting.

"You're not asleep, are you?" Jane's voice was dark with suspicion.

"With this sting? Certainly not." To prove it, Lambert took his hat off and propped himself up on an elbow to peer at Jane. "Are you?"

"Not yet. I suppose we should be going soon." Jane looked regretful.

"Of course. Quite right." Lambert subsided again and put his hat back over his face. "Immediately." After a long pause, he added, "It *is* nice here. Pretty."

"It wouldn't hurt to spend a little time studying the maps, I suppose." Jane brought out the map case and before long the picnic things were out of sight under layers of unfolded paper. Much rustling ensued.

Struck by a sudden suspicion, Lambert put his hat aside, propped himself up again, and asked, "You're not really using that ivory thing to choose the route, are you?"

The Bartholomew's map was obscured by the more specialized maps. The spindle dangled from Jane's hand, swinging in a tidy arc. She looked embarrassed. "I thought it couldn't hurt to check. If we had to choose an alternate route for some reason, it might be helpful to know how the spindle behaved."

"I am not letting a child's toy decide my route for me."

Jane's voice frosted. "You being the final arbiter of all things, of course." She put the spindle down and rubbed her fingers briskly.

"Don't be silly. That's not what I meant at all. But at least flip a coin or something." All tranquility gone, Lambert sat up straight. That made his wasp sting throb viciously, so he resumed his earlier treatment, dabbing gingerly at the spot with the linen compress.

Jane did not seem mollified. "Oh, it's silly to take something domestic seriously, is it?"

Lambert didn't try to conceal his impatience. "Look, it's not just domestic, is it? It's *Amy's*. Amy is a wonder and a marvel, but she reads tea leaves. She read my fortune in the lumps on my head, for pity's sake."

"I thought so." Jane's delight was obvious. "What revelations did she bring forth? Did Amy predict you would live a long life and achieve great fame?"

"Do I detect the note of a fellow sufferer?" Lambert asked. "No fame for me. So much for my career in show business. No, I'm going to take a long journey over water, marry well, and have a tidy crop of children. She must have mixed the pair of us up."

"Really?" Jane's eyes blazed with glee as she reached out to him. "Let me check and see."

"Hey, wait a minute." Lambert parried her halfhearted effort to feel his scalp, fended her off successfully, and put her firmly back on her side of the great wall of tea things. "That's personal, a man's scalp is. Private and personal. Otherwise, there would be no need to wear a hat."

Jane sobered. "Has she ever read the irises of your eyes? Long appraising glances, with much scolding if you dare blink?"

"It seems I've been spared something, thank God." Lambert gazed at Jane. "Why? What did she tell you about your eyes? That they're gray?"

Jane nodded. "Gray *and* remarkably fine. Don't forget that. No, Amy is an authority on using the irises of your eyes to evaluate your health. She diagnosed me immediately. I'm addicted to stem ginger cake and three-volume novels."

"And are you?"

"Oh, utterly. I'm surprised she refrained from examining you. Your superb vision must have intrigued her."

"At the moment, Amy would have her work cut out for her getting this eye open far enough to peer into." Lambert refolded the compress and placed a cooler side on his abused eyebrow.

For the first time, Jane looked and sounded truly sympathetic. "It must hurt."

"Like the devil," Lambert agreed. He was too tired and cross to attempt polite dishonesty.

"Good for you," said Jane. "I deplore a Spartan."

"Thanks."

"No, I'm complimenting you. I've always wondered about that Spartan boy who let the fox gnaw his vitals. How could you ever trust someone like that?"

"Well, if straightforward moaning is anything to go by, I'm the most trustworthy person you ever met." Lambert thought it over. "If you deplore a Spartan, why were you such a stoic yesterday when we brought you back from the police station?"

Jane made a vague gesture of dismissal. "Fussing."

"You're against it?" Lambert ventured.

"That's right." Jane relented. "Though I must admit you didn't fuss a bit. You were very helpful. Thank you."

"You're welcome. Next time, allow me to recommend a bit of straightforward moaning. It can be very refreshing."

"I knew you must be a terribly straightforward person," said Jane. "It's always nice to have one's snap judgments confirmed. First impressions are so often the most accurate."

"So they are," Lambert agreed. "The moment I met you, I thought, now, *here* is a good eater."

"Oh, very droll." Jane's rendition of Porteous was dead on. "Very droll, dear fellow."

"Not bad," said Lambert. "I did notice your remarkably fine eyes, of course. I noticed them immediately. But I have to admit I also noticed you are a young woman who appreciates her food."

"Since you remind me, I don't mind if I do." Jane wrapped up and stored away the remaining slices of stem ginger cake, then helped herself to the last sandwich as she set to work putting everything back in the baskets. Lambert handed her things and Jane packed them away neatly. "So much for your career in show business, you said. What will you do now that the Agincourt Project is over? Go back to the Wild West Show? Or go home to Wyoming?"

"I haven't had a chance to make up my mind," Lambert answered. "I'm not absolutely sure Kiowa Bob would take me on again, but I know I don't want to go back home to Wyoming."

"Not take you on again? With your eye? He'd be a fool not to," said Jane indignantly. "There can't be many people who can shoot the way you do."

"There's more to sharpshooting than marksmanship," Lambert replied. "There's showmanship. Making easy things look hard."

"What could possibly be easy about it?"

"Shooting glass balls with buckshot, for one thing," Lambert answered. "You can make it look harder by taking your shot from the saddle at a full gallop. But you only have to nick a glass ball to shatter it. It looks fine, but it *is* relatively easy."

"For you, perhaps."

"I've always been best at the distance shooting, standing on solid ground. Very boring for an audience, that kind of thing. Made it tricky to get the right sort of act going. I started out with pure shooting, and I was good enough that Kiowa Bob signed me. But he made me work up a different gag."

"What's a gag?"

"Oh, just a fresh angle on the basic act. The first shows I did, we were out West, touring our way to the East Coast by stages. Nothing funnier to that kind of audience than the greenhorn out to show off, so Kiowa Bob had me dress up like a city slicker." Lambert smiled at the memory. "We worked up a challenge—a volunteer from the audience could try his hand at target shooting—but the only volunteer Kiowa Bob ever picked out of the audience was me. I had a big pair of round spectacles with plain glass in them, so it looked like I was blind as a bat, but I could still see to shoot. I parted my hair in the middle and stuck it down with pomade, then put on a derby hat about a half size too small, so it fell off all the time. I had a cheap suit with the trousers and the sleeves cut just too short. Oh, I made a beautiful picture."

"But you hit the target?" Jane asked.

"I hit lots of things. Some of it was rigged—I fired blanks and the boys pulled trip wires to get chicken crates to fly open, or hats to fly off. I would act scared and try to throw the pistol down on the ground, then pretend it was stuck to my hand and I couldn't stop firing it. Finally, Kiowa Bob would calm me down and point me at the target and we'd have a shooting contest."

"And you won."

"Not always. It depended on the audience. The farther east we went, the less people laughed at city slickers, so I finally had to give up playing the greenhorn. That's when I put on the full bib and tucker—Stetson hat and leather chaps and a Colt Peacemaker strapped on my hip. It's not the way I dressed at home, believe me."

Jane blinked. "Isn't it? I thought all cowboys dressed that way?"

"But I wasn't a cowboy. I taught school."

Jane gave a crack of laughter. "You are a schoolteacher too?"

"That's right. Gave me kind of a turn when Amy told me that's what you do."

"Where do you teach?"

"Nowhere. I signed a two-year contract to teach at the country school nearest to our home place, but I could not weather it. After the first three months, I was wild to leave, but what could I do? A signed contract is a signed contract." Lambert sighed. "Then my friend Albert asked me to go with him to try out for Kiowa Bob. I went along for moral support, and had no intention of auditioning myself. Once we were there, however, I was weak. Albert persuaded me to try what I could do, and Kiowa Bob hired me. I never went back to the school."

"You ran away from school to join the Wild West Show?" Jane's eyes were wide. "What did they do?"

"My mother finished out the school year and did so well they took her on to work out the rest of the contract. The school board was mighty happy, as she is nine times the schoolteacher I ever was. My mother was mighty unhappy. She was disappointed in me for running out on a legal obligation and she's still somewhat annoyed with me about it. That's why I would rather not go home for a while yet."

"Do you mean to tell me you're not wanted dead or alive after all? How very disappointing." Jane seemed amused, not disappointed. "What subjects did you teach?"

"All of 'em." Lambert thought it over and revised his claim. "Somewhat."

"You do have teaching credentials, don't you?"

"I had just enough education to qualify for the position," Lambert replied, "but my best qualification was the ability to discipline the older students. Some of those boys are big."

"What does your mother do with them?"

"They don't give her any trouble. She just gives them that Look." To give Jane an idea of the Look in question, Lambert arched one eyebrow and gazed fixedly at her.

Jane was dubious. "Hm. It doesn't seem to work on me."

"I don't have the eye for it. My mother does."

"You do have an eye, though." Jane looked thoughtful. "I have a confession to make. When we met, all I cared about was finding a way to meet Nicholas Fell so I could deliver Faris's message. But by the time you showed me St. Mary's, I knew that Glasscastle must be even narrower and more wrongheaded than I'd always thought. Vision like yours, and all they can think to do with it is make you shoot a gun. It's criminal."

"But that's what I do," Lambert reminded her. "I'm a marksman."

"That's not *all* you do. In its most basic form, there are two elements to magic." Jane counted them off on her fingers. "Perception and will. I don't know anything about your capacity for magic. Even if I did, it would be folly to speculate. But given your powers of perception, I find it intriguing to speculate about your will."

Lambert stared at her. "You think I could do magic?"

"I didn't say that. In fact, I would go to great lengths to avoid saying that. But I think studying magic might be an idea worth examining. Now that you're finished catering to Voysey's whims with the Agincourt Project, you might give it some thought."

Lambert hesitated a moment, then said, "I can't go to Glasscastle."

Jane nodded. "It's no bed of roses, I know, but think about it."

"It's not that I don't want to. It's that I can't. I'm an American."

Jane looked confused. "What has that to do with anything?"

"Americans can't do magic. Canadians can't either. Voysey says it's bred out of us because of the ocean voyage. No one with magical aptitude can survive it."

"Can't they?" Where on earth did he get that idea?" Jane demanded.

"Voysey says they don't fully understand why yet, but the people who have magical aptitude have trouble crossing water, just like you do. No one with magical aptitude could survive the crossing to the New World. So there was no one left to hand on the aptitude to his descendants."

"Nonsense." Jane put her hat on, adjusted the angle, pinned it firmly in place, and cast the great net of her veil over all. Deftly she knotted the veil beneath her chin to anchor the whole works. "If that's what the Vice Chancellor of Glasscastle thinks, I don't think much of Glasscastle."

"That's what Voysey told me. It's his theory, anyway. But there's the Latin requirement besides. No one gets in without demonstrating proficiency in Latin. I don't have any."

"That's a stumbling block, I agree. As for your Mr. Voysey, he can think what he likes and concoct any theory he pleases. All the same, there are Canadian students—and Americans—at Greenlaw and they do perfectly well. I think Voysey must be mistaken. I wouldn't take his word for anything. Now, back to business." Jane tugged a map out of the stack before her. "I intend to abandon you heartlessly at a railway station along the way to Ludlow. Since I am rather fond of you, I will let you help me pick which one."

"Not using the spindle for such an important decision?" asked Lambert. "I'm surprised at you."

"Good idea." Jane retrieved the spindle and held it out to him, but she did not extend her arm very far. "You try it."

Lambert had to move much closer to reach the spindle. He took it from Jane's hand and dangled it by its horsehair tail. Resigned to making a fool of himself, he asked, "How do I work this thing?" Jane was so close he could feel her warmth.

"Just hold your hand still and clear your thoughts. I'll manage the rest." Jane settled herself mere inches away. "Close your eyes."

Lambert held his hand still. In a matter of moments, his fingers went to sleep. Stubbornly, he held on. Silence ruled for the space of several minutes. At last, Lambert couldn't stand it any longer. "Well?" He opened his eyes to find Jane right in front of him, her remarkably fine eyes as wide with surprise as he'd ever seen them, her nose a scant inch from the tip of his own. Lambert dropped the spindle as they both started violently and drew apart, Jane with the speed of a scalded cat.

"Leominster," said Jane, a little too loudly. "I'll drop you in Leominster. You can easily get the train from there."

"Leominster?" Lambert stared at her. What had just happened here? He shook his hand and rubbed the circulation back into his fingers.

Jane busied herself folding the maps and stowing them in the case. "The spindle hung steady long enough for me to take a good look at the map," said Jane. "Leominster is much the best place for me to leave you."

"Is that what you were doing? Looking at the map?" Lambert thought it over. "You don't want me with you when you arrive in Ludlow."

Jane lifted her chin. Her tone was airy. "I may, on occasion, seem to be mildly eccentric, but even I know where to draw the line. Bad enough I drive my brother's motor car. I cannot possibly turn up at a respectable place to stay for the night with a personable young man in tow. My reputation wouldn't stand it."

"Oh, just personable, eh? Nice of you not to flatter me. Do you think it will be any better if you turn up unchaperoned?"

"Perhaps not," said Jane, "but I'm used to creating that particular sensation."

"I'm supposed to be in Ludlow to help you. How will I know where to find you if we arrive separately?"

"I'll stop at the Feathers. Choose a room for yourself elsewhere. If we don't meet by chance, look for me at the church. I'll make a point of admiring the misericords there before today's evensong." Jane seemed pleased by the prospect. "I do appreciate a good evensong service."

Lambert helped Jane stow her baskets among the luggage in the back of the motor car. "What *are* misericords anyway? Which church? What if there's more than one? England is brimful of churches. Makes me wonder what you people have on your conscience."

"Look for the church with the best architecture. Ask someone. After all, you're traveling to improve your mind. They'll expect to be asked about the most improving spots for you to visit. The misericords are carved ledges under the seats in the choir. Monks leaned on them to rest when they were praying. Stout fellows, those monks. Even with a nice wood carving to brace yourself against, that amount of prayer would be hard to endure. Just ask the verger or someone to show you where they are."

"How do you know there will be misericords? You don't know which church it is, do you?" Lambert pulled the canvas cover taut as Jane tied it down over her cargo.

Jane managed the knots adroitly and tested her work with a brisk tug at each. "Ask for the oldest, least restored church. If they don't happen to have any misericords, they'll have a particularly good window or some rare vaulting. Every church has its point of pride. Find it and I'll find you."

"All right. The oldest church in town, before evensong. But if we don't meet there, I'll send you a message at the Feathers."

"No need for that." Cargo stowed and canvas tied, Jane pulled her gauntlets on and clambered into the driver's seat.

Lambert stood by the crank. "Every need. I don't want to let the sun go down without knowing exactly where you are and what the plan is."

"You know the plan. Find Robin and find Fell." Jane waved her hand impatiently to signal she was ready for him to turn the crank. "Find out what's going on."

"That's the plan now." As he bent to the crank, Lambert did not try to keep the gloom out of his voice. "I'm sure it will have changed by the time we get there. Who knows how many times?"

At six o'clock, Jane drove into Ludlow alone. The streets seemed steeper than they actually were, an illusion Jane blamed not on her fatigue but on the narrowness of the streets and the overhang of the half-timbered buildings that loomed on either side. In places the upper stories of the black-and-white houses leaned toward one another, as if longing for the far-off day when they could yield to gravity and meet in midair. The Feathers Inn was among the most elaborately fronted. Its black timbering was a bold tracery against its pristine whitewash, as different from the simpler houses as Spanish blackwork embroidery from a hemstitched dishcloth.

With great caution, Jane steered the Minotaur through the Feathers' arch to the coach yard within. It would never do to scrape the paint now. With deep relief for the respite after a long day's drive, she consigned the motor car to the staff of the Feathers, who showed it all the reverence and respect they could not show her.

Jane knew she'd been right to set Lambert down near Leominster station. Even arriving alone, she created a mild sensation. Fortunately, Jane was no stranger to the phenomenon and she used her force of personality to make things run smoothly as she booked a room and oversaw the transport of her luggage. It was possible that her stay in Ludlow would be lengthy. She'd tried to consider every eventuality when she packed. Firearms she'd left to Lambert. Otherwise, she felt prepared for any contingency.

The inn, despite its elaborate facade, concentrated more on home comforts than the latest of modern conveniences. Jane found her room quiet and comfortable, a haven of peace after the day spent at the wheel. Once she had freed herself of goggles, gloves, hat, and veil, she sank gratefully into the armchair at the window. There was time to spare for a visit to the church. She didn't want her meeting with Lambert to be cut short by evensong. But there was no reason to rush off immediately. Nothing more peculiar in the behavior of a newly arrived traveler than to dart out without bothering to wash or rest a moment. The Feathers prided itself on the comfort it offered its guests. It would be criminal not to enjoy it, if only briefly.

Jane permitted herself a moment of relaxation. It really was a most comfortable armchair. It might have been made to her measurements, it suited her so well. She closed her eyes.

To be quite still, just for a moment, was all Jane wanted in the world. A moment to think, to set the events of the day in perspective, was all she needed. To clear her thoughts, not only of the demands of the journey but of her own irrational impulses.

Jane knew she had been wrong to snap at Lambert. She should have thought to tell him to avoid the ferry. Mocking his inability to read a map had been childish. In her own defense, Jane had to admit neither of them had been at their best. They had both been hungry, thirsty, and tired. Lambert's midmorning lager hadn't helped things either.

What Jane could not excuse, no matter how she tried, were her irrational impulses. Jane had enjoyed watching Lambert as they picnicked in the shade of the Minotaur. He had a nice face and a nice voice. She had noticed when she met him that his eyes turned just slightly down at the outer corners, as did the left corner of his mouth. But when she was looking him over after the hornet sting, she had noticed for the first time that the right corner of his mouth turned just slightly upward and when he was telling stories it would quirk up into a half smile when he reached a self-deprecating part. Jane had found herself paying more and more attention to that upward quirk as the picnic had gone on. By the time she ordered Lambert to try the ivory spindle, Jane had been visited by not one irrational impulse but two in rapid succession.

The first impulse, to which she'd so nearly yielded, had been to kiss Lambert as he sat there with his eyes closed, concentrating on the spindle. She'd been on the very verge of acting when Lambert had opened his eyes and found himself nose to nose with her. The second impulse, to which she had yielded with disgraceful haste, had been to pretend she'd never had the first impulse, no, never, not in a million years. Jane was pretending with all her might, but she could not quite decide which impulse she regretted more.

Jane sighed. It was nice to be quiet, even if only for a moment. The room was utterly silent. Indeed, the whole inn seemed as quiet as if everyone in it had fallen asleep for a hundred years. It must be unusual, mustn't it, for such a prosperous place to be so quiet at this hour? What time was it? Jane didn't have the energy to look for a clock. The chair was so comfortable. It might have been made for her. A moment longer sitting there would be so pleasant. Only a moment more.

"But O my virgin lady, where is she?"

Lambert waited in the splendid confines of St. Lawrence's church, Ludlow, inspecting stained glass, misericords, monuments, and all, until evensong began. He took a seat then and waited through the service. The scale of the place was grander than the chapel of St. Mary's at Glasscastle, though the ornament was not as rich. The candles did not burn as brightly to Lambert's eye, nor were the voices of the choir as sweet to the ear. After the choir and congregation filed out, he dawdled until the verger approached him.

"Do you need help, sir?" The verger's steely eye warned Lambert not to try any fancy stuff.

Lambert did his best to look as though he'd come to Ludlow specifically to be improved. "No, thanks. Just admiring the misericords."

"Lovely work, isn't it?" the verger agreed. "The finest you'll ever see."

"You haven't seen a young lady admiring them recently, have you?" Lambert held his hand level with his upper lip. "About this tall. Dark hair and gray eyes?"

If anything, the verger looked even more disapproving. "No young person of any such description has been admiring the misericords. Come back in the morning, if you must. The light is better then."

Meekly, Lambert let the verger escort him out of the church. The doors were locked behind him. St. Lawrence's was saved from its admirers for another night. Stained glass and carved wood, not to mention the odd candlestick, were protected for another day.

Lambert was worried about Jane's tardiness. He'd followed her instructions. The train from Leominster to Ludlow had set him down in late afternoon. He'd walked up to the town on the hill and booked himself a room over a pub. The rest of his day had been spent in getting the lay of the land, learning which church was most likely to be the kind of rendezvous Jane had in mind, and fixing the pattern of the city plan and the local landmarks in his mind's eye so that he could find his way through the streets and passageways. It had been pleasant work. Time hung heavily enough on Lambert's hands that he purchased a two-penny booklet on local history and sat on a bench near St. Lawrence's to study it.

Ludlow, the booklet had informed him, crowned one of the green hills of southwest Shropshire and was crowned in its turn by the vast sprawl of Ludlow Castle, stronghold of the Egerton family, now the Earls of Bridgewater, who had been lords of the marches for centuries. Even before the Egertons won it as reward for their faithful service to Queen Elizabeth, Ludlow Castle had been a strategic point. It had been from Ludlow Castle that young King Edward V had set forth to ride to London for his coronation, a ceremony that had never taken place. The booklet did not go into detail about why not, but Lambert had the vague recollection that wicked uncles were involved.

Lambert had been distracted from his booklet by the sound of church bells. Time for bell-ringing practice, apparently. The cascade of notes Lambert associated with bells at Glasscastle was a more haphazard affair here. Sometimes the fall of notes dried up for several minutes at a time, only to resume in a completely different pattern. There was none of the sense of deliberation and little of the order and inevitability of Glasscastle bells.

Still, it had been agreeable, sitting in the shade, listening to the rehearsal, letting the world go on without him. Lambert was in a brown study, staring at nothing, by the time the bell ringers fell silent. Eventually they emerged from the church, walking in twos and threes as they argued over how many pints of ale they were going to put away. Idly Lambert watched them go. His attention sharpened only when he recognized the last of them to leave, a more than ordinarily tall man, his bearing regal, his demeanor striking despite his simple clothes. The last time Lambert had seen the Earl of Bridgewater, he had been urbanity itself at Fell's club in London, but he looked even more at home here.

Lambert's stare seemed to draw Bridgewater's attention. As if he sensed a watcher, the tall man glanced around as he walked. He spotted Lambert, and to Lambert's utter astonishment, approached with a friendly smile.

"Mr. Lambert, isn't it?" Bridgewater held out his hand as Lambert rose to his feet.

With a sense of disbelief, Lambert shook hands. It was like shaking hands with King Arthur. "I'm surprised to meet you here."

Bridgewater looked puzzled. "But I live here."

"You live in the castle." Lambert gestured toward the church. "I meant, here."

"I can't always be here to take my turn," Bridgewater said, "but when I am at home and a practice is scheduled, I try to do my part."

Lambert blinked. "You're one of the bell ringers?"

"Yes. Why, are you surprised? It's wonderful exercise, for the brain as well as for the body."

"Is it? I had a notion the big attraction was the excuse to drink beer afterward."

Bridgewater chuckled. "Oh, that too. I think a pint or two is definitely in order."

"I won't keep you, then," said Lambert.

Bridgewater's courtesy was flawless. "Won't you join me?"

"Thank you, no." Lambert didn't want to high-hat his lordship, but he was reluctant to miss his rendezvous with Jane. "I appreciate the invitation, though."

"Are you sure you won't? You're a friend of Nicholas Fell's, after all. If I may make a bold statement, any friend of his is a friend of mine."

For a moment, Lambert was tempted, very tempted, to tell Bridgewater why he was in Ludlow, and to enlist Bridgewater's help in the search for Fell. Better to discuss it with Jane first, perhaps. Lambert hesitated and the moment passed.

"Another time, perhaps," Bridgewater said. "Enjoy your stay here."

"Thank you, I will. It's good country hereabouts." Lambert glanced around. "I saw what looks like a fine brook for trout down that way."

Bridgewater looked amused. "If anyone asks, you have my permission to fish it, but I advise you to be careful how you refer to it. That's not a brook. It's the River Corve."

Lambert couldn't stop himself. "You call that a river?"

"Indeed we do." Bridgewater's amusement grew.

"The other one rattles along at a tolerable rate," Lambert conceded. "You *might* call that one a river."

"We do. It is the River Teme," Bridgewater said.

"The Teme might qualify," said Lambert, "although back home it would hardly be rated a creek. But the Corve is not a river."

"For your own protection, I advise you to keep that opinion to yourself. Our traditions are nearly as old as our waterways. I fear you may bruise some feelings if you apply your standards to our rivers."

"I don't mean to be discourteous," said Lambert. "If people in these parts are used to calling a creek a river, I will try to play along."

"Oh, it isn't the people you need to worry about," said Bridgewater. "It's the rivers themselves. Very sensitive, some of them. You wouldn't wish to provoke a flood, would you?"

"You're right. I wouldn't." Lambert took his hat off and bowed slightly. "You win, sir. I've told a few stretchers from time to time, but never one as neat as that. My hat is off."

"I am entirely serious, I assure you." Bridgewater fairly exuded sincerity.

Lambert put his poker face back on. "Yes, sir. I'll remember. Don't speak disrespectfully about the rivers here."

"Not where they can hear you, at any rate," said Bridgewater.

Bridgewater had taken his leave and Lambert had sat down on his bench again. While he had waited for Jane, he had plenty of time to soak up the peace of the place. He put away his booklet and watched the birds. As the evening began to draw in, swifts and swallows came to hunt insects, and their darting flight was all the entertainment Lambert needed to pass the time until evensong began.

Lambert's appreciation for the beauty of the place had dwindled as evensong came and went with no sign of Jane. The afternoon hours had passed as effortlessly as the rivers that skirted Ludlow. Now time seemed to drag past.

Where was Jane? Lambert asked at the fancy inn on the other side of town, the one she'd planned to patronize. He described her. He described the Minotaur. Nothing. Alarmed, Lambert made inquiries with the police. No motor accidents had been reported anywhere between Ludlow and Leominster. Lambert officially notified the police that Miss Jane Brailsford and a motor car licensed to her brother Robert Brailsford were missing. The police were courteous but promised nothing.

Much later, Lambert clambered to the foot of the city wall and sat in the long grass, looking south, away from the town. He ignored the fact that he had his back to the most important parts of Ludlow. Behind him to the north lay the city, the castle, the great sweep of the countryside off to Wenlock Edge. Here on the south side, there was only the River Teme and the wooded hills of Whitecliff beyond.

Lambert didn't care. He liked it there. It was quiet and it smelled good. That mattered more than usual, after the long day spent rattling along in a motor car and then breathing the institutional vapors of a railway carriage, seasoned only by the odd puff of coal smoke from the locomotive.

The time he'd spent at the police station had done nothing to ease his mind. The constables had their routine. Lambert was sure they would take Jane's disappearance seriously, once sufficient time had elapsed. Meanwhile they had assured him they would make their customary inquiries. Lambert took this to mean they would do nothing until compelled. Eventually, Lambert's anger had burnt itself out and, disgusted, he'd left the police station to send a telegram to Amy. That had been a difficult message to write. He'd tried to make it the most soothing telegram possible, given the disturbing circumstances. She deserved to know the true state of affairs, but he didn't want her to leave Glasscastle.

Lambert soaked in the peace of the evening. The loudest sound was the river running over stones, the next loudest, the silvery rattle of crickets, and then came the rustle of the trees. Where was Jane now? What could she hear, what could she see where she was?

The stones at Lambert's back held the warmth of the summer day for a long time. Eventually, the cool of the evening penetrated, reminding him of his bruises. Lambert admitted to himself that sitting in the grass thinking wasn't going to do him any good. Whatever had happened to Jane, Lambert was the only person in the world who had a chance of helping her. No one else even knew she needed help.

Whoever had taken Jane had to have some connection with whatever had become of Brailsford and Fell. Even Lambert's imagination staggered at the thought of three separate and unrelated disappearances.

A prudent man would wait for morning and decide on a plan of action after a good night's rest. Lambert knew with utter clarity that he wasn't going to be prudent. Jane had been missing long enough. Time to find her, and Fell, and Brailsford. Lambert pushed himself to his feet and turned back to the town. The best way to work off his fatigue and aggravation was to take it out on someone else. The perfect frame of mind, he thought, to begin his own search for missing persons. He would start at the Feathers.

It took time and beer, but by last orders, Lambert found a corruptible groom. After Lambert had bought him enough pints and handed over enough shillings to prime the pump, the man said, "The mad lady, right? That's who you're talking about, isn't it? She's gone back to the home."

Lambert fought the urge to shake the man. "Gone back home?"

The groom was scornful. "No, gone back *to* the home. The rest home. The sanatorium. The loony bin. Whatever you care to call it. She wasn't twelve to the shilling, was she? Stole the family motor car and went for a drive. She might have killed someone. You could, easily, running them over with a great powerful thing like that. Her family sent four men to fetch her. They carried her out in a chair. It took two men just to drive the motor back. Big tips all round to make sure there were no complaints here, no alarming stories to get back to the other guests. Bad for business, that. Madwomen on the loose."

"What did the men look like? Can you describe them?" Lambert demanded. "Where did they take her?"

The groom hesitated, as if taken aback by Lambert's ferocity. "I only saw the men who came for the motor. They were nothing special. Just what you'd expect. I don't know what mental asylum she escaped from. Couldn't have been far, could it? She might have landed in a ditch somewhere, driving that whacking great thing. Why do you want to know?"

"Are you joking? Do you often have a madwoman on the loose around here? It's only natural I'd be interested, isn't it?" Lambert kept his tone level. "Lucky her family found her before someone was hurt. How did they know where to look for her?"

The answer was prompt and profoundly indifferent. "Don't know, don't care." The hope for more money gleamed clear as the groom asked, "Will there be anything else you would like to know?"

"No, thanks. That's all." Lambert turned to go.

The groom's interest was sharp both in eyes and voice. "Why are you asking all these questions? Know her, did you?"

"I'm keen on motor cars, that's all," said Lambert. "Saw her at the wheel earlier in the day. Quite a sight she made."

The groom nodded sagely. "We'd best accustom ourselves. Madwomen everywhere these days."

"Madmen too," Lambert agreed.

Reluctantly the groom smiled agreement. "More all the time."

The next morning, Lambert's day began badly. Tired after his night spent asking questions at the Feathers, he reported the answers he'd found to the police, who were hard put to conceal their lack of interest, though they promised him all possible cooperation.

Lambert kept his patience on a tight rein so as not to lose it. When he had done all he could with the police, he yielded to the temptation he'd had the day before and went to ask the Earl of Bridgewater for help.

It took more than a clean collar to gain admittance to Ludlow Castle. Fortifications that had held the high ground for seven hundred years were manned by well-trained staff. No one disturbed the Earl of Bridgewater unless he wanted to be disturbed. Lambert wrote a note to send in with his card.

Forty minutes later, word came back. His lordship would receive his visitor in the library.

As he followed the footman up staircases and down hallways, Lambert compared the massive walls of Ludlow to the architecture at Glasscastle. It felt less like walking into a labyrinth of stonework and greenery and more like walking into a root cellar. The heat of the day yielded to the thick walls at once. By the time Lambert was shown into the library, the cool of the place bordered on chill.

"Wait here," said the servant.

Lambert waited. The library had been furnished by someone who liked books and didn't mind climbing ladders to get to the highest shelves. There were deep armchairs with good lamps nearby. There were two vast library tables with enough curios, photographs, and keepsakes to make the place seem inviting, yet still provide room to work. There was a monumental fireplace and some windows, small and high. Otherwise the walls were an expanse of bookshelves.

As Lambert tried to work out the system used to order the books, the door on the far wall opened. The Earl of Bridgewater entered and greeted Lambert warmly. Judging by the way he was dressed, he'd either just been riding or he meant to go riding very soon.

"Haven't they brought up a tea tray yet?" Bridgewater asked. "Please forgive me. The staff are not quite at their best these days. There was a burglary here a few weeks ago and we seem to be devoting more attention to preventing another than to basic courtesy." Bridgewater saw Lambert was seated comfortably, rang for the tea tray, and settled himself in a chair opposite.

"A burglary?" Lambert asked. "A man would have to be near as foolish as he was dishonest to try breaking in here."

"I would have said so myself." Bridgewater's long face was a picture of chagrin. "Whoever it was, he combined foolhardiness and courage sufficient to make away with a few small things, easily replaced, but full of sentimental value."

"I'm sorry," said Lambert.

"I blame myself. One cannot ignore the changes in the world just because one wished the old ways still held. Now, what is this urgent business that brings you to me this morning?"

Lambert stuck to the essentials. "Nicholas Fell is missing. So is Robert Brailsford. Miss Brailsford—that's Robert's younger sister—came to Ludlow with me to find them. Now Miss Brailsford is missing too."

Bridgewater regarded Lambert with astonishment. "My good man! You have notified the authorities?"

"I've notified authorities until I'm blue in the face. At Glasscastle, I told Stowe of St. Joseph's when Fell disappeared. Here in Ludlow, with three people gone, I can't seem to get the police to take me seriously at all. They listen, they nod, they're polite enough, but they don't do anything."

"Good heavens." Bridgewater turned as the door Lambert had come through opened and a servant arrived with a tea tray. "Foster, as soon as you've seen to that, send along to the police station and let them know I wish to speak with the man in charge."

Without a flicker of curiosity, the servant acknowledged his new orders and withdrew.

"Permit me to talk to the police. We'll see whose face goes blue." Bridgewater poured out tea for Lambert. "But for now, please continue."

Willingly, Lambert went over his interrogation of the staff at the Feathers. Bridgewater was an excellent listener. With searching questions, he brought out every detail of Lambert's story.

"It shouldn't be too hard to trace a Minotaur, given enough time and men," said Bridgewater. "And I think we might have luck with the lunatic asylum. I can dispatch a servant to ask the local physicians where they send their patients. If that doesn't turn up anything useful, we'll send to London for more." He poured out tea. "This will take time, you understand."

"I know. But I'm not sure how long I can make myself sit still." Lambert accepted the cup he was handed but refused the little pastries that accompanied the tea. "Maybe I could ask around myself. Might get answers faster that way."

"That's true. But there is something to be said for being known locally. You've asked me to help. Please permit me to do so." Bridgewater settled back to enjoy his own tea and pastry. "I am proud to be able to help Nicholas Fell and his friends. Thank you for enlisting me in your cause."

"Thank you for listening to me," Lambert countered.

Bridgewater looked pensive. "Can you think of any reason these three people in particular should disappear? I understand that Miss Brailsford was searching for her brother. But what connects the Brailsfords with Nicholas Fell?"

"It's obvious, isn't it? The Agincourt device," said Lambert.

Bridgewater quirked an eyebrow. "Perhaps I flatter myself, but I fancy that if anyone could interest Nicholas Fell in the Agincourt device, I could. I tried and failed. I confess it is his disappearance that troubles me most."

Lambert put his teacup down untouched. "To be honest, Miss Brailsford's disappearance worries me considerably more."

Bridgewater winced. "I'm sorry. Of course. I misspoke. The abduction of the young lady must be our first concern. Fell can take care of himself. As can Robert Brailsford. It is the girl we must seek most urgently. If the police won't detail enough men, I have servants to help. We'll start with Ludlow itself, then fan out to cover every inch of the surrounding countryside. It will take time, but it is vital to be thorough."

Bridgewater's sternness surprised Lambert. "You make it sound like you're organizing a search party."

"Precisely so. I only hope we are not already too late."

Lambert thought for a moment. "You've never met Miss Brailsford, have you?"

"I have not had that good fortune," said Bridgewater, "although I know her brother rather well."

"Trust me, Miss Brailsford can take care of herself better than Fell and

Robert put together. When I said her disappearance worries me, I meant it worries me that she was on her guard, ready for trouble, and still she disappeared. Do you have any idea how difficult that must have been to arrange?"

"To be honest, I fail to see any difficulty. Of the three, I think it would be easiest by far to subdue a young lady."

Lambert chose his words with care. "Miss Brailsford was trained at Greenlaw. Now she teaches there."

Bridgewater's eyebrows climbed. "Miss Brailsford is a witch of Greenlaw?"

"Yup." Lambert gave him a moment to let the idea soak in.

"Ah. I see." Bridgewater chose a framed photograph from those on the table beside him and held it out to Lambert. "My grandmother."

Taken aback by the non sequitur, Lambert found himself examining the likeness of a middle-aged lady dressed in a fashion sixty years out of date. Despite the frills and full skirts, there was something austere in her expression, something like sadness in her eyes. The way she carried her head, the arch of her brows, and the proud set of her jaw were very like Bridgewater himself. "I see the resemblance," he said politely.

"She was a witch of Greenlaw," Bridgewater explained.

"Oh." Lambert took another look at the lady before he handed her back. What a pity photography hadn't been invented in time to capture her likeness when she had been Jane's age. He tried to imagine the years away but he couldn't do it. There was no girl left in her, just the habit of command. "Then you understand."

"I do. Although my grandmother did not believe in Greenlaw's use of a strict curriculum in magical education. She felt the rigidity of her training cost her a good deal of her power." Bridgewater smiled faintly as he replaced the photograph. "Even so, she was a force to be reckoned with."

Lambert could just imagine. "What about you?" Bridgewater aided the scholars of Glasscastle even though he'd never studied there. Did he regret his decision now? It was none of his business, but Lambert could not help asking. "What do you think of magical education?"

Bridgewater sobered. "I think there is more to magic than any one person can ever live long enough to understand. The wise men of Glasscastle have been studying it for centuries. Their efforts do them credit, but how can they truly teach what mankind understands so little?"

"They understand more than anyone else does," Lambert said.

"Pygmies placed on the shoulders of giants see more than the giants themselves. Left to themselves, how far might giants see?" Bridgewater's faint smile was back. "I'm sorry. You must not tempt me to ride my private hobby horse when we have a witch of Greenlaw unaccounted for."

Lambert brought himself back to the point. "Right. So we're up against someone who can overcome Jane's kind of power and formal training. The police may be able to help locate her, but I don't think that's going to be good enough."

Bridgewater frowned. "You say the authorities at Glasscastle are aware of the situation?"

"They know Fell has disappeared. They haven't heard from Robert Brailsford at the time I left, but they didn't seem to find that as alarming as I do."

"What influence I have with them is at your disposal. I'll send a wire at once." Bridgewater moved to a worktable and took up a pen.

"Thank you." Lambert rose. "I appreciate all your help, but in the meantime, I need to do something. At least let me start hunting for asylums."

"I understand." Bridgewater thought for a moment. "You might start with Dr. Hanberry. He's the best medical man here in Ludlow. Meanwhile, you know where to find me. Keep me informed. If nothing else, I can act as liaison with the authorities."

"Well, if you can get the authorities to handle this properly, I'll tip my hat to you."

"Speaking of hats," said Bridgewater, "I'll ring for Foster. You'll want to be on your way."

"That's right." Lambert shook hands with Bridgewater. "Thank you for everything."

"My dear boy, when a man who shoots the way you do asks me for a favor, I make it a rule to oblige him." Bridgewater accompanied Lambert to the door as the servant arrived. "Mr. Lambert needs his hat, Foster. Show him out when he's ready. Oh, and let it be known that he is to have any assistance he requires. Understood?" To Lambert, he said, "Remember, keep me informed."

"I will. Thanks."

Back in the streets of Ludlow, Lambert found his way to the red brick building that held the office of the best medical man in Ludlow.

"If I may ask, why do you wish to see Dr. Hanberry?" the young man who booked the physician's appointments asked. His expression suggested anyone suffering from a measly insect sting could just take himself off and stop wasting important people's time.

Lambert opted for honesty. "I want to ask him about insane asylums. I was told he was the best man to consult locally. Where would he send a patient of his? Is there a place hereabouts?"

Warily the young man eyed Lambert over his pince-nez. "Is this question a personal one? That is, are you interested on your own behalf?"

"I'm asking on behalf of a relation of mine," Lambert said in as reassuring a tone as he could manage.

"There's no need to trouble the doctor. He sends his patients, on the extremely rare occasions when he must," added the young man, looking down his nose as well as over the neat little optical contraption clamped to it, "to St. Hubert's. It's a very exclusive institution."

"I'm sure it is," Lambert agreed. "I suppose Dr. Hanberry must be very important, to get his patients admitted there just on his say-so. I'm sure you're a big help to him."

The young man found nothing odd in Lambert's clumsy flattery. "It is an excellent facility. As such, it is in great demand. I wouldn't count on admission there. Not without a referral from a qualified practitioner." His tone made it clear that the likes of Lambert, no matter how violently insane, would never be admitted there, no, not while there was breath in his body.

"I'm sure only the most select madmen are admitted." Lambert took his leave and stepped out into Broad Street with a light heart. He had a place to start. Find that very exclusive madhouse, St. Hubert's, and he could make a start on the hunt for Jane.

St. Hubert's, Lambert discovered, after consulting his two-penny booklet and asking a few questions at the pub where he was staying, had begun life as a priory. Monks searching for a safe place to pray had built a Gothic masterpiece on a hill among greater hills, an island of serenity in the wilderness, a holy grove blessed with a holy well. Over the centuries, the priory had been worn down like a bar of soap until there was nothing left but picturesque ruins. One hundred years ago, it had enjoyed a renaissance when the spa craze drove investors in search of ever more therapeutic waters. The holy well had inspired a massive building intended to house the sick who would come to drink the healing waters. The trustees would have done better to bottle the water and ship it to the sick, so few wealthy invalids came to stay. In three years, the despairing investors had sold the place to a company that enclosed the grounds securely and turned the imposing structure into an asylum for the mad.

St. Hubert's hadn't been a fashionable facility for long, just since the 1880s, when a pair of London physicians had taken it over and invested a great deal of money in what amounted to home comforts. Since the modernization, the place had become so exclusive that hardly anyone remembered it was there at all. Lambert was able to get directions from his host at the pub. His route lay across the Teme and southwest among the wooded hills, to what amounted to a fortress in a forest.

As part of the modernization of the priory, a substantial stone wall had been constructed around the grounds. The only gate, a monumental affair of mock-Gothic ironwork, was posted No Admittance. To judge from the size of the sign, the height of the gate, and the sharpness of the spikes atop it, the owners meant business.

A court order would open those gates, Lambert knew, but court orders, even when the Earl of Bridgewater was asking for one, took time. Lambert couldn't wait for a court order. He didn't want to take the time to argue about waiting for court orders, either. So he'd put everything he knew in writing, addressed the letter to the Earl of Bridgewater, and sent it from the pub to the castle by way of his host's young son.

Lambert climbed over the wall at a secluded spot, and dropped down into the wood on the other side. The landing thumped the Colt Peacemaker against his ribs. Lambert tucked the weapon away more securely and for a full minute stood motionless, watching and listening with every sense strained.

He was in a well-kept woodland, the earth under his feet soft and yielding with a cushion of long-fallen leaves. The place smelled good, a cool amalgam of leaves and earth. It felt good. Lambert didn't trust that feeling. Overhead the trees interlaced their branches in arches that made a tapestry of leaves against the sky. Beyond the tree branches, the sky was pearly, a high overcast taking on the mutable tints of the failing daylight.

There was underbrush, but not enough to make walking difficult. Grazing animals probably kept the worst of the scrub down. Lambert told himself he'd know what kind of animal soon enough. From where he stood he could see oak and ash trees. The breeze was so slight only the very top branches were stirring, so no rustle of leaves mixed with the intermittent birdsong. The soundless motion of the branches far overhead added to Lambert's faint sense of uneasiness.

Lambert reminded himself that if this place were like the greens of Glasscastle, any trespassing spell would have acted the moment he dropped down off the wall. Since nothing had happened, he was safe to proceed. Probably. Lambert took a tentative step away from the wall. Still nothing happened. He walked as quietly as he could but every step seemed loud in the silence. If he kept going uphill, leaving the wall behind and keeping the setting sun to his right, he should be walking south toward the priory. The wood was thick enough to shut out the long view in every direction. After fifty yards, when he looked back the way he'd come, he couldn't even see the wall.

For the first time since Lambert had come to England, he had the feeling of unbounded wildness, limitless space given up to nature. But for the grazing (done by deer, Lambert surmised from the droppings he found as he walked), the place looked as it might have centuries before. The monks of St. Hubert's might have walked in this very place. If they had, Lambert wished they'd made more of an effort to leave a path.

It took Lambert a long time to be sure that he'd walked too far. The slope of the hillside had changed slightly. The angle of light through the trees had sharpened as the sun dropped. But there was no priory. There wasn't even the wall on the far side of the wood. There was just the wood. It couldn't go on indefinitely. It couldn't stretch for miles. But that was how it seemed.

Lambert arrived at a clearing where the oak and ash trees drew back enough to give him a good view of the sky. Here and there at the edge of the open space were beech trees, silvery columns among the gloom. The sun was gone and dusk was going. He wouldn't have even the fading twilight much longer. But if he had his distances and directions right, he should have reached the far wall long since. Lambert glanced around the clearing, half hoping his bearings had been wrong and that he'd been walking in circles. He brought out his compass and what it told him made the nape of his neck bristle. Either he had gone mad, or the laws of nature had been suspended. No matter which way he held the little device, the needle pointed exactly toward the *N* for north.

Beyond one of the beech trees, from the deepest shade, came the sound of footsteps, more than one pair, shuffling through the long grass. An asylum guard? An inmate of the asylum? Lambert retreated, finding a beech tree of his own to stand behind as the footsteps approached. Motionless, he leaned against the smooth bark to watch and wait.

Two men walked into the clearing. They were young, so young that they looked unaccustomed to the formal suits they wore. Something about the way they walked out of the woods as if they owned them told Lambert that these were young men of privilege. Something about the way they carried themselves was oddly familiar. Their trousers were cut with the slight fullness that undergraduates of Glasscastle affected. Their straw boaters were appropriate to the season for students of Glasscastle.

The taller spoke to his companion and his accent and inflection convinced Lambert that he was observing two Glasscastle undergraduates in the wild. Lambert recognized them, belatedly, as Herrick and Williams, the string bean and the potato who had come to search for Fell in his quarters at Holythorn two nights before.

String bean said, "Season of mists and mellow frightfulness, that's what. Here we are again, dash it."

Potato didn't seem bothered. "All right. I'll give you that one. Your turn to pick a direction."

"Thanks very much. There's only the one direction left. We've tried east, west, and south."

"North it is, then. Since up and down would be impractical."

As they approached, Lambert stepped noiselessly out into their path. "Excuse me. Can you tell me if I'm too late for visiting hours?"

Both young men maintained their placid demeanor but Lambert read the sudden improvement of their posture as a sign of their surprise.

"Oh, I should think so," said Herrick the string bean, with an involuntary glance over his shoulder.

"We were just leaving," said the potato Williams.

"Not inmates, then?" Lambert inquired mildly. He wondered how long it would take the young vegetables to remember that they had met him before. "I thought you might be."

"*We're* not," said Williams. He started off eastward but looked back when he noticed his companion was still staring at Lambert.

"I know you, don't I?" Herrick asked. "You're the American. You live with Sabidius—I mean, Mr. Fell. Have you found him yet?"

"Not yet. Have you?"

"What are you doing here?" demanded Herrick. "Who brought you? Lambert, that's your name, isn't it? What's your game? Who sent you here?"

"No one." Lambert said placidly. "I brought myself."

"Now, now. Let's not ask questions we'd rather not answer ourselves," Williams said to his companion. To Lambert, he added, "You'll forgive us, I hope, for using noms de guerre. It's highly illegal of us to be out of bounds, even between terms, so we'd rather not use our real names. On the whole, we'd rather you forgot you ever met us. But since that doesn't seem likely, we would be obliged if you would call me Polydore and my curious friend here Cadwal. For all practical purposes. We'll have to deal with the impractical purposes as we come to them." Williams the potato, who wished to be known as Polydore, held out his hand and Lambert shook it. Herrick, now Cadwal the string bean, followed suit and for a moment the three young men inspected each other suspiciously.

"I'm here because I'm interested in St. Hubert's," Lambert said. "Just another American eager to see the Old World firsthand, that's me. Now it's your turn. What are you two doing here?"

"We're here because we can't find the way out." Polydore's frankness was engaging. "We thought it would be simple to scale the wall, find our tutor, and bring him to a proper sense of his duty. That must have been yesterday. It seems as if we've been here about a year."

"We gave up on that scheme some time ago," said Cadwal. "If Mr. Fell is here, we can't find him. We've been walking back to the main gate since midday. Just at the moment, that plan isn't looking too clever either."

"What makes you think Fell is here?" Lambert asked.

"Mr. Fell to us," said Polydore scrupulously.

"We may not be Fellows of Wearyall yet," said Cadwal, with patience so exaggerated it bordered on rudeness, "but we are students of Glasscastle. We have our ways."

"You know, I've been wondering. Is it the study of magic itself that gives people airs, or is having a big head a prerequisite to get into Glasscastle?

Don't bother to answer," Lambert added hastily, as Polydore appeared to be giving the matter serious thought. "Just tell me straight. What are you up to?"

"We came to find Mr. Fell," said Cadwal. "We haven't succeeded."

"Now we're in retreat," Polydore confided. "Orderly. Dignified. But retreat, definitely retreat."

Cadwal's indignation rose. "Mr. Fell is our tutor. We've spent months writing papers for him and since January he's ignored us completely. Bad enough this spring, when he hid from us in his study. We gave up on following protocol. Finally we beard him in his rooms and that's when we find out he's absconded completely. To run away is simply unacceptable. We've taken leave from chantry duty to track him down and bring him to his senses. Failing that, we're going to turn him over to the proctors and have him relieved of his position."

"Covert leave," Polydore added. "So we'd rather not come to official attention until we're safely back at the university."

"I told you Fell was missing, possibly abducted. Where did you get the idea he has absconded?"

"You're his friend. We assumed you were exaggerating," Cadwal said. "To protect him, you know."

"Let's not quibble over semantics," said Polydore. "He isn't where he should be, doing his duties at Glasscastle."

"Mr. Fell is here." Cadwal looked confident. "Somewhere."

"How do you figure that?" Lambert persisted.

"We'll share our reasoning with you," said Polydore, "just as soon as you tell us what you're doing here."

"I told you. I'm here for visiting hours."

"Of course you are." Polydore became conspiratorial. "Who are you visiting?"

"Mr. Fell?" suggested Cadwal.

"For all I know, you two are running this whole show and you just told me all that bunkum about being lost to get me to trust you."

"Didn't work very well then, did it?" Polydore's round face grew more hopeful. "You don't have anything to eat, do you?"

Cadwal said, "You can't eat here, I keep telling you that. Haven't you read anything?"

"You ate your share of the sandwiches quickly enough," snapped Polydore.

"Sandwiches we brought ourselves," Cadwal reminded him. "That's all we can eat here. Anything else would be dangerous."

"Through *le Forêt Sauvage* with Baden-Powell himself," said Polydore gloomily. "Just my luck."

Lambert attempted to bring them back to the point. "Look, if you won't tell me why you think Fell is here, at least tell me what you know about the layout of this place."

Cadwal produced a battered map. It was a proper hiking map with a linen backing, worn to the point of utter limpness. Lambert spared a moment's wistful regret for one of the Minotaur's acetylene lamps, and then lit a match.

The grounds of St. Hubert's priory were marked near the frayed edge of the eastern boundary of the map. Neither the dimensions of the markings nor the contours of the topographic lines corresponded to the landscape Lambert had walked through. The match went out and he folded up the map. It wasn't worth wasting a second match on. "Something's wrong here. The map is old. Things must have changed since the area was surveyed."

"Look around you," said Cadwal. "Some of these trees have been here since Magna Carta."

"Longer than that," said Polydore. "Something's wrong, that's certain. Only it's not the map that's off. It's this place. On Saxton's map, drawn in the sixteenth century, this place isn't called St. Hubert's at all. It's called Comus Nymet. Nymet comes from *nemeton*, the old word for a holy grove. Does that give you an idea of how long this wood may have been here?"

"He means a grove holy to druids," Cadwal added.

"Druids?" Lambert suspected he was subject to an elaborate leg-pull. He knew students of Glasscastle took their entertainment in some esoteric forms. Hoaxing the American had to be a possibility.

"This place was a focal point for local legends until the Egerton family enclosed it toward the end of the seventeenth century. Before that, there were all kinds of stories." Cadwal looked thoughtful but said nothing more.

"Stories about druids?" Lambert asked.

"No druids. Not for the last eighteen centuries or so," Polydore conceded. "But lots of complaints of demonic possession, angelic visitation, things of that nature. Stolen livestock," he added after a moment's further consideration. "Indecent exposure. Public drunkenness." He trailed off.

"In short, *le Forêt Sauvage*," said Cadwal crossly. "And here we are in the middle of it. No fire, no shelter, and nothing to eat. You know, I'm not terribly keen on spending another night in this place."

"It isn't my favorite milieu either." Polydore turned to Lambert. "The question is, what are we to do about it?"

"You haven't gone north yet, have you?" Lambert considered showing them his useless compass but left it in his pocket. "I came that way. I think."

Cadwal and Polydore became distinctly uneasy. "How did you know that?" Cadwal asked.

"I heard you talking about it," answered Lambert. "Not very stealthy, are you?"

"We weren't attempting stealth," said Cadwal stiffly.

"Do you think we ought to?" Polydore seemed to find the idea intriguing.

"You've been here longer than I have." Lambert knew he sounded sarcastic but he couldn't help it. "What do you think?"

"We'll go north," said Cadwal. "We'll go the way you came in."

"I climbed over the wall. The two of you should be able to manage it."

"We'll go for help," said Polydore.

From the expression on Cadwal's face, Lambert guessed that Polydore would have his work cut out for him persuading Cadwal to do anything but go straight back to Glasscastle, where they belonged. "If you do, head for Ludlow Castle and tell the Earl I sent you. Maybe you can tell him what makes you so sure Fell is here. What kind of place is this *Forêt Sauvage*, anyway?"

"There's some kind of misdirection spell on this wood," said Polydore, "but we can't determine what sort. Curious, that, because it's one of Cadwal's specialties, detecting and analyzing spells."

"We can both tell there is one," Cadwal volunteered, "but that's all we can be sure of. It's most annoying."

"We've been wandering around on the outskirts of whatever it is ever since we got here. We did a series of location spells before we crossed the wall. We were positive we had a fix on Mr. Fell's presence here before we came in. By chance, a hat of his came into our possession a few months ago. It was a hat he felt strongly about, and we were able to work that link into a most effective finding spell." Even in the dark, Polydore's pride was clear. "As soon as we were in the wood, however, all our spells failed. We have no idea where he is now. Nor can we be quite certain where we are. That's the one problem with a good, efficient form of magic. When it fails, it leaves you helpless."

"You don't need magic to know where you are." Lambert looked up through the beech leaves toward the darkening sky. "Not while there are stars up there."

"Stars aren't all that's up there," said Cadwal. "It was overcast last night."

"Cloudy again tonight, from the look of it," said Lambert. "I don't think it will rain, though."

Polydore asked Cadwal, "Shall we give north a try?"

"Why not. If you're sure it's this way," Cadwal replied.

To Lambert, Polydore said, "You could come along with us and make sure we don't get lost. We could probably use your help to get back over the wall too."

"I'm not ready to leave yet."

"Please yourself," said Cadwal. "Just don't eat anything while you're here unless you brought it with you. The literature on the subject is quite specific." He followed Polydore out of the clearing and the pair of them trudged slowly out of earshot, chatting incessantly.

Lambert started gathering downed branches for firewood. It didn't suit him to go blundering around in the dark. He would build a campfire. That would do for a start. Then he'd see what came to him out of the wild wood.

The fire cheered Lambert considerably. He'd taken care to keep it a small one, just big enough to boil a kettle. Too bad he didn't have a kettle, nor much of anything else.

Lambert spent most of his time at a distance from the fire, his back to the light, watching the darkness. There wasn't much to see. He listened. The rustle of the leaves far overhead and the rustle of the fire behind him fit together in a way that calmed him.

Lambert thought of the bench in the garden outside Wearyall. The music of the chant went on there still. It existed, even if he had strayed too far to hear it.

Could Jane hear the rustle of leaves, where she was? Could Fell?

Belatedly, it occurred to Lambert that now he was missing too. He was glad Amy didn't know it. It wouldn't calm her Lucia di Lammermoor frame of mind any. But maybe everything was all right, with Jane, with Fell, and with Robert Brailsford. Maybe none of them felt any more lost than he did, waiting in the dark. Maybe all three disappearances had as logical an explanation as his own.

Lambert spared a thought for Upton. What would that wise man have made of all this? Ivory spindles and motor cars and a lunatic asylum. Useless to speculate, Lambert decided. A wise man would never find himself trespassing on the grounds of a lunatic asylum.

After midnight, something approached from the west. For a moment, Lambert thought it might be Cadwal and Polydore returning. It wasn't. It was only a deer. There was a moment when the light steps paused, as if uncertain whether to approach or flee, but the moment passed, the steps moved on, and Lambert was alone again in the rustling forest.

Lambert remembered Cadwal's warning about the perils of the forest. He hoped Cadwal and Polydore had found their way to safety. Reinforcements would be useful. In the meantime, he was glad to be alone. With Cadwal and Polydore along, he was convinced there would have been regular debates on the nature of stealth, the need for it, and the lack thereof.

It was late summer, so the nights were still shorter than the days. It was not long before the darkness began the shift toward dawn. Cadwal and Polydore had not returned. Lambert could only hope they hadn't lost themselves again. Lambert let the fire go out. Back to a beech tree, he sat, half dozing, and waited. Whatever he encountered on his own walk through the woods, Lambert wanted light enough to see it by.

"Not that Nepenthes which the wife of Thone
In Egypt gave to Jove-born Helena
Is of such power to stir up joy as this,
To life so friendly, or so cool to thirst."

Night yielded at last. Lambert was glad to see it go. He yawned, stretched until every bruise protested, brushed the worst of the twigs and grass from his clothing, and wished hard for breakfast. Even a cup of tea would have tasted good. His forehead still felt tender but the pain of the sting was gone unless he prodded it, an act of foolishness from which, after the first gingerly exploration, he refrained. The few aches that lingered from his encounter with Midsummer Green and the man in the bowler hat had been submerged completely by the discomfort of a night spent in the open.

When full dawn came, Lambert found it unsettling. The sun rose in the east, no doubt about that, but the rising light showed him his sense of direction had been off. His idea of east was ninety degrees away, so that what he'd considered to be east was really south. Internally realigning his sense of the world with a mental somersault, Lambert made himself accept that what he'd considered to be north had been east. Usually confident in his own grasp of the world around him, Lambert was shaken by the experience. If his internal compass could be so far off, what about his sense of time and distance? Nothing could be taken for granted in this place.

Lambert took extra care to orient himself before setting forth from his beech tree. His plan was to quarter the wood, searching it systematically.

Before he'd gone a single step, the angle of the morning light brought him another revelation.

The dew on the grass in the clearing gleamed silver. But it didn't gleam everywhere. There were two strips, parallel paths each as wide as his palm, where the grass had been pressed down by the passage of something heavy. The distance between the parallel paths was the distance between the wheels of a carriage. After careful inspection, Lambert decided that the marks were no mere cart track. What had passed through that clearing had been far heavier. No road in, no road out, but all the same, a motor car had been driven past.

Lambert tracked the marks through the wet grass and into the trees. It must have been hard for whoever had driven the motor car to thread a route among the trees. Lambert had to cast back and forth occasionally to pick up the trail. As he searched, he recognized blue-eyed grass, the folded-heart trefoil of wood sorrel with its reddish stems, and the straplike leaves of bluebells—all that remained once they had flowered. Did snowdrops blossom here, as they did at Glasscastle, a remnant left by the monks who had built the place originally? If monks had built the place. Had there been something there first, something even older?

Lambert paused when he reached a patch of mud that held a clear impression of a tire track. He could not be sure he'd been that way on his fruitless exploration the day before, but he thought he had. He remembered no mud of any kind, nor any such track. And such a track. Hours of wrestling with a jack had brought him nose to nose with that particular pattern of tread three days before.

Lambert followed the traces of the motor car into another clearing. There he found the Minotaur, with its sheet of canvas still lashed taut over Jane's luggage, drawn up on a sweep of lawn bordered by beech trees. Centered in that lawn was a house the size of the Metropolitan Opera House. Lambert backtracked into the trees to take a long look at the place before he decided on his next move.

St. Hubert's was small in comparison to the hospitals Lambert had seen in London, but it loomed large in its clearing. Three stories high on a foundation that added another half story, it stretched over one hundred feet across the broad frontage, as silent and secure as if it had been locked up tight for years.

Though it was still early morning, Lambert was surprised by the desolate air of the place. He had expected some sign of occupation. Even the mad require breakfast. Lambert thought wistfully of the contents of Jane's picnic basket, probably still under the canvas with the rest of the luggage. They'd finished all the sandwiches, but there had been some stem ginger cake left.

Lambert worked his unobtrusive way around the looming pile of St. Hubert's, staying out of sight. He took his time and it was midmorning before he came back to his starting point, none the wiser about the best way into the building. In all that time, he had seen no one. It disturbed him, the quiet of the place. Yet it was not utterly quiet. There was birdsong and occasionally the soft rustle of the trees. But nothing from the outer world intruded—no train whistle, no cattle lowing, not so much as the bleat of a sheep. It bothered Lambert considerably.

When another half hour or so had passed, Lambert gave up hope of any sudden inspiration. There was simply no good way to enter St. Hubert's undiscovered. There was no bad way. There was just one way. Lambert would have to use the front door.

With great reluctance, Lambert left the tree he'd been sheltering behind and crossed the clearing. There were four broad stone steps before the door and he climbed them silently to try the latch. Locked. No surprise there.

Lambert raised his hand to knock at the rough-hewn oak but before he had a chance to try his knuckles, the door opened. Morning light raked in over Lambert's shoulder to reveal a portion of the dim interior. Adam Voysey stepped aside to usher Lambert into an empty entrance hall.

"Welcome to Arcadia, Samuel. I'd begun to think you weren't coming." Voysey beamed at Lambert.

"Voysey." Lambert stared across the threshold. "What are you doing here?"

Voysey beckoned him in. "Come in, come in. Come in, you must be famished. I've been watching you for hours, all admiration. You really are cautious, aren't you? Excellent quality, discretion, but you can't lurk in the shrubbery forever. Come in and sit down. I was just about to have elevenses."

Lambert considered his reluctance to obey Voysey and cross the threshold. It wasn't as if he hadn't just spent hours planning how best to enter the place. He'd learned all he could from observation. He needed to get inside. "Thanks." Lambert followed Voysey in. "Why aren't you at Glasscastle?"

The entrance hall was stark, spotless, and utterly unfurnished. It was cooler even than the morning outdoors. Drafts stirred across the empty floor like cold hands clutching at Lambert's ankles.

"Just at the moment, I'm here for the Bombay toast." Voysey led the way down the entrance hall and into a small room that seemed to be doubling as both dining room and study. "I can't remember. Do you eat anchovies?" Voysey began folding up the map that covered the table in the center of the room. Within moments, all papers had been cleared from the table to a sideboard.

"Not really. Anchovies are what put me off patum peperium." Lambert took the chair he was offered. "They smell like something you'd use to doctor a sick cat." To his unease, he found himself disoriented again. He thought the cluttered little dining room was on the east side of the house but he couldn't be sure. The matter was of no importance in itself, but his continued failure to orient himself bothered him. "What are you doing here?"

"No anchovies, then. Excuse me, I'll just have a word with the cook. No reason you shouldn't have cheese on toast instead." Voysey left through another door.

Even with daylight to help him, Lambert couldn't place himself accurately. The faded curtains at the windows smothered most of the light as well as all of the view. If Voysey had been watching Lambert's approach, it hadn't been from the windows in this room.

The sideboard looked as if it had been stacked with books long before Voysey had moved his papers there. In the teetering pile, some of the papers were edging perilously outward. Lambert recognized among them a familiar dog-eared corner. He tilted his head for a closer look. The corner belonged to the hastily folded plans of the Agincourt device he'd found in Nicholas Fell's study and given to Robert Brailsford. Lambert felt the back of his neck prickle as it had when he'd realized his compass no longer worked. It was a bad feeling. Familiarity only made it worse. With a deft tug he removed the plans from the stack and pocketed them. He gave the remaining papers and books a stern look. None of them cascaded to the floor.

Soundlessly, the door opened and Voysey was back. "Everything's fine. Elevenses will be here soon."

Somewhere not far away, a dog howled. Lambert cocked his head to listen. It sounded as if it came from upstairs. It sounded like a substantial dog. Possibly even a wolf.

Voysey smiled at Lambert's reaction to the howl. "Cook has a dog. A hound, really. I can't say I blame her. The place is rather remote. It was chosen expressly for its secluded location."

"So you're here eating Bombay toast in the middle of nowhere," prompted Lambert. The plans seemed to burn cold in his pocket, proof that Robert Brailsford had been here before him. "What brings you here?"

"My dear Samuel, I would go to almost any length for Bombay toast if it were correctly prepared."

"What are you doing here?"

Voysey sobered. "You'll notice I haven't asked you that, dear boy. I'm glad to see you. We could use your help. You've solved the puzzle. That will persuade my colleagues that you're worthy to join us."

The service door opened and a woman dressed as a cook brought in a tray. She served them with mute efficiency and left. There was Bombay toast for Voysey, cheese on toast for Lambert, and the perennial, the inevitable, the ubiquitous pot of tea.

Lambert's stomach rumbled at the mere sight of the cheese on toast. He reached for a fork. He'd never seen cheese on toast look better. The dark crustiness of the grilled cheese hinted at the molten texture within. He could imagine without effort the mixed delights of the first bite, crisp yet tender, sharp yet rich. The aroma made his mouth water.

This cheese on toast looked the way cheese on toast would look if it were served in heaven. It dawned on Lambert that there was more to his fascination with the plate before him than mere hunger could explain. He remembered Cadwal's warning and put the fork back.

Lambert's stomach protested again. He steeled himself to ignore the dish. Cautiously, he tried another question. "Why did you call me in for target practice after the Agincourt Project had concluded?"

Voysey's expression as he put down his fork was blissful. "Just the right amount of curry powder. Cook really understands these matters. Aren't you even going to taste your cheese on toast?"

"Aren't you going to answer even one of my questions?" Lambert asked.

"Very well." Voysey was affable. "I was testing you. To see if your interest in the project was genuine. It is. Your help with the project to that point had been invaluable. Now I am in a position to expand the role you may play."

"The Agincourt Project is finished," Lambert reminded him. He remembered Stowe. "Unless you are pursuing an ancillary line of thought."

"Your own words, Samuel?" The suggestion seemed to amuse Voysey. "In fact, I am. One in which I hope to enlist your aid on a more theoretical level.

Now, you haven't touched your tea and I can guess why not. I know something that tastes far better with cheese on toast." Voysey rang for the cook. When she appeared, he said, "A pint of ale for my friend Sam, if you please." To Lambert he added, "No shortage of cakes *or* ale with Cook, I'm pleased to report."

When the pint of ale was put before him, Lambert found it a compelling sight. It was in an ordinary pint glass, but as it caught the light the brown ale glowed a deep reddish gold. Lambert knew without thinking that the glass would be cool to his touch, but just cellar cool, no more than that. Not too cold. It wouldn't do to kill the flavor. He even knew how the thin foam would feel against his lip as he took the first taste, a fleeting kiss before the tingle of the ale itself.

With difficulty, Lambert looked away from the glass and kept his eyes determinedly on Voysey. "No, thank you."

"What may I offer you instead?" Voysey's courtesy was unimpaired. His patience, apparently, was unending.

"Nothing, thank you." Lambert's stomach rumbled yet again, a protest which gave his words the lie. Lambert ignored it. "I'd rather hear your explanation in full."

"How persistent you are." Voysey was benevolence itself. Lambert had never seen him so at ease, so genial. "You know the purpose of the Agincourt Project is to create a weapon. Our enemies build armies and navies. We match them. But armies and navies have been the rule for centuries. There is no winning that kind of footrace. The finish line is not a fixed point." Voysey allowed himself a few more bites of his meal. "We require a new kind of weapon."

"Won't you still need an army or a navy to use it, whatever it is?" Lambert asked. "Some of those brave men you mentioned when we were last at Egerton House?"

"For the protection of the empire, we seek an advance upon the outworn tools of war." Voysey grew earnest. "An evolutionary advance, if you will. We seek a weapon that will aid the empire as simply and dramatically as the longbow aided our side at Crecy and Agincourt. My task—our task, rather—was to choose the most suitable of the designs suggested, to verify every aspect of the theory involved in the magic behind it, to build a prototype, and to test it until it will work as intended without fail. You were recruited to help with stage three of the project. Now stage three is finished. We arrive at stage four. The prototype has been built and we are testing it here."

Lambert thought it over. "Why out here? Why not test it at Glasscastle?"

Voysey dismissed the suggestion with a wave of his hand. "Glasscastle is much too public for this endeavor. Testing requires perfect privacy."

"Why, doesn't it work?" Something in Voysey's pleased expression made Lambert abruptly certain that the exact opposite was true. "Does it work too well? That would be a drawback. Turn it loose in Glasscastle and someone is bound to notice. Nobody gossips like an undergraduate."

"It is a powerful weapon," Voysey conceded. "It doesn't do to take unnecessary risks."

"You don't really believe that you can test a cannon for long without attracting attention? Even out here in the woods, people are bound to notice someday."

Voysey was taken aback. "Is that what you think we've been working on all this time? A cannon?"

"No ordinary cannon, or you wouldn't be thinking of it as an ultimate weapon. But yes, a sort of a cannon. A big one, I reckon." Lambert tried hard to keep himself from even thinking of the plans in his pocket, the plans that made it all too clear that there was nothing of the cannon about the Agincourt device.

"The initial proposal for the project was for a cannon. Indiscriminate destruction administered at a distance." Voysey's distaste was evident. "Finer minds prevailed. The result is a weapon that owes nothing, thank goodness, to the idea of artillery. It is a purely personal weapon, and highly accurate. That's where you've been such a help. Measuring your perceptions taught us much about the scientific principles of accuracy."

Though Lambert guessed the admiration in Voysey's tone was calculated to flatter, it gave him a stab of gratification anyway. Exasperated with himself, Lambert replied drily, "You've taught me a lot too."

"Oh, Samuel, if only I'd been permitted to tell you all this at the start. It's most unfortunate." Voysey put his knife and fork down with a sigh of satisfaction. "You're not going to eat anything, are you?"

"I'm not hungry," Lambert lied.

"Nor drink anything?"

Lambert shook his head.

"Most unfortunate," Voysey repeated sorrowfully. "I suppose the folklore must be universal, if you've run across the notion."

"'The serpent beguiled me and I did eat.' I am tolerably familiar with that one."

Voysey looked thoughtful. "There's probably even some Red Indian legend about a captive princess who is taken to the underworld."

"She's called Persephone," Lambert said. "As long as she leaves the pomegranates alone, she's fine."

"But Persephone didn't leave the pomegranates alone, did she?" Voysey frowned. "Perhaps I've misjudged you. All this time you've struck me as an obliging chap, Samuel. Eager to learn and fundamentally unspoiled. Yet now I wonder. I don't think you've been quite straight with me, as your idiom has it. Perhaps you've embraced civilization more thoroughly than I suspected. Perhaps I should have tempted you with caviar and champagne instead of simple wholesome food."

"Caviar and champagne are simple and wholesome," Lambert pointed out.

"But you wouldn't accept either from me, would you?" Voysey looked sorrowful again.

"Not just now, thanks."

Voysey studied Lambert with utter solemnity. "If I cannot tempt you in the traditional way, so be it. I do have a bit of information you might find of interest. I have had some discussions with the Provosts of Wearyall and St. Joseph's. There is a distinct possibility that with my recommendation, you will be accepted as a student of Glasscastle."

"That's not true." Lambert couldn't keep the note of exasperation out of his voice. No temptation was too obvious for Voysey, it seemed.

"No, I assure you. I'm telling the truth. With my recommendation, you could be a student for the Michaelmas term."

"There are rules. You took pains to explain them to me from the start. Remember?"

"Don't you understand yet? Rules need not apply to you, not ever again. Listen, Samuel. With my help, nothing is impossible." Voysey's eyes shone. "It's what you've wanted from the first time you walked through the great gate, isn't it?"

Lambert didn't trust himself to say anything. His exasperation had turned to anger.

"You've dared to let yourself dream, haven't you? A free man in Glasscastle, the equal of any man there? You would be at liberty, no door closed to you, no knowledge too arcane. Go anywhere, say anything. Glasscastle would be yours."

Lambert shook his head. He didn't want Glasscastle on those terms. To be the exception to every rule? To be there as some kind of curiosity? He'd had quite enough of that. He wanted to deserve Glasscastle, to belong there, and he didn't believe for one instant that Voysey was capable of bringing that about. The best wizard in the world couldn't cast a spell so Lambert knew Latin. No, Voysey was a liar. Easy to see it now. So why did the words still ring in his ears?

On that thought, Lambert remembered Jane's words when she made it clear what attending Glasscastle meant to her. Sourly, he quoted her to Voysey. "'To get up at some unearthly hour of the morning and sing myself hoarse for the greater good of the community? To eat gruel at two meals out of three?' Gosh, what an offer. No, thanks."

Voysey looked amused. "Isn't it strange, Sam. I would have guessed that you would give up all hope of heaven to do those very things. The more fool I. I'm afraid you offer me no alternative, then. If you won't help me test the Agincourt device willingly, it must be unwillingly. I *am* sorry."

Voysey did not sound sorry. He sounded quite pleased. From a black case that might have held a doctor's medical supplies or a surgeon's instruments, Voysey produced a device of ornate design, shiny as a new trumpet. He trained the object on Lambert.

There were a few things in the world that Lambert disliked more than patum peperium and having his fortune told. Pain and thirst and hunger were on the list. But of all the things that Lambert hated, number one, top of the list, was to have a weapon pointed at him.

Before the gleaming object drew level, Lambert threw the pint of ale at Voysey and ducked under the table. There was a satisfying crunch of glassware overhead as he scrambled through the table legs and darted for the door to the hall.

Voysey swore. "To me!" he shouted. Footsteps neared from the passage beyond.

Lambert didn't wait to see who answered Voysey's call. He scrambled out into the corridor and made for the first flight of stairs he came to. After all the time it had taken him to win his way inside St. Hubert's, he wasn't about to leave until he'd had a chance to look around. If he had to hide somewhere first, so be it. At top speed, Lambert climbed the stairs and set about losing himself in the gloomy halls of the asylum.

Flight after flight, landing after landing, Lambert climbed the ever-steeper stairs until the sounds of pursuit had faded behind him. Resolute, Lambert drew the Colt Peacemaker he'd brought with him and kept it ready, cold in his sweating hand, as he moved cautiously onward. It took a moment or two for Lambert's vision to adjust to the gloom. Ears straining, he paused to listen. If there were any small noises native to the wood and stone and tile of the place as he moved up and up through the levels of the building, he couldn't catch them. All he could hear was the rustle of his clothes with each careful step he took, that and his own breath, his own heartbeat.

He found himself in a sour-smelling hall lined with doors, an observation grille set into each door at eye level and a wide slot at the bottom of each, the better, perhaps, to slide a tray of food through. Warily, he worked his way along the corridor before him, peering through the grille into each room as he came to it.

The first room was empty but for a cat curled up asleep on a folded blanket. There were food and water dishes at hand and a tray of sand in the corner. The animal did not appear to have suffered any neglect. All the same, Lambert was disquieted by the situation. He tried the door. A cat locked in a room alone. It didn't seem right. A cat so soundly asleep that it didn't bother to look up when someone was at the door? That was downright unnatural.

The next room held a bedraggled spaniel. The food and water beside it seemed untouched. The dog looked up as Lambert tried the latch, then dropped its head back to its paws as if resigned to solitude. Not a whimper, not a bark. Lambert's disquiet grew.

Lambert tried the third door along and felt the back of his neck prickling again at what he found there. The room held a full-grown deer, a four-point stag. The animal rushed the door as Lambert tried the latch. The thump as it hit the door echoed dully down the corridor. It was the first noise he'd heard for some time and it made Lambert jump. As he watched through the grille, the stag pressed near, great eyes wide and nostrils flared in fear. Each breath, soft as it was, came clear to Lambert's ears. It was unnatural to see the stag so close, so still. Every line of the creature was made for speed. To stand so close that he could see individual hairs of its coat filled Lambert with wonder and dismay.

Something of the stag's unease communicated itself to Lambert. He remembered the sounds he'd heard the night before, a deer passing in the dark beyond his ring of firelight. But had those sounds really been made by deer? Was there something more at work here? The oddity of a stag indoors didn't account for all the strangeness he felt. The place smelled wrong, it felt wrong, and only the chill of the weapon in his hand kept Lambert from yielding to the impulse to retreat. He wanted to hide until he understood more about what he was facing, but the only way to learn more was to hold fast and go on.

Lambert thought of Cadwal and Polydore. Had those young men escaped over the walls of St. Hubert's? Were they still looking for the way out? Or had something quite different happened to them?

The stag stayed near to the door, a most unnatural proximity. Lambert put his face close to the grille. He kept his voice down as much out of embarrassment as caution. "Cadwal? Polydore? Fell?"

There was no response. Lambert rested his forehead against the grille, scolding himself for expecting any. Fancifulness was one thing. This was idiocy above and beyond the call of duty.

The stag backed away, lowering its head for another assault on the door.

"Don't do that. You'll only hurt yourself." Lambert took a closer look at the door, cursing the gloom in the corridor. It made it almost impossible to see the details of the knob and keyhole. Touch told him what vision couldn't. Locked was locked. After a brief debate with himself over the merits of using the gun on the lock, Lambert moved on.

The rest of the rooms held one creature each. More dogs, more cats, another deer, a young doe this time. "Jane?" Lambert whispered. No response. He found one badger and a disgruntled-looking seagull. The last room, just before the staircase at the far end of the corridor, held a single armchair. Seated in the armchair facing the door, palms flat against the fine upholstery, back straight, with chin resolutely up, was Jane Brailsford.

Lambert gazed at her, speechless with relief at finding her safe. Jane gazed back, fine eyes wide. The silence held between them until it spun Lambert's relief to foreboding. "Are you all right? Has he hurt you?"

"I'm fine." Jane's voice shook a little. She took a deep breath, let it out, and said quite normally, "It's just taking me a while to break this spell."

Lambert made a small, involuntary sound of relief. "God, you had me worried." He rattled the lock and swore under his breath. "I don't know why. I told Bridgewater you could take care of yourself."

"Where have you been?" Jane looked happy to see him, but she sounded cross.

"Admiring the misericords, what do you think?" Lambert brandished the Colt Peacemaker. "Cover your ears."

"I can't." Jane sounded, if possible, more peeved than before. "If I could move, would I be here? This armchair has a spell on it that I don't recognize, and I haven't been able to break it yet."

"If you can't move, how can you talk?" Lambert shot the lock out, put the gun away, and opened the door. He put his arms under Jane's and hauled at her. Nothing doing. He gave up, stepped behind the chair, and began to push her toward the door. Luckily, the chair legs had casters. It was slow going but not impossible. Not quite. "You're heavier than you look, you know."

"Fool." Jane sounded cheerful. "I can talk because Voysey wants me to answer his questions. He can't get his magic to work properly on me and he wants to know why."

"Why?" Lambert couldn't spare the breath for a longer question. He had the armchair out in the corridor and poised at the top of the stairs. No course of action from there looked appealing. Jane had to be freed from the chair. There was no alternative. He leaned against the wall and watched Jane as he caught his breath.

"According to the literature, the key is chastity. He can't turn me into an animal unless I've"— Jane cleared her throat— "been unchaste." Her voice was calm but her color deepened as she blushed.

Lambert felt his own ears heat, as if in sympathy. "That's about the biggest piece of foolishness I've heard yet."

"I agree. So did Fell, apparently. Where is he, do you know? Voysey told me he's about the place somewhere."

"It's like the London Zoo in this place. But I haven't seen anyone but you. What's Fell doing here?"

Behind them, Voysey spoke, obviously amused. "I thought I'd help him concentrate exclusively on his research. So many interruptions back in Glasscastle, you see. Very bad for his work."

"Oh, it's you." Gun in hand, Lambert turned to confront Voysey. To his surprise, Voysey seemed to be alone. Lambert leveled his weapon at Voysey. It violated every rule he'd ever been taught, aiming at a man. "What took you?"

"Just recruiting a bit of help." Voysey was cheerful. "Not that I need any, it seems."

"There are two men coming up this staircase behind you," announced Jane. "They don't seem to be armed, unless you count the collar and lead they're each carrying."

"They won't need weapons," Voysey assured Lambert as he leveled the Agincourt device at him. "Not when I'm finished with you."

Lambert dared not turn his back on Voysey to confront the men coming up the stair. "Don't come any closer," he called. "I'm armed and I haven't had breakfast. So don't cross me."

"They've stopped," Jane reported. "But they're still there. They don't seem impressed with your warning."

Lambert moved the armchair so Jane had her back to the wall. It was still too close to the top of the stair to suit Lambert, but there wasn't much room for maneuvering and the chair was too awkward to handle easily. He stood between the armchair and the men on the stair and stared, weapon leveled over Jane's head, at Voysey. "Do you choose what animal I turn into, or may I make a request?"

"Oh, the choice is yours," said Voysey. He kept the brass device leveled at Lambert's head. "The phenomenon derives from something implicit in your own nature, whatever the animal turns out to be. I have nothing to say in the matter. Robert Brailsford turned into a border collie. I had expected something far more impressive. Still, it suits him. Relatively high intelligence, a keen sense of duty, and a glossy black coat with touches of white. My first successful transformation."

"What have you done with him?" Jane demanded.

"What were the unsuccessful transformations like?" Lambert asked.

Voysey ignored Lambert. "He's around here somewhere. Cook gives him kitchen scraps."

Jane growled low in her throat, a sound of rage and disgust muted by helplessness. "He trusted you."

Voysey looked regretful. "Not entirely. By the time he questioned me about the plans of the prototype I had planted in Fell's study, your brother had serious misgivings about the whole project. He meant to warn the Earl of Bridgewater, but I insisted dear Robert remain here."

"Who's the four-point buck down the hall?" Lambert asked.

Voysey thought it over. "The vicar, I think. No one you know, at any rate."

"Where are the inmates of this asylum?" Lambert asked. "What have you done with them?"

"So many questions, Samuel," Voysey chided. "You're not playing for time, by any chance?"

Jane looked fierce. "What did you do to them?"

"Nothing, I promise you." Voysey smiled at Jane. "To tell the truth, they didn't seem particularly mad to me. I sent them home. Let their families deal with them."

"To you, no one seems mad." Jane's disapproval was evident. "I suppose that makes perfect sense. Compared to you, they were probably quite sane."

"Now, there's no need to be insulting. Are there any other questions?" Voysey prompted. "No? Very good." He pointed the elaborate bundle of brass cylinders at Lambert.

Lambert fired. The report and recoil made him wince. Even in self-defense, pulling the trigger made him feel sick. His father's words came back to him, relic of the first time he'd ever touched a weapon. *Never aim a gun at anyone unless you're fixing to kill him.* He turned to cover the staircase, lest Voysey's men dare rush him. There was only one man left. On the step beside him, a rat terrier gave a single sharp bark and then retreated down the stairs, leaving only a collar and lead to mark the place where he'd been standing.

"Missed." Voysey was studying the device, scowling. "It's never done that before."

"You or me?" asked Lambert. He stared from the Colt Peacemaker to Voysey. Both seemed to be in proper working order, which meant there was something very wrong somewhere. To judge from the expression on Voysey's face, he was thinking much the same thing about Lambert.

Jane's voice was crisp with annoyance. "You both missed. He *is* a wizard of Glasscastle, Lambert. You might give him some credit—for an instinct toward self-protection, if nothing else."

"You mean he's made himself bullet-proof?" That was easier for Lambert to believe than that he'd missed at such short range.

"I do. You're lucky you didn't hurt yourself, the way the bullet ricocheted."

"Are you all right?" Lambert leaned over Jane, his face only inches from hers.

Although her fine eyes were full of emotion, outwardly Jane seemed as composed as ever, only the edge in her voice betraying her agitation. "I think so. It's difficult to be sure, since I'm frozen from the shoulders down. I'm not bleeding or anything, am I?"

"You look fine. Just fine." Belatedly, a thought struck Lambert. "Why am I fine? Why aren't I a rat terrier?"

"He missed you, that's why." Jane sounded puzzled. "That must be why." Much more slowly and thoughtfully, she added, "Mustn't it?"

"I can't have missed you." Voysey had finished his inspection of the device. Now he aimed it at Lambert again.

"Careful with that. You're going to run out of henchmen." Lambert was aware of the man behind him retreating a half dozen steps so that he was far enough down the staircase to be out of the line of fire. "I think you ought to worry about ricochets too, Voysey. Wonder what kind of animal you'd make."

"Snake," said Jane instantly.

"Really, Samuel." Voysey's tone was exaggeratedly patient. He sighted with care. "I've taken every precaution." He lowered the device and gave it a violent shake. "Blast!"

"Why, Lambert," Jane sounded pleased. "At this rate, you'll get an armchair of your very own."

Lambert didn't risk a glance down at her. All his attention was on the man in his sights. "What are you talking about?"

"Don't tell me you're a virgin too?"

Lambert grimaced. He couldn't think of anything to say that wouldn't make the guess into a certainty. He felt his face and neck grow hot.

"You are." Jane called to Voysey, "Score one for field testing. Imagine coming across this little problem in the field. This could change military recruitment standards drastically. Not to mention the demand for camp followers." Jane grew abruptly serious. "*Run,* Lambert," she said, her urgency unmistakable as she pushed herself to her feet. Silently, she confronted Voysey, who gaped at her.

"You can't—" Voysey began. "I forbid you!"

Lambert reached for Jane's arm. He intended to run with her. They had to retreat together down the staircase no matter how many of Voysey's henchmen lurked there. But there was no arm. There was not even the fabric of a sleeve to grasp. He pawed at empty air.

Jane stood silently before Voysey, waiting for his response. She was still touching the chair.

Lambert tugged at Jane's gown, or tried. There was nothing to meet his touch, though every detail of vision told him Jane stood there. She might have been a ghost, she was so insubstantial.

"Go," cried Jane, her voice trembling with strain.

Lambert gave up. He turned tail and ran down the stairs.

Jane's departure from her room at the Feathers, mere hours after her arrival in Ludlow, had been ignominious. The armchair held her fast and clouded her mind. She was intermittently aware of her surroundings despite the pins and needles and eventual numbness that kept her helpless. She knew enough to understand that strong men were required to lift her, chair and all, down the stairs and into a horse-drawn van they had waiting. She knew enough to try to enlist help from the servants at the inn. All she could do, however, was sob and scream. The men said she was mad and in the silent faces that watched her struggles, she could see they were believed.

Nothing she tried helped. Everyone, even the men who hoisted her unwieldy chair, believed her to be mad. Nothing Jane could think of disabused them of the notion. Eventually she stopped fighting.

When Jane was locked up alone in her empty cell, in relative comfort thanks to the armchair, she marshaled the strength she had left. She knew of no spell that could hold her indefinitely, provided she brought the right kind of knowledge to the task of breaking it, so long as her strength held out.

Jane settled in to fight the spell that held her. The task required exacting concentration. Jane grew impatient with herself as her mind wandered from the analysis of the spell to futile worries.

Why was she in this ridiculous situation? Who had brought her here? What did they want and when were they going to want it?

Useless fretting, Jane scolded herself, and went back to work.

After an amount of time that seemed like hours but that Jane assured herself could hardly have lasted sixty minutes, the door of her cell opened and Adam Voysey came in. He looked much as she'd seen him last, quietly pleased with himself. In the crook of his arm he cradled a gleaming metallic device about eighteen inches long. It was tapered, roughly the shape of a toy cannon, and had a narrower cylinder of equal length bracketed with it.

There were a few smaller cylinders, some curving off in a purposeful way, as if they had been grafted from an unsuccessful musical instrument. Voysey patted the bright metal tubing with an air of proud possession.

"Welcome to the Agincourt Project, Miss Brailsford." Voysey was as polite as ever. "I'm delighted that you will be able to participate in the field testing."

"Well, I'm not," Jane said tartly. "What do you think you're doing?"

"I'm about to test the weapon," Voysey replied. He lifted the device to his shoulder and sighted through the narrower cylinder. As the mouth of the weapon was leveled at her, Jane could glimpse reflections within, as if there were lenses mounted deep inside.

"Don't point that thing!" Jane could only shout.

Voysey lowered the weapon and regarded Jane with deep satisfaction. "You can stop whining. I'm finished."

Jane goggled at him. "You haven't done anything."

"No, I haven't. There's one theoretical constraint confirmed. Though if it *had* worked on you, it might only have confirmed the rumors about young women who travel alone."

Voysey's smugness snapped Jane's already threadbare patience. "Stop talking to yourself and let me go."

Voysey left while Jane was in full spate. Eventually her voice gave out, her rage ran down, and she let the silence in the room have its way.

Jane had spent the time after that in vain attempts to free herself from the spell that bound her. Night yielded to day. Day gave way to night. Jane knew she had slept, but her uneasy rest was very like the nightmarish hours of wakefulness, so she did not know how long. Night yielded again to day, and somewhere in the middle of that endless morning, she'd looked up to find Lambert at the door of her cell, peering at her through the grille.

Relief flooded Jane. She hadn't known until that moment just how frightened she had been. There was too much she didn't know. She couldn't gauge the odds. But with Lambert here, already working on the lock, surely the odds were in their favor?

Lambert was staring at her as if she were his best hope of heaven. When he broke the silence at last, his voice was so deep and hoarse it was as if he were slowly remembering how to speak. "Are you all right? Has he hurt you?"

"I'm fine—" Jane broke off, horrified by how weak she sounded. She pulled herself together. "It's just taking me a while to break this spell."

"God, you had me worried." Lambert was fussing with the lock. He muttered something cross and then said, more audibly, "I don't know why. I told Bridgewater you could take care of yourself."

Jane's sudden impulses returned in full cry. She wanted to put her arms around Lambert and hug him until his ribs creaked. She wanted to shout at him to hurry. *Stick to the point*, she reminded herself. *Stay calm. First you need to break the spell.*

12

*"List, list, I hear
Some far-off halloo break the silent air."*

Lambert kept an eye out for henchmen, but made it down to the next floor without meeting any. He ducked out of the stairwell and found himself in a corridor identical to the first he'd explored. Doors lined the dark hallway. Lambert knew what he would find in those rooms and he weighed the alternatives before him. Voysey would find some fresh weapon, magical or material, to use against him if he stayed. If Lambert fled, he would leave Voysey possessed of a powerful, if unreliable, weapon. Jane would be at Voysey's mercy. Assuming Voysey's word could be trusted, he would leave Fell captive somewhere on the premises and Robert Brailsford stuck in the form of a border collie. Lambert could not keep himself from imagining Amy's response to that last bit of news. The very thought of it made him close his eyes and shudder.

Voysey had to be stopped. Lambert had been an idiot not to wait for Bridgewater, and a bigger idiot to think he could handle things on his own. An army wouldn't be out of place, under the circumstances. Lambert would have to get to Bridgewater and anyone else he could enlist to help. First order of business was to escape. If he could find a window he could fit through, Lambert would risk the leap. Any disorientation he felt leaving the grounds would just have to be dealt with. Lambert refused to concede that it might take him as long to get away from St. Hubert's as it had to get in.

Lambert hunted along the corridor for a suitable window. Every room he peered into had its window barred. After the first half dozen, he didn't bother to slow down for more than a glance through the grille. Halfway along the hall, he heard music. It was scratchy and faint but there was no mistaking the source. One of the locked rooms contained a gramophone.

Lambert let his curiosity lead him along until he was peering through the grille into a room that seemed less gloomy than the others. The music stopped. For a long moment, he watched the occupant in silence.

Nicholas Fell sat at a table covered with paperwork. On the floor beside him a gramophone was spinning itself ever more slowly into stillness, the melody yielding to the crackling silence at the end of the disc. Fell was watching the gramophone record intently.

To Lambert, Fell seemed almost exactly as he had seen him last. He needed a shave and a clean collar, no question. But his friend seemed completely unscathed. Fell looked as calm as ever when he glanced at the door. "Hello, Lambert. What on earth have you done to your eye? No—don't bother—"

"Wasp. What on earth are you doing here?" Lambert shot out the lock before Fell could finish his sentence, opened the door, and crossed to check the bars on the window. One was enticingly loose.

"I'm Voysey's prisoner," Fell replied. "I was about to say, don't bother trying to rescue me. I'm afraid I'm not able to leave."

For the first time, Lambert noticed the water carafe, glass, and empty plate on the floor behind Fell's chair. His heart sank. "You didn't fall for Voysey's toasted cheese trick, did you?"

Fell looked irritated. "I've been here long enough to die of thirst, Samuel. Water, I had to have. No trickery was involved."

"But you ate something. That plate's empty." Lambert worked at the loose bar.

Fell sounded, if possible, even more annoyed than he looked. "I did eat something, unfortunately, although I cannot tell you what. It resembled chicken sandwiches, but it tasted dreadful. Until Voysey's spells are broken, or until he chooses to release me, I must remain here."

"If that's so, why did he bother to lock the door on you?" Lambert kept working on the loose bar. "It was Voysey who brought you here?"

"Voysey's minions, to be precise. He had more than one man in a bowler hat, it turns out, and cantrips aplenty." Fell added, "I've never liked Adam Voysey, but I must admit he makes a capital jailer, most accommodating to my requests for equipment. No interruptions to speak of. I've been able to get on with my work at last."

"Why did he bring you here?"

"Voysey disapproved of my sociability. He wants me left alone to work."

"Funny way of working you've discovered. But I meant, why did he bring you *here*? Why this place?"

"I can only presume Voysey prefers seclusion for his research. He has a point. It is galling to be forced to stay here, but at least I've been able to concentrate on my work."

Fell's air of conscious virtue annoyed Lambert. "Oh, is that what you've been doing? Listening to gramophone records while Voysey's turning people into animals?"

"Does he have it working now? He's succeeded in turning people into animals?" Fell sounded intrigued. "Anyone I know?"

"What difference does it make?"

"There's no need to raise your voice."

Lambert turned back from the window to snarl at Fell. "He's transformed Robert Brailsford into a dog. Would it matter more if he'd turned the Earl of Bridgewater into an alligator?"

"I understand your agitation but there's no need to be brusque. Voysey has stolen the Agincourt device to use for his own ends, the slyboots. At least he lets me get on with my work."

"He put a spell on Jane too."

"Reckless fellow! What did he turn her into?"

"Nothing. It didn't work on her. He tried to turn me into an animal too but he missed—or the weapon jammed—or something." Lambert went back to struggling with the barred window. Unwilling to repeat Jane's diagnosis, he hoped the heat he felt suffusing his face could be explained by his persistent efforts at the window.

"Voysey didn't miss, whatever happened," Fell said. "The whole theory underlying the device was that it relied on the selection of a single mathematical point as its target. The selection of the point was derived from your own perceptions. How often do you miss?"

"Not very often," Lambert conceded. Strange sounds distracted him from the window bar and he looked over his shoulder. "What are you *doing*?"

Fell had bestirred himself sufficiently to lift the needle, rewind the gramophone, and start the gramophone playing again. "Research." He sat back in his chair but his eyes did not stray from the turntable. The morning-glory flair of the gramophone's trumpet brought forth measured beauty.

Lambert didn't try to hide his disgust. "Listening to pretty music?"

"Listening to time," Fell corrected. He pointed at the turntable. "Look while you listen. This is time, Lambert. Look closely and think while you look. What do you see?"

"A gramophone record."

"Don't be so bloody-minded. Keep looking. Now, what do you see?"

Lambert tried to see things the way Fell might. "I see a disk on a flat surface. A surface that spins. There's a label, 'Little Fugue in G minor.' Want me to read the rest?"

"Your vision is remarkable, but no, thank you. What else do you see?"

"I see a needle tracing a groove carved in the disk to reproduce the noises made when the groove was cut."

"Excellent. The groove you see, Lambert, is a spiral. That groove is time. Time made manifest. I've been looking at armillary spheres too long, thinking in circles. Perfect circles aren't what we're dealing with here."

"Time is a spiral?"

"It might be." Fell's eyes blazed with his enthusiasm. "Under certain conditions, it might be."

With an effort, Lambert kept his voice down. "I hate to be the one to break it to you, but time is not a spiral. Nor is it a circle. Nor is it an octagon, nor a dodecahedron, nor any other geometric form. Time is what we are wasting here. I need help to handle Voysey. If you aren't willing to interrupt the concert to help me with this window——" At Fell's unenthusiastic expression, Lambert nodded to himself, and continued, "That's what I thought. If I ever get this thing wide enough to squeeze through, I'll have to leave you here."

"That's what I've been trying to tell you." Fell's air of mild apology had never been more pronounced. "How little one man can ever truly know another, despite sharing the same living quarters. I had no idea you even knew the word dodecahedron, Lambert. Go, by all means. I'm sorry I've delayed you. The chance to work undistracted is a novelty. I've made enough progress to give me hope. I may be able to alter the imbalance before I yield to the need to become a warden."

With a pang, Lambert remembered Fell's unwilling admission of the discomfort his resistance cost him. "Is it very bad?"

"It's nothing I can't manage. After all, what's the alternative?"

"The alternative is, you turn into a warden without adjusting things first. That's probably what it's going to take to settle Voysey's account. If a warden can't do it, who can?"

"A warden could sort Voysey for you." Fell sighed. "I'm working as fast as I can. It's simply not my bailiwick. I've always considered myself more the researcher than the theoretician, more the careful historian than the clear-eyed visionary."

"That reminds me. Two of your students were here looking for you." Lambert went back to his work on the window. "You haven't marked their papers, I gather. They're not pleased."

"Students? What are they doing here?" Fell looked unhappy. "I suppose I should be glad there are only two. Who are they?"

"Cadwal and Polydore, they call themselves. They didn't want to use their real names away from Glasscastle, something to do with taking covert leave. Cadwal is the string bean and Polydore is the potato."

"Herrick and Williams?" Fell looked, if possible, more distressed. "Haven't I finished going over their work with them? Hell."

"You may not hear from them anytime soon. Even if they managed to escape, they may be reluctant to come back here. It's possible that they didn't make it over the wall. Last night I heard something in the dark. I wondered if Voysey might have turned them into deer or something."

Fell laughed hollowly. "The perfect host."

Voysey spoke from the doorway. "Why, thank you." He beckoned Fell and Lambert toward him. "Since you've been so reckless about destroying the locks, Samuel, I'm going to have to ask you both to move to another room. You'll find it a bit more crowded, I'm afraid, Nicholas. Jane will be there too. If you put your firearm down on the floor and step away from it, Samuel, you'll have both hands free to help Nicholas carry his papers and equipment."

Lambert's heart sank. Voysey and his henchmen were there in too great a force to resist. All he could do was follow Fell's lead and obey.

Lambert was surprised by the dispatch with which Voysey's henchmen escorted them to the cell he and Fell were to share with Jane. Similar efficiency had been shown in the preparation of the cell. Like all the other rooms he'd seen, the walls and floor were tiled. The corner with the washstand and chamber pot was screened off in the name of privacy. There were a pair of narrow camp beds. There was a tray on a small table bearing a plate of what looked like excellent chicken sandwiches, a pot of what looked like tea, and the usual array of cups and saucers. Fell's worktable, chair, and gramophone were moved in along with him. Fell was back at his studies as soon as his notes were in front of him. The one remaining article of furniture in the room was Jane's armchair.

Jane herself seemed hardly able to bear the sight of Lambert and Fell, let alone Voysey and his henchmen. She sat frowning, pale and silent.

"I'm sorry I didn't get away," Lambert murmured, when Voysey and his men locked up and left them. "I found Fell instead. I let myself be distracted. My fault."

Jane said, "You did the best you could. Sorry I couldn't come along. It was all I could do to create the illusion that I'd broken Voysey's spell. I could make myself fade so only the illusion of me was visible, so you would think I was free. But that's all. Now I'm paying for my effrontery."

Lambert remembered the aftermath of her interrogation at the Glasscastle police station. "Headache again?"

"It's not just that. There's been a slight complication." Slowly, Jane lifted her right hand. Her true right hand remained on the arm of the chair. The illusion of her right hand passed through Lambert's arm without any sensation at all.

"What the——" Belatedly, Lambert noticed that Jane was accompanied by her own full-length illusion. At the moment, both were seated in the armchair. Only the gesture of her hand differentiated the true Jane from the illusion. "Did Voysey do that?"

Jane looked chagrined. "I did it. When I created the illusion, I had to exert more force than usual—I assumed I needed it to counteract Voysey's strength. Now I can't seem to undo it. Some kind of split seems to have occurred. Not all the energy I put into the spell is still mine to manage. It's as if something somewhere is—leaking. Most unsettling. Worse than that, it takes most of my concentration just to keep it under my control. Even if I don't try to control it, it's still consuming my energy."

Rapt, Lambert watched the pair of them. "How long can you keep it going?"

"I don't know. But what happens if I let it—her—go? She may fade out eventually, but how long will that take? How much of my strength will she take with her when she goes? I've never encountered anything like this before." Jane's distress was evident in her voice.

"That's why I couldn't feel you, back by the stairs." Lambert thought it over. "It—she can't be touched, can she?"

"No, she can't."

"Can she touch?"

"No. No voice, either. She's just for the look of the thing."

Lambert didn't try to conceal his disappointment. "So she might be able to walk through the wall but she couldn't do anything to let us out once she got there."

"Alas, no."

As fascinated by it as he was repelled, Lambert watched the illusion match Jane's resigned expression. "How does she know what to do?"

"How should I know?" Jane sounded tired. "If I let her go, it might satisfy your curiosity. But what will I do if she doesn't come back?"

"It takes effort on your part to keep her with you, though?" Lambert ventured. "Won't you have to rest eventually? Better to experiment a bit now, while you have the strength."

"I'm beginning to understand how you were able to work with Voysey so long," Jane said acidly. "This fascination with field testing." She relaxed and let out a deep sigh.

The illusion of Jane rose to her feet and took a step away from the chair. The vividness of the semblance paled as the distance between them increased. By the time it reached the door, the illusion was almost sepia toned. The lines and shapes were the same; only the colors had faded. Lambert found it easier to deal with the unease the thing's presence provoked in him if he thought of the illusion as a kind of moving photograph.

"Go on," Lambert urged as the illusion hesitated at the door. "You can do it."

The illusion lifted a monotone eyebrow in perfect imitation of Jane and circled back toward Jane's armchair. On the way, it walked behind Fell, who was muttering to himself, his fingers stuffed in his ears as an aid to concentration. It touched his shoulder, to no avail, and then leaned over him to look at the papers strewn all around him. The illusion pointed at one of Fell's computations and shook its head reprovingly.

Lambert felt his jaw drop. He recovered himself enough to ask, "She can't speak, but she can read mathematical formulas?"

"If she could hold a pencil, she could correct them." Jane was looking more wan than ever. She closed her eyes. "Yes, that's an obvious enough mistake."

"You can see what she sees?" Lambert demanded.

Jane opened her eyes to stare at him. "Apparently. I've told you. I've never heard of anything like this before."

For the first time, Fell looked up from his studies. His hands dropped from his ears and he pushed himself away from the worktable. "What are you doing?" He gazed from Jane to her illusion and back again, dismayed by the illusion's interest in his work.

The illusion of Jane studied Fell's calculations unhurriedly and then looked up with an ironic smile. This time it rolled its eyes a little as it shook its head.

Diverted, Lambert murmured in Jane's ear, "Is that what you're like underneath all the manners?"

"I hope not," said Jane. "I think it's just her way to make up for being speechless."

Fell seemed to find the illusion's facial expressions less annoying than Lambert did. He took up a pencil, found the spot in the calculations where the illusion had pointed, and challenged, "Well, what's wrong with it?"

The illusion tapped the numbers above it on the page.

"Oh." Fell scratched out a line and began to work the calculation again. "*Oh*. How's that? Better?"

The illusion nodded. Jane kept her eyes closed as she nodded her own agreement.

Lambert grew accustomed to the illusion as it worked with Fell and Jane. As he watched them, he felt useless, shut out of the proceedings. At this rate, he was going to be bored into watching the label spin round on the gramophone record. He sat on the floor beside Jane's armchair and let his head rest against the arm. Now that he had time to think about it, he was tired and hungry and his shoulder ached a little where one of Voysey's henchmen had twisted it manhandling him into the cell. He didn't have enough education to be any help to Fell. He didn't know the first thing about helping Jane. The best thing he could do was stay out of the way and try not to distract them.

Lambert shifted restlessly. His attempt to find a more comfortable position brought the sound and feel of crumpling paper from his pocket. Belatedly, he remembered the plans he'd stolen from the sideboard. Plenty of time for a closer look. He brought out the papers and unfolded them.

The plans consisted of three large sheets of paper with mechanical drawings of the Agincourt device as a whole and in parts. The views of the whole, full front and broadside on, were clear enough. There was a kind of a gun sight, a trigger mechanism, and among the bundle of cylinders, one that served as a barrel. The details of the cylinders absorbed Lambert. One was completely hollow. One held mirrors. Another contained lenses. A fourth appeared to be a brass tube designed to encase a wooden cylinder sixteen inches long. This tube was labeled "Egerton wand."

"Egerton," Lambert said aloud. "That's who enclosed St. Hubert's, isn't it? The Egertons?"

"That's right." Fell sounded abstracted. Intent on the joint scrutiny of his calculations, he seemed to answer with less than half his attention.

"What is an Egerton wand?" Lambert asked.

"It's not *a* wand, it's *the* wand," Fell replied. "The Egerton wand belongs to the Egerton family. It's an artifact of supernatural origin treasured by the family that owns it, the way the Musgrave family prizes the goblet they call the Luck of Edenhall. The Egerton wand appears in Brown's *Glossary of Legendary Motifs* under 'Comus.'"

With exaggerated patience, Lambert said, "Since I can't look up the reference just now, would you mind telling me?"

"Can't it wait?" Fell looked up from his papers. "Oh, very well. If you insist." He folded his hands and gathered his thoughts. "Once upon a time, when the forest stretched all the way from the mountains of Wales to the Severn Plain, powerful things dwelt in the deep woods. Some were good and some were bad."

"Whoa." Lambert held up a hand to stop him. "I didn't ask for a fairy story."

"On the contrary." Fell was clearly nettled. "You asked about the Egerton wand."

Jane had closed her eyes. "To be honest, I could use a bit of rest. Tell us a fairy story, by all means."

"Fine." Fell took up his tale again. "One of the bad things in the wood was a shape-shifter. The antiquarian who recorded all this centuries later called the shape-shifter Comus. No proper antiquarian ever failed to trace his subject all the way back to a classical source. In this case, the antiquarian dutifully claimed that Comus's mother was Circe and his father was Bacchus. That's nonsense. Whoever Comus was, whatever he was called in his own day, his parents were neither Roman nor Greek. He was British through and through."

Lambert remembered Polydore. "Comus Nymet? That's what this place was called once."

"I wish I'd known that." Fell said. "Comus was a brute. His favorite occupation was to waylay young women. In the prettified version of the story, published about a hundred years ago, he accosts a girl on her way to market and bargains with her, offering good luck and long life in return for her virtue. This is a whitewashed version of the story, needless to say. In the Anglo-Saxon version, he offers to buy her virtue and when she refuses, he tries to rape her. In every version, the girl runs away. She throws herself into the river rather than submit to him."

"Did the merciful pagan gods turn her into a trout so she could swim away?" Jane asked. "Or was she considered a Christian martyr and venerated at the nearest holy well instead?"

"I'm coming to that." Fell continued, "In subsequent accounts, Comus accosts any girl who takes his fancy. In addition to his indecent offer, he threatens the victim with his shape-shifting spells. In these later stories, only those who accept his offer are subject to his power. If the girl refuses him, he cannot change her shape. In some cases, the girl escapes. In every instance of a successful escape, the girl resists Comus and calls upon the local water spirit for help. The water spirit intervenes and the girl escapes. Through the association of ideas, the water spirit is conflated with the original girl of the oldest legend. We have the familiar motif of transfiguration: not girl into trout but girl into water spirit."

"Poor girl," said Jane. The illusion looked as if she agreed.

"Sounds like an opera," said Lambert.

"Now, much more recently, only half a dozen centuries ago, another girl was waylaid in the area. Things have changed dramatically. Much of the forest has been cleared. The Normans have fought their way to a standstill trying to subdue the Welsh. Great castles have been constructed, including the one that still stands at Ludlow. Law, of a kind we would dimly recognize, holds sway over those who lived in these hills."

"Law." Jane snorted. "*Oyer* and *terminer* for some. Not all."

"Better law for some than law for none." Fell was tart. "This time, when the girl fled the shape-shifter, she did not run to the river. She ran to the local authorities to lodge a complaint. The authorities didn't believe her. In fact, they gave her a month in jail for slander. But the pattern had changed, you see. Comus was still the same, shifting his shape and trying to bargain. But this time, the girl appealed to a civil authority, not a divine one."

"They let her down," said Lambert.

"Alas, they did. In time her sentence was up and she was free to go. According to one account, she turned to the spirit of the river and invoked its power in her studies of magic. She worked to protect others from Comus's influence and for a long time, there are no instances of the shape-shifter accosting anyone. According to this account, when the woman died, her magical powers augmented those of the river spirit."

"What a pretty story." Jane's acid tone made it clear she was still brooding on the injustice done the girl. "So inspiring."

Fell kept on with his lecture. "Another few centuries go by, flying fast as days now, until there is an Earl of Bridgewater in Ludlow Castle, holding the marches for the king. This man had three children, two sons and a daughter. One day out hunting, they went astray, first from the hunting party, then from one another. You see the pattern, don't you?"

"Couldn't miss it," Lambert said.

"Comus accosted the girl while her two brothers were searching for her in the forest. He charmed her first and threatened her second, but the girl knew her local history and she called on the spirit of the river to protect her. Comus could not harm her, but neither could she go free, for Comus put a spell on the girl to keep her prisoner in a chair. There she might have stayed forever, watching the revels of Comus and the unfortunates he'd bargained with and caught. Fortunately for the girl, her brothers were located by the search party. Together the whole group found the girl, interrupting the revels. Comus and his merrymakers ran away, but not before the brothers fell upon him and wrested his wand away. With the wand, the brothers freed their sister unharmed. The Earl's three children returned together in triumph to their father's castle."

Jane stared at Fell, as did her illusion. "I don't believe it. A happy ending?"

"Decidedly so. The wand was held in fear and reverence, counted as one of the treasures of the family, and kept safe." Fell regarded Lambert with great self-satisfaction. "It is now known as the Egerton wand."

"What happened to Comus?" Jane asked.

"He ran away. Without his wand, he was all but powerless. He dwindled to a story for scaring children at bedtime. In time he faded away completely, nothing left but a bibliographic listing in *Brown's Glossary of Legendary Motifs*. No more assaults. No more abductions. The young women of Shropshire have been growing more dauntless with each passing year. They'll be driving motor cars next."

Lambert thought it over. "All right. How much of that yarn is true?"

"Who can say?" Fell returned to his calculations. "None of it, perhaps. Perhaps it's all just a fairy story."

"It must be," said Jane, "if they lived happily ever after."

That brought Fell's attention back from his paperwork. "In fact, they did—eventually. All three of the Earl of Bridgewater's children lived to prosperous old age. We could look them up in the parish records and prove it. But there's a story associated with that fact, and it's not one Brown dared to include."

"Go on." Jane and Lambert both prompted Fell.

Fell appeared to enjoy every moment of the coaxing. At last he yielded to their curiosity. "Very well. This story is not one you may repeat. There is no documentary proof and any references to it are to this day met with charges of libel. Once upon a time, a few years after the Egerton family encountered Comus, the Civil War began. You see, King Charles misunderstood the nature of law completely. He bungled things so badly, he had to go to war against his own people."

Jane cleared her throat and said gently, "I'll explain the origins and causes of the Civil War to Lambert later, just in case he's unfamiliar with ours. You can get on with the story."

"Please yourself." Fell was mildly affronted. "The Egerton family, albeit far richer than most, was no different from many other families. One brother sided with Parliament, the other with the King. There was no way to stay out of the conflict. Lady Alice Egerton found herself confronted with the prospect of losing at least one brother, possibly both. So much is undeniable. It's the next bit that will bring out the libel suits. To protect her family and to preserve the castle they counted as their home, she took up the wand and studied magic in order to exploit its power."

"Where did she study?" Jane demanded. "She couldn't just pick up the wand and teach herself to use it."

"I know." Fell held up his hands to still her protest. "I know. It's impossible. Still, there are all manner of magics and all sorts of wild talent. The fact remains, Ludlow Castle was never besieged. Her brothers survived the war unharmed. Lady Alice was revered for her wisdom and power. The Egerton family fortunes have flourished ever since. Witness the evident accomplishments of the current Earl of Bridgewater, who would be Lady Alice's many-times-great-nephew. The man is Il Cortegiano brought up to date. He has climbed mountains, sailed more than one seacoast, mastered painting, poetry, change-ringing, and eleven languages. Men like him have never been common, but there hasn't been a throwback of his magnitude in over a hundred years."

"The Egerton wand belongs to the Earl of Bridgewater?" Lambert frowned over the drawings in his lap. "What's it doing in the Agincourt device?"

Fell pushed his chair back and Lambert knew that for once he had his friend's undivided attention. "What are you talking about?"

Lambert pointed to the labeled detail. Fell, intrigued, took up the plans and spread them across his worktable as Jane and her illusion craned to see.

"Comus was unable to do more to the Earl's daughter than confine her to a chair. Chastity is still a shield in someone's theoretical framework," said Fell.

Lambert winced.

"The constraints still apply," Fell continued. "You tell me the weapon Voysey constructed had no effect upon Miss Brailsford. That curious armchair is the only thing that constrains her. Frankly, I'd be surprised to learn Voysey was solely responsible for that armchair."

"You haven't answered Lambert's question," said Jane. "How did this artifact come to be incorporated in the Agincourt device?"

Fell tugged at a corner of his mustache. "I'd like to ask Bridgewater that. In fact, I have several questions I'd like to ask him."

"Bridgewater delivered that lecture you attended in London," said Lambert. "Does he know mathematics, in addition to all his other talents?"

"By Jove, I'd quite forgotten my calculations for a moment. Bridgewater is an authority on the history of the armillary sphere, not the uses of it. He may know more of mathematics than you do, Lambert, but I'm afraid I found him a sad disappointment." Fell put the plans for the Agincourt device aside and turned his attention back to his papers. "Thanks for the reminder. I must get back to work."

"I knew it couldn't last," Jane said gloomily.

"I should have known." Lambert folded the plans and put them back in his pocket. "I guess I'll go back to being seen and not heard."

Fell looked up at Lambert, his eyes piercingly bright. "What did you say?"

Jane raised an eyebrow. "He heard something. That's progress of a sort, I suppose."

"You said something about being seen but not heard." Fell's eyes narrowed. "But what if you had said 'heard but not seen'?"

"If I had said that," Lambert answered cautiously, "I would have made no sense."

"No novelty there." Fell stroked his mustache thoughtfully. "Not you specifically, Lambert. People in general seldom make sense. Fortunately we're so used to that fact, we understand one another quite well despite it."

"I'm not so sure I do," said Lambert.

"I've been concentrating on calculations that I can see." Fell flicked the sheets of paper spread before him. "The key was right in front of me the whole time I was watching that gramophone record spin. Mathematics can be heard as well as seen."

"Music?" Lambert glanced over at the gramophone. "Bach's Little Fugue in G minor?"

"Music of the spheres," Fell replied, abstractedly.

Lambert eyed him narrowly. "What are you talking about?"

"Thank you for the idea, Lambert." Fell seemed to be looking at something far away. "Now if I could have just a moment or two without further distractions." His voice trailed off as he returned to his work. A few moments later, Fell's absorption in his calculations could have been no more complete if he'd been alone in the room. Eventually, Jane and her illusion went back to watching for errors. Lambert paced until he wore out his fit of restlessness, then went back to sit on the floor and rest his aching head against Jane's armchair. At least the gramophone had run down.

Lambert stirred. From the pain in his neck as he straightened, he deduced that he'd dozed off leaning against Jane's armchair. He took his time about yawning and stretching and rubbing his eyes. There was nothing in particular to do, after all, but sleep. He just hoped he hadn't been snoring too loudly.

There was sunlight from the single barred window, but it was the diffuse light of a cloudy day. Lambert's sense of direction was no better than it had been in the woods. He couldn't tell which direction the window faced, nor could he see anything from the window but trees. The disorientation nagged at him. Without his internal compass to guide him, Lambert found his surroundings difficult to believe in. He might have been on a stage set or in an artist's studio. The light was wrong and he couldn't be sure of the way in which it was wrong, nor was he even certain why he thought so. The discord of the place was too basic for him to identify. He only knew it disturbed him.

Jane and Fell were still at it. Fell had moved his worktable over to Jane's armchair so that she could see his calculations better. The illusion of Jane was still there, smiling down on them benignly. Jane, looking more wan than ever, was reading the notes Fell held up for her inspection. Fell was looking harried. He'd pushed his chair away from the worktable. It was the scrape of the chair legs on the floor that had awakened Lambert.

"You aren't following my logic," Fell informed Jane.

"No surprise there," said Jane. "I don't think there is any to follow."

Lambert rubbed his sore neck. Clearly, he hadn't missed a thing.

Fell said, "You don't see the greater structure. Perception and will are the foundation of all magic. I can't correct the imbalance until I can perceive it. The only way to do so fully is to find an adequate description of the structure of the world as it should be, our world nested in the center of the celestial spheres. Then, if I can manage to describe the structure of the world as it actually is since the imbalance occurred, I need to exert sufficient will to perceive those two structures as they coincide."

"I thought you said the imbalance is a distortion of time. You've been describing space." Jane could not gesture toward the calculations so the illusion of Jane did it for her.

"Where does magic come from? Why should human perception or human will have any influence over anything? It comes from the juxtaposition of the celestial structure of the world, perfect spheres nested in the harmony modeled by the armillary sphere, and the structure of the actual model of the planets circling the sun. Every true perception implies both.

The degree of will required to employ that influence varies according to how great or small the differences are in that juxtaposition."

"They teach these matters differently at Greenlaw," said Jane.

Fell ignored her. "I can't reset a clock until I know the correct time. I'm trying to juxtapose the model of the world we have at the moment, the model that contains the implicit imbalance, with the model of the celestial structure. Instead of perfect spheres, I'm trying to find a way to use a spiral. If I could only perceive both those structures simultaneously, I'd be prepared to will them to coincide."

Jane looked cross. Her illusion looked mulish. "You can't use a spiral."

Fell retorted, "*You* can't. I must at least try."

"Parallel lines do not meet. They never meet. They can't. The spheres can't be anything but what they are. Spheres." Jane all but shouted the last word.

Fell was patience incarnate. "The spheres met once. Or we wouldn't have had the rift to begin with."

"The rift was created by a warden. Wardens' magic is different," Jane said.

Fell's harried expression returned. "Don't presume to tell me what wardens' magic is and isn't. I've studied the sources. I know what wardens have done and can do, time out of mind."

Jane's voice was ice. "They balance. They don't juggle."

"The greatest warden is the one who does the least, I know. But I'm not a warden yet. I can only use the tools I have."

Jane sighed and leaned back to gaze at the ceiling. Her illusion looked at her, concerned. "This will never work. You're never going to get there."

"Not with these constant interruptions, no," agreed Fell. "Still, one must grasp the nettle."

"Grasp the right nettle, as long as you're at it," said Jane. "Make up your mind. Your use of points seems to be Euclidean. You assume points exist independently of the planes you are describing. That's what you meant, isn't it? But in the rest of your work, your planes are constituted of points. Two different conceptions—Oh, forget it. You could keep a team of mathematicians, real mathematicians—*accurate* mathematicians—at work for years on end and never arrive at a useful model. You're wasting your time here, Fell. You're wasting everyone's time."

"Is that why Voysey has been such a perfect host?" Lambert asked.

Fell's attention snapped to Lambert as if he'd forgotten he was there. "What do you mean?"

"Voysey had you brought here and made sure you had to stay here. But he let you have your work and he gave you time to get on with it. He gave you a gramophone and some records to play. Doesn't that seem fishy to you?"

Fell looked thoughtful. "You have a point."

"If Voysey had any worries about you, it wasn't that your work would interfere with his," said Jane. "He's been letting you amuse yourself with it. To keep you out of his way, I assume."

"Or to keep Fell out of someone else's way," Lambert suggested. "If you had succeeded in getting Fell to act as a warden, would that be something that Voysey could handle?"

"Probably not," said Jane.

"But Voysey knows you failed. Fell still doesn't want to be warden. Who would be the next person to try to persuade Fell to act?" Lambert asked. "Maybe Voysey brought Fell here to keep him away from whoever that is?"

"If that's the case, Voysey wouldn't have shut us up together unless he were absolutely certain that I had no chance at all of persuading Fell to act as warden. Ever." Jane looked decidedly peeved. Her illusion added ferocity to Jane's expression.

Jane went on. "Voysey is just as sure that you'll never get anywhere with your calculations. And there, he's quite correct. You have to give up, Fell. Doing it your way won't work."

"The fact you were able to find a few errors in my calculations doesn't qualify you as a critic."

"Any competent individual could find errors in your calculations, sir." Jane leaned on the courtesy until the rudeness beneath it emerged. "Face it. You're the warden of the west. Accept that and act accordingly."

Fell resumed his work. "A time will come when I can't resist any longer. That time isn't here yet. While I can work, I must work."

The illusion of Jane looked as cross as Jane did. There was a strained silence in the room.

Lambert crossed the room to peer through the grille in the door. The corridor outside was empty. "What do you suppose Voysey plans to do with the Agincourt device now he has it working?"

"The same thing I would do, I suppose," Jane replied. "Apply it selectively until the world ran according to my instructions."

"Is that really what you'd do?" Lambert asked. "Rule the world?"

"I prefer to think of it as refining the world," said Jane, "but I admit I can think of far more effective ways of doing it. It's not much of an ultimate weapon, is it?"

Fell looked up from his work. "The initial idea the committee had for the Agincourt Project was to create a large-scale device with enough range to deliver an indiscriminate transformation spell at a distance. None of this turning one man into a dog and another into a horse. A whole battalion turned to pigs, that was the original aim."

Jane said, "I thought you weren't involved in the project. How do you know all that?"

"I was invited to participate and I attended more meetings than I care to think about before I succeeded in getting myself removed from the committee," Fell replied. "I wish I had sixpence for every committee meeting I've had to attend in my time. Repetitious nonsense. Hours of my life wasted. Hours that will never come again."

Lambert paced from the door to the window. "Wait. Voysey altered the weapon to make it less effective?"

"More accurate. I don't know about less effective." As Fell spoke, the air pressure in the room changed. Although the window was closed and the door locked, although there was no breeze, the papers spread out before Fell stirred as if a wind caught them. The atmosphere seemed to prickle with energy.

"What the dickens—" Jane began, just as Fell said, "By Jove!"

"What the hell is that?" Lambert raced to the grille and strained to see out into the corridor.

From near and far came the sound of many dogs barking, accompanied by the sounds of other animals disturbed. The restlessness in the air built, as if a storm were about to break, but there was no change in light, inside or out, to account for the sense of gathering darkness.

"Is this Voysey's doing?" Jane asked. Her words were lost in the roll of thunder that followed. While to all appearances the world was unchanged, the deep growl of thunder heightened the prickling unease in the air. The barking turned to howling, both distant and near by. Though there had never been a breeze, as the roll of thunder faded, something stirred in the room and Fell's papers went drifting to the floor.

"That's their defensive spell broken," said Fell. He rose and stretched luxuriously. "It seems to have broken the spell on me as well. I gather your pair of truants escaped to summon help after all, Lambert. Well done."

From an indeterminate distance, it might have been from half a mile away or it might have been from just downstairs, came a shout—a multitude of voices ringing out as one. The shout held one note and no more, one sound and no more. Yet the note rang and reverberated, fed on itself, doubled and redoubled, until the very stones of the place sang an answer.

The shout and its echoes ended sharply, as though cut off, but the restlessness ended with it. Silence hung in the still air. So profound was the quiet, Lambert wondered for a moment if he'd lost his ability to hear.

"Quick, Lambert, try the door," ordered Jane. "That was the Yell Magna. If it was properly done, it could open every lock for a mile."

Lambert did his best, but the door was still locked. "Who *was* that?"

"The scholars of Glasscastle. They created the Vox Magna." Fell was gathering up his papers, trying to restore them to some kind of order. "Only schoolboys call it the Yell Magna. Silly bit of slang."

"*That* was the scholars of Glasscastle? What, all of them?" Lambert came to help with the papers. As he and Fell worked, a new sound floated up from below, a fluting whistle repeated again and again, sometimes alone, sometimes from several whistles at once. "And what is *that?*"

"It sounds like a policeman's whistle." Jane cocked her head. "Times one hundred."

"It can't be," Fell replied. "The police force is forbidden to use the Vox Magna to gain entry unless they have a warrant to do so."

"Then we must assume someone has bothered to get a warrant." Jane leaned back in her chair. "Thank goodness."

Lambert went back to the grille. From down the corridor came a fresh disturbance. Someone was singing, a tenor voice holding just one note for eight counts. There followed several measures of rest, during which came the sound of a door opening. Then the note returned, eight counts long.

As the singer came into view, Lambert recognized Polydore. At his heels, the animals he was freeing followed. There were spaniels and pheasants, cats and rats, deer and deerhounds together, each utterly indifferent, so it seemed, to the other animals around him.

Polydore stopped at the cell across the corridor, called through the grille, "Herrick, is that you?" He sang out a single note, an A, and the door unlocked itself. Polydore held the door open while a yearling fawn emerged and joined the thronging animals. "Mind the badger."

Polydore turned and saw Lambert staring at him through the grille. "Why, it's the American. What a pleasant surprise." He crossed the corridor and peered past Lambert into the cell. "You have found companions, I see. How nice to meet you again, Mr. Fell. It's been too long. And how delightful to encounter two young ladies here. Twins, I take it?"

Lambert wasted no time on explanations. "Open the door. Please."

Polydore smiled at his intensity. "I can't. It's locked."

"You can. I saw you do it. Sing it open."

"I'm not singing," Polydore explained modestly. "Technically, I'm directing the residual energy of the Vox Magna. It does sound as if I'm singing, I grant you that."

"You sound wonderful," Lambert assured him. "Caruso should look to his laurels. Please unlock the door. We can't let Voysey get away."

"If it were just you and the ladies, I'd be delighted to oblige," Polydore said. "As it is, I'm afraid I have no intention of unlocking the door for Mr. Fell. He's far too elusive. Almost as elusive as Mr. Voysey, it seems."

Lambert tightened his grip on the bars. "Where is Voysey? Have they caught him?"

"No, but they've found the Agincourt device. It looks as if Mr. Voysey may have turned it on himself to escape the consequences of his actions."

"Not likely," Lambert scoffed.

"Whatever he did, Mr. Voysey will be found. The hunt is most definitely up." Polydore's cheerfulness increased. "Scholar or stag, he'll be brought to bay."

Fell came to Lambert's side. "Look, Williams, I'm terribly sorry I haven't kept to the schedule for your tutorials. I'll make it up to you. I promise I can explain everything. But do please unlock the door."

"Apology accepted. Though it is a bit late. Please don't excite yourself, Mr. Fell. I'm not the one you'll have to explain things to," Polydore said. "There's going to be an inquiry back at Glasscastle. The authorities are very curious about your role in Mr. Voysey's scheme."

Fell backed away from the door as if the bars had burned him. "You're right to leave us just as you found us, Williams. Voysey kept us prisoners here. If he could have turned us into animals, he would have, same as everyone else you've found."

"You found your friend, then." Lambert waved vaguely in the direction of the yearling fawn. "Is he all right?"

"Yes, I think so." Polydore looked pleased with himself. "He was helping me climb over the wall, you see. I'd just reached the top when they caught him. I couldn't do anything to stop it. I had to go for help."

"What did Bridgewater say?" Polydore's guilty expression made Lambert press the point. "Didn't you go to Ludlow Castle to ask for help?"

"I'm afraid not," Polydore confessed. "I was in such a hurry. I just went to the nearest telegraph office instead. I sent a wire from Ludlow and Mr. Porteous and Mr. Stowe came by the next train. They put the Earl of Bridgewater in the picture, and after that, we had police reinforcements streaming in. Quite exciting."

"Can they change them all back?" Lambert asked. "Have you found Brailsford?"

"Not yet. They won't change anyone yet," Polydore explained patiently. "Even if there weren't doubts about whether Voysey is among them, they wouldn't try. Technically, everyone is evidence. Dear old Herrick—I mean Cadwal—is just exhibit A until the inquiry concludes."

"You can't leave them like that," Lambert protested.

"I can't leave them locked up, no," Polydore agreed. "That's my assignment, springing them all. The Fellows of Glasscastle will make sure none of them stray. You'll have to excuse me. I must get on with it." He left them there and resumed his progress down the hall, singing and unlocking, with an ever-increasing flock of animals trailing behind him. Every creature in his train gave the badger a wide berth.

"Hell," said Lambert, leaning his forehead against the door in despair. "We'll never get out of this place."

"Don't be silly." Jane had brought her illusion close to her side. "They're going to let us out any minute. It won't be long until they come to take Fell into custody."

Fell turned back to her, rigid with indignation. "I haven't done anything. You know that."

"That's exactly the point," Jane said tartly. "You haven't done anything. It shouldn't be difficult to explain that to the authorities, should it? You could have taken action against Voysey at any time. He's no match for a warden. But you chose inaction. Didn't you?"

"You're going to tell them about my calculations?" Fell looked horrified at the prospect.

"Oh, I should think you'll be the one to tell them," Jane replied. "How else will you be able to account for your time here? Let alone your neglect of the students you're supposed to be helping."

"Are you that petty? Because I won't leap in unprepared and accept the role of warden when I'm ordered to, you'll refuse to speak in my defense?"

From down the corridor came the sound of approaching policemen. Lambert called out to them through the grille.

"Oh, I'll defend you with my last breath," Jane assured Fell. "Unfortunately, from what I've seen of Porteous and from what I've heard of Stowe, I can't imagine that the great minds of Glasscastle will pay the slightest attention to what a weak and feeble woman thinks."

"Weak and feeble, my eye," said Fell with disgust, as the authorities arrived to take him in charge.

"I'll take that as a compliment," said Jane. To a passing police constable, she called, "Oh, sir, would you please ask someone from Glasscastle to come and break the spell on this chair? I'd be so grateful."

It took some time for Jane's request to reach the right authority. Lambert stayed with her, despite his sense of disloyalty at letting Fell be taken back to Glasscastle without him. It seemed even more disloyal to leave Jane alone with her illusion. There was no sign of the Earl of Bridgewater, so at least Lambert was spared the difficult task of explaining why he'd gone off to St. Hubert's all alone. At last Porteous arrived, wheezing slightly from the stairs. Even in his black frock coat, old-fashioned hat, and unmistakable sense of self-importance, he looked formidable.

"Now where is this spell to be broken?" Porteous asked as he entered the cell. He saw Jane and her illusion. "Good gracious, there's two of you. A *duplicare* spell gone awry, is it?"

"Not that spell," said Jane hastily. "Please let that one alone. I can manage it by myself. I need your help with Voysey's spell, the one that keeps me in this chair."

"Ah." Porteous was already running one broad palm across the back of the armchair. "Indeed you do require assistance." After a moment's investigation, he stood squarely before the armchair, lifted his hands, and intoned, *"Audi me, audiuva me."* He took a triumphant step back as Jane rose. "Rather a complex bit of work."

Jane's illusion sank down into the vacated chair with every appearance of relief.

Jane drew a shaky breath and walked slowly across the room and back, testing her limbs. "Thank you," she told Porteous. "That's much better."

Porteous beamed. "Think nothing of it. Delighted to be of service. I suppose this is a practical demonstration of the relative merits of magic used in Glasscastle over magic as it is taught at Greenlaw, isn't it?"

Jane's smile grew a little forced. "Just so. Now surely your skills will be needed elsewhere. There must be spells to be broken from one end of this place to the other."

"We're letting as many of them stand as we can," Porteous confided.

"Even Robin?" Jane asked.

"I'm afraid so. Evidence for the inquiry, you see. Transporting them to Glasscastle will be a challenge, but well worth the effort. When we remove the spells, we want the purest restoration possible. As it is Glasscastle magic, it will work best to remove it at Glasscastle."

Jane's worry was clear. "Are you sure?"

"That's the conclusion the Provosts have reached," said Porteous. "I have every confidence in them."

Lambert held the door for Porteous. Jane thanked Porteous again as she sent him on his way. Once he was finally out of earshot, she muttered something under her breath.

"Sorry, what was that?" asked Lambert, smiling as he leaned close. "Didn't quite catch it."

"Oh, I should think you could guess." Jane looked up at him and Lambert saw that all the forced cheerfulness she'd mustered for Porteous was gone, along with the annoyance Porteous had provoked in her. She was completely grave as she gazed at him in silence, her fatigue unmistakable.

Lambert looked back at her. He gave a start of surprise when she reached out and touched him, just the lightest brush of her palm against his cheek. Her hand was very cold. Lambert looked at her inquiringly.

"I couldn't touch you before," said Jane. "I've been wanting to."

Lambert felt as puzzled as he had when Jane had let him try the spindle over the map. Greatly daring, he took her hand in his to warm it. She let him, for a moment. Then Jane pulled away and turned all her attention to the armchair. "I promised myself a good look at this thing before we go."

"Want to borrow my penknife again?" Lambert offered, bewildered by her change of mood.

"Yes, thanks." Jane used the knife to tease a few threads of upholstery from the underside of the chair, but did no other damage before she returned it to Lambert.

"Find anything interesting?" he asked.

"I don't know yet." Jane ignored the illusion as she inspected the armchair minutely. "Strange that Porteous should be so sure everything is Glasscastle magic."

"Well, it would be, wouldn't it? If Voysey created it?"

"I suppose so. Still, it was excellent advance planning on Voysey's part to catch me off guard at the Feathers." Jane tilted the chair until her illusion left it indignantly, then she overturned it and studied the underside. "Neat work."

"Just as well it was Glasscastle magic, or Porteous might not have been able to free you so easily."

"It was easy, wasn't it?" Jane said, absently.

Suspicion sent a chill down Lambert's spine. "You don't think he helped to set the spell up? That Porteous knew how to break the spell because he helped create it?"

"No." Jane pushed the chair upright again but she took care to seat herself in the chair Fell had used. "But I do think someone helped Voysey. Someone powerful."

To Lambert, she looked smaller than usual, and extremely tired. He didn't like it. "I think we should get out of here. Find somewhere that the water is safe to drink, the food is safe to eat, and the furniture doesn't have quite such a grip."

"Good idea." Jane rose, looked back at the armchair thoughtfully, and started for the door. Her illusion trailed along a pace behind. "I could just do with a cup of tea."

Lambert stifled a groan at the thought. "Your motor car is outside if you feel up to driving. At least, when I got here it was outside. If it's still there, no one can stop us using it." He felt confident about making that statement. Anyone who did try to stop them would have one cross American to reckon with.

"I can drive. If I can rely on you to manage the crank for me to start her up?"

"Of course." Lambert held the door for both Jane and her illusion. "What about your double? Hadn't you better do something about it before anyone takes fright or decides to see a doctor about his eyes?"

"She might prove useful," said Jane. "I'm going to need a chaperon, after all. Anyway, at this point, it will take more strength to end the illusion than to continue it. Best to wait until we're safe somewhere and the driving is finished before I make up my mind. I've grown rather fond of her."

"Strange to say, so have I," said Lambert. "She's very restful company."

Jane's illusion looked pleased.

It was blue twilight by the time Jane settled herself behind the wheel of the Minotaur. The illusion was with her, a faint sapping of her concentration that went almost unnoticed in the wide variety of Jane's more physical discomforts. She was hungry and thirsty and dirty and tired and sore, she'd come close to making a fool of herself with Lambert, and worst of all, her clothes were a disgrace. No question about it. Informal travel did not agree with her. Perhaps it was a bad idea, a motor car of her own. Perhaps she should avoid all travel in the future. Perhaps she should find her way back to Greenlaw and stay there, term in and term out. Travel was simply not worth the filth and fatigue.

Lambert was rummaging in the wicker chests stowed in the back. Just as Jane was about to ask what on earth he thought he was doing, he returned.

"Split it with you?" Lambert was holding out the last of the stem ginger cake, darkly sticky in the paper wrapping.

"Oh! Yes, please." Glad she'd managed to restrain the urge to carp, Jane seized her half and ate it greedily. Heedless of the breach of etiquette, she even licked her fingers afterward. It put heart into her, but she dearly wished for a decent cup of tea to accompany it. "That was delicious. Thank you."

"As good as I thought it would taste," said Lambert, and went to light the lamps fore and aft. He cranked industriously until the motor caught, and slid in beside her. "And I thought of it a lot."

"I thought of soap and hot water," Jane confessed.

There wasn't enough light left to see it clearly, but from the smile in his voice, Jane could tell Lambert's mouth had crooked up at the corner. "I could use a dose of that too. Let's go find some."

Jane felt uncomfortably exposed, driving without hat, veil, goggles or gloves, but she didn't want to waste another moment searching for her things. Even with acetylene lamps ablaze, and half the scholars of Glasscastle on hand to counter the misdirection spell on the place, Jane found it difficult to thread her way between the trees to the gate.

Only when the Minotaur was purring along the road to Ludlow did Jane dare to relax her grip on the wheel and drive more naturally. "Comus Nymet. Thank goodness we've seen the last of that place."

"Have we?" Lambert sounded skeptical.

"If I have anything to say about it, we have. Beastly place." Jane took a turn with such care she had to downshift to compensate for her loss of speed. Despite the relief she felt at being free of the crooked house in the crooked wood, she knew she was losing her strength rapidly. "I wish we'd seen the last of Ludlow too, but I don't think I can drive much farther."

"Ludlow will be fine." Lambert's calm was reassuring. "I'd like to have a word with Bridgewater if he's back at the castle there. Thank him for his help."

Jane took a firm line. "If you go, you go without me. I'm much too filthy to meet anyone at the moment. One look at me, and his lordship's servants would send for the police."

"You may have a point there. We'll have to find rooms somewhere, then."

"I refuse to stay at the Feathers again. It will have to be the Angel for me. Where would you like me to put you down?" Jane asked Lambert.

"Nowhere." Lambert's voice was calm but firm. "I'll find another pub after we get you settled at the Angel."

There were some points Jane was never too tired to argue and propriety was one of them. "It will be far better if I arrive alone."

"It would be, but you aren't alone, are you? As long as you have your double to attract attention, who's going to notice me?"

Jane had been almost unconscious of her illusion, who was now driving the Minotaur with her, coinciding in every detail but for the fact that Jane was windblown and dusty and the illusion wasn't. "You have a point. I'll have to keep her with me exactly and stay in the shadows myself."

"Good idea." Lambert was calmer than ever. "I'll do the talking. If the place passes muster, I'll even help bring up your luggage. But you're staying nowhere unless I get a good look at the armchairs first."

As good as his word, Lambert inspected the room he booked for Jane, supervised the arrival of her luggage, and left to see to the safe disposition of the Minotaur before heading to his own rest.

By the time she and her illusion were alone in her room, Jane was so tired that fifty enchanted armchairs could not have kept her awake. She performed a sketchy toilet and retired. Never had a mattress felt so comfortable, nor an eiderdown so soft.

*"Be with his bare wand can unthread thy joints,
And crumble all thy sinews."*

It was late morning, bright, breezy, and cool, when Lambert returned to the Angel Inn, the second-best hostelry in Ludlow. Lambert had chosen to spend the night in plainer surroundings, opting to hire a room, tiny but spotless, over another pub. Breakfast at the pub had been wonderful. Portions were substantial. Everything that was supposed to be hot and crisp had been hot and crisp. Everything that was supposed to be steaming and strong had been steaming and strong. Everything that didn't come with butter came with cream.

After his meal, Lambert felt qualified to face fresh perils, including Bridgewater's staff. His call at Ludlow Castle was fruitless, however. His lordship was not at home, the butler informed Lambert. Lambert wrote a note of thanks and left it for the butler to deliver. Probably just as well. Lambert didn't like to leave Jane to her own devices for too long.

When Lambert joined her, Jane was supervising the rearrangement of her luggage in the back of the vehicle. Her illusion was on hand, though it was careful to stay quite still and keep in the deepest shade. Lambert was glad to see that yesterday's exhausted girl with the cold hands was gone. After a good rest, Jane looked her usual self again, brisk and bright. She was sporting her full motoring regalia, tinted goggles and all.

Lambert greeted her as she tipped the groom who had been helping with the luggage. "You look wonderful, Miss Brailsford."

"Thank you. In fact, I do feel a bit full of wonder." Jane paused to admire the morning. "Sometimes on days like this, I feel I could move mountains, or at least rearrange them in a more becoming pattern."

"I take that as proof that you slept well and had a good breakfast." Lambert moved to the front of the vehicle, preparing to do his duty at the crank. "All settled up and ready to go back home?"

"All settled up," agreed Jane. She walked into the shade and let her illusion walk out with her, discreetly coinciding in every detail as she climbed into the driver's seat. "Ready to go back to Glasscastle?"

Lambert cranked until the motor turned over and then took the passenger seat. "Not your home, Glasscastle. I understand. Where is home for you?"

Jane's eyes, intent behind her goggles, held his for a long moment. "For now, Greenlaw is my home. Where is your home?"

"For now?" Lambert hesitated. Already his work at Glasscastle had come to an official end. Before the day was over, he might see its unofficial end. Yet something in his heart made Lambert answer finally, "Glasscastle. For a little while longer."

"And after that?" Jane's eyes were as gentle as her voice.

"I don't know." Lambert made himself smile. "I'll have to see."

Jane smiled back. "Sometimes I catch myself thinking it's such a pity you are a man. But then again——" She broke off, as if taken aback by what she had been about to say.

"Then again, what?" Lambert looked at her curiously.

All Jane's attention was on the motor car as she put the Minotaur into gear and started on her way. A bit gruffly, she answered, "Then again, maybe it isn't."

That it was not quite five o'clock when the Minotaur drew up at the great gate of Glasscastle owed more to Jane's utter disregard for the laws against driving to the common danger than it did to Lambert's navigation. Their traveling luck had improved, Lambert decided.

"At last." Jane, her illusion held so close a casual onlooker couldn't see it, was out of the dusty vehicle as soon as she'd shut off the engine. She pulled off her goggles and ran to the gatekeeper. At the gatekeeper's refusal, she turned to beckon Lambert to sign for her admittance.

Lambert followed more slowly. "Are you sure you want to leave the Minotaur right there by the bench?"

"It will be fine there for the moment." Jane composed herself while Lambert signed the visitors' book, but impatience shimmered around her like heat off a roof. "I must see Robin as soon as possible."

"We don't even know that they've brought them all back yet. That was a lot of livestock for anyone to move," Lambert pointed out. "Mixed stock, at that." He was just glad he wasn't the man in charge of the herd.

The gatekeeper spoke up. "The transformations, you mean? They're back. Came by special train last night. They've been quartered on Midsummer Green. It took hours to change the trespassing spell so they would all be safe on the grass. Quite a sight, it is. There's no end to the number of would-be gawkers I've had to turn away." The gatekeeper's expression made it clear that he would be only too glad of an excuse to turn Lambert and Jane away too.

"Excellent. Good work. Keep it up." Jane swept Lambert after her through the arch. Once inside Glasscastle, she stopped in her tracks. "Oh, dear."

Before them, scattered across Midsummer Green, tranquil in the steeply angled shadows and deep golden sunlight of the summer afternoon, were the denizens of St. Hubert's. There were not just deer, cats, rats, and dogs of every description. There was a badger, a seagull, several hedgehogs, and a fox. The serenity that kept them in place was as palpable as the scent of fresh-cut grass, a drowsiness that was almost audible in the perfect silence. They were people shaped like animals, not true animals at all, but they were remarkably calm people.

A handful of undergraduates displayed the only signs of energy. Prompt to exploit the novelty of being able to walk on the grass, they'd brought cricket gear and set up an impromptu pitch. Play had not yet commenced, due to a spirited disagreement over who would umpire.

Caught up in the peace of the place, Lambert started to yawn and stifled it. "What a spectacle. All we lack are some of the buffalo from the show."

Porteous, carrying a black leather satchel the size of a violin case, joined them in time to overhear Lambert. "It does resemble one of the more detailed Netherlandish *Adorations of the Lamb*, does it not?" Porteous paused to reconsider. "Perhaps I mean *Adoration of the Lambs*. No. I certainly do not. Adorations, definitely."

"Is that Robin with Amy?" Jane asked, at the same moment Lambert asked, "Where's Voysey?"

"Please." Porteous held up his hands. "One at a time." To Jane, he said, "I believe that is your brother, *couchant* just over there." He pointed to a black-and-white border collie lying at the feet of Amy Brailsford, who was sitting on the grass, resplendent in white linen. "We sent for her. We thought your brother would prefer it that way." To Lambert, he said, "We aren't positive by any means, but we think Voysey is the fox." Porteous patted the satchel at his side. "We're safe enough. He'll not get at that infernal device of his again."

"Where's Fell?" Lambert and Jane asked together.

"Now that's a curious thing. We took him under our care, for his own protection, you understand?" Porteous paused to make sure that they did indeed understand. "But now we can't seem to find him anywhere."

Jane and Lambert exchanged horrified looks.

Porteous looked rather horrified himself. "Yes, I know. He can't have escaped on his own. Someone must have helped him." He hailed Jack Meredith as he passed. "Any sign of Fell yet?"

"Hello, James." Meredith answered Porteous as if he were the only one there. "They're still searching the Holythorn quad, but no. Not yet. Another hour, perhaps." He walked away without waiting for more questions.

"That's strange." Porteous was looking at his pocket watch. "It's past five o'clock. Did you hear the bells strike the hour?"

Lambert ignored the older man's fussing, annoyed at the way Meredith had given him the cut direct. The message was clear. Now that the Agincourt Project was over, now that he was of no immediate use to Glasscastle, Lambert was no longer of any interest to Meredith.

"My dear child, what are you doing?" Porteous was staring at Jane with a combination of outrage and repulsion. "You assured me you could manage your *duplicare* spell by yourself."

Lambert put Meredith's discourtesy out of his mind and turned back to see that both Jane and her illusion were now clearly visible. The illusion was frightened. It had already faded to sepia, and was walking rapidly away from Jane across the velvety turf of Midsummer Green.

The effort it took to exercise her magic within Glasscastle had turned Jane herself pale. She was ashen, as white as whey under her veil. Plaintively, she tried to call her illusion back. The illusion walked on, ignoring her. Jane gave up and followed it across the green.

"See here, you can't do that," Porteous called after her. He turned to Lambert. "She can't *do* that."

But Jane was following the illusion toward the quadrangle in front of Wearyall. Both were walking, but the illusion was walking faster. It moved with the air of someone who was being pushed along by a high wind, or pulled along against her will. The hem and cuffs of the motoring coat it wore, a faded duplicate of Jane's, seemed to flutter and blur at the edges, as if some unseen force consumed them. Jane followed, first on grass and then on gravel.

Lambert saw what was coming and felt every bruise he carried come to life in empathy. The spell on Midsummer Green had been adjusted, but every other green in Glasscastle was as dangerous as ever.

Lambert grasped Porteous by the elbow and jostled him after Jane and her illusion. "Come on. The illusion can walk on the grass of any green, not just Midsummer. Jane can't. Unless you catch up with Jane, the illusion will give Jane the slip when she can't go any farther without a Fellow of Glasscastle as escort."

Protesting vigorously as the satchel banged his thigh every step of the way, Porteous yielded to Lambert's urging. "It's past five o'clock," he protested.

"It's been a long day for me too," Lambert replied, "but you have to keep up with Jane."

"You don't understand. Listen!" Porteous shook off Lambert's grip and sketched a gesture that took in all of Glasscastle. "Why have the bells stopped?"

At last, Lambert noticed the silence. The drowsy serenity of Midsummer Green grew deeper still as they skirted the quadrangle in front of Wearyall College. "I don't know why. Just hurry up." Lambert hustled Porteous along at a half run that brought them to Jane's side.

"No chanting, either. This is bad," said Porteous. "This is very bad."

Lambert kept after him. "I don't care. Keep going."

It was all too easy to keep up with Jane now. Her pursuit of the illusion had flagged until she could hardly take two steps together. The illusion cut across the green of St. Joseph's quadrangle and increased its lead. Lambert let Porteous go and took Jane's arm. He felt her sag against him, still walking, but only with his help. Her breath was coming fast and shallow, her skin waxen and damp with sweat. Lambert tried to halt her. Jane forged on.

"Easy, Jane." Lambert steadied her. "Just hold up for a minute. Catch your breath before you go on."

Jane's words came out in gasps. "I can't. She *pulls*. She's draining me." She staggered on, panting.

"Something's wrong," said Porteous. "No bells. No chanting. That means something's gone wrong with the wards themselves."

Together they followed Jane's illusion through the gates of the botanical gardens, through the sudden chill shade of the triumphal arch, and into the sun-baked afternoon heat of the herb garden. The illusion, now pale almost to invisibility, moved faster as it crossed the rose garden to the second gate. They lost it for a moment, too faint to see in the dark blue shadows of late afternoon, but when they joined it in the walled labyrinth, there it was, moving swiftly through the pattern of the boxwood hedges.

Lambert stopped at the mouth of the labyrinth. When he had accompanied Fell there, days before, the hum of Glasscastle's wards had been a steady drone, a single constant note. Now there was utter silence. No hum. No bells. No birdsong. Lambert's heart sank.

"The wards are down," said Porteous. He sounded as if he were praying. "The whole place is open."

Jane dropped to the ground at Lambert's feet.

Lambert knelt beside her. "What's wrong?"

Jane's eyes were terrible. "It's too strong."

"*What* is?"

"The drain. It—pulls." Jane made a dreadful soft sound—pain stifled. "It has her now."

Lambert looked up from Jane to see where the illusion was. He had to rise to his feet to see over the boxwood hedges. Difficult to be sure, for by this time the illusion was little more than a troubling of the air, but he thought he saw it move into the hexagonal center of the labyrinth as it faded completely. Eyes strained to catch further sight of the illusion, Lambert realized he could see, drifting in the center of the labyrinth, what he had never beheld before.

Glassy, transparent, visible only as their motion caught the angled sunlight, barriers drifted around the hexagonal heart of the labyrinth. Walls hitherto unguessed-at were there, hidden in light, revealed by light. Lambert watched as they shifted, stately as clouds drifting across the sky on a fine afternoon. He perceived that the full scope of the maze took in not only the labyrinth itself and the garden that surrounded it but the stones and spires of all Glasscastle, university and town alike. The walls were held within walls, barriers within barriers, as neatly as the rings of an armillary sphere nested.

The illusion had moved into the precise center of the labyrinth as it disappeared. Where had it gone? *Had* it gone?

Lambert kept his eyes fixed on the hints of light that showed where the barriers were drifting. He did not look down as he stepped into the pattern of the maze. He did not spare a thought for Porteous, left beside Jane. The gleam of the transparent barriers was all that drew him. At last, he would see the heart of Glasscastle.

No bells, no birdsong, and no sense of time passed as Lambert made his way to the center of the labyrinth. He might have crossed it in a few strides, the journey went so quickly. He might have been crossing it for years. Rapt, he set foot on the flagstones at the edge of the central hexagon. He felt the scrape of them beneath his boots, yet he saw no flagstones. The hexagon before him was open to the sky, a well of green translucent glass that fell away out of light into unimaginable shadows. But the well was not empty.

When he looked down, Lambert felt his heart lurch with dread and with surprise. Below him, six feet down and drifting slowly downward, Fell was caught in the translucence of the well. Holding him there, gathering power as he gathered light, was the Earl of Bridgewater.

Bridgewater was more Merlin than Arthur now, with his hat gone and his silver-streaked hair flowing almost to his collar. He grappled Fell to him, using both height and strength to subdue his captive. Bridgewater spoke slowly, with great effort, as if to soothe Fell. "Steady. Nearly ready now."

Jane's illusion was gone. Forever gone. Lambert knew it without knowing how. The drowsing silence had pulled it to Bridgewater and Bridgewater had consumed it. Much of Jane's strength had gone with the illusion, strength that now belonged to Bridgewater. More strength was going, pulled inexorably into Bridgewater's light.

Lambert knew without analysis that Glasscastle itself was adrift, its power and serenity pulled into Bridgewater's orbit. As the transparent barriers continued to drift, gleaming in the fading daylight all around him, Lambert knew that Fell was adrift too. Bridgewater held him fast. It was Bridgewater's grasp of Fell's strength that had given him the foothold he needed to win Glasscastle. There was a piece of Bridgewater's magic in everything, and every tendril it sent forth was a taproot, draining the magic, drawing it back for Bridgewater's use.

Lambert could see it all in the way Bridgewater held Fell, a puppeteer with his puppet well in hand. Lambert could see it all in the way Fell blinked up at him, as if blinded by dazzling light.

Fell's voice was a rasp of pain, a husk of sound. Only the acoustics of the well gave the words strength enough to reach the surface. "Samuel, are you there?"

From childhood memory, a scriptural reference stirred and surfaced. Lambert knew the books of Samuel, his namesake, best of all. The mere recollection calmed him: *The Lord called Samuel and he answered: Here am I.* "Here am I. Hang on." Lambert found himself short of breath. "Just hang on."

Not a rasp. A scrape. "I will. But you——" The voice hesitated, grew minutely stronger. "You must hurry. Kill me before he gets it all."

Fell's words struck Lambert like a blow. *Kill* Fell?

Bridgewater tightened his hold on Fell.

Fell made a sound. It was not a word. It wasn't even the shape of a word. It was a sound of pain, frustration, and despair. After that sound, there was nothing. Only silence.

Still Lambert hesitated. The silence grew. The light was fading. Even as Lambert watched, Fell and Bridgewater sank farther out of sight into the depths of the well. He tried to say "Hang on" again but the words didn't come. His mouth was dry. His eyes were wet.

There was only silence. No chanting. No bells. No birdsong. Lambert turned and ran. All he saw was the labyrinth before him. All he heard were his own swift footsteps. That and the scrape of his panting breath, the beat of his leaping heart as he raced from the core of the labyrinth to the labyrinth's mouth.

At the labyrinth's entrance, Lambert tripped over Porteous, who was still leaning over Jane. "My dear child," the booming voice beseeched. "My dear child, you must try to breathe. That's it. *Try.*"

Lambert dared not spare a glance at Jane. He ignored Porteous and went straight for the black satchel. The latch yielded to force and he pulled the two halves of the top apart with a snap, as if opening a doctor's medical bag.

The Agincourt device, absurdly ornate, lay gleaming within. Lambert clawed it out, turned it over in his hands, hefted it, and looked through the sight. The image was inverted. Very disconcerting, to see the world turned upside down. From the outside, the device seemed just as he remembered it. He wished he'd had a better view when Voysey had aimed it at him.

To Porteous, Lambert snapped, "Have you disarmed this thing?"

Porteous gaped at him. "No. We don't know how. We haven't had time to learn."

Before Porteous had finished speaking, Lambert was back in the maze. He wanted to hurdle the hedges, to cheat the long switchbacks, but he knew better than to try to cut corners. There was meaning in the intervals of the pattern, just as there was meaning in the intervals of St. Mary's arches, and meaning in the intervals of the chants.

Lambert ran as fast as he could through the maze. This was a pattern he understood. He knew he had to stick to it, every step. It was part of the game. Just as in baseball the infielders threw the ball around the horn after a putout, each putout a different pattern but every pattern counterclockwise; just as the third baseman, and only the third baseman, was to touch the ball last on the return to the pitcher, this was inevitable, a pattern he knew to the marrow of his bones.

It mattered that Lambert follow the pattern. It mattered that he take each step in its proper order. The desire to break the pattern was part of the pattern, and that temptation augmented the power the pattern held. Turning and returning, Lambert ran back to the heart of the maze.

It took forever. It took five minutes. It took fifty years. Lambert reached the heart of the labyrinth, looked deep into that well of glass, raised the Agincourt device, and took aim. The frantic beat of his heart made it hard to keep his hands steady, to keep the target in its sight. His breath tore in and out. He tasted blood.

Lambert dropped to his belly on the ground, propped his elbows to steady his aim, and forced himself to breathe evenly. His pounding heart made the device seem to pulse in Lambert's grasp. From this angle the drifting barriers were harder to see, slower and more random in their movement. There was no possibility of calmness, no chance of deliberation. He had Fell in his sight. Lambert moved just enough to draw a bead on Bridgewater's head.

If this doesn't work, I'll have to try it on Fell. And if that doesn't work, I may have to try to kill Fell after all.

His father's words came back to him. *Never aim a gun at anyone unless you're fixing to kill him.* The memory settled him down. He steadied his breathing.

The gleaming shift of a barrier held Lambert up another five heartbeats until it cleared his view. He pulled the trigger. The device made a noise Lambert had never heard before—a piercingly sweet note just beside his ear—the only sound left in the world. Something inside the device shifted subtly and then it felt as inert in Lambert's hands as a bugle or a flute. Lambert closed his eyes. He held his breath until spots danced on the inside of his eyelids.

When Lambert had to breathe again, when Lambert had to look, Bridgewater was no longer there. In the depths of the glassy shaft he could see only Fell. Fell was holding something under one arm, something a little smaller than a football. Lambert could just make out that it was a tortoise. He knew, without any idea how he knew it, that until he'd fired the Agincourt device, the tortoise had been Bridgewater.

Fell called up, "Don't shoot. It's only me." He was calm but hoarse. He sounded far away.

Lambert lowered the Agincourt device. The silence wasn't draining into the well any longer. Nothing was draining anywhere. The gleaming barriers, and the whole world with them, simply drifted. The cylinder that had held the Egerton wand had split from one end to the other and there was nothing inside but dust. Lambert watched the dust sift out of the flawed brass and disappear into the sunlight. That was the sound he'd heard when he fired at Bridgewater, the final strain on the Egerton wand as it shattered.

"I've broken it," said Lambert, forlornly.

"I broke it," Fell replied, "when the answer came to me. It wasn't the spheres I needed to realign. It was the space between spheres. The shape of the intervals. The silence between the notes."

All the while he spoke, Fell was climbing toward the surface on a stair Lambert couldn't see. He took it a step at a time, as though his knees hurt him, or as if he were very old. Bareheaded, unshaven, with a tortoise tucked under his arm, Fell ascended. As he rose, the aimless drift of the barriers slowed and became deliberate motion, even as the barriers refined themselves back into invisibility.

Fell reached the surface and stepped out of the well. As he did, the flagstones were firm underfoot again, the glassy depths lost to sight under the familiar stones. From the towers of Glasscastle, bells began to ring. They did not strike the hour and stop. Instead they rang out every quarter they'd missed in the draining, drowsy silence. Bells answered bells. The birdsong returned. From every quarter the measured music of Glasscastle rang and redoubled.

Fell paused to listen, or maybe just to rest his knees, when he stood face-to-face with Lambert in the heart of the labyrinth. The light of the afternoon sun was in his eyes as he gazed at Lambert, his expression lit with intense interest and concern

"Are you all right?" Fell asked.

Lambert was listening too. It should have been impossible to hear the chants from such a distance, but he thought he could feel them in the marrow of his bones. "I am. Are you?" Lambert countered.

Fell's assent was in his expression. He said nothing, but led Lambert through the pattern of the maze at a stately pace. When they reached the mouth of the labyrinth, Fell placed the tortoise in Porteous's satchel, latched it, and handed it to the astonished Porteous.

Porteous accepted it without protest. He dropped back a deferential pace as Fell walked past. Lambert looked askance at such respect from one man to the other. Porteous looked at Lambert with mild embarrassment and a faint air of apology. "He is the warden, you see."

"He is?" Lambert watched Fell walk away into the rose garden as he helped Jane to her feet. That was it, then. The glow he had seen in Fell's eyes was not merely a fresh angle of the sun. There was a fire within him now, a pattern that gave a sense of rightness and fitness to Fell's every move.

"My goodness," said Jane faintly, gazing after Fell, "he is, isn't he?"

But he still walked like an old man, Lambert thought.

"That's Bridgewater in your satchel there," Lambert informed Porteous. "I had to use the device on him to save Fell."

Horrified, Porteous gazed down at the black case he carried. "This is Lord Bridgewater?"

"He's a tortoise now. But I'd keep that thing latched all the same," Lambert advised.

Jane was looking pale and sick and she sounded shaken. "No wonder the Egerton wand found its way into the Agincourt device. Bridgewater must have arranged it himself."

Lambert held up the device and shook it. A few grains of dust drifted out. "It's broken. The Egerton wand has been destroyed."

"Such a pity." Jane sounded much more like herself. "I wanted a look at that wand."

Porteous eyed the device warily. "If the wand's destruction saved Glasscastle, then it was a small price to pay."

As Lambert and Jane and Porteous followed in Fell's wake, first through the rose garden, then through the herb garden, then back through the quadrangles to Midsummer Green, Fell's stride smoothed and loosened. His head came up, as if he were listening to more than the bells. By the time he reached Midsummer Green, he seemed younger than his years. His energy made every step inevitable. His progress was a dance of grace that looked like a wise man walking. The bells announced him. The hours and quarter hours lapped and overlapped into cascades.

Porteous lifted a hand in recognition as they halted on the grass at the edge of Midsummer Green. "That's the bells of St. Mary's ringing the changes." He listened to the fall and rise of it a while, a shy smile widening by degrees until he was beaming with pleasure. "They're ringing Spliced Surprise Major. Lovely."

Stowe, Stewart, Russell, Meredith, and many other Fellows of Glasscastle waited and watched with them. Fell's arrival among the creatures and the cricketers scattered upon Midsummer Green attracted great attention. Before anyone could summon help, Fell was beyond their reach, encircled by the press of the beasts.

To Lambert's eye, Fell did nothing. He said nothing. He merely stood in the middle of the green, arms loose at his sides. It did not happen gradually, creature by creature. It did not happen in any order that Lambert could detect. One moment the creatures were there and the next, all transformations were unmade and Fell was surrounded by naked men and women.

"See here!" Porteous stood at gaze for a moment, jowls wobbling, then turned to Jack Meredith. "Send for blankets at once. This is indecent!"

There was nothing indecent about it to Lambert. He saw Cadwal, naked and unashamed, exchanging a few words with a man who had been a gray tabby. Robert Brailsford was locked in his wife's arms and she in his. Compared with the misgiving Lambert had felt at his first encounter with the transformed animals in the cells of St. Hubert's, the sight of men and women in their own skin was a great relief. Lambert looked again. Where there had been a red fox, another Jack Meredith sat naked on the grass, bewildered.

Lambert looked back at the Jack Meredith who stood beside Porteous. Instead of an efficient researcher, Voysey stood in his place. Fell had broken one more transformation spell.

"*There* you are." Lambert dropped the Agincourt device, put up his fists, stepped close to Voysey, and took a swing.

Agile in body as in mind, Voysey ducked the blow, turned, and ran. Within three strides, he was well into the crowd of naked people.

"Stop Voysey!" Lambert gave chase, dodging and bumping through the crowd. "Stop him!"

Voysey darted this way and that among the press of the newly transformed, staggered as he tripped over a cricket bat someone had abandoned on the grass, recovered his balance, and ran on. Lambert, in hot pursuit, hesitated at the cricket bat, but only to stoop and scoop up a discarded cricket ball from the grass nearby. He set himself, shut away the oddness of the ball he held—wrong weight, wrong feel—gauged Voysey's speed and direction, reared back, and fired the ball. All his strength was behind the throw. All his accuracy was in it.

The cricket ball caught Voysey square in the back of the head. It made a wet, unpleasant sound. Voysey went limp as he fell, arms at his sides, and toppled headlong, like a tree going down. When Lambert reached him, Voysey's face was in the grass. He was unconscious but still breathing, for the moment rendered harmless. Lambert bent to retrieve the cricket ball while watching Voysey for any twitch of movement. No sign of consciousness.

With great pride and no small amount of relief, Lambert said, "You're *out*."

Jane joined him, her hat askew and her veil fluttering loose behind her. Together they stood over Voysey. "That," said Jane, as she surveyed the inert figure with satisfaction, "was grossly unsportsmanlike."

"Thank you." Lambert looked down into Jane's pale face. "I did my best."

"If he revives, or if further drastic action should be required," said Jane, "just remember, it's my turn next."

Cadwal and Polydore, naked and clothed respectively, were among the eager volunteers who took Voysey into custody. Porteous's orders eventually resulted in blankets for all. When Fell rejoined Jane and Lambert, he had Robert and Amy with him. Though Robert wore only a blanket, he wore it toga style, folded and draped with his customary air of elegance, precision, and savoir faire.

"Just the people we were longing to see," called Amy. "You did it!"

"Fell did it," Lambert replied.

Fell looked somewhat sheepish. "It wasn't difficult."

A little awkwardly, Jane embraced Robert. "I'm so glad to see you. Really you, I mean."

Robert returned the greeting, then pulled free. "Forgive me, but we must go now. I must see to Amy. She's been under a great strain."

"Of course. Mind your bare feet. I've left the Minotaur just outside the gate."

Robert nodded absently to Lambert and Fell, and hurried Amy off, still dignified despite everything.

"That's a great relief." Jane produced a handkerchief and permitted herself a brief sniffle before she put it away again. "Splendid."

"You might want to make an exit, Fell," Lambert warned. "I see Cadwal and Polydore and they're heading your way."

"Thanks for the sharp eye, but it's time I apologized to them both and settled what's to be done with their work." Fell moved to meet them.

"It's a miracle." Lambert watched Fell go. "What next?"

"Sorry to intrude. But that's our ball, sir," said one of the undergraduate cricketers.

Lambert returned the ball without hesitation. "Next time don't just leave your things lying around underfoot. Somebody might get hurt."

"Lucky for you they did leave their things lying about," Jane said. "I wonder what the precise term is for that. Head before wicket? Robin would know."

Lambert scrutinized Jane with care. "You're looking better."

Although Jane was still oblivious to her dishevelment, she sounded more like herself and her eyes were bright again. "I feel better. But I think I ought to go and see about Robin. It can't have been easy for him, all this."

"I'll walk you there, if you have no objection."

"That would be kind." Jane straightened her hat and fell into step beside Lambert as they strolled away in Robert and Amy's wake. "What do you plan to do after that?"

Lambert held out his palm and pretended to study the lines there. "Unless my luck has changed considerably, it will be time for yet another lovely cup of tea. After that, I haven't the slightest idea. Possibly take a long journey over water. Fell will have his hands full now he's really the warden. He will probably want me out of his way. I suppose I'll have to give some kind of account of myself for the inquiry. The Provosts will have a field day, won't they? They're sure to haul us all over the coals. Once that is over with, I don't know what I'll do. What will you do?"

Jane's color was much better and she was able to match Lambert's pace without apparent effort. "Michaelmas term doesn't begin for weeks yet. I'll make sure all my luggage is as it should be. Some things probably just need a good clean. One or two bits will never be the same, so I might as well get rid of them. When I'm presentable again, I'd like to pay a call on my old nanny. She keeps a bookshop in Malmesbury and I've always meant to visit her there. Then I suppose I'll visit my parents. Perhaps call upon Aunt Alice— she's my very best aunt—in London. After that, I might buy myself a Blenheim Bantam after all. Finally, home to Greenlaw. I'm not looking forward to the trip over on the ferry."

"You won't be staying here very much longer, then?" Lambert didn't try to hide his disappointment.

"I won't be leaving tomorrow, if that's what you mean. You're quite right about the hearing. I have no intention of leaving Glasscastle until I've learned every last detail of Voysey's and Bridgewater's misdeeds. After that, however, I think Amy and Robert might be glad of a bit of peace and quiet. They've earned it."

"What about you? Haven't you earned a bit of peace and quiet?"

"Oh, I've had my share," said Jane. "I have always found that a little peace and quiet goes an extraordinarily long way with me. I like a bit of excitement, don't you?"

"Depends on the kind," Lambert said cautiously. "I've had enough to last me lately."

"True." Jane thought it over. "I just count myself lucky I wasn't one of those poor devils caught in the center of Midsummer Green without a stitch on."

"Virtue *is* its own reward," said Lambert wonderingly.

"You sound as if you didn't believe that until now."

"Let's just say, I've never seen it demonstrated so plainly."

"I hope you never do again." Jane touched Lambert's sleeve. "Do you have time for a brief detour before we leave the grounds?"

"I have nothing but time." Lambert thought it over and added, "Unless you want to stop somewhere for a nice cup of tea. Then I'm busy."

"No tea for the moment." Jane led Lambert into St. Mary's. "I just wanted to take a last look."

Once inside, the bright fall of bells was somewhat muted. Despite the need to make himself heard over the ringing of the changes, Lambert kept his voice soft. "Not your last, surely. You'll be back again."

"Inside St. Mary's of Glasscastle? I doubt it. I almost hope not. I doubt I can ever return to Glasscastle without remembering—" Jane broke off. In silence, she led Lambert along the south aisle and they looked up, marveling at the light that lingered in the heights above.

"Remembering what?" Lambert murmured at last.

Jane's voice, when she finally spoke, was uneven. "How it felt when she—when my illusion was consumed. I put a great deal of my strength into that illusion. To have it torn away—" Jane didn't finish.

It was drawing to the end of a bright day. Here and there the wash of daylight across the vaulting was still adorned with red and gold as the setting sun angled through the stained glass. The raking light made the shadows they walked through seem all the deeper when Lambert spared his neck and glanced down to watch where he was going.

"Perception and will," said Jane, half to herself. "The men who built this place believed God created the world according to a model in His mind. We can look at what has been created and learn from it. If we study the proportion and construction of the world around us, we can find a hint of the divine order of the model."

"Was that what Fell was trying to do?" Lambert looked around. "It's hard enough to find a trace of the divine in what's in front of us. I don't give much for anyone's chances of figuring out the divine order."

"Let's sit down for a moment. I could use the rest." Jane led the way to the spindly chairs ranked in the nave. When they were seated, she looked up. "Fell was trying to halt the river in its bed. Those who built this place knew that there are patterns in the world and they used those patterns here. Porteous was right about this place. There's music all around us here. Every arch, every vault, it all means something in terms of space. The nave to the transept is a musical fifth."

"Is this like the music in change ringing?" Lambert looked up and around. "I can see the proportions in stone, but I can't hear the music they represent. I can hear the bells, but I don't grasp the melody. I can listen to the chants, but I don't understand the structure of the music."

Jane was silent for a moment, letting the bells fill the space before she answered. Finally, she said, "You would find the pattern in time. After all, to us mere mortals, what is music without time? Those who built this place were telling us a story outside of time, so they give us these images arranged by the way their internal meaning echoes back and forth. It's all happening all at once, like scenes in a stained glass window. The order that matters here in the stone isn't chronological. It's eternal."

Someone began to practice the organ. The fluting notes of the stopped diapason floated up inquiringly over a single deep note that held on and on beneath everything.

"'The playing of the merry organ, sweet singing in the choir,'" Jane observed. "We are granted a choice of musics."

Lambert recognized the words of the Christmas carol despite Jane's difficulty in carrying the tune against the one the organist played, let alone the orderly cascade of the bells. "We've already seen 'the rising of the sun and the running of the deer.'"

"They didn't run. I found them all quite overwhelmingly dignified. Particularly Robin, of course." Jane seemed amused at the thought.

"What do you think they'll do to Voysey?"

"If they have any sense of symmetry, they will turn him into an animal and do it in such a way that no one can ever turn him back."

"And Bridgewater?"

All Jane's amusement fled. "He can stay a tortoise for the rest of his life. I understand they live a long time."

"In the end, we've accomplished nothing," Lambert said. "The Agincourt Project was subverted. The Agincourt device is broken. The men who turned the project to their own ends have been shown up as blackguards. Fell is the warden, but did he really repair anything? Even if he did, were all those calculations of his nothing but a waste of time?"

"Fell changed something. The bells told me that. I think he mended matters." Jane brightened. "I only know one thing for certain."

Lambert took the bait willingly. "And what is that?"

Pride shone from Jane. "I did what *I* set out to do."

"Oh, good. I'm glad for you." Lambert rolled his eyes.

Jane sobered. "I haven't thanked you for trying to move that armchair. I appreciate that."

"It was a botched rescue." Lambert renewed his interest in the vaulted ceiling. The afternoon light had dimmed a little, he thought.

"It was impossible. You tried just the same. Admirable. Don't look so flustered. I'm serious."

"Oh, yes. Utterly sincere." Lambert returned her gaze. "Oh. You are."

"You did very well." Jane's eyes were steady on Lambert's. The look held.

"You did indeed." A booming voice from the direction of the porch drove them apart as Porteous joined them. "I hope I'm not intruding."

"Oh, no. No, not in the least." Lambert realized he was stammering and silenced himself.

Jane looked peeved. "Things must be going well if you have time to spend admiring ecclesiastical architecture."

"Things are going extremely well." Porteous seemed disposed to take all the credit himself. "However, I came looking for you, Lambert."

"How did you know I was here?"

"I have my ways." Porteous glowed with satisfaction. "I have my little ways. Not much goes on here to which I am not privy. I have come to invite you to take sherry with me tomorrow. With the transformations restored, thanks to our Fell, the inquiry will be more simple than we'd feared. I think by five o'clock tomorrow, we should be able to clear up the details once and for all. Please come to my rooms at St. Joseph's. Bring Fell with you, if he'll come. I've sent invitations to your brother and his wife as well, Miss Brailsford, and I hope you will join us too."

Lambert and Jane accepted the invitation. Porteous looked pleased. "Excellent. I must be off. Five o'clock tomorrow, then. Plenty of work to be done first."

Jane let Porteous leave St. Mary's before she rose herself. "There are things to be done. If you promise to go quite slowly, I'll hold you to your offer of a walk to Robin's house."

"I promise." Lambert accompanied Jane out of St. Mary's as the organ practice resumed. Overhead the change ringing came to a triumphant close. They left the organist in sole possession of the place. As Lambert signed them out in the visitors' book, the half hour struck. All the bells of Glasscastle, in their proper pattern and order, chimed their notes and fell silent. Time was marked as it should be once again.

The Brailsford house was quiet when Jane let herself in. Though Jane didn't see anyone anywhere, she had the feeling that all was right with this particular world. The sense of domestic calm was unmistakable. Her luggage was back in her room, contents unpacked. Some items of clothing had already disappeared, she assumed for cleaning. Everything remaining was in perfect order.

Moving as slowly as if she were ninety, Jane tidied herself and changed from half boots to a pair of house slippers. Hot water and lavender soap had never seemed such welcome luxuries. From its hiding place in her wash stand, she brought out the Royal Worcester plate and the bottle of ink. Murmuring softly but distinctly, she poured out the ink rim to rim. This time her sense of Glasscastle's bounds was like a waterfall thundering nearby. With all her remaining strength focused on maintaining her concentration, Jane managed to find her way from the gloss of the ink to the matte of the black and through the blackness to a place where she could hear Faris Nallaneen's voice, bodiless in the chamber of her ear.

"Well done, Jane."

"You know what happened?"

"Couldn't see a thing. You were too close to the wards of Glasscastle. But I felt it when it came right. We all did."

"It worked? Fell was able to correct the distortion?"

"He did it. Time still runs. Yet it runs more smoothly. It's not just the relief of having four wardens again. He did it."

Faris's words were already dwindling. This time Jane knew it wasn't Faris's fatigue she sensed but her own. Her concentration was flagging. The roar of the bounds was almost painful. "Sorry. I must stop now." Before the words were out, the ink had dried from rim to rim.

Jane left the plate where it was. With uneven steps she walked to the bed. Without a thought for the hour, she lay down and slept.

14

"But now my task is smoothly done,
I can fly, or I can run
Quickly to the green earth's end,
Where the bowed welkin slow doth bend,
And from thence can soar as soon
To the corners of the moon."

Lambert enjoyed the walk back to Fell's rooms at Holythorn. There was no need to shorten his stride for Jane any longer, so he could step out at his own pace. The air was soft and sweet. Every twig on every branch seemed etched against the sky. At each quarter hour the bells of Glasscastle struck, and in each note of their pattern was a reminder of what had been threatened, and a sign of what had been restored. Lambert's heart lifted at the sound, even as he remembered that his work in Glasscastle was finished. Before long, he must leave it behind.

After that, each stage of the walk assumed a melancholy significance. How many more times would he approach the arch of the great gate, Lambert asked himself. How many more times would the gatekeeper greet him as he dipped the pen and held it out for Lambert's signature in the visitors book? How many more times would Lambert be permitted to pass through the gate into Glasscastle, and to crunch his way along the gravel paths that marked the narrow way open to him from the broad precincts that were not?

Back at his rooms, the state of disarray in Fell's quarters was about what Lambert had expected. There was still a half-smoked cheroot in the ashtray and the clock was ticking away. There were signs of Fell's return. The door to his room was open and Lambert could see garments scattered across the bed in a way that suggested Fell had gone for a bath before changing for dinner.

On the floor just inside the door, Lambert found four neatly addressed envelopes, two for him and two for Fell. Fell's valise was right where he'd left it, in the center of the carpet. Belatedly, Lambert remembered his own small valise. It was probably still in the Brailsford motor car. He put Fell's mail on the mantelpiece and opened his own. One was a summons to the Tegean Theater, where the inquiry would open at nine the next morning. The other was the sherry invitation Porteous had promised. Both were in the same handwriting.

The card tray bore two items, a playing card and a visiting card. The visiting card was from Louis Tobias. The name was vaguely familiar. It took Lambert a moment to remember Cromer and Palgrave's dinner guest from Farnborough. Apparently he'd paid a call on Fell after Lambert's departure. Lambert wondered how the two men knew each other. Fell had never mentioned an interest in aviation. Still, when Fell was concerned, anything was possible. The playing card was perfectly ordinary, a three of hearts, unmarked in any way. Lambert frowned at it and put it back in the tray. He would ask Fell to explain it to him later.

In his own room, Lambert pulled off his collar and dropped it in the wastebasket. A bath would be a good idea. So would dinner. Lambert sat on the edge of the bed to take off his boots. The mattress was far more comfortable than he remembered. Lambert forgot about good ideas. Instead he stretched out on the bed, boots and all, and dozed off.

Fell's return woke him. In shirtsleeves, Lambert staggered out to the sitting room they shared. "There you are," said Lambert to the door of Fell's room, and yawned prodigiously.

"Yes, I am." Fell emerged, hair still gleaming wet. He too was in shirtsleeves, but his shirt was clean and pressed. Under the cleanliness, there was fatigue, but on the whole Fell looked more energetic than Lambert could ever remember seeing him. "I'm sorry I couldn't express my gratitude earlier. I was preoccupied. But allow me to thank you now. You never made a more timely shot."

"I'm only sorry it took me so long."

"Time seemed to run slowly to me too. Perhaps with good reason." A bit abstractedly, Fell looked across the room.

Lambert followed the direction of his gaze and saw he was staring at the clock. "Did you ever finish your calculations?"

"My calculations were only an aid to my perceptions, so perhaps fortunately, I didn't have to. When you took Bridgewater out of the equation, I was left in the center of Glasscastle's wards. There was energy in abundance. Without Bridgewater there to devour it, power was drifting aimlessly. I had to try to balance it."

"You succeeded."

"I did. When I found my way out of the wards, I started something. By the time I finished walking the labyrinth, order had been restored. I could tell."

"How did you do it?"

"Jane told me my planes were constituted of points, yet I assumed points existed independently of the planes. She criticized me for confusing two different conceptions. But that made me rethink my perception of points. What if they were something like musical notes? What if they had their own resonance? What if that resonance was the music of the spheres? Once I perceived it, it was as if more strength than mine augmented my will." Fell uttered a deep sigh and fell silent. After a thoughtful pause, he added, "May I never again be so comprehensively frightened. Thank you."

"You're welcome." Lambert remembered cause for gratitude of his own. "Thank you for letting me stay on a bit now that the project is over."

"Letting you—" Fell looked appalled. "Don't be ridiculous. You must stay."

"Thanks, but even if you are the warden of the west, the Agincourt Project is over. I'll pack up soon. It may take me a day or so. I don't know just what I'm going to do next."

"There's no need for haste." Fell turned to the mirror over the mantel and concentrated on it fiercely as he did up his collar and started on his tie. "You can't possibly do anything before the inquiry is concluded, so take your time making up your mind. I have an idea I want to discuss with you myself."

"Porteous seems to consider the inquiry tomorrow a formality. He's invited us for sherry afterward." Lambert held up both cards. "Louis Tobias called. I didn't know you two knew each other. But what is this?"

"Tobias and I belong to the same club. We met at a Royal Society lecture on botany, of all things." Fell inspected the three of hearts and put it back in the tray. "No idea about the playing card, I'm afraid. It doesn't seem like something Tobias would do, leaving it. Perhaps it came from an undergraduate who fancies it symbolizes something. The Black Spot, perhaps."

Lambert took the pitch and changed the subject. "A strange bunch, those undergraduates. Will you be called to speak at the hearing?"

"I suppose so. I hope Porteous is right about the brevity of the inquiry. Voysey's fate may be easy to determine. I doubt Bridgewater's will be so simple. Aside from the moral implications, he's one of the richest men in England. For one thing, what becomes of his personal property while he is a tortoise? Someone will have to be named a trustee. Think of the legal wrangling." Fell studied the angle of his bow tie and was satisfied enough with his reflection to leave it alone and put on his coat.

"Is that something Glasscastle has jurisdiction over?"

"I'm not entirely sure. Glasscastle is occasionally called upon to advise in matters of crime magical. In this instance, the crime concerns the security of Glasscastle itself. I don't think the university should yield jurisdiction. Bridgewater struck at the heart of Glasscastle. Glasscastle must teach him what that means." One moment Fell stood there, faultlessly dressed for dinner, more elegant than Lambert had ever seen him. The next, Fell threw himself into his armchair and the crisp crease of his trousers was gone forever. "Sit down. It makes me tired to watch you stand there swaying."

Lambert settled into the chair opposite, enjoying the return of his friend's familiar rumpled aspect. "Was that what Bridgewater was after? The power of Glasscastle?"

"Not exclusively. Glasscastle was a means to an end for Bridgewater. He meant to use it to augment his own power."

"Wasn't that a bit risky, taking on the whole university?"

"If anything, it made the enterprise more attractive to him. Bridgewater loved a challenge. I suppose that was part of Voysey's appeal. He represented a challenge since he had something Bridgewater greatly envied."

"Bridgewater envied Voysey?" Lambert considered the two men and marveled. "What for? Did it matter so much to Bridgewater that he was getting old?"

Fell hooted. "Oh, Bridgewater envied Voysey, but not for his youth, I assure you. Bridgewater envied Voysey because Voysey had Glasscastle. Voysey studied here, rose fast and far even in the ranks of the Senior Fellows, and was responsible first for Holythorn and then for Glasscastle as a whole. In Bridgewater's view, Voysey was the very lord of Glasscastle. A place Bridgewater had not even dared ask to attend, for fear he'd be refused."

Lambert thought it over. "I guess I can understand that. But Bridgewater almost made it sound as if he didn't want to go to Glasscastle in the first place. As if he thought it might limit his power."

Fell raised an eyebrow. "Interesting. Does it remind you at all of the fox and the grapes?"

"Bridgewater might have envied Voysey's influence, but I don't think he had much of an opinion of the wise men of Glasscastle. He called them pygmies."

"Cheek." Fell looked kindly at Lambert. "Voysey went after your fascination with Glasscastle, did he?"

"Voysey offered to arrange for me to be admitted as a student. I knew he must be lying. From things he said when I first arrived, from what I've seen since, I figured I could never be accepted here."

"*Never* is a big word," said Fell. "You mustn't assume—"

Lambert cut in. "*Not* just because I'm American. There's more to it than that. I don't know any Latin. I don't have a 'background.'" Lambert added darkly, "Whatever *that* means. Money, I reckon."

Fell began, "It's complicated—"

Lambert snorted. "Yeah, that's what I thought."

"Generally, it has to do with one's social class. But money can enter into it, yes. Among other things." Fell, with uncharacteristic tact, changed the subject. "Voysey never expected the ministers to choose the Farnborough project over his. When he received word that the funding had been redirected, he had to adjust his timetable. He combined the prototype with the Egerton wand. To his great satisfaction, the device worked."

"Was that what he was working on the day he and Wright had me firing the Baker rifle?" asked Lambert.

"That was a pretext to keep you busy during Voysey's last attempt to remove me." Fell took out a cheroot and toyed with it. "Our intruder in the bowler hat was Voysey's first attempt. In the last attempt, he made sure he sent more men and more cantrips. Voysey's henchmen took me to St. Hubert's specifically to keep me in isolation."

"Because Voysey wanted you kept out of the way in case anyone persuaded you to be the warden before he was good and ready."

"Quite so. As we surmised, Voysey was worried that I would abandon the idea of resisting the wardenship before he was in possession of the device. He thought keeping me at my calculations would be the best way to keep me from interfering."

"I thought Voysey didn't believe in wardens."

"Bridgewater persuaded Voysey that he could think of the wardenship in whatever terms pleased him, so long as I was kept from accepting my responsibilities. Apparently Voysey never suspected Bridgewater possessed so much wild talent. If he had, he might have been more circumspect about linking the power of Glasscastle to the Egerton wand."

"Didn't either of them fear that once you were given a chance to concentrate on your work, you would finish your calculations and correct the imbalance?"

"No," Fell said tartly. "Apparently no one considered that possibility for a moment." As if stung by the reminder, Fell lit his cheroot and puffed smoke indignantly.

"Didn't Voysey guess that Jane came here expressly to persuade you to assume the wardenship?"

"Voysey learned that Miss Brailsford was a friend of the warden of the north. He believed that my next caller was likely to be the warden of the north herself. Small chance I would have been able to resist her persuasion in person. This was Voysey's judgment, of course. Between us, I think I'd have had no trouble ignoring her, even now that I've had a chance to communicate with her directly. She's strident, no question, but she's not completely immune to reason."

Lambert reminded himself, with difficulty, that the undistinguished man before him was truly the new warden of the west. "You don't seem much different now."

"I'm not." Fell attempted a smoke ring. "I don't miss the sensation of resistance, I assure you. It was a drain. And not the only one. Just as I lost the ability to resist Bridgewater's pull on my strength, I lost my ability to abstain from the wardenship any longer. It all rushed in. Until you took action, it was all rushing out. Straight into Bridgewater. A most unpleasant sensation."

"Until I tried to get away from Voysey at St. Hubert's, I never took lethal aim at anyone," Lambert confessed, "let alone pulled the trigger. It wasn't any easier the second time than it was the first, even if it was a different weapon."

"Thank you for doing it. The relief was considerable, I assure you."

"What would have happened if I hadn't?"

"Who knows? Bridgewater had the wards of Glasscastle down and me in his power. Jane too, for that matter. It would have been very hard on all of us if he'd gone on much longer." The understatement hung there like one of

Fell's misshapen smoke rings until Fell tapped the ash off his cheroot into the seashell ashtray. "There's something I wanted to ask you about."

Warned by Fell's change of tone, Lambert braced himself for a total change of subject. "Yes?"

"How does it happen that a fine young man like you achieves the great age of—" Fell hesitated. "How old *are* you?"

"Twenty-three," Lambert answered with reluctance. "Why?"

"You have achieved the great age of twenty-three without so much as a single amorous dalliance?" Fell's disbelief flavored every word.

Disgusted, Lambert corrected his friend. "What you mean to say is, how can I still be a virgin? Not that it's any of your business. Women don't exactly grow on trees, you know."

"They do in London. In certain locales, they positively teem. I don't imagine any other city lacks them either."

"I don't mean that sort of woman." Lambert sighed. "They're all clean and half of them are virgins, to hear them tell it. Oddly enough, I don't believe them. I don't want to pay for a few minutes of pleasure and contract a social disease that will last for the rest of my life. I'd sooner go to the opera."

"You're a strange young man," Fell observed. After a few meditative puffs on his cheroot, he added, "There are other kinds of women."

"So there are," Lambert agreed. "The kind who view a wedding ring as essential equipment. Time enough for that when I've seen a bit more of the world. I could have stayed in Wyoming if that was all I wanted out of life."

"I thought you liked Wyoming?"

"I do. But when I lived there, I'd never heard of Glasscastle. Who knows what else I've never heard of?" For the first time, Lambert felt a sense of optimism about leaving Glasscastle. If the world could hold something as wonderful as Glasscastle, who knew what else it contained? Who knew what other surprises life had in store for him? "It's a big world."

"So you're off in search of high adventure?" Fell made the suggestion sound like something out of a dime novel. "Exploring forgotten corners of the Old World looking for excitement?"

"No, not for excitement. I've had enough of that to last me." Lambert thought it over. "If there are other places like Glasscastle out there, maybe those forgotten corners are worth exploring too."

"Wait a moment. You aren't suggesting that Glasscastle is a forgotten corner of the world, are you?"

Lambert ignored Fell's indignation. "It's funny. I never thought of getting an education when I was back home. It never crossed my mind. When I first came to Glasscastle, I just thought it was pretty here. Not a patch on Wyoming, you understand, but pretty. Then I heard the chants. It wasn't until peace soaked into me that I noticed what I'd been missing." Lambert struggled to express himself. "There is a calmness here I've never run across anywhere else. A clarity." Lambert gave up the search for the right words and let his voice trail off to silence.

Fell grimaced. "How, knowing Porteous, can you say that and keep a straight face?"

Lambert didn't let Fell's joking deter him. "You know what I mean. It's in the air here. There's such a thing as truth. People care what it is. For all the time they spend reading and arguing and making up new theories and torturing each other with them, they're only doing it to get at the truth."

"I think you take an overly optimistic view of academic life."

"Maybe I do. But all the same, there could be other places where that's the rule. Who knows? There might be. Miss Brailsford doesn't say much about Greenlaw, but it sounds as if that's the way things are there. Maybe there is somewhere I could go. Somewhere else. Somewhere I would fit right in."

"But you won't look for that place back home in your own country?" Fell asked.

"Home in my own country?" Lambert could not keep the wistful note out of his voice. "Don't get me wrong. I am American. But if Glasscastle isn't my own country, I guess I haven't found my true home yet. I have to keep looking."

The clock on the wall struck the hour and the bells of Glasscastle, near and far, began to echo it. The bells seemed unusually sweet and clear to Lambert. He put it down to fatigue.

"I can hardly blame you for this sudden case of wanderlust, as I suffer from the same complaint. Our paths diverge, that's all. A pity." Fell stood and shrugged into the black academic robe he wore as a Fellow of Holythorn. The smooth fabric concealed a multitude of rumples and Fell looked almost elegant again. "I'll be late for dinner if I don't leave now. I am bidden to Mount Olympus itself. Stewart of Wearyall wants to curry my favor, even if Stowe of St. Joseph's doesn't, so they're asking for my guidance on who should be named Provost of Holythorn now that Voysey is disgraced. They're in a hurry to settle that little matter so they can go straight for each other's throat over who will be chosen the next Vice Chancellor."

"Flattering," said Lambert. "Try not to overdo the nectar and ambrosia. Do you think they want you to be next Provost of Holythorn?"

Fell paused, thunder-struck. "By Jove. What a revolting thought. It would be just like them. As if I don't already have more responsibility than I need. No, Brailsford is their man. That's what I'll advise. If we of Jove's nectar sup, I assure you I will take pains to sup in moderation. As for you, my advice is have a good dinner and a proper night's rest. The Tegean opens bright and early. The inquiry will too."

Promptly at nine the next morning, Lambert arrived at the top of the steep steps that led to the carved and gilded doors of the Tegean Theater. He was far from the first arrival. As the doors opened to let their party file in, Lambert joined Robert and Amy Brailsford, Nicholas Fell, and Jane, who looked her trim Parisian best. The night's rest had restored all her vitality and she seemed to look forward to the proceedings as if to a high-stakes horse race in which she was sure she had backed the winner.

"Whom will they call first?" Jane asked the group at large. "Does the defendant begin?"

"The Provosts and Senior Fellows are here to find out what happened and to decide if there is reason to file charges. If they determine that a crime has been committed, and that the defendants should be brought to trial, they will refer the cases to the appropriate court," Robert Brailsford answered. "Voysey, at least, has been examined and has delivered his testimony in full."

Fell added, "Poor devil isn't permitted to sleep until he does. That's him under guard. The restraining spells they've used on him are what give him that cobweb effect. Bridgewater is in the terrarium on the table beside him."

"Devil is the word." Amy was uncharacteristically stern.

"They deny the man sleep? That's medieval," Jane protested. "It's cruel and unusual punishment."

"I don't think he's worthy of your pity. Voysey brought all this on himself." Amy said, "I'm just glad there's something they could do to compel the beastly man to cooperate."

"You thought he was charming," Jane reminded her.

Amy's eyes flashed. "Honors even, so did you."

"I did not! I thought he was patronizing and vain."

While taking the seats the ushers had allotted their party, Lambert and Robert insinuated themselves between the ladies and put an end to their conversation.

The Tegean Theater was stark simplicity in comparison to the theaters Lambert was used to. No velvet, no gilt. The stage was nothing but a bare wooden platform surrounded on three sides by the space allotted the audience. High above, the ceiling was painted with gods in a chariot riding through a handsome assortment of clouds. The plaster walls were ornamented with sculpted laurel garlands, white against white. The windows high above, already opened from the top in anticipation of the heat to come, circled the room with light. With no curtains and very little furniture, sound reverberated. To the audience, even the squeak of a footstep on the planks of the wooden stage was audible in the last row.

With the booming rap of a beadle's mace, the proceedings were brought to order. Stewart and Stowe, the Provosts of Wearyall and St. Joseph's, presided over the inquiry. The places that would have been filled by the Provost of Holythorn and the Vice Chancellor of Glasscastle were taken by Russell and Porteous. The four of them, robed and hooded in full academic garb trimmed with ermine and velvet, sat in a row at the center of the dais. Lambert compared the splendor of the academic robes with the war bonnets and ceremonial costume of some of the Indian chieftains in Kiowa Bob's show and decided the chiefs would have looked right at home in such getups.

The defendants were held to the left of the dais, facing the Provosts. Voysey was seated comfortably enough, though cobwebs seemed to hold him in his chair. On the table beside him rested a glass box containing the tortoise that had been Bridgewater.

Ranged around the other three-quarters of the circular space were rows of chairs for the audience. Only a third of the chairs were full.

"Closed inquiry," Robert explained when Lambert asked. "Admission by invitation only. Otherwise the place would be crammed to the gunwales with journalists."

The beadle's mace rapped again. "The inquiry calls Robert Brailsford to be questioned."

Robert sidled along their row of chairs, came down the steps, ascended to the stage, took his place standing before the Provosts, and was sworn in. Bareheaded and simply dressed, Robert Brailsford held his own before the Provosts.

The Provosts consulted one another in murmurs. Finally the question was boomed out by Porteous. "Robert Brailsford, will you tell the Provosts why you left Glasscastle for Ludlow without troubling to leave any official notice of your departure?"

Robert answered readily. "I did not know whom I could notify without betraying my knowledge of the attempt to abduct Nicholas Fell. When Samuel Lambert gave me the plans he found on Fell's desk after the intrusion, I was alarmed. The highly classified nature of the information surprised me. At the first opportunity, I visited Fell's study myself. Among the papers there, I found what I believed to be a cipher letter selling the plans to the German secret service."

This news caused a mild sensation in the audience. The rising whispers sounded like wind in the trees to Lambert. At a Provost's request, the beadle rapped for order and got it.

Porteous's next question boomed out. "If the letter was written in cipher, how could you know what it said?"

"It was a childishly simple code, character substitution without altering word length." Robert looked apologetic. "Any schoolboy could have deciphered it in five minutes. The clumsiness of the effort put me on guard. I thought it had been planted there, along with the plans, to cast suspicion on Fell's disappearance. Accordingly, I took the letter and the plans with me when I went to consult Lord Bridgewater."

"That is why you went to Ludlow, to call upon Bridgewater himself?" Russell asked the question. Compared to the booming of Porteous, he sounded like a choirboy.

Robert was candid with Russell. "I certainly intended to. His lordship was not at home. His secretary referred me to St. Hubert's and like an idiot, I went. My suspicions of Voysey's malfeasance were confirmed when Voysey held me prisoner there."

"Unfortunate that you hadn't shared your suspicions with anyone before your departure," Porteous observed.

"It was." Robert looked up into the audience to where Amy was watching him with a proprietary air. "I won't make that mistake again."

Amy's expression changed to one of unqualified approval.

"At the time you confronted Voysey at St. Hubert's, were you aware that he had the Agincourt device in his possession?" Stowe asked.

"If I had known, I would have been a great deal more circumspect. To the best of my knowledge, no one had yet built a working prototype of the device. Voysey's claims surprised me and I admit I scoffed at him." Robert lifted his chin, as if his collar had abruptly grown too tight. "As it happened, my first sight of the finished device was the last thing I saw before I was transformed into a beast."

"You were but one among many to be changed," Stewart reminded him. "No need for embarrassment."

"To be frank, I don't feel any embarrassment." Robert seemed to consider the matter. "Residual fury, perhaps."

"Understandable, given the circumstances," said Stowe. "What were Voysey's claims?"

"He was very proud of having tricked Lord Bridgewater into abetting his schemes. It was only Bridgewater's assistance that made the working device possible. Both men shared a devotion to the expansion of imperial interests that I consider unwholesome." Robert sniffed. "I knew Voysey had played on Bridgewater's patriotism and his respect for Glasscastle as an institution of magical research. Bridgewater not only provided private backing for the project, he exercised considerable influence in government circles as well, all of which he used in Glasscastle's favor."

"To return to the cipher letter," Porteous said, "did Voysey say anything to lead you to believe that he himself had engaged in dealings with the German secret service?"

"On the contrary. From what Voysey told me, he contrived the cipher letter purely to incriminate Fell. Selling secrets to the Germans was the worst crime Voysey could imagine."

"Did Voysey say anything that led you to believe that the Earl of Bridgewater had dealings with the Germans?" Porteous asked.

"His lordship's worst enemy could not make such a claim and expect it to be taken seriously," Robert replied. "As I see it, both Voysey and Bridgewater are far too partisan to consider such measures."

Russell frowned and leaned forward. "Too partisan? What do you mean by that?"

Robert said, "I should have said too patriotic."

"Surely it is impossible to be too patriotic?" Russell asked.

"That judgment must depend upon your view of the actions taken by the defendants," Robert countered smoothly.

Stewart cut the exchange short. "Thank you. That will do."

The Provosts dismissed Robert. The audience shifted, murmured, and coughed as he resumed his seat. The beadle summoned the next witness, Meredith.

Meredith stood in the spot Robert had vacated. He looked uncomfortable, Lambert thought, perhaps because he was dressed more formally than usual, full academic robes over an immaculate suit.

Porteous, once again, spoke first. "John Meredith, will you describe from your perspective the events of yesterday?"

"From my perspective?" Meredith thought it over. "You woke me up in the middle of the night, that's my perspective. That idiot Williams had wired from Ludlow with some madness about a working version of the Agincourt device. I was scarcely back from London, where I've been wasting days trying to get an appointment with Lord Fyvie. Small chance of that!"

"Please——" Stewart held up a hand to stem Meredith's tirade. "May we confine ourselves to the events of yesterday?"

Meredith calmed down. "Very well. I suppose I might have been asleep for three hours when Porteous woke me. He said the Agincourt device was working. Williams had seen it used with his own eyes. I tried to tell him that if anyone had done such a thing, I'd know about it. He paid no attention to me, as usual. Next thing I knew, I was squashed into a train compartment with Porteous and Stowe while we argued about the best spell to use once we got there."

Porteous looked indignant but before he could speak, Stowe asked, "At what point did you appreciate the degree of Voysey's involvement?"

"We were halfway there before anyone mentioned that Voysey was involved at all." Meredith looked annoyed. "Up until then, I had a hazy idea someone had managed to break in and steal the device. Indeed, even after I heard the accusations against him, I could scarcely believe Voysey was responsible for such a thing."

Stowe cleared his throat, and asked, "At what point did you encounter Adam Voysey?"

"At the precise point that I appreciated the degree of his involvement," said Meredith, bitterly. "We had successfully deployed the Vox Magna to break the protective spells on St. Hubert's. I was among the first group of Fellows to enter the place, an advance search party. The moment I opened a cupboard door and saw the muzzle of that infernal Agincourt device pointed at me—that was the exact moment when I realized everything I'd heard about Voysey was true. The moment after *that*, of course, he turned me into a fox."

Stowe asked, "Were you at any time aware that Voysey transformed himself to resemble you?"

Meredith looked disgusted. "I wasn't aware of a bloody thing until I came to my senses on Midsummer Green, naked as the day I was born. Any further questions?"

"Er, no. Not at this time." Mildly apologetic, Stowe dismissed Meredith.

The beadle thumped again and called Nicholas Fell. After Meredith's neat appearance, Fell provided a striking contrast in his academic robe. Fell stood before the Provosts waiting for their first question as patiently as if he were waiting for a train he didn't particularly want to catch.

This time Russell spoke for the Provosts. "Nicholas Fell, please explain to the Provosts why you neglected your duties as a warden, as well as your duties as a Senior Fellow of Glasscastle, to pursue a personal interest in mathematical calculations which you are not qualified to make?"

"My dear Provosts," Fell replied, after a long dispassionate look at each of them, "I respectfully decline to do so. Whatever my reasons, they were sufficient given the limited knowledge available to me at the time."

"An interesting point," Stowe said. "Are we to infer that you now have more knowledge available to you?"

Fell looked bored. "You may infer that I found Mr. Russell's question impertinent."

"Is that why you decline to answer? Because you consider yourself above being questioned?" Russell asked.

"Clearly you have a fondness for impertinent questions," Fell countered. "Are you capable of asking any other kind?"

"Gentlemen, let me remind you we are not here to be rude to one another," Stewart cautioned. "We are here to get at the truth. You are uniquely situated to help us, Mr. Fell. Will you do so?"

Fell looked mollified. "I will help if I can."

"Perhaps we can dispense with questions and get on with it." Stewart's glare quelled any incipient protest from the Provosts. "Mr. Fell, from your perspective—what happened?

"I'll tell you what I *think* happened," Fell said. "Some of it I've known for some time, idle talk being what it is. Some of it I learned from conversations with Voysey while I was his captive at St. Hubert's. Some of it I've taken the trouble to find out since Lambert rescued me and saved the wards. Most of it I learned from Bridgewater's close embrace. While he was draining my strength, his concerns were evident to me."

"What, ah, concerns were those?" Stewart looked as if he weren't sure he wanted to know the answer to his question.

"For one thing, he wanted to save the world." Fell smiled bitterly.

"In what sense?" asked Russell.

"In the literal sense. He intended to keep the world safe personally, once the British Empire controlled it—under his supervision, of course."

"Really. How did he think he was going to accomplish that?" asked Stowe.

"Through me. In his view, I was ignoring the power of the wardenship. If I wasn't using it, someone should. What I was wasting, he was welcome to. In his estimation, of course."

"Ah, yes. The wardenship." Porteous sounded pleased. "Modern theories notwithstanding, we see before us the new warden of the west. I felicitate you, sir."

Fell looked a trifle sheepish. "You are too kind. However, the events we are discussing took place before I accepted the wardenship. For reasons I won't enlarge upon at this time, I wished to abstain from the wardenship. I might have reconsidered the matter if I had known how my reluctance played into the hands of Voysey and Bridgewater."

"You hold them both equally responsible?" asked Stewart.

"I blame Bridgewater more, for he understood the wardenship, while Voysey honestly believed it to be a matter of folklore until Bridgewater persuaded him otherwise. Bridgewater wanted me to continue to abstain from the wardenship while he looked for ways to get at the power through me. That's why Bridgewater invited me to be his houseguest when I attended his lecture in London."

"Yet you declined that invitation," said Stewart. "Did you have some reason to suspect Bridgewater's interest in you?"

"I suspected nothing," Fell replied. "I had work to do. Bridgewater was at least as interested in forging a connection to the power of Glasscastle's wards as he was in exploiting the power he believed me to be ignoring. That is why Bridgewater permitted Voysey to incorporate the Egerton wand into the Agincourt device."

"I understand why Voysey wished to incorporate the Egerton wand," said Stowe, "but surely Bridgewater prized it himself? Why did he consent to let the wand be used in the Agincourt device?"

"The Egerton wand gave Bridgewater a link to the device. It was a significant source of power to Bridgewater, but he could reach the power he wielded without it. Once the wand was incorporated into the device, he could reach the power of Glasscastle. At least, he could reach as much of the power of Glasscastle as Voysey could access. It was a singularly ineffectual ultimate weapon, the Agincourt device. One reason was that Bridgewater was drawing power out of it only a bit more slowly than Voysey was putting power in."

"Voysey accepted the wand and incorporated it into the device. Why?" asked Stewart.

"Power like Bridgewater's wand? Voysey was sure that Glasscastle magic subordinated all others. The wand was a source of energy and no more, as far as Voysey knew." After a moment, Fell added, "There was another reason Voysey wanted to use Bridgewater's wand, a less pragmatic one. Voysey knew that Bridgewater envied him. Voysey enjoyed that. He wanted to keep Bridgewater involved, close at hand, always mindful of Voysey's superiority."

"Why did Bridgewater permit that?" Stowe asked. "If Bridgewater's power was so great, why did he wait so long to attack the wards of Glasscastle?"

"Bridgewater dared not approach the wards of Glasscastle until Voysey used the Egerton wand. Not until then was he able to draw power from Glasscastle, through Voysey and finally through the wand," Fell said. "Even then, Bridgewater was careful. He was escorted through the gate during the confusion caused by the arrival of the animals from St. Hubert's. I was under escort as well. It took Bridgewater hours to find a way to free me. In the end, he used main force to bring me with him to the garden."

"Any Fellow of Glasscastle could have escorted him there," said Russell. "Why did Bridgewater trouble to free you in particular? Because you are the warden of the west?"

Fell regarded Russell solemnly. "If I had accepted that responsibility, Bridgewater couldn't have forced me to go with him. I was still resisting.

Therefore Bridgewater planned to use me to reach the power I refused to touch myself, just as Voysey was the straw through which Bridgewater sucked at the power of Glasscastle."

"Bridgewater brought the wards of Glasscastle down just before five o'clock," said Porteous. "Their silence was our first warning of Bridgewater's intent. If you knew he was conspiring with Voysey, why didn't you warn us?"

"I didn't know," Fell said simply. "I was surprised to learn the plans for the Agincourt device specified the Egerton wand. Until then, I had assumed Voysey was working alone. The spell on the armchair at St. Hubert's seemed a bit sophisticated to be Voysey's handiwork, but I didn't know the role Bridgewater played until he took me into the garden."

"When he did so," Stowe said, "when you believed you understood Bridgewater's intent, did you believe you had reason to fear for your life?"

"On the contrary." Fell chose his words with care. "I was afraid that my life would last too long. If I died before Bridgewater reached the power of the wardenship through me, the wardenship would pass to someone else. There's no way of telling who. But I thought it would be better to shut the door Bridgewater had opened. To close the connection between us. Before it was too late. That's why I asked Mr. Lambert for his help."

"Did either Voysey or Bridgewater, at any time, threaten your life?" asked Russell.

"Oh, no. They each abducted me, but neither had any intention of killing me," Fell replied.

"Are there any other charges you wish to bring against either defendant?" Stewart asked.

"Beyond the abductions?" Fell thought it over. "In a way, I am grateful to Voysey. He permitted me time to devote myself to my work undistracted. He could even be said to have contributed, however indirectly, to the reasoning process that made it possible for me to assume the wardenship. Bridgewater, on the other hand, used us all unscrupulously. To further his own ends, he stole every scrap of power that he could. He gutted Glasscastle. Had he not been transformed into a beast, I don't doubt that he would have committed many more crimes."

"So you wish Bridgewater to be punished more severely than Voysey?" asked Stewart.

"My wishes are not your concern. Your concern is the law. But please, don't make the same mistake Voysey did. Don't overestimate the power of

Glasscastle. Fear Bridgewater. Use him fairly, punish him as the law requires. But fear him."

The audience murmured among themselves. The Provosts received Fell's speech in utter silence. They looked at one another, stirred uneasily in their chairs, and said absolutely nothing, even to each other. After a full minute in which the only sound was an amalgam of indecipherable whispers and speculation from the audience, Fell asked, "If there's nothing more, may it please you to excuse me?"

"By all means," said Stewart.

Fell left the dais and resumed his seat.

In his most ringing tones, Porteous asked, "Do the defendants wish to address the Provosts at this time? If you have anything to say in your defense, please do so."

Voysey spoke. "I cannot rise to my feet to address the Provosts as properly as I might wish, for these cobwebs prevent me. Forgive me, I beg you. My fellow defendant can rise to his feet, and very different feet they are, but he cannot address anyone at all. Forgive him, I beg you. You have my sworn testimony, so I won't weary you with repetition. I will thank you for the testimony I have heard this morning. Until now, I had no idea of the true depth of Bridgewater's duplicity. What I did, all that I did, was for the greater glory of our empire and the greater good of the university. That I was made a puppet to serve Bridgewater's ends is bitter to me indeed, but I cannot deny it. Please believe me most sincerely repentant. If my deeds put Glasscastle in danger, I deserve to be punished. I only ask that whatever you do to me, you do to Bridgewater also. When I serve my sentence, my patience and remorse will be the greater, knowing that as I suffer, he suffers too, and with better reason."

Not so much as a creak of wooden flooring broke the silence that followed. The audience was subdued. The Provosts were impassive. Kiowa Bob's Indian chieftains could have done no better, Lambert reflected.

Little by little, the silence faded, eaten away by the small noises any large group of people makes. Someone coughed. Someone whispered. Someone's chair squeaked as it moved slightly on the waxed wooden floor. Whispers became murmurs. Murmurs became soft conversation. At last the beadle rapped for order.

After a long bout of their own murmuring, the Provosts confined the rest of the proceedings to questions concerning the precise nature of the laws Voysey and Bridgewater had broken. Three legal experts were called and questioned about an assortment of crimes. The experts were in agreement. Voysey and Bridgewater could both be charged with subverting a government weapons project and with abduction. Bridgewater had also attacked the wards of the university with intent most malicious. Ample grounds existed to bring the defendants to trial.

At the conclusion of the expert testimony, the Provosts conferred briefly. Their impassivity and the measured dignity of their nods and murmurs reminded Lambert more forcibly than ever of Indian chieftains. All they lacked was a pipe of peace.

Stowe nodded to the beadle, who rapped for attention. Stowe spoke. "This inquiry is now adjourned."

Stewart added, "The public will be informed of our verdict at the earliest opportunity. Meanwhile, all onlookers are free to go."

Since it was already lunchtime, this decision was welcomed by everyone. Lambert was surprised that Fell cheerfully joined him and the Brailsfords to eat lobster salad and drink champagne. Amy and Robert had prevailed upon Jane to extend her stay with them for a few more days, and all three were in a merry mood. It was a festive meal. At the end of it, Amy presented Lambert with a fine gold watch chain adorned with an all-too-familiar ivory fob.

"Mrs. Brailsford, I can't accept this." Lambert looked up from the ivory spindle to protest. "It was your grandmother's. A family heirloom. And the chain is much too fine—"

"Do shut up, Lambert," Jane advised. "Say thank you first, and accept it graciously. But then keep quiet."

Lambert obeyed her to the letter.

Delighted by his capitulation, Amy took his hands in hers. "We're so grateful to you for all you did for us. You rescued Robert and you saved Glasscastle and you risked your life riding along to protect Jane when she was off with the motor car."

"*I* rescued Robert," Fell pointed out sotto voce, just as Jane protested, "He was *not* protecting me."

Amy turned Lambert's hands over and inspected his palms with an air of rapturous pleasure. "Oh, how nice. I see you're still going to take a long journey over water. You will marry well and have—" She took a closer look at his right hand and seemed to be counting under her breath. "Yes, seven children."

Lambert put Jane's advice to use again. He thanked Amy politely, extricated himself from her grip, and kept quiet.

Robert took pity on Lambert and changed the subject. "With the Agincourt Project concluded, you don't yet know what you'll be doing next. Whatever your immediate plans, I assume you wish to return to Wyoming soon."

"I wasn't planning on it," Lambert said noncommittally.

"So Jane was right." Robert looked surprised. "She told me why you couldn't return. I don't mind admitting I found it difficult to believe her."

Lambert looked from Robert to Jane. The disappointment he felt surprised him. He'd never have taken Jane for a tattletale. Though why shouldn't she share the joke of Lambert's past with her brother? She couldn't know how deeply it embarrassed him, although he wouldn't have thought it beyond her to guess.

Jane spoke while Lambert was still hunting for words to hide his hurt surprise. "Robin says he found it difficult to believe me. What he means is, he accused me of making the whole thing up. As if I would," she added airily.

"Jane! Did you have the audacity to tell him the same story you told me, about Minnie and the Bandit Ramerrez?" Amy turned from Jane to regard her husband with affectionate reproach. "Robert, you must stop working so hard. If you took time away from your duties now and then to keep up with cultural matters, you might have recognized that farrago of nonsense Jane told you."

"I said I found it difficult to believe," Robert protested. To Lambert, he explained, "Jane claims you dare not return to Wyoming, where there is a large reward for your capture, as you are secretly the Bandit Ramerrez and wanted by the forces of law and order."

"Hold on, there——" Lambert began, pushing his chair back from the table.

"Indeed?" Fell regarded Lambert with keen interest. "You have never mentioned this to me."

"Oh, Robin." Jane frowned at her brother. "I thought you were listening to me. I said it is *believed* that Lambert is the Bandit Ramerrez. There's a difference."

"It's all hogwash," Lambert declared.

"It's all from *The Girl of the Golden West*," said Amy, patting Robert's hand. "Come with me when I go to Covent Garden and perhaps you won't take things so literally next time Jane chooses to amuse herself at your expense."

"*The Girl of the Golden West?*" Fell repeated the words wistfully.

"Puccini wrote it," Amy told him. "You might consider going to the opera once in a while yourself."

Lambert relaxed back into his seat and looked at Jane. "You never let on you'd seen that one."

For a moment, Jane regarded him so gravely that she reminded Lambert of the exhausted girl he had known at St. Hubert's. "There are a lot of things I never let on about," she stated. Then Jane beamed at him and her gravity melted into mischief. "I just couldn't resist the chance to try Robin's patience. You wouldn't think it to look at him, but he can sometimes be endearingly gullible."

Lambert realized he was gaping at Jane stupidly when she frowned a little and asked, "Do you feel all right? You haven't eaten something that disagreed with you, have you?"

"No, no." Hastily, Lambert said, "I just—I just figured something out, that's all."

Jane blinked. "I see." It was all too clear she didn't see.

Lambert did his best to reassure her. "You can go back to teasing your brother. I'm fine."

Jane turned her attention back to Robert and Lambert let out a deep sigh of relief. That smile of Jane's had knocked him for a loop. It made Lambert understand something he should have figured out a long time ago. There was something more than friendship in his feelings for Jane, and whatever that something was, Jane felt it too. In that moment of mischief, something had passed between them, as tangible as static electricity, as true and sweet as a chord of music. Whatever it was, it frightened Lambert half to death.

After lunch, the Brailsfords went back to the Tegean Theater to await the Provosts' verdict. At Fell's request, Lambert stayed behind while Fell slowly smoked a cheroot.

"There's something I want to ask you about." Fell looked uncomfortable.

"What is it?" Lambert was wary, remembering the personal turn the conversation had taken the last time Fell had used those words. He was still reeling from his fresh knowledge about Jane. This wasn't a particularly good time to be cross-examined.

Fell cleared his throat and tugged at his mustache. "I wonder if you'd be interested in joining me on a long journey over water?"

"Huh?" Lambert stared at his friend. "I mean, I beg your pardon?"

"I am the warden of the west," Fell said. "If the historical accounts are reliable, wardens are able to travel over water without the least distress. Quite a change from what magicians experience, I gather. I'm eager to put it to the test. I've always wanted to see a bit of the world. More than this particular corner of it, green and pleasant though it is. As I am warden of the west, it seems appropriate that I investigate the west. The golden west."

"You want to go out West?" Lambert tried to picture Fell's response to his first look at Wyoming. He tried to picture Wyoming's response to its first look at Fell. The effort to keep a straight face all but staggered him.

"I want to sail to North America. Once I'm there, I'd like to travel. By train, not motor car," Fell added as an afterthought. "Will you accompany me?"

Lambert hesitated. He knew he had to leave Glasscastle soon. He hadn't thought beyond that. In his days with Kiowa Bob's show, touring from London to Paris to Germany, he'd promised himself he'd see the rest of the world on his own before he returned to the United States. Constantinople, St. Petersburg, Normandy—none of those places seemed very likely now. But was he ready to head for home so soon? He struggled for an answer but none came.

"It's all right." Fell seemed to sense his indecision. "Think it over."

"Thinking won't help," Lambert admitted. "I can't go back. Not yet."

"It's nothing to do with a price on your head, is it?" Fell asked, smiling wryly.

Lambert smiled back ruefully. "I just can't."

"I understand." Fell clapped him on the shoulder. "I'll write."

Lambert and Fell had rejoined the Brailsfords in the hard little chairs of the Tegean Theater by the time the Provosts issued their verdict. Stowe, chest puffed out until his snowy shirt parted the front of his academic gown, read out the findings in a voice as loud as Porteous's, though it was about half as deep.

Adam Voysey was declared stripped of every shred of power and authority with which Glasscastle had ever invested him. He would be remanded to police custody. Until such time as appropriate sentence were passed upon him by a suitable court of law, Bridgewater was to remain a tortoise. Both men were to be brought up on charges of subverting a project vital to imperial security, Voysey before the Court of the King's Bench and Bridgewater before a jury of his peers in the Court of the Lord Steward.

The chief malefactors dealt with, the inquiry turned its attention to the petty criminals in the case. The man in the bowler hat was to remain in the trance inflicted upon him by his employer, Adam Voysey, until such time as the spell could be broken. Then he would face charges for his deeds, including trespassing, attempted abduction, assault, and damage to university property. Among the undergraduates of Glasscastle, miscellaneous charges of truancy, dereliction of scholarly duty, and willful property damage at St. Hubert's were dismissed. Glasscastle would be held harmless in the case of all complaints from those who had been transformed into animals and back again. The trespassing spell on Midsummer Green would be restored to its original strength and purpose. In the meantime, sports in general and cricket in particular were forbidden there. All unauthorized pedestrians were hereby warned to confine themselves to the gravel paths.

Finally, the Provosts of Glasscastle wished to confirm that the warden of the west, denounced by the forward-thinking as a remnant of folk belief, existed in truth. It was Glasscastle's proud boast that the new warden of the west, Nicholas Fell, was one of their own. Doubtless, the Provosts announced, he would fulfill his duties—all his duties—illustriously, to the greater glory of Glasscastle.

By three o'clock, the Provosts had declared the inquiry concluded and the investigation closed. The theater was cleared. All members of the colleges of Glasscastle were to return to their duties.

There was plenty of time to talk the news over before they joined Porteous for sherry in his rooms.

Porteous was more expansive than Lambert had ever seen him. His good mood might have owed something to the splendid comfort of the rooms he occupied in St. Joseph's, well shaded, quiet, with just enough summer-scented breeze through the open windows to be pleasantly cool even at the height of the afternoon. The furnishings were Georgian, the tapestries on the wall Jacobean, and the carpets Persian. The sherry would not have been out of place on Mount Olympus itself.

Robert and Amy stayed close together, close enough to touch. Fell kept his distance from the entire group. Lambert found himself morbidly aware of every step Jane took. He tried to mask his response to her by focusing fixedly on Porteous instead. Porteous, if he noticed anything, merely took Lambert's interest as his due.

"I'm delighted you could all accept my invitation." Porteous gazed affably around at the five of them. "I have a proposal to put before Mr. Lambert and I hope you will all join me in urging that he accept it."

Lambert put his glass down and set himself to listen to Porteous with close attention.

Porteous cleared his throat. "Mr. Lambert, I hope that you will give the Provosts of Glasscastle great pleasure by consenting to attend a short cere-mony in the Wearyall College chapel before hall this evening. There you will be invited to matriculate as a student of Glasscastle. Stowe, Stewart, Rus-sell, Brailsford, and I approve wholeheartedly of the idea. We trust that you will accept our invitation."

Amy gave a little handclap of delight, and exclaimed, "Oh, how splen-did." Robert beamed. Jane did too, and the smiles made their family likeness more marked than usual. Fell said nothing but watched Lambert intently, as if studying his response to the offer.

Lambert was glad he'd put his sherry down. Otherwise he would have dropped the glass for sure. "You—you want me to be a student of Glasscas-tle?" He could not have heard correctly. "That's impossible."

Porteous said, "You've taken an unorthodox path to our door, but what of that? If the Agincourt Project accomplished anything, it has been a testimo-nial to the excellence of your perception."

Lambert hardly knew where to start. "But—to begin with, I'm an Amer-ican."

Porteous frowned. "So you are. What of it? We haven't had an American student for many years, but there was no difficulty the last time we did."

"No more difficulty than the usual students pose," said Fell.

"There is almost always an American or two at Greenlaw," Jane said. "Fortunately, for as a rule, they bring excellent gramophone records."

"Yet you claim Greenlaw teaches decorum," said Robert, shaking his head in mock reproof.

"Before or after they teach you the two-step?" Amy asked Jane, playing along with her husband's reaction.

"At Greenlaw, my fellow students taught me to dance the mazurka, the ziganka, and the sword dance," Jane declared. "All the faculty ever taught us was the danse macabre—that was at comp time."

With difficulty, Lambert tore his attention from Jane, and said, "Voysey explained to me that Americans have no magic. Because of emigrating across the ocean. It's evolutionary."

Porteous smiled. "Voysey told you that, eh? An opinionated fellow, young Voysey. No shortage of convictions there. He had his theories and he held them fast. In time, he might have made them policy. As yet, however, there is no rule in the statutes that pertains in any way to Americans."

"Hardly surprising," said Jane. "I don't know when the statutes were written but I'd be surprised if Glasscastle had even heard of America, let alone spared a thought for her citizens."

"The greater part of the statutes were recorded in 1559, at the time of Elizabeth's first Parliament," said Robert. "There have been amendments since, of course."

"Oh, of course." Jane nodded. "One or two, at most, I should imagine."

"One or two hundred, more likely," said Amy. "I've read them, you know. A good wife makes it her business to learn about the challenges her husband faces."

"Never mind about statutes. What about the Latin requirement?" Lambert demanded.

Porteous allowed himself to be distracted from the sherry. "Ah, yes. Latin. You'll have to learn it while you study magic. It would be simpler if you knew it before you started the chants, but it can't be helped. Provided you pass the proficiency test before you finish your studies, we are prepared to waive the requirement for your entrance."

Lambert gaped at him, looked at Fell, then back at Porteous. "What about background? Voysey said Glasscastle demanded its students have the right background."

"I defy Voysey, or anyone else, to find anything whatsoever about background in the written statutes. If you have been invited to matriculate, you must have the right background. Because, you see, Glasscastle is always right." Porteous's smugness was palpable.

"Oh, very true," said Fell, a touch sarcastically.

Jane looked amused, her attention firmly back on the matter at hand. "Yes, that's right, isn't it? How convenient."

Robert and Amy looked on approvingly.

Fell cleared his throat and caught Porteous's eye.

"Oh, yes. One more thing," Porteous said. "We thought the fees for tuition might pose some difficulty, so we have taken the liberty of arranging a loan for you. The terms are quite reasonable, I assure you."

Lambert was at a loss. "I don't know what to say. I could be a student of Glasscastle?" Could he have found his own country after all? "A true student? Not just here to help out with odd jobs?"

"A true student," Porteous assured him.

Lambert was still dubious. "So there won't be any more tests of marksmanship?"

Robert said, "With the funding for the Agincourt device removed, we have no need of marksmanship. Nor will we be seeing any more government research projects, I'm afraid. Tobias and Sopwith will have their work cut out for them to meet the expectations they've created for their aviation experiments at Farnborough. Frankly, I don't envy them the task."

"A student of Glasscastle." Lambert whispered the words but even to his own ears, they didn't seem quite real. He shook himself and said it again more loudly. "A student of Glasscastle."

Fell smiled at Lambert.

"Aviation," breathed Jane, eyes wide. Then, even more softly, with such deep feeling it approached reverence, she added, "*Aeroplanes.*"

Robert looked alarmed by her response but said nothing.

Amy looked from Robert to Jane and back again. "Robert?" She turned back to Jane. "What do you mean, *aeroplanes*?"

"You will need to tell us precisely why you wish to become a student of Glasscastle. You are somewhat older than the usual applicant, but that might prove a point in your favor," Porteous said. "It sometimes takes the younger fellows a few terms just to settle down and study properly."

Lambert's stomach seemed to be tying itself into a succession of knots. "I don't know what to say."

"No need to say anything. Not at this time. Just have your answer ready by the time you join us in the chapel at seven." Porteous clapped Lambert on the shoulder and called for more sherry all around. "Oh, and it's a formal occasion. So do dress accordingly."

Lambert looked at Fell, who was smiling ruefully down at his untouched glass. After failing to catch his friend's eye, Lambert turned to Jane, who was smiling at him. The smile put new life into the knot in his stomach. "What shall I do?"

"Accept, of course," said Jane. "You've been pining to study at Glasscastle ever since you arrived. Amy had told me all about it by the second day I was here."

Lambert blinked at the thought of Amy and Jane talking about him, then managed to say, "Oh, I pined all right—when I first got here." He hesitated. "I've been put in my place so many times since then—To hell with them," he finished, under his breath.

"Obviously, you've made them reconsider. No mean feat, that." Jane sobered slightly. "Glasscastle wants you, Lambert. If I know anything about you, I know that you want Glasscastle the way I want Greenlaw. This is your chance. Take it."

For a long moment, Lambert looked into Jane's eyes. Silence drew out between them until at last, Jane broke it. "Think it over. You have lots of time."

"Oh, lots. Until seven o'clock," Lambert said gloomily. It was too much time—yet it wasn't near enough, not when it was impossible to think straight. His heart wanted to leap out of his chest. His pride was afire. He had made them all change their minds. His brain told him that there would be plenty of drawbacks to signing on as a student of Glasscastle. For one thing, when would he ever get the chance to see Jane again? Confused, he turned to Fell. "What do you think?"

From the amusement in Fell's eyes, he had been watching Lambert's every thought chase itself across his face. "What I think is of no consequence. The important thing is what you think. Take as much time as you need to be sure of your decision. But choose what you truly want and consider why you want it. You chose well when I tested you with the golden West. Now choose again." Fell lifted his glass. "Ladies and gentlemen, I give you a toast—to the very good health of Samuel Lambert."

At seven o'clock, Samuel Lambert found himself listening at the door of the chapel of Wearyall College. How often had he heard the chanting from his bench on the far side of the cloister garden wall? How often had he heard the voices raised as one, though not raised far, as he heard them now, through the heavy chapel door? How would they sound when he was inside, when he heard them fully? How would they sound to him when he was among them, no longer an outsider?

Lambert hesitated. He was wearing his best clothes and found them uncomfortable, even as the August heat faded toward evening. Fell had knotted the white tie for him and pronounced him acceptably formal. Could he really stand to be dressed up regularly? Top hat, white tie, and stiff shirtfront dressed up? Could he bear the foreign customs for the full three years of a Glasscastle education? Could anything live up to the expectations Lambert had? Could he be sure he wasn't dooming himself to disappointment and disillusion? Could he be sure of anything?

The urge to hear the music more clearly spurred Lambert on. He opened the door and stepped inside. Wearyall Chapel was not as grand as St. Mary's, but it seemed more beautiful to Lambert, for the early evening light through the windows was augmented by candles. Somewhere incense was burning, a tendril of pure sweetness that matched the music. Lambert couldn't see where the students were, but their chanting made his throat go tight. He took off his hat.

Alone, Lambert walked down the nave to the altar. There, flanked by candelabra, stood James Porteous, jovial as Old King Cole, and Cecil Stewart, almost as rosy after his inroads on Porteous's excellent sherry. Nearby, but clearly a mere onlooker, Nicholas Fell stood. All three men were magnificent in full academic regalia. Under his arm, Fell had a book and bundle of black fabric. He kindly took charge of Lambert's top hat, putting it safely aside.

"Welcome, Samuel Lambert," said Porteous as he handed Lambert a candle in a wooden cup. "Do you come seeking power?"

"No." The word came out a crooked whisper and Lambert cleared his throat. "No, sir."

"What do you seek?" asked Porteous.

Lambert hesitated, trying for words with which to capture the feeling the music gave him. "Knowledge, sir. Understanding." The wooden cup gleamed with use. Lambert wondered how many hands had held it before his.

"What more?" asked Porteous. His hand was still outstretched toward Lambert's unlit candle and the jovial look had faded.

Lambert didn't try to guess what Porteous was waiting to hear. He couldn't guess. He didn't want to. He only wanted to speak the truth. "That's all, sir. I want to learn. I want to work. And I want to learn to make that music. I want to chant."

For the first time, Stewart spoke. "Can you sing?"

"Not like they do in the opera," Lambert answered. "But I can sing hymns as well as anybody."

Porteous looked inquiringly at Stewart. "For knowledge? For understanding? To learn and work and sing? Will that do as an answer?"

Stewart considered. "It's a bit vague."

"It's honest." Fell moved toward Porteous and Stewart. "There's this, as well." In his outstretched hand he held a playing card, the three of hearts. "When the wards were mended, I returned to the rooms I share with Lambert. He showed me this and asked if I knew what it was. Where did you find it, Samuel?"

"In the card tray." Lambert was startled by the scrutiny he was getting from Porteous and Stewart. To Fell, he said, "You told me some undergraduate must have left it as a joke."

Porteous frowned. "It's a perfectly ordinary playing card."

"Yes. But it's the three of hearts," said Fell.

Stewart stared at Fell. "You wouldn't by any chance be able to prove this?"

Fell looked rueful. "If I had thought to fabricate anything, I would have come up with something a bit more convincing than this, I assure you. There's nothing out of the ordinary about this card. But it is the three of hearts."

"Upton's card," said Porteous.

"What does that mean?" Lambert asked, frowning.

"In the grand scheme of things, absolutely nothing," said Fell. "I could have planted it myself. But I haven't been able to find anyone who knows anything about how the card came to be in my tray. And Upton used a three of hearts as his badge."

"Upton has been dead for forty years," said Lambert.

"That's why we are a bit nonplussed," said Stewart. To Porteous, he added, "I accept the young man's answer if you do. Administer the oath."

Porteous brought forth a book. "Do you, Samuel Lambert——" As he opened the book, a playing card fell from between its pages and landed on the floor facedown. Porteous paused, staring.

"If I pick that up," said Fell thoughtfully, "will you promise not to suspect me of fabricating this one too?"

Stewart bent down and took up the card. It was the three of hearts. He showed it to Porteous. "Well?"

"That settles it." Porteous cleared his throat and resumed. "Do you, Samuel Lambert, swear to protect Glasscastle and to defend the university from all dangers and dishonors?"

"I do," said Lambert. What was in the words to make his heart beat faster?

"Do you swear to devote yourself to the studies that Glasscastle imposes, and to fulfill the duties Glasscastle demands?"

"I do."

"Do you undertake to be faithful and to bear true allegiance to Glasscastle and to observe the statutes of the university?"

"I do."

Porteous nodded to Fell. Fell handed Porteous the book he'd had under his arm, then shook the folds out of the undergraduate's gown he carried. With a gracious nod, Porteous presented Lambert with the book.

" '*Scito te in Matriculam Universitatis hodie relatum esse, sub hac conditione, nempe ut omnia Statua hoc libro comprehensa pro virili observes.*'" In his most stentorian tones, Porteous read from the book he held.

Lambert took the book, risked a glance at the spine, which read *Statutes of Glasscastle University*, and then returned his full attention to Porteous in time to meet Porteous's most penetrating stare.

"I asked you if you promise to observe the statutes of Glasscastle University to the best of your ability?" asked Porteous.

Lambert tightened his grip on book and cup. "I do."

Porteous reached out and held his open hand, palm down, six inches above Lambert's candle. Lambert caught his breath as the black twig of the candle wick blossomed into flame.

"Welcome to Glasscastle," Porteous said to Lambert, all his joviality back in place.

"Welcome to Glasscastle," said Stewart. "As Provost, I welcome you to Wearyall College. We have work for you here, Mr. Lambert, plenty of hard work."

"Thank you, sir," said Lambert. He nodded awkwardly to Porteous. "Thank you, sir."

"Congratulations," said Fell, holding out the undergraduate's gown. Lambert had both hands full, but with Fell's help and a lot of concentration, he managed to shrug his arms into its loose sleeves without dropping either the burning candle or the university statutes, and without setting anything on fire. "Welcome to Glasscastle."

"Thank you, sir," said Lambert, half strangled by emotion.

"Don't thank me," said Fell. "Thank Upton."

When Lambert emerged from the chapel of Wearyall College with Fell, Porteous, and Stewart, he found Jane waiting for him. Her brother, Robert, was along as her escort. There was a soft breeze, just enough to rustle in the trees overhead and to lift the edges of the gossamer fine scarf Jane wore around her shoulders.

"You did it," said Jane. "You are one of the students here. You belong to Glasscastle now."

Stewart clapped Lambert on the shoulder as he moved past to join Porteous in conversation with Robert. "You belong to Wearyall now, for three years."

Lambert smiled and called after him, "For three years, with luck."

Fell paused on his way by Lambert just as Lambert looked down at the candle in his hand, wondering what to do with it.

"Don't put it out," Fell told him. "Bad luck. Just let it burn. The longer it lasts, the better the omen for your studies here."

Fell walked past the little group of Brailsford, Porteous, and Stewart, headed in the direction of the Winterset Archives. That left Lambert in the shelter of the college chapel porch, face-to-face with Jane. He held out the copy of the university statutes for Jane's inspection. "I have my work cut out for me, that's for sure."

"What a lot of rules to follow. Imagine Amy reading all of them." Jane glanced through the pages. "I see you won't be allowed to bring a rapier and dagger to your tutorials. That will be a sacrifice. Particularly if you have Porteous as a tutor." She closed the book and handed it back.

"I still can't believe it." Lambert gazed from the book to the candle in wonder. "I'm a student of Glasscastle."

"And not just for three years, either. For the rest of your life. No matter what happens, Glasscastle is going to change you." Jane looked sad. "It's a pity. I quite like the way you are now."

Lambert tucked the statutes under his arm and thought it over. "Maybe you're right. Maybe I can't study magic without changing a little bit. Maybe you can't study anything without changing a bit. Maybe everyone changes—but when they do, it's mostly to get more like themselves. So just think. In three years, you'll be even more like Jane Brailsford than you are now."

Jane gave way to quiet laughter. "Don't say that to Robert and Amy. They wouldn't find it a pleasant prospect."

"I do." Lambert let the words rest between them for a long moment. When Jane said nothing, he went on. "It's not as if I'm going to start smoking cheroots, you know, or carrying on about how Glasscastle is always right."

Jane widened her eyes. "But Glasscastle *is* always right."

"You don't believe that and neither do I. Just out of curiosity, is Greenlaw always right?"

Jane's air of simple innocence altered slightly, just enough to make her look even more simple. "Well, of course it is."

"Really? What if Glasscastle and Greenlaw disagree? Who is right then?"

"Both," said Jane promptly, all show of simple-mindedness abandoned.

Lambert frowned. "That requires mental gymnastics that I'm not equipped for."

"Give yourself a year at Glasscastle. You'll be surprised," Jane advised.

"It's different though, isn't it? Greenlaw magic? Even the little I saw of it—your illusion, for example. It's not like Glasscastle magic, all organized and harmonized. It's more personal."

"More individual, perhaps," Jane conceded. "I don't have—I can never have firsthand knowledge of how true Glasscastle magic works, so I can't be sure how it compares. But Greenlaw magic is highly individual."

"So Glasscastle magic is more powerful?" asked Lambert. "It must be, mustn't it? Since more people are involved in each spell?"

"If you like to think so. That would probably be a useful opinion to take with you to Glasscastle. But be careful with it when you go out into the world. Don't trust it completely. It's only an opinion, after all."

"You're telling me Greenlaw magic *is* more powerful than Glasscastle?"

"It's only my opinion," Jane said, apologetically. "Rest assured, even I don't trust it completely."

Lambert looked into Jane's remarkably fine eyes for a long moment. Out of nowhere, he heard himself asking, "If I write to you at Greenlaw, will they deliver my letters?"

Jane's surprise was obvious. "Of course. Why shouldn't they?"

"If Greenlaw is anything like Glasscastle, they guard themselves from outsiders."

"They do guard themselves from outsiders, but don't take the parallel to extremes. No one sees a need to interfere with mail delivery."

"If I write to you, will you write back?"

Jane let that question go unanswered, studying Lambert as closely as if she meant to memorize him. "Write to me and see," she said finally.

"I'll write to you. Promise you'll write back."

Jane looked nettled. "You aren't the only one with duties and responsibilities, you know. I'll be working hard too. You have to write me a letter worth answering. If it's full of cheroots and complaints about the food, forget it."

"I will write you a real letter, I promise. Now promise me you'll answer."

"Oh, you're going to be persistent, are you?"

Lambert nodded.

Jane took a step closer and touched Lambert's forehead, the slightest brush of gloved fingers over the spot where the wasp had stung him. "That looks much better."

"You'd never know it happened," Lambert agreed. "It was the deuce of a nuisance at the time, but you can't use it to distract me now. Promise you'll write to me."

Jane's eyes held his, clear and grave. "I promise nothing."

She was so close to him, closer than they'd been over the maps and the ivory spindle on the way to Ludlow. Lambert bent his head a little, just to see her that much more closely. His mouth was dry as he murmured, "I'll promise, then. I'm going to be persistent."

Jane smiled at him. She touched him again, just a moth's brush of fingertips at the corner of his mouth, but said nothing.

Lambert could muster no more than a whisper. "*Jane.*"

Jane whispered back, and her tone held a world of tenderness that lifted his heart. "*Lambert.*"

"*Jane!*" Robert Brailsford stood in the path, rigid with disapproval. Lambert and Jane sprang apart as if electrified. The university statutes slipped and landed with a substantial thump on the chapel doorstep. "What are you doing?"

Behind Robert, Porteous and Stewart withdrew tactfully and set off in the general direction of dinner.

"While we were motoring to Ludlow to rescue you," said Jane, utterly composed, "Mr. Lambert was stung by a wasp. I wanted to assure myself he was healing properly."

Lambert retrieved the book of statutes and clamped it securely under his elbow. He drew himself up to his full height, squared his shoulders, and met Robert's eyes. "I hoped to persuade Miss Brailsford to correspond with me while she is at Greenlaw."

Robert regarded him gravely. "Indeed."

"Robin." Jane's tone was crisp and cautionary.

"Jane." Robert was just as crisp. "We don't wish Mr. Lambert to be late for his dinner, do we? In any event, Amy will be expecting us for our own dinner."

"We certainly don't want to be late for that," Jane said dryly.

"I certainly don't," Robert replied. "Congratulations on your matriculation, Mr. Lambert. Come along, Jane."

Jane hesitated a moment, then followed her brother as Lambert called a farewell after them. Lambert tucked the university statutes more firmly under his arm. With his free hand, he sheltered his candle for the careful walk back to Holythorn. Despite the soft breeze, he meant to keep the flame safe. He planned on it burning for a long time.

It was early morning in late September, on the first day of Michaelmas term at Glasscastle. As returning students greeted one another throughout the halls of Wearyall, St. Joseph's, and Holythorn, boisterous amusement and waggish backchat were the order of the day. In the garret room allotted him as a first-term student, Lambert stood on a chair in an effort to peer out the window and get his bearings.

The space was little more than a box room, a glorified cupboard under the eaves. Slanting oak beams waited for Lambert to forget their existence and bash his head on them. A narrow bed was tucked in one corner of the room, a writing table, already almost hidden by a stack of chants and Latin primers, lurked in another.

On that stack was a letter from Nicholas Fell, received only the day before. In it, Fell shared with Lambert his impressions of the luxurious and speedy trans-Atlantic crossing he'd enjoyed aboard the *Titanic*, his description of the traveling tumult that was New York City, and his low opinion of the complexities involved in booking train tickets from New York City to Laredo, Texas.

On top of the letter from Fell was one from Jane, written from Greenlaw. Her safety was implicit in the letter's existence, her arrival mere postscript to Jane's enthusiastic description of her unorthodox journey home. Not all travel was a tiresome medley of road dust, railway soot, and seasickness. Some forms of transportation were much worse, seasoning personal misery with physical danger. Colonel Sam Cody had taken her on as a passenger. Together they had flown across the Channel to France. Fine weather and good mechanical luck had combined to bring Jane safely home to Greenlaw by aeroplane.

Atop Jane's letter lay a single playing card, the three of hearts. It was Lambert's good luck piece, no matter how it came to be in Fell's card tray.

The room's best feature was a skylight. Lambert had inspected its leading and frame with care. He could see it had leaked recently and he guessed it would continue to leak regularly throughout the winter. He didn't care. The sunlight that filled the room would be worth the occasional effort of emptying a few rain buckets. The only other window in the room was right up in the gable, its diamond-paned glass almost completely obscured by ivy.

Once he had the gable window pried open a few inches, Lambert sawed patiently at the ivy with his penknife. When the window was clear, he wedged himself into the narrow frame and leaned out into the morning.

Far below, students in the quadrangle of Wearyall College could be heard but not seen. Tree branches and the angle of the slate roof hid the ground from him. In recompense, the roof held interest of its own. Lambert felt sure that it would not take him long to learn the ins and outs of every form of rain gutter, the location of every other skylight, and the properties of every sort of moss that flourished on the slates.

It was halcyon weather, perfectly cloudless and boundlessly blue. After relentless days of rain at the end of August, the return of dry weather came as a godsend. In the morning sunlight, Lambert could see every detail of the roof and chimney pots of the deanery of St. Joseph's, and beyond that the looming silhouette of the Winterset Archive. Beyond that was only the sky. Only the whole world.

For a solid quarter of an hour, Lambert looked out upon his own true country, savoring the sounds of the place as he memorized the color of the sky. He heard distant laughter and talk, bells and birdsong, and when the breeze was right, faint strains of chanting. The blend made a music that opened his heart and stung his eyes a little.

At last Lambert came back inside, latching the window and climbing down off his chair lightly out of respect for the furniture's decrepitude. He couldn't stare out the window forever, after all. He was a student of Glasscastle, free and equal. Lambert squared his shoulders and let the thought soak in. He was a student of Glasscastle and he had work to do.